HERO DE NOVO

888-555-HERO #3

SUZAN HARDEN

This is a work of fiction. All characters, organizations and events in this novel are products of the author's imagination and are not to be construed as real. Any resemblance to persons, living or dead, is entirely coincidental.

HERO DE NOVO (888-555-HERO #3)
Copyright 2019 by Suzan Harden
All rights reserved

ISBN-13 - 978-1-938745-47-8
Published by Angry Sheep Publishing
Findlay, Ohio

Interior Design by QA Productions
Cover Design by For the Muse Designs

More books by Suzan Harden

(Each series is in suggested reading order)

Bloodlines

Blood Magick

Zombie Love

Zombie Confidential

Zombie Wedding

Amish, Vamps & Thieves

Blood Sacrifice

Love, War & a Bulldog

Zombie Goddess

Ravaged

Sacrificed

Reality Bites (Coming Soon)

Ghouls in the Grocery (Coming Soon)

Resurrected (Coming Soon)

Seasons of Magick

Spring

Summer

Autumn

Winter

Justice

Sword and Sorceress 28 ("Justice")

Sword and Sorceress 30 ("Diplomacy in the Dark")

Justice: The Beginning

A Question of Balance

A Modicum of Truth

A Matter of Death (Coming Soon)

A Touch of Mother (Coming Soon)

888-555-HERO

Hero De Facto

Hero Ad Hoc

Hero De Novo

Miscellaneous

Sword and Sorceress 31 ("Pig-Headed")

Sword and Sorceress 32 ("Unexpected")

For more information or to join her mailing list, visit Suzan's website at www.suzanharden.com

Or check her out on Twitter (twitter.com/Suzan_Harden) or Facebook (www.facebook.com/SuzanHardenWriter).

Legal definition from the *Merriam-Webster Dictionary*:

De Novo – over again; as if for the first time

Chapter 1

Rey Garcia stared at the woman with the gun, her words ringing through his head. *They brainwashed Captain Justice to kill my ex-boyfriend. The Ghost Owl.*

No. Tim couldn't be dead. And how could I have killed him if I was a prisoner in this Corvus lab?

Despite the sick feeling in his stomach at the strange woman's words, Rey tried to laugh, but pain shot through his side. The monster's claws had cut deep enough to see bone, but he was pretty sure they hadn't puncture his lungs. He wouldn't have been able to draw a proper breath for his weak chuckle if they had.

"C'mon. The Ghost Owl is a Canyon Pointe urban myth," Rey said. "How could Captain Justice kill a children's tale?" Despite the drugged haze the morning he was abducted, he definitely remembered the man who looked just like him. *Dios*, if his doppelgänger had killed Tim, how could he live with himself? Bile rose in the back of Rey's throat. And if the imposter had infiltrated his real life, that meant Aisha and their baby were in danger as well.

The woman gave him a suspicious look.

"I grew up on the east side of the Pointe." He shrugged. "Everyone knows the story. Jatz'om Kuh, the Ghost Owl, is nothing more than the Robin Hood tale for this century."

"No, he exists. Here." The woman poked around the shelves of the lab some more. She pulled out a set of scrubs and shoved them at Rey. "These will work until we get to the mainland."

"The mainland?" He accepted the wad of blue-green clothes. "What mainland? There aren't any islands in Lake Del Oro."

She paused and stared at him. "You really have no idea of where you are, do you?"

He shook his head.

"We'll discuss it once we're out of here." She continued rummaging through equipment and supplies.

"No. We need to discuss it now." He was fairly certain he heard the rhythm of the sea, but it could be the Gulf of Mexico or the Pacific Ocean for all he knew.

A shiver ran through him. What if Corvus had taken him from the U.S.? How would he ever get back across the border? Harri Winters, one of his attorneys, had pulled a lot of strings to make it look like he was born there, even though Mama had said more than once she had carried him to the U.S. from Honduras. But he hadn't carried any ID the morning he was abducted. No superhero in their right mind would carry their civilian ID with them when responding to an emergency.

The woman sighed and shook her head. "We're on an abandoned oil rig off the coast of Java."

"What?" His heart sank at his predicament. "You mean as in the capital island of Indonesia Java?"

"Why are you stalling? You said you were worried about Corvus agents coming back here." She stopped shuffling through the last supply cabinet. Again, the suspicious look from the woman.

"I am, but for all I know, you could be one of them," he said.

"How'd Corvus get you here?"

"I'm not sure."

When she raised her gun and pointed it at him again, he tried to look non-threatening. He couldn't risk injuring his only potential ally.

"The last thing I clearly remember is getting a text about an emergency and to come into work early." He shook his head. "I got dressed and was flying—" He swallowed hard at his slip. "Down the freeway." He hated lying to anyone, but as both Aisha and Harri repeatedly pointed out, total honesty could be a detriment in the superhero business.

Her eyes narrowed. "Are you registered?"

Dios, she was sharp. But given her admitted rage at Captain Justice, telling her he was the real thing wasn't smart.

"My attorney was working on it before Corvus abducted me." Which was true if he stretched the definition of truth. He sighed. "I'm not even sure how long I've been here, much less if it was really Corvus." The head of the top secret organization had taken a personal interest in Rey years ago. He couldn't imagine General Trubble not coming in to gloat over Rey's capture. But as far as Rey knew, Trubble had never come here.

The stranger lowered her weapon again.

Rey ran his tongue over his dry lips. "What happened to the Ghost Owl in this epic battle between him and Captain Justice? If the real guy is as good as the myth—"

"The Ghost Owl wasn't a super." The woman slid into an undamaged chair and popped a flashdrive into a port on the last functioning computer work station. "He had enough tricks up his sleeves to fool a lot of people, but in the end, he was a mortal man."

"So are you going after Captain Justice?"

"Not exactly." The woman sagged in her seat. "According to the rumor mill, an unknown female super claiming to be the Ghost Owl killed him."

"A woman? But you said . . ."

The stranger looked at him and rolled her eyes. "I know, right? So insecure she couldn't create her own super persona? What a pussy!" She turned back to the monitor.

"But you just said the Ghost Owl was your ex-boyfriend, and you don't know who she is?"

"I'm guessing she's a family member." The woman's fingers danced across the keyboard. "An illegitimate daughter or something."

"If Captain Justice is dead, there's no one to exact your vengeance on," Rey said.

"I'm going to find this woman, and then I'm going after Corvus, like I should have done years ago."

"What's your issue with Corvus?"

"Besides the possibility they were the ones who were mind-controlling Captain Justice?" She whirled on the chair to face him. Anger sparked in her eyes. "Those assholes used the Supervillainy Act of 1947 to take my daughters from me."

CHAPTER 2

Aisha Franklin stared at her to-do list on her computer screen. So much for any relaxation over the upcoming Labor Day weekend. Tim was still insisting on getting the patent filed on the new exoskeleton suit he'd built with Miguel and Francisco. Harri had pretty much destroyed the original in her battle with the man pretending to be Captain Justice. Tim wanted to do a presentation on the suit to NASA in two months, which Aisha personally considered a little too ambitious, considering he just got out of rehab after the imposter Captain Justice tried to kill him.

Taking a deep breath, she tried to roll back the fury and grief flooding her. Not an imposter. A brain-washed evil twin.

How the hell did her life get this screwed up?

Her only consolation in the mess their lives had become was Black Death hadn't been sitting outside their office building for the last two months. The last thing their assistant Patty needed was her super ex-boyfriend stalking her. Sometimes though, Aisha wondered if Harri had made a mistake by siccing Black Death's boss from Corvus on him. If the super was still sitting on their street in his old Honda, they knew where he was.

Aisha tapped the key to bring up Tim's application. If either NASA or the ESA picked up the exoskeleton for use on the space station, the licensing fees would cover Francisco's education, room and board through a couple of doctorates. She smiled to herself. That's assuming their building manager Miguel could come to terms with the idea of his soon-to-be eight-year-old son going off to college, even though his oldest son Domingo would accompany his baby brother next fall.

Rey had already set aside some of his money for Dom to pursue his business degree. It only made sense for him to attend college at the same time as his baby brother.

Harri managed to pit the federal and the state governments against each other over the damage caused by the fake Captain Justice, which meant Rey's estate was intact. And Aisha had negotiated more licenses for memorial memorabilia once the FBI had declared Captain Justice dead. All the proceeds went into a trust governed by Miguel, Tim, and Harri along with Aisha. For once, she was thankful for her law partner's insight. Harri had insisted Rey include a clause providing for any of his children in his will long before Aisha herself knew she was pregnant.

The expected tsunami of agony at missing him rolled over her again, and she blinked away the tears as she rubbed her abdomen. Her baby bump was starting to show. And Rey would never have the chance to see his son.

She touched the jade amulet at her throat that hung from a titanium chain.

Miguel had brought it to her loft the other night when he came up to talk about Francisco's education. He'd found the amulet in a box of his late wife Beatrice's belongings. It was the original one Rey had taken off in a child's fit of pique over bath time. The jade piece's original leather thong was too short for an adult.

She and Miguel had talked for a long time that night. Jokingly, he said if she could be a surrogate mom for Francisco and thirteen-year-old Javier, he'd act as her baby's surrogate dad.

Then they both had a good cry.

The man they knew and loved was gone.

Rey was gone.

Byron Trubble, head of the black ops group known as Corvus, claimed Rey had been kidnapped without his authorization.

Aisha didn't believe him.

Trubble had also told Harri everyone at the facility where Rey had been held was dead.

That part Aisha did believe. She had no doubt Trubble had killed everyone to cover up his mess. Or he had Professor Paranoia, the supervillain Trubble had hired to run the lab, murder them.

Her office phone buzzed, interrupting her maudlin thoughts. She sniffed back the tears before she answered.

"Aisha, your sister's on line one," their assistant Patty announced. "Do you want me to put her through?"

"Yes." She had a pretty good idea what the call was about. Maybe dealing with family issues would get her mind off her own problems.

The receiver buzzed and clicked. "Hey, LaShun, what's up?"

"Oh, so I'm finally good enough to talk to?"

Aisha rolled her eyes even though LaShun couldn't see her and leaned back in her office chair. "I've texted you when I can. It's been a little busy around here."

"So we've seen on the news." LaShun laughed. "How's living the high life with all the studly superheroes around?"

Fresh grief brought a lump to Aisha's throat.

"Ah, crap," LaShun muttered. "I stepped into it, didn't I? I take it you knew Captain Justice pretty well?"

Damn. Leave it to her big sister to stumble over the truth in the dark.

Aisha forced a laugh. "More like Harri wanted to adopt him."

LaShun snorted. "Like she has a maternal bone in her body."

Time to change the subject. "I'm assuming you're calling about Mom and Dad's upcoming anniversary. Did you need more money?"

"Yeah, it's about their anniversary, and no on the money." There was a sucking sound on the other end of the line. LaShun must be baking and licking the batter off a spoon. Or her finger. She did that whenever she was nervous or upset. "Did you know they were seeing a marriage counselor?"

"Are they? Good. I suggested it to Dad after their blow-up here back in May."

LaShun's sigh sounded relieved. "I told Mom the same thing when she showed up in Portland without him. The kids were bummed Dad wasn't with her."

"Really? You suggested they see someone?"

"Why does that sound so strange to you?"

Aisha laughed. "Because you always take Mom's side!"

"And you always take Dad's," LaShun shot back. "Martin was the swing vote. He told them they weren't invited to his wedding if they were going to act like spoiled, nasty children."

"I doubt Renata would have let him disinvite his own parents."

LaShun snickered. "Or maybe he realized she'd force him to go to Vegas if he did."

"That's because our baby brother is more invested in having the fairytale wedding than our future sister-in-law," Aisha added.

"Anyway," LaShun continued. "Back to Mom and Dad. She called this morning. The therapy must have worked because they want to renew their vows for their forty-fifth anniversary, instead of just doing a family dinner. Since their anniversary is on a Thursday this year, she wants to throw an engagement party for Martin and Renata the following Saturday, so we all aren't making two trips down to Atlanta."

Wow. Not only Mom, but LaShun thinking ahead? Maybe some of that therapy was wearing off on her big sister.

Aisha pulled her planner up on her computer monitor. "Okay, marking those dates on the calendar."

"Also, I haven't gotten an RSVP from Harri. She's not pissed at Mom and Dad, is she? They're both pretty embarrassed they blew her off when they were in Canyon Pointe."

"No, she's not. The invite's probably in the mess of paperwork on her desk. I'll nag her about it." Aisha hesitated a second before she asked, "What about Jeremy and Leo?"

"I already talked to Leo, and he can't get Jeremy to come. I don't know why he thinks Mom and Dad wouldn't approve of their marriage. They were pretty hurt Jeremy didn't invite them."

"Whoa! Roll that back. Leo and Jeremy got married? When the hell did this happen?"

"I know something you don't know?" LaShun cackled.

"Quit dancing around your kitchen, bitch, and answer the question." With everything that had been happening in hers and Harri's lives, Jeremy must have been scared to share his little bit of good news.

"I think they both realized they've got a good thing. They were looking for a house together, and a week ago Saturday, they decided to make it official down at Judge Inunza's office."

"Thanks for making me feel like a total shit." New tears formed in Aisha's eyes. She'd been so consumed with her own petty problems she hadn't paid any attention to the life of one of her best friends. "I'll talk to Jeremy, too."

"Or you could sic Harri on him."

Aisha laughed. "I thought you wanted him to come."

At the knock on her office door, she looked up. Harri Winters, her law partner, stood in the doorway with a large file and a serious expression.

"Speak of the devil. Harri's in my office with her 'we need to attorney' look. I'll call you later tonight."

"You'd better, then you can tell me about her new boyfriend. Leo was pretty coy about it. Love you."

"Love you, too." Aisha set the receiver back in its cradle and held up a finger when Harri opened her mouth. "Before you get started, Mom and Dad's forty-fifth anniversary is Thursday, September 6th, you're invited for their vow renewal along with Martin's engagement party the following Saturday, and LaShun's ticked you didn't RSVP for the original dinner."

Harri's jaw snapped shut. She closed the office door quietly behind her before she plopped in one of the visitor chairs. "That's only a week away. Have you told them about the bun yet?"

Her ponytail swung as she inclined her chin toward Aisha's abdomen. Her new chunky highlights shone bright against her dark hair. Harri had finally given in about letting Jeremy color her hair after the receptionist at Tim's physical therapist's office had asked if Harri were Tim's mother.

Aisha rubbed her bump. "What do I tell them? That my son's dad is already dead?"

"Sweetie, that baby is their grandson." Harri set the file on the chair beside her and leaned her elbows on Aisha's new desk. "You're past your first trimester. It's time to tell your family."

"I just turned forty-one, and I'm not married." Aisha shook her head. "If I wear some baggy clothes—"

"Then they're definitely going to know something's wrong. Baggy's not your style." Harri shook her head again. "And I may have to bow out. We don't have your maternity leave replacement set up yet—"

"Wait!" Aisha sat up straight. "What happened to Susan Kennedy?"

"Nothing." Harri used her fake soothing voice that drove Aisha insane. "She had to delay joining us for a week." She waved at the stack of paperwork on Aisha's desk. "But word's getting out about us, and we've received a dozen requests for legal services this morning alone."

"So, what you are doing a horrible job of saying is it's not smart for both of us to be out of town right now." Aisha eyed her partner. "How about you go to Atlanta instead and I mind the law firm?"

"Oh, no, no, no!" Harri sat up straight and waggled an index finger at Aisha. "You are not using me as an excuse to avoid your family. Besides, isn't Jeremy invited?"

"He is, but—" Aisha hesitated. She hated spilling, but if Harri already knew. "Did you know he and Leonardo tied the knot?"

"I . . . yes," Harri murmured. "If it makes you feel better, I wasn't invited either."

"But they told you. Why didn't anyone tell me?" Aisha threw up her hands. Her eyes burned. Dammit, she was getting emotional over something so ridiculous. Stupid hormones. She reached for a tissue. "Why am I the last to know?"

"Because . . ." Whatever Harri was about to say changed into a supercilious smile. The one she'd been wearing since the federal government presumed Rey was dead. The one that needed to be smacked off her face.

Aisha clenched her fists in her lap. She'd worked too hard to get her powers under control. At least she didn't float to the ceiling every time she got upset any more.

"Why don't you come over for dinner tonight?" Harri said with her fake brightness. "I'll call Jeremy and tell him to bring Leo."

"I don't know what's worse—being the fifth wheel at your dinner or the fact that you can't cook."

Harri looked down for a moment, but when her gaze returned to Aisha, some of the old Harri shone through. "You can't spend every night moping in your loft."

The intercom buzzed before Aisha could think of an appropriate rejoinder. Patty wouldn't interrupt unless it was important.

"Guys, Tim needs you two in the basement. Like now. There's a big problem with Qiang. Arthur is already on his way down."

The word "problem" probably didn't cover whatever was happening downstairs. Qiang Reilly, AKA the superhero known as Sparx and one of their firm's clients, was usually too proud to ask for help. And for her to go to their security chief, who was the former vigilante known as the Ghost Owl, much less accept assistance from their IT manager Arthur, who was the former supervillain Professor Venom, meant things were very, very bad.

"On our way." Aisha stood. "C'mon. I'll fly us down."

"No, you are not," Harri growled. She was up and out the door pretty fast for someone with no powers.

Aisha followed her into the reception area. "Aw, come on! I need to practice. What if I only have them another five months?"

Patty grinned as they approached her desk. "Still won't let you fly her around, huh?"

"Shut up, or you're fired," Harri snapped as she raced past.

"Don't worry," Aisha added as she strode by their assistant. "I'll rehire you."

Patty chuckled behind them while Harri punched in the security code for the basement entrance.

Aisha closed the door behind them, vaulted over the railing, and floated down to the concrete floor twelve feet below. She had the code punched in and the second security door open by the time her partner jogged down the stairs.

"After you, madam." Aisha gestured inside the old fallout shelter with a flourish.

"Show off," Harri muttered.

Once through, Aisha resealed the door and reset the basement level security alarm. Angry voices echoed down one of the side hallways.

"That doesn't sound good," she murmured.

"What doesn't sound good?" A perplexed expression twisted Harri's face.

"Tim and Arthur arguing." Aisha strode in the direction of the fight.

"Wait! Slow down!" Harri jogged up beside her. "Tim and Arthur are arguing?"

"Yeah." Aisha slowed her pace. It had nothing to do with superpowers. Her legs were simply longer than Harri's. "You can't hear them?"

"Damn you and your super hearing," Harri growled.

They reached the next security door. Harri made a point of pushing in front of Aisha to enter the code.

Her unplanned pregnancy had been a sore point with Harri, but the unexpected triggering of superpowers by Aisha's hormones seemed to send her best friend over the edge. Not for the first time, she wondered why Harri had wanted to open their boutique law firm specializing in the representation of supers when she had resented them long before the asshole pretending to be Rey had pounded her boyfriend to a bloody pulp.

Harri wrenched the door open and winced at the obvious shouting, except

Qiang had joined in the fray with the mix of English and Vietnamese obscenities. It was the fourth super who drew Aisha's attention.

The one who wore her beloved Rey's face.

She flew across the room and grabbed the man by the throat. His eyes widened, and his hands locked on her wrist. When she slammed him into the thick concrete wall, a puff of gray powder rose. She cocked her right fist back.

"No!" Harri inserted herself between Aisha and the imposter and tried to shove her back. "Aisha! You're not a killer!"

"Get out of my way, Harri!" Aisha glared at the man who probably had murdered Rey and nearly succeeded with Tim.

"He was under a supervillain's influence, and you know it," Harri snapped. "It wasn't his fault!"

"Look, I don't blame you." The man she only knew as Hunahpu released her wrist, and his hands dropped to his sides. "I deserve whatever punishment you want to dish out, but help me find my brother before you kill me."

"What?" Aisha said at the same time as Harri, who turned to face him.

"You heard Xquic when she took me." Disbelief and worry crossed his face. Maybe he was concerned they would commit him to a psychiatric facility for talking about a Mayan goddess like she was real.

Except Aisha and Harri had an extended conversation with the woman claiming to be Xquic.

"Sh-she is certain Xbalanque, er, Reyes is still alive," Hunaphu finished nervously. "She detected his . . . essence or whatever you want to call it."

"Then tell me where he is," Aisha hissed.

"I don't know. Xquic doesn't know either. She couldn't pinpoint his location, and she wants him back alive as much as you do."

"Why couldn't she locate him? She's supposed to be a goddess."

He fumbled under the collar of his cream-colored polo shirt and produced a leather thong. At the end hung a piece of jade, green with a curved white streak. The Mayan symbols for love and protection were carved into the stone.

The same symbols that had been carved into Rey's amulet. Only his had a straight blue streak through the stone.

"The protection spells she placed on our talismans hide us from everyone's sight, mortal and immortal. She sensed him for a day, but before she could triangulate his position, she lost him. She believes he's regained possession of his amulet."

Aisha's heart jumped. No. She slammed the door on that glimmer of hope. She couldn't bear dealing with the loss of Rey again. And for all she knew the man in front of her lied, playing some game with her head. But damn, how she wanted his words to be true.

Slowly, she released Hunahpu and took a step back. "Or he's already dead."

"Don't say that." Harri's shoulders sagged. "Tell her she's wrong."

Hunahpu shook his head, his attention focused on Aisha. "No, he isn't dead. Our grandfather is the Mayan lord of the Underworld. If Reyes were dead, he'd be holding it over our mother's head."

"He's lying!" Arthur's anguished cry sent an answering tremor through Aisha.

She turned toward him. Sparx held him back as best she could on one leg. From the size of the gash on her thigh and the amount of blood dripping down her costume, she couldn't put any weight on the other leg. Arthur trembled so bad Aisha doubted he noticed the superhero's grip on his arms.

"Aisha?"

She faced Tim. The former vigilante superhero everyone else knew as Jatz'om Kuh, the Ghost Owl, sat in his wheelchair. The wheelchair Hunahpu had put him in. Tim was still facing another surgery on his left leg. The one Hunahpu had practically crushed while he pretended to be Captain Justice.

"Let's hear him out." Tim gazed thoughtfully at Qiang before his attention returned to Aisha. "Sparx wouldn't have brought him down here if she weren't convinced of his sincerity." A wry smile quirked his lips. "The only one harder to convince than Sparx is Harri."

Harri stepped from between Aisha and Hunahpu and gave him a vicious grin. "And if I don't like what I hear, I won't stop Aisha from killing you. Got me, jerkwad?"

"Yes, ma'am." No mocking in his expression. If he were faking the total sincerity on his face, he was one hell of an actor.

Aisha glared at the super. It was their grade school playground all over again when she had been the new student, and the other girls had been picking on a much smaller one named Harri. This time though the stakes were a hell of a lot higher than bloody noses and scraped knees.

"I hope you really do understand my partner," she said softly. "Because there won't be enough of you for your people, whoever they really are, to fill a copper pot when I'm done if you're lying about this."

CHAPTER 3

Harri breathed a little sigh of relief when Aisha released Hunahpu's throat and backed away. If the two of them got into a fight here in the basement, they could bring the whole building down.

And kill everyone else in the process.

"Sit down, and start from the beginning." Harri jabbed an index finger in the direction of one of the wheeled stools. "Who are you really?"

He crossed to the stool and sat. "Who I thought I was and what I am are two different things." He raked both hands through his dark hair. "I was raised as Steve Connors up in Seattle. My parents, well, the folks I know as my parents, adopted me when I was a few weeks old."

"Did you know about the adoption?" Harri grabbed another stool and perched on it.

He chuckled. "When your dad's Caucasian, your mom's Asian, and you're neither, you figure out pretty quick you're adopted."

"How was the adoption handled?" Harri asked.

"It was a private one." Steve drew and released a deep breath. "According to the attorney who handled it, the woman who was caring for me was my aunt. She claimed her sister had died in an accident and her brother-in-law had been killed during the troubles in Honduras."

He shrugged. "The attorney did his homework. She had birth certificates for herself and her alleged sister. A U.S. birth certificate for me. A death certificate for the sister. He even called the U.S. consulate in Honduras to try to confirm my supposed father's identity. He and his pregnant wife were on a list of people applying to get the hell out of Honduras. My alleged father disappeared a few days later, but the consulate had a record of the wife being granted a visa. Now, I find out it was all bullshit."

"When did you learn you were a super?" Harri asked.

He smirked. "When I was ten. My dad, well, my adoptive dad's boss and his family came to our house for dinner. The boss's son was twelve. The jerk pushed me off the platform for my treehouse."

"No one saw?" Sparx asked. She sat on one of the worktables with her injured leg propped up while Arthur examined and cleaned her wound.

"This would be easier without the spandex on," he grumbled.

"I want to hear this," she snapped.

"To answer your question, Miss Sparx, no," Steve said. "I threatened to hurt him if he told anyone. And I agree with Mr. Arthur. You need to get that cut taken care of. If it's all right with Miss Harri, we won't continue until you come back."

Harri had spent more than her share of time in depositions as a Canyon Pointe city attorney. Either this kid was the real deal, or he'd win next season's best actor award. Of course, there was an easier way to find out the truth about his story.

"Tim, you want to show Arthur where your medical supplies are and maybe scrounge up some extra clothes for Sparx?"

Arthur opened his mouth to protest that he knew where everything was in the Owl's Nest, but Sparx jabbed an elbow into his rib cage. Harri knew from first-hand experience how hard the superhero could hit.

On the other hand, Tim's dark blue eyes twinkled. He must have been trying to come up with an excuse to get himself or Arthur to a computer without being obvious.

"This way," he rolled past everyone and out the door.

"We'll be right back," Sparx added, but her comment was directed at Steve.

"Don't worry. He's not going anywhere," Aisha said sourly.

Arthur helped Sparx get vertical, and they followed Tim. Arthur not-so-casually hit the basement intercom button when he walked past the doorjamb.

Steve looked at Harri. "They're going to verify my story, aren't they?"

"Yep." Harri crossed her arms.

"None of you like me," he stated. A line creased the space between his dark eyebrows.

"No," Aisha answered.

"Xquic said I hurt my twin brother's friends when I was under a sorcerer's spell." Steve's fists tightened against his thighs until his knuckles were pale mountains poking from his tan flesh.

"It was more the trying to kill us that pissed us off," Harri said dryly.

"Shit," he muttered. "She left that part out."

"You don't remember anything that happened back around the end of June?" Aisha asked.

Steve waved toward the intercom. "Is it okay to answer if the other three can hear us?"

"Go ahead." Tim's voice had a tinny quality through the speaker. So did Sparx's laughter.

"The last events I remember clearly happened the day I arrived in Honduras." His hands relaxed. "After college graduation, I wanted to do a year in the Peace Corps before I started on my Masters degree. I went to take a shower at the hostel before the welcome dinner."

Harri could see what was coming. "You took off your original amulet."

He nodded and touched the small lump under his shirt. "Mom and Dad said it was the only thing I had left from my biological mother. Sometimes, I've taken it off before to shower at home and at college. Why would that one time have mattered?"

The stricken expression on Steve's face was so close to Rey's. It made Harri re-evaluate her opinion of the man. This was probably how Rey would have turned out if he'd given half the opportunities his brother had.

"Geography and some planning on your nurse's part," Aisha said softly.

Harri tilted her head and regarded her partner. "You think she ditched Steve on purpose?"

Aisha shrugged. "If you were on the run with your goddaughter, what would you do?"

Harri nodded as she caught up with Aisha's conjecture. "Find the safest place to stash her and lay down a false trail. Get the bad guys as far from her as I could."

"She might not have known the Conners' names or where they lived," Aisha added. "If the bad guys caught up with her and tortured her, she'd never be able to give them any information."

"Crap." Harri rubbed her temples. "That doesn't explain why Steve could take off his amulet but Rey couldn't."

"Triangulation" came Arthur's tinny voice over the intercom. "The bad guys were probably getting blips all over the place between Steve, his nurse, Rey, and Maria. Steve's nurse may have even gone to another continent. For example, the parrot-lizards can't teleport by themselves. They would have to find a way to cross the Atlantic if she went to, say, Paris. Maybe the signal is weaker the farther away it is. That would make it harder to determine direction."

"Ugh," Harri muttered. "I'm getting a headache from all this."

"Good thing I brought you coffee and Vitamin I," Tim said cheerily as he rolled back into the lab.

Behind him, Arthur helped Sparx into the room. A little flicker of jealousy ran through Harri at Sparx wear Tim's clothes. But the swath of gauze covering most of her thigh mitigated some of Harri's illogical reaction.

Sparx had forgone her cowl besides the rest of her superhero togs. That was weird. She was pretty damn anal about guarding her secret identity, especially since she had a special needs son and her elderly parents at home.

"Vitamin I?" Steve asked with a confused expression.

"Ibuprofen," everyone else answered in unison.

Tim grabbed the travel mug in his chair's cup holder and handed it to Harri along with a bottle of pills. She popped off the bottle lid and shook out two ibuprofen capsules before she chased them down with a swallow of an Italian roast with a splash of milk at the perfect temperature.

"What? I don't get any?" Aisha asked in mock dismay.

"I don't have any decaf down here, and you can't take ibuprofen right now." Tim shrugged. "Sorry." He turned to Steve. "Excellent grades at Harvard by the way."

The kid blushed just like Rey would have.

Harri choked on her mouthful of coffee. "Harvard?" she said between coughing bouts. Sparx slapped her back a little harder than necessary.

"That's enough," Harri snapped.

"Just don't want both of my attorneys in the hospital at the same time." But Sparx didn't look the least bit sorry. She was never going to let go of the fact she'd been bested by a non-super.

Though in all fairness, Harri had been fighting for her life at the time. Corvus had extorted Sparx into killing Harri by threatening Sparx's family. Harri glared at Sparx's back as Arthur helped her over to a third stool. Nope, she definitely didn't regret fighting dirty that night. Sparx needed to get over herself.

"What was your major?" Aisha asked.

"Dual degrees in business and accounting," Steve said sheepishly. "What did Rey study?"

"Philosophy and literature," Harri answered. It wasn't a true lie. Rey had been reading Aristotle and Homer when he disappeared.

But she knew Steve's type, had grown up in that privileged world herself, and her protective streak when it came to the people she cared about surged to the surface. She'd been working hard to keep it under control. The last time she even mentioned Patty or Aisha needed some rest, Aisha threatened to drop her into Lake Del Oro from ten thousand feet. Patty vowed she would be Aisha's alibi.

"When did you tell your adoptive parents about your powers?" Aisha asked quietly.

"Two weeks ago when Xquic left me on their doorstep."

From the mix of relief and sadness in his tone, Harri could guess the next answer, but she asked the question anyway. "Why didn't you tell them about your powers before now?"

"Part of me was afraid they'd send me back to child services." He shook his head, and the brilliant gold of his eyes dulled. "I couldn't tell them the whole truth even now. I mean, who would believe this crazy story about Mayan gods? So, the statement I gave the state department and the FBI was I had been mistaken for the son of a Honduran superhero and kidnapped. One of the supervillain's minions realized they'd made a mistake, and she helped me escape."

"And what story did you tell your parents?" Tim appeared highly amused by Steve's tale though he kept a straight face.

"A little bit more of the truth." A rueful smile tilted the left side of Steve's mouth. "That I'd been kidnapped by enemies of my biological father. I found out he was a superhero who had been assassinated, but I resembled him enough that his former associates figured out who I was and rescued me. I met my biological mother who told how she thought she was sending me and my twin brother to safety by getting us out of the country. She then helped me leave Honduras and return to the U.S. And I told them I wanted to go to Canyon Pointe to see if I could find my brother."

Steve shrugged. "Mom and Dad weren't happy about me coming down here, but they gave me access to the money they'd set aside for my masters degree with the promise that I call them every day."

"And how did you just so happen to stumble into Sparx?" Arthur spat. He was not taking this well, but then Rey was probably the first real friend the former supervillain had. Harri couldn't fault Arthur's loyalty.

Steve held up his hands. "Total accident. I flew into Canyon Pointe last night. By plane," he added belatedly at the looks he got from everyone. "I'd planned to call Winters & Franklin since they are listed as Captain Justice's reps this morning, but I was wide awake before your office opened. All I did was step out of the hotel for a walk to clear my head, and I stumbled into the middle of the battle between Sparx and Steelrose."

"Steelrose?" Tim's eyebrows rose. "She's out of prison?"

"Yeah," Sparx said sourly as she waved at her injured thigh. "She decided to celebrate by robbing the Canyon Bank branch over on High Street and MLK."

"Poor girl." Harri grinned. "Did you have your morning jog ruined?"

"I take supervillains more seriously than I do middle-aged attorneys," Sparx shot back.

Harri bit her tongue to keep her normal sarcastic response in check. Sparx was only three years younger than her and Aisha, but getting into a fight with a client in front of Steve wasn't the image she wanted to project. Not to mention the stupidity of quarreling with a paying client out of pride.

Sparx's attention returned to Tim. "Captain Mojave handled the assist and the cleanup while I brought Steve here. Didn't want to take the chance of someone recognizing him on the street."

"But I'm—" Steve looked down at himself. "—dressed in regular clothes."

"Rey is too well known in Canyon Pointe," Harri said. "Both in his civilian identity and his superhero persona. Did Xquic give you a starting point of where to look for him?"

Steve pulled out his wallet and removed a slip of paper. "The writing on the scrap of cloth she gave me is in ancient Mayan. It's back at my hotel if you want to see the original. One of my friends took it to his Mesoamerican history professor at the University of Washington. Here's the original symbols and our number they translate into, but I have no idea what it means." He handed the piece to Harri.

She held out the paper and examined the neat black writing on the white sheet. No reason to waste time running back upstairs for her reading glasses. The numbers didn't make any sense though. They weren't a phone number or an address.

Tim wheeled closer to her stool and looked over her arm. "Those almost look like map coordinates. Arthur?"

Arthur kicked another rolling stool over to the desktop computer, sat, and started banging on the keyboard. At least, he was taking out his anger by physically abusing the furniture and not melting anything with his acid formula. "Ready."

Harri held out the page so Tim could read off the numbers for Arthur. Good to know she wasn't the only one too proud to get their reading glasses.

Arthur turned away from the monitor, frowning. "It's a private ranch about an hour outside of Denver." He and Tim stared at each other.

"Son of a bitch," Tim muttered.

"What?" Harri's attention flipped between the two men.

Tim's expression turned bleak. "That's a property Corvus controls."

"The facility where Trubble said the staff was slaughtered?" Aisha asked.

"Possibly." Tim rubbed his chin.

"I could take Steve to the location—" Harri started.

"We need to talk first. Partner-to-partner. Upstairs." From Aisha's scowl, this wasn't going to be a pleasant discussion.

CHAPTER 4

Sympathy sparked in Rey at the expression of rage on the woman's face. Once he'd gotten over the fear after his mother's murder, a similar fury had taken him. He'd flown as far away as he could.

But there wasn't much a seven-year-old could do on the streets of Portland for a living by himself. Between speed and flight, he evaded the cops, but he'd resorted to shoplifting when he couldn't get enough change for food through begging or scrounging through dumpsters.

The superstrength had taken him by surprise when he hit puberty. The one convenience store owner who'd caught him still haunted his nightmares. He hadn't meant to hurt the man. He simply jerked his arm in an effort to escape, and the owner flew across two aisles and crashed into a glass door in the refrigerated section. Milk, soda, and blood mixed in an ugly puddle on the floor.

The man survived, but Rey hadn't been able to make things right. Not until he'd started earning endorsements as Captain Justice.

One night, he'd left the bag of cash on the convenience store owner's doorstep and rang the doorbell. The man's wife opened the door and peered fearfully at the plain canvas bag before she called for her husband.

He knelt, unzipped the bag, and checked the contents. Tears first ran down his face, then his wife's as they read Rey's note that simply said, "I'm sorry for hurting you eight years ago."

Tim was right. No one ever looked up. The couple never saw Rey hovering over their neighbors' roof. It wasn't enough for the pain and suffering he'd caused the couple, but it was a start.

And maybe he could do something to help this woman.

She had turned back to the computer, her fingers typing furiously.

He pulled on the scrubs and cleared his throat. "I know you have no reason to trust me, but is there something I can call you besides 'Miss'? My name is Rey."

She looked up at him and chuckled in a low throaty way. "Hello, Rey. I'm Monica."

When she turned back to the monitor, he bent as much as his injury allowed him and peered over her shoulder. "'Gemini Project'? I've never heard of that in Corvus's files."

Monica gazed up at him, suspicion back on her lovely features.

Oops.

Maybe part of the truth would suffice.

"One of my closest friends used to be a supervillain." When she reached for her gun again, Rey held up a hand. "He's gone straight, except for hacking into the Corvus servers to keep an eye on them."

Her right eyebrow lifted. "You sure your buddy isn't playing both sides?"

"I'm sure he isn't." Rey smiled at the memory of the night Arthur had asked him for courting advice when it came to Patty. "He's very much in love, and he's keeping clean because of her. But he keeps an eye on Corvus because they tried to frame him for attempted murder and the fire that destroyed the Canyon Pointe City Hall earlier this year. That's how Seismic Shift ended up in jail."

"Sounds like they picked the wrong guy to set up," Monica commented.

"They did it because they didn't think he had any friends." Rey straightened. His breath hissed out of him at the pain.

She turned back to the monitor. Her back muscles tensed under her clothes.

Shit. He'd said the wrong thing again.

"I'm sorry your friends didn't stick up for you when Corvus took your children," he murmured. "Maybe if you talk to my attorney, she can help you get them back."

A bitter laughter ripped out of her throat. "It doesn't matter anymore. They're already over eighteen."

"All right. I'm going to shut up now."

She looked over her shoulder at him. "It's old news, but I shouldn't be taking it out on you."

When she turned back to the monitor, she muttered, "There we go." She pulled her flashdrive from the USB slot and stood. "I've already taken care of the other servers. Think you can destroy this desktop, too? Make it look like it happened during your battle?"

Rey nodded. The last thing he wanted was Trubble to get his hands on any information regarding Rey's personal biology.

Assuming the jerk didn't already have it.

Rey inclined his head toward the door. "You might want to step outside so the debris doesn't hit you."

Monica didn't argue with him. She left the lab and pulled the door shut behind her.

He grabbed the swivel chair she'd been using and swung. The monitor shot across the room and shattered against the titanium wall that had formed part of his cage. Next, he jumped and came down on the desk with all his strength. The desk itself crumbled, the computer tower's plastic exterior fractured into thousands of pieces, and the only thing left of the metal inside was molded into two large footprints.

Rey went to the cabinet with spare scrubs and pulled a drawstring from another pair of pants. The woven cord wasn't the sturdiest of holders for his amulet, but it would have to do for now. He threaded the cord through the hole in the stone.

After a second's consideration, he grabbed one of the flashdrives out of the supply closet. It was the same type as the one Monica had used. He threaded it onto the cord and tied everything around his neck. He couldn't let anyone have his personal information. He needed to swap the blank one with Monica's copy when he had the chance.

When he opened the lab door, the awful scent of gasoline filled the air of the hallway. The walls and edges of the floor had an oily sheen to them. How much had Monica used that the gasoline hadn't evaporated?

She appeared at the end of the hall and waved at him. "Come on, Rey! Let's go!"

He ran a couple of steps across the section of floor not soaked in gasoline, but pain shooting across his ribs sent spots floating across his eyes. For some reason, he didn't want to fly in front of Monica. Maybe he didn't trust her as much as he wanted to. He settled for a fast walk.

She led him outside, and it wasn't the fresh ocean air that caught in his throat. They really were on what looked like a decrepit drilling platform. But looking closer, someone had cleverly painted the exterior to look like rust and salt water scaling.

He followed her to a ladder that extended down to the water. What looked like a very expensive speedboat was tied to the bottom rung.

"Can you make it down without help and without destroying my getaway vehicle?" Monica grinned at him.

He nodded and started making his way down. About halfway, he realized she wasn't on the ladder.

"Monica!"

Her head appeared over the edge of the platform. "What's wrong?"

"Aren't you coming?"

"Of course, silly." Her grin turned almost maniacal. "You need to get down there and settled. I'm just taking care of the last details."

Setting fire to the rig, he realized belatedly. Maybe he had more of the gaseous drug still in his system than he'd realized.

Rey loosen the knots holding the boat to the oil rig, in case Monica had misjudged her pyromania, before he settled in the seat at the back of the boat.

A huge *whoosh* sounded above him, and flames shot to the height of the derrick. Monica appeared at the ladder and climbed down. Faster than a normal human, he noticed.

If she was a super, that would explain Corvus's interest in her daughters. But she hadn't shared, so he decided not to say anything.

She pulled the lines loose and into the boat with her. She took the seat behind the wheel and ignited the engine. Waves of heat rolled over them from above.

"Now where to?" Rey shouted over the roar of the engine.

"A safe harbor," she called over her shoulder.

Worry wiggled up Rey's spine. Normally, he could rely on his powers and his friends to get himself out of a jam. But he was hurt, and he had nothing but Monica's word concerning his location. Even if she were telling the truth, he'd be hard-pressed to fly across the Pacific Ocean when he was healthy.

He'd have to use his brain and wait for an opportunity to contact someone at the Lechuza Building back in Canyon Pointe. Hopefully, he didn't get into more trouble before then.

CHAPTER 5

"I don't like the idea of leaving you here alone with him," Aisha muttered after she and Harri retreated upstairs to the conference room for a partner discussion. At least, it was more of a neutral location than either of their offices, but neither of them sat. She didn't even know why she was trying to talk some sense into Harri. The woman was the proverbial immovable object.

"Steve's not going to do anything." Harri crossed her arms, almost as if she heard Aisha's thoughts. "He has a vested interest in stopping the people who brainwashed him—"

"He is not Rey!" Aisha ran her hands over her hair to keep from strangling Harri. The feel of her dreds still threw her off, but she couldn't afford to get her hair cut every week. And she knew damn well that Leo was undercharging her for the henna coloring as fast as her hair was growing. Stupid pregnancy hormones. "None of you can treat him like he is!"

"I know he's not," Harri snapped. "Give me a little credit. But if there's any chance of finding Rey, I'm going to use Steve."

Aisha stared at the carpet. She could barely see the toes of her shoes. It wouldn't be much longer before she couldn't see her feet at all. She'd always envisioned sharing the changes to her body with her baby's father, and this argument with her best friend slashed at her raw emotional scars. She took a deep breath and released it.

"Look, I've already resigned myself to the fact the man I love is never coming home and I'm raising this baby by myself—"

"You've really given up?"

Aisha looked up at her partner. Harri's stricken expression said just how much she was buying the asshole's Kool-Aid.

"I can't—" Aisha swallowed the lump in her throat that threatened to choke her. "I can't go through losing him again. Please don't ask me to do that."

"I'm not asking you to," Harri murmured. She uncrossed her arms and held out her hands. "I'm asking you to have faith in me."

"When did we switch personalities?" Aisha shook her head.

"I've always been the crusader." An impish smile tilted Harri's mouth.

"No, I mean, when did you start having hope and when did I lose mine?" Aisha's eyes burned. She wanted to believe. Lord knew how she wanted to believe. But if her hopes were dashed again, she'd totally lose her mind.

"Let me check this out for my own sake," Harri said. "I'm the one who dragged Rey into the superhero world. Please, girl, don't fight me on this one. I don't want my godson to think I didn't try to help his daddy."

Crap. Aisha closed her eyes. She should have known this was as much about Harri's guilty conscience as it was any wishful thinking.

Once she was sure she wouldn't start bawling, she opened her eyes and nodded. "All right, but I expect you back here before I have to leave for Atlanta."

"Sooner if I can. Scout's honor." Harri saluted her.

Aisha laughed and shook her head. "Says the woman kicked out of our troop for telling off our den mother."

"Do we have to rehash that particular affair of my dad's every frickin' month?"

"Quit making oaths on the scout honor code and I will."

Harri threw her hands in the air. "Fine. You win."

⁂

Except Aisha didn't really win after all. Harri managed to book herself and Steve on an afternoon flight to Denver. While Harri took Steve back to his hotel to collect his things before their departure, Aisha drove Qiang home.

"This morning's incident didn't cause too many issues with your boss, did it?" Aisha glanced at the superhero sitting in the passenger seat of her new hybrid. It was a far more sensible car than her destroyed BMW.

It was a sensible car for a single mother. A single mother just like Qiang.

"Reality just hit you, didn't it?" Qiang said softly.

"What?"

"I had the same look in the mirror after Kevin's accident. All this power at my fingertips, and I couldn't save the man I loved." Leave it to Qiang to understand exactly what Aisha was feeling. And she was probably going to have a baby that was even more special needs than Qiang's autistic son.

Life simply wasn't fair.

Aisha glanced at Qiang again, but the other woman was staring out the passenger window. "You didn't answer my question about your boss."

Qiang turned toward her, a grimace twisting her face. "Yeah, my days off are starting to cause problems."

"We can file a leave of absence in the national superhero registry—"

"It's not just the superhero stuff. Connor is having problems at school." Qiang's heavy sigh emphasized the weight on her shoulders. "And my mother had a mild stroke two days ago."

Shit. This was bad.

Aisha's favorite coffee chain was two blocks away. She checked her mirrors before she signaled her left turn.

"Where are we going?" Alarm rattled Qiang's voice.

"We're going to get a cup of coffee and have a talk."

"But—"

"You've been there when I needed you for personal crap, Qiang." Aisha shot the other woman a no-nonsense look. "I'm going to do the same for you whether you like it or not."

CHAPTER 6

"Turn left in one half mile," the GPS navigator ordered.

Harri hated the damn things, but she had to admit they came in handy in unfamiliar terrain. And she needed to have a word with Arthur when she got back. The drive out of Denver was a lot more than an hour.

"Should we go back to the highway and get a hotel room? It'll be dark soon."

For a split second, Harri would have sworn Rey sat beside her in the rental car, his skin glowing in the beams from the setting sun. He would have been just as cautious, always conscious the people around him weren't invulnerable like he was.

Except he wasn't so invulnerable after all. And despite Aisha's protests about Steve, part of Harri was protective about him, too.

"I want to find the place first," she said. She hit the turn signal even though they hadn't seen another car for the last ten miles.

"But you'll stay in the car, right?"

"You are as annoying as your brother," she grumbled. Weeds had encroached on the edges of the asphalt road they turned onto, and tree branches joined overhead, forming a dark tunnel. Unlike her ancient Honda, the daytime running lights automatically switched to the brighter nighttime driving headlights. "Since when did you become so protective?"

Steve exhaled. "I would hope he would be as protective of my parents if they were in trouble."

"I'm not Rey's mother," Harri muttered.

"You act like it."

"And I'm not in trouble."

"Yet."

She glanced at Steve. His bright, charming smile was almost like Rey's, but Aisha was right. There was a subtle difference. It didn't have the innocent quality. No, this was the smile of a cocky Harvard graduate who had everything handed to him in life. It reminded her too much of her dad.

Or Tim.

And that comparison wasn't fair to any of the men in her life.

"Rey would help anyone in trouble, regardless of who they were," she murmured.

"That's good to know." He waited a moment before he added, "But you folks still don't trust me."

"After what happened back at the beginning of July, we're going to need some time."

"I . . . understand."

Harri felt sorry for the kid. From his tone, he didn't understand. Not really. Either he was the best actor on the face of the planet, or he really didn't remember what had happened when he'd pretended to be Rey.

But Sparx said she didn't remember trying to kill anyone when she'd been under the Honduran supervillain Professor Paranoia's control. As much as Harri and the superhero disliked each other on a personal level, Sparx wouldn't a lie.

Especially not about anything that might affect her kid in any way, shape, or form.

"Your destination is on the right," the navigator proclaimed.

Harri pressed the brake, and the rental car rolled to a stop. Through a break in the trees, a wild, overgrown meadow glowed golden beneath the setting sun. They had a half hour of light left at most, and she really didn't want to go traipsing through an unknown area in the dark. Who knew what critters lurked in the high grasses, much less what booby-traps Corvus might have set?

"Does that look like a road to you?" Steve pointed at a spot a few yards ahead.

Harri let off the brake and let their rental coast to the spot he indicated. He was right. A dirt lane lay between a few trees. Weeds nearly covered it. It would have been easy to miss even in the middle of the day.

Beyond the little grove that guarded the road, a bar gate blocked access to the meadow. A couple of signs were attached to the gate. One said, "Private property." The other warned, "No trespassing." In other words, nothing to make it stand out from all the other farms and ranches they'd passed once they left the Denver suburbs behind.

"You want me to open the gate?" Steve looked at her expectantly.

They were in the middle of nowhere with no backup. If it were her ex-husband sitting beside her, he'd be chewing her a new asshole for going into a potentially dangerous situation with a questionable ally. But the need to find out what the hell had happened to Rey and Steve was an itch she couldn't reach. At least, not by sitting safely in the rental car.

She backed the car enough to turn onto the dirt lane and stopped in front of the gate. "Let's take a quick look, and come back in the morning."

"All right." A thread of anticipation ran in Steve's voice. "What would Rey do for you in this situation?"

"Fly reconnaissance." The words were out of her mouth before she could stop them.

"Okay." He pushed the door open, climbed out, and drifted upward out of sight.

"Shit," she muttered as she pressed the button to kill the engine. "Way to go, Harri." She shoved open the driver's side door. "Get a civilian outed as a super before you've even signed him as a client." She climbed out of the car and shaded her eyes against the low sun.

The grass behind the gate waved in the slight breeze. All except one patch, which rose straight up.

Because a man in gold and brown camouflage was attached to the grass. Or more accurately, the grass was attached to his poncho and helmet.

A click sounded behind her, and something very hard nudged the small of her back. "Call off your super, Winters, before someone gets hurt."

CHAPTER 7

Rey didn't realize he'd fallen asleep until someone was calling his name and shaking his shoulder. He jerked upright and pain shot through his right side. "What is it? Is it the baby?"

Instead of Aisha, a pale face peered at him through a darkness that was punctuated by twinkling lights. "Sweetheart, we haven't known each other long enough for that to happen." Monica straightened and shrugged. "Not that you aren't cute, but I've got a feeling you aren't much older than my kids."

"It-it was just a dream," he muttered and scrubbed his scratchy eyelids.

"Uh-huh." She crossed her arms. "Does your significant other know you're a super?"

Rey closed his eyes and exhaled. Of course. Monica may not be a telepath, but she'd been on the streets long enough to learn how to read people very, very well. He opened his eyes and looked up at her.

"Yes, she does."

"Does Corvus know she's knocked up?"

"I don't know." He had no idea how long he'd been imprisoned either. He cleared his throat. "I know this sounds like a stupid question, but what's the date?"

She chuckled. "Considering we're past the International Date Line, it's almost dawn on August 29th."

"What?" Rey jumped to his feet. Once again, agony ripped through his side, and he stumbled.

"Take it easy, kid." Monica caught him before he hit the deck of her boat. She was definitely stronger than her lithe build indicated. "You're not doing yourself any favors moving around like that. Think you can make it up to the pier. It's only a few rungs, but we need to get that injury taken care of, and I don't think it'll wait until high tide."

"Where are we?" He shuffled to the ladder with her help. Around them, a variety of personal-type boats bobbed in the water.

"Singapore. I've got contacts here that can get us back to the U.S. while staying off Corvus's radar."

"I can't pay you back until we get home. I don't have my ID or—"

"Kid, I only take money from my enemies." Her dark eyebrow lifted. "Are you my enemy?"

"I hope not," he said fervently.

"Good, because with friends I trade in favors. Someday, I'll ask for your help when I need it. For now—" She grinned and slapped his left buttock. "—up the ladder!"

He prayed she couldn't see his blush. Aisha would never have done something like that, in public or in private. He never quite understood what a classy lady like her saw in him. His thoughts only fed into his guilt. She probably thought he'd abandoned her and their baby, just like Harri said he would do.

When Rey reached the top of the ladder, a man waited on the pier. A local from his appearance. The stranger frowned at Rey.

He glanced down at Monica. "There's someone here."

"I know," she said before she slapped his bare foot. "Move your cute ass. I'm not hanging on the ladder all day."

Rey climbed onto the pier. The stranger's expression switched to a full-on scowl, but he broke into a broad smile when he saw Monica. He said something in a language Rey didn't understand.

She answered the stranger in kind, then said, "English if you don't mind." She inclined her head towards Rey. "My big fish doesn't know Mandarin. Rey, this is Ke."

Ke's chin jutted toward Rey. "Damn, Missy, did you hook him in the side?"

Rey reached for the spot where his scrubs covered his makeshift bandages. Warm stickiness met his fingers.

"I didn't do it," Monica said dryly. "But yeah, my big fish needs a little first aid."

Ke shook his head. "You out there picking fights with pirates again?"

"Something like that." She smiled. "Let's debate this somewhere else."

But Ke never asked Monica any more questions on the ride in his cab. A soft gray overcast turned lighter as the sun rose. He pulled into an alley in a not-so-nice part of the city and stopped in front of a vaguely blue door.

"Are you sure this is a safe place?" Rey leaned over as best he could in the back seat of the cab to check the roofs around them. Nothing obvious caught his attention, but this was totally unfamiliar territory.

"Would you rather go to a proper hospital?" Again, her raised eyebrow seemed to mock him.

He sighed. Of course, he couldn't. A super in a foreign nation without appropriate ID, much less a visa, was tantamount to an act of war.

"No." He pulled the lever of the door and carefully climbed out. The buildings were covered with soot and dirt, yet everything had a wet sheen to it, including the handful of doors he could see besides the one that really wanted to be blue.

Monica joined him. The cab accelerated down the alley before it turned left and disappeared from sight, leaving them alone and quite visible in the alley. Appearing unconcerned, she knocked a specific pattern on the door. As they waited, Rey scanned the rooftops again.

"Why do you keep doing that?" she asked.

"Doing what?"

"Looking up."

Rey shrugged only with his left shoulder. "Something my mentor taught me. Humans never look up."

The streets' neon lights reflected off the damp pavement and walls. The wild colors also reflected from Monica's narrowed eyes.

"And your mentor is?" she snarled.

"One of my attorney's other clients." He gave her what he hoped was an apologetic smile. "I'm sorry. I'm not supposed to be talking about him outside of her office."

"For someone who claims he's a victim, you sure do have a lot of secrets." But her body relaxed.

"It's the world we live in—"

The almost blue door swung open. An elderly woman glared at him and spouted something in Mandarin to Monica. At least, Rey assumed it was Mandarin. The language sounded an awful lot like what Ke spoke earlier at the pier. Finally, Monica gestured emphatically, and the woman stepped aside to let them inside.

The receiving area was stacked high with boxes bearing some type of Asian writing. Once the elderly woman shut and locked the door, she gestured for them to follow her. She led them through the stacks of cardboard and down a narrow hallway.

"Are we in trouble?" he whispered to Monica.

"Less than we were yesterday."

"Yesterday?"

She nodded. "I had to island hop to avoid some patrols and one ship I'm pretty sure contained pirates. You slept through the whole thing. With that nasty cut in your side, I figured you needed the rest."

The hallway dead-ended in front of a wooden panel. The elderly woman slid it into the wall. Once again, she beckoned Rey and Monica to step inside.

Worry stabbed Rey's nerves. The room was smaller than the ancient elevator in their building back home in Canyon Pointe. There were no obvious doors or windows.

He grabbed Monica's arm. "What's going on?"

"Calm down, Rey." The corner of her mouth twitched. "She's only scanning us for weapons."

He followed her into the little room and glared at the old woman. She stepped inside, slid the door closed, and glared right back at him. The walls vibrated with an odd hum, and the single overhead light turned a greenish color. He counted approximately five seconds before the light changed back to its yellow-white glow at the same time the hum stopped.

The entire back wall slid aside to show a much more modern and brightly lit area. In fact, it looked like a combination of Tim's labs and Jeremy's costume workshop. People bustled to and fro, working on pieces of outfits hanging from mannequins or constructing odd little gadgets on the tables full of equipment and parts.

A much younger woman in a lab coat and glasses stepped forward, a bright smile on her face. "It's been a while, Missy!" She gave Monica an enthusiastic hug which was returned. "I thought you'd never return to pick up your new costume."

"I'm going to need a little more than the costume, Kwan Li." She pulled the flashdrive out of one of the Velcro pockets on her tactical pants. "I've got something new for the auction block."

Kwan Li squealed in delight and reached for the drive.

Monica held it out of her reach. "You still owe me the payment from the last auction."

"Spoilsport." But the younger woman didn't seem upset. She made a beckoning gesture and headed down the closest aisle on the right. "Let's get a private room and talk business." She glanced over her shoulder. "Do I need to find a place for your new boytoy until we're done?"

"Boytoy?" Rey said indignantly.

"Rey's my new partner," Monica interjected smoothly. "That's another thing we're going to need—new papers for him. He's on Corvus's radar."

The younger woman abruptly halted, and Rey hissed in pain at his effort to keep from running into her. She pivoted and cocked her head.

"I'm guessing your new partner needs some medical attention as well, Missy?"

"Yes, please," Monica said. Her grin would have put the Cheshire Cat's to shame. "If it's not an inconvenience."

<hr>

Rey hated to admit it, but he was glad when the two women decided his medical care was their first order of business. After the injuries he'd seen his friends handle, he didn't know how they suffered through the pain, much less the treatment. The worst physical sensation he'd experienced before this was hunger.

No, the worst were the cuts on his arm the last time the monsters had gotten close to him. He'd forgotten what pain felt like in the nearly three years since that encounter.

Kwan Li led them to a very white room with three very white futons and three equally white ottomans. However, the futon cushions were actually covered in vinyl, which probably made it easier to clean off the blood.

Monica leaned against the wall to watch the proceedings. Kwan Li bade Rey to remove his scrubs top. He didn't have to fake pulling the cotton off carefully because of the pain, but he managed to keep the flashdrive behind his amulet.

Kwan Li poked at the nosepiece of her glasses as she peered closer at his chest. "That's an awesome carving. Is it an antique?"

"I don't think so," he replied. "Just a keepsake. It's the only thing I have left from my mother."

She nodded before she ordered him to lay down on his left side on one of the futons while she lifted off the top of the closest ottoman and pulled out a bright red toolbox. He carefully moved the amulet out of her way. He just hoped he'd kept the flashdrive hidden.

Kwan Li replaced the top, kicked the ottoman closer to him, and sat on it. After she donned protective gloves, it only took her a few seconds to cut off his makeshift bandages, but his invulnerable skin didn't apply to his body hair. He bit back a shout when she ripped off a huge swath of his chest hair along with the duct tape.

Kwan Li ignored the tears leaking across his nose as she wiped the slashes across his ribs with several antiseptic pads. She pulled a suture kit out of her big red toolbox. Both he and Monica shook their heads and said, "No."

"You're kidding me?" Disbelief made a crease between Kwan Li's fine eyebrows.

"Hey, if you want to destroy a perfectly good suture pack trying, be our guest," Monica said.

The younger woman muttered something under her breath that Rey didn't understand. She dropped the pack back in her toolbox and fished around before she produced a small tube.

"Seriously?" Monica stared at the tube. "You're going to superglue him back together?"

"This is specifically formulated for wounds," Kwan Li said primly. "And it's the only way to treat supers with unusual skin properties."

She carefully held the edges of the first slice together and squeezed the tube along the wound. The glue acted as she said. Soon, blood no longer oozed from the cuts.

"I understand why you would partner with an invulnerable super," Kwan Li said as she replaced the cap on the tube and tossed it back into her red toolbox. "But what are you into that something actually hurt your boy Rey?" She looked up at Monica.

"It has nothing to do with her." He slowly and carefully sat up. "These monsters killed my mom fifteen years ago, and they've been after me ever since. Corvus was stupid enough to keep me in one place for too long, and the personnel at the lab where I was being held paid for it with their lives."

"Monsters?" Both of Kwan Li's fine black eyebrows rose above the frames of her wire-rim glasses.

"Some kind of genetic hybrids," Monica said. "Our guess is they're keyed to his scent." Damn, she was good at coming up with a decent lie on the fly.

"So, these things won't show up here?" Kwan Li asked.

"Not if you can get us the papers we need to get out of Singapore in the next couple of hours." Rey smiled. "And as long as I go out the same door I came in, they'll follow my trail away from you and your people."

She nodded. "Very well then. Missy, take the top off the ottoman by you."

Kwan Li gathered the bloody bandages and the rest of the trash, including the scrubs shirt he had been wearing, while Monica did as she was asked. Kwan Li dumped everything inside the ottoman. She stripped off her surgical gloves and tossed them inside as well.

"Computer, shut down fire suppression in Treatment Room Two," she said.

"Fire suppression shut down confirmed," a male voice answered from hidden speakers.

Blue flames danced along Kwan Li's fingertips. She flipped her hand, and the fire dropped into the ottoman. The contents popped and crackled as the blue fire consumed them. The acrid scent of burning plastic tainted the air. Overhead, fans hidden behind the ceiling panels whirred to life.

Kwan Li faced Rey. "I guarantee *all* of my clients' privacy and security."

"Until it becomes more profitable not to?" Rey asked.

"You're a cynical one, aren't you?" The amused expression Kwan Li wore since he first met her faded into something far grimmer. "I don't betray my own kind."

The odd light in the anteroom made more sense. "You weren't scanning us for weapons. You were making sure I was a super."

No, they couldn't have scanned him. Rey tried to keep a neutral expression on his face. Tim and Arthur had tried several different methods, but he didn't give off the weird energy other supers did. But Serena back home had known what he was.

Of course. It was the elderly woman. The lights and sounds had been for show.

Kwan Li looked at Monica. "This one's smarter than your usual tagalongs. You should keep him."

"How about my payment and the paperwork I requested?" Monica said.

"I'll have to deduct the medical service, your travel goods, and the paperwork from your current auction money balance," Kwan Li replied.

"Fine." Monica drawled out the word like a recalcitrant teenager, which brought a smile back to the younger woman.

"I'll send someone in so your boy doesn't look like a raggedy man in his photos. And I'll see if I can scrounge up some decent clothes for you and your new partner while I'm at it." Kwan Li pivoted and flounced out of the room.

Once the door closed, Rey carefully pushed himself upright, rearranged his amulet, and checked his wounds. They were still sore, but blood no longer seeped from them. The glue formed a flexible seal.

He looked at Monica. "Why do they call you Missy?"

"You're from the U.S., right? Trying to get registered?" Her purple irises twinkled under the overhead lights. "That means you've studied the supervillain database."

"You're not a bad person," he said softly. "It wouldn't be the first time the government got things wrong. So if you don't want to tell me, I understand."

"Oh, sweetie, someone's going to out me to you eventually." She grinned. "Missy is short for Miss Purrception."

Chapter 8

Not wanting to get shot in the back, Harri raised her arms. "You with Corvus?"

"Call off your super now, Winters." Another poke in her spine emphasized his warning.

A high-pitched whistle she recognized filled the air. "Well, we've got a problem because he's not mine."

She dropped to her right. By the time she poked her head above the weeds, Steve had disarmed both guards and secured their hands to the bar gate with the straps of their rifles.

"You all right, Ms. Winters?" Steve called out.

"Nothing my dignity can't endure," she said, brushing dirt off her jeans. It was true. The first time Rey rescued her, she was burned, bruised, and throttled despite the kid's best efforts.

Harri strode over to their prisoners. "You two mind telling me the purpose for the guns?"

"This is private property," one of them snarled, the one who jammed a gun in her back from his voice.

"So the sign says," she replied dryly. "But given Corvus's lack of concern for my private property, I tend not to care about Trubble's privacy or that of anyone who works for him."

"Harri, would you mind releasing my men?" The familiar voice came from behind her. She and Steve turned. Five figures walked toward them, all in fatigues, but it was the center man who drew her attention.

"Well, if it isn't Crazy Jim," she said with mock enthusiasm. "To what do we owe the dubious pleasure?"

Valentine "Crazy Jim" Delante was one of Corvus's top operatives. For years, he'd masqueraded as a homeless man in Founder's Green between the county courthouse and City Hall. He was in the process of strangling Harri when Rey had stopped him with a little extra prejudice.

This time though, Crazy Jim's hair was cut in a short military style, his front teeth weren't blacked out, and he didn't smell like months of unwashed clothes and body. All five people carried weapons, but none of them were pointed at her or Steve. Crazy Jim's neutral expression didn't fool her for one moment. He was the most dangerous man here.

"What are you doing here, Harri?" He almost sounded bored.

"I could ask you the same thing," she replied mildly. "Why would Trubble make you clean up his facility? Or were you the one who made the mess?"

Crazy Jim ignored her jibes and looked Steve up and down. "I see you found your missing super."

"No thanks to Corvus." She smiled, the same nasty one she used on super-villains in court back when she had been city attorney. "In fact, he remembered where he had been held despite the drugs and Professor Paranoia's brainwashing. So, why'd your boss go to all the trouble of lying to me?"

Crazy Jim shrugged. "I don't know if he lied to you or not. My orders were to extend all courtesy if you, Franklin, or the Ghost Owl showed up here. Frankly, we've been expecting the Ghost Owl for the last eight weeks." He looked at the two strapped to the gate. "Guess we need to do some more security drills."

"Then why'd you have us training for a ninja instead of Captain Justice?" The operative who had poked Harri with his gun glared up at Steve. "Aren't you supposed to be dead, Tighty Whitey?"

Steve opened his mouth to respond to the insult, but Harri shook her head sharply. The kid rolled his eyes at her, but he wisely kept his mouth shut.

This is why I don't have children. She clenched her fists to keep from smacking the attitude out of Steve. How the hell did Miguel manage it with four boys?

She turned back to Crazy Jim. "So what is the courtesy you're supposed to extend?" She cocked her head. "Besides pointing guns at us?"

Crazy Jim scowled at her two prisoners. "Well, if they were that stupid, then they can sit out here and think about their screw-up. Is it safe to assume you want to examine our facility?"

"I think that's a safe bet," she replied dryly. "Though I'm assuming you've already cleaned up the body parts."

"Don't worry. We stored them neatly." Crazy Jim's grin would have made a serial killer wet his pants.

Harri just hoped she and Steve wouldn't be joining the body parts permanently.

CHAPTER 9

At eight the next morning, Aisha forced herself to go downstairs to the office. With Harri still in Colorado, their little law firm couldn't afford the other partner hiding under her covers.

No matter how much Aisha wanted to.

But her talk with Qiang yesterday reminded her that she wasn't the only one with major personal problems. In the end, Qiang simply needed someone to vent to. Between her son, her parents, her day job, and the superhero gig, she was stressed to the max. And with her overload of responsibilities, the poor woman didn't have time for any social outlet.

Which meant she needed whatever side income through licensing her superhero persona Aisha could provide for her. Which also meant Aisha needed to get her ass downstairs even though she had practically no sleep. Not with the nightmares about Rey.

Aisha walked into the reception area, waved to Patty, and headed straight for the break room. The pricey espresso machine was probably the best investment she had made in the law firm.

But something didn't look right at Patty's desk.

Aisha walked backwards and stared at the woman sitting beside their assistant. "Susan?"

"Long time, no see, Franklin!" The redhead rose, strode over to Aisha, and hugged her. She took a step back. "Congratulations on the little one!"

"Harri said you couldn't start until next week." Aisha tried to make her bleary brain work.

Susan Kennedy rolled her eyes. "I was doing some contract work for Mother Defiant in Hermanville. Her previous attorney was trampled by a triceratops during Professor Triassic's attack back at the beginning of July. Everything was fine between us until our old boss Howard Dewey had a little talk with Mother behind my back."

"Shit," Aisha muttered. "I'm so sorry." Their former boss badmouthing

Susan as well as Aisha didn't surprise her one bit. When would he realize it just made him look like a jealous dick?

"Oh, I got the non-refundable retainer upfront from Mother." Susan grinned. "And I told her when she got tired of Dewey & Cheatham of ripping her off, I'd help her find new representation." She shrugged. "Once she finds out how Dewey nickels and dimes his clients, I'll get the phone call. Happens all the time. Anyway, I'm free early, so I thought I'd surprise Harri, but apparently, I just missed her."

"Yeah, she's out today." Aisha turned to Patty. "Do you have the employment contract?"

"Right here." Their assistant grabbed the folder on her top tray.

"Harri said something about room and board being included?" Susan asked. "It would be great not to live out of my suitcase for a while."

"There's an unoccupied apartment on the fourth floor." Aisha smiled. "Why don't we get some coffee and I'll show it to you while we talk?"

Aisha sipped her mocha while Susan checked out every nook and cranny of what was originally supposed to be Patty's apartment. Harri claimed she asked Patty if she was going to move in here or back to her old apartment after her ex-boyfriend Cade Wilson, AKA Black Death, stopped casing both buildings. Allegedly, Patty said she and her baby daughter were going to remain in Arthur's spare bedroom for now.

If things were getting serious between Arthur and Patty, maybe she should offer to babysit Grace one night so the couple could have a proper date. Lord knew she needed the practice with an infant. A slight flutter in her abdomen seconded the notion. Aisha smiled and rubbed her baby bump.

"Wow! This place is amazing!" Susan's pumps clicked against the hardwood as she strode back into the main living area. "What's the rent if I want to stay here after my employment contract is up?"

"How about we wait and see if you want to join the firm? Besides—" Aisha waved her free hand to indicate the whole building. "—after six months with us, you may—"

The main door for the apartment crashed open. Tim zipped inside on his motorized wheelchair, a Taser in his hand. Arthur poked his head and arm around the door jamb, also armed with a Taser.

"—run screaming for the hills." Aisha finished. "What the hell are you two doing?" She glared at the men as she set her mug on the island counter.

Even Tim appeared sheepish as they both lowered their weapons. "Sorry, the motion sensor for this apartment went off. I knew it wasn't the kids because Francisco was with us and Javier's at school."

"I punched in the correct security code." Aisha crossed her arms and tapped the right toe of her Jimmy Choo Roma flats.

"Yeah . . ." Tim set the Taser in his lap and ran his hands through his red hair, making it stand up on end. He probably hadn't taken a shower or slept since Harri left. "Since no one is living here, an alert that a code was entered goes down to my computer, which switches the motion detectors back on to confirm someone is in here."

"And you couldn't have just asked Patty who was up here?"

"Told you," Arthur muttered. Tim shot him a dirty look.

"Since you're both here—" Aisha turned back to Susan. The other attorney had one hand over her mouth, obviously trying to stifle her laughter. "Susan Kennedy, the idiot in the wheelchair is our head of security Tim Canyon. The one trying to keep the baby out of the line of fire by hiding behind the doorjamb is the head of our IT department Arthur Drallhickey."

Arthur stepped the rest of the way into view. As Aisha suspected, the baby was snuggled in his chest harness.

"And the adorable two-month-old is Grace," Aisha finished.

"Harri said Ms. Kennedy wasn't going to be here until next week." Tim looked a little peeved.

"Thanks to my ex-boss, Susan was released from her previous contract earlier than expected," Aisha said sourly.

"Is it always this exciting here?" Susan asked.

"This is mild," Arthur stated. "You should have been here the time Screaming Orgasm walked in on a fight between Rey and Aisha while Rey was in his underwear."

Aisha buried her face in her hands. This was going to be a very long day.

CHAPTER 10

Rey wasn't sure how long he'd napped on the white futon when their hostess returned to the white room. At least, Kwan Li sent one of her people to trim his hair and beard, and he'd been allowed to clean up before the nap, but he was still in the blood-stained scrub pants.

He accepted the passport and driver license Kwan Li held out for him. He examined them before he eyed her. "James Davis? Doesn't he write the comic strip about the lazy cat?"

She looked at Monica. "I take back what I said about him having some brains."

Monica set aside the fashion magazine she'd been reading and grinned. "I just keep him around as arm candy."

Kwan Li slung a dark blue carry-on bag from her shoulder and handed it to Rey. The red one she handed to Monica. "You each have two changes of clothes, credit cards in your ID's name, clean phones, and the requested cash. The remainder minus my fee was wired to your Cayman account."

"You know I'm not going to give you the flashdrive until I have confirmation," Monica said slyly.

"So picky." Kwan Li gave her a cheeky grin before she sashayed out of the room.

Once the door closed, Rey looked at Monica. "Are you two an item?"

"Why?" She stripped off her black t-shirt. "You want in on the action?"

Rey tried to look anywhere but at her ample assets in a sheer black bra. "No, thank you. You just seem to flirt a lot with her when you said you wanted revenge for your ex-boyfriend's death."

"Ah, sweetie, am I making you uncomfortable?" Yes, she was definitely laughing at him.

"As you pointed out, I have a significant other." His skin heated, and definitely not in the good way. If anything, it made him wish he had a moment of privacy to call Aisha to make sure she was okay.

In his peripheral vision, Monica picked up the third futon and propped it on its side between them. "Is that better?"

"Yes, thank you." He unzipped the carryon and pulled out the clothes. Kwan Li had even provided a pair of athletic shoes and a clear plastic zippered bag with a toothbrush, toothpaste, and an antiperspirant stick. He considered tossing the blood-stained scrub pants, but he didn't want any more of his genetic data spread around, considering God only knew what Corvus had planned to do with it. Carefully folding them so the blood wouldn't contaminate the other clothes, he placed them in the bottom of the carryon.

That left the problem of how to get the flashdrive from Monica. He dressed and removed the cord from his neck. It would be better if he tried after she gave it to Kwan Li. He and Monica would hopefully be long gone before Kwan Li discovered the switch.

He slipped the spare flashdrive in his jeans pocket before he retied the amulet around his neck. It only took a moment to repack the carryon.

"You decent?" Monica called out.

"Yes, thank you."

She peered around the futon back. "You are really too good to be true."

"I hope my significant other believes that when I get home," he murmured. The shoes were a half size too small, but they were serviceable as long as he didn't wiggle his toes and tear through the leather.

She put the futon back in its original spot. Unlike the tough woman image she projected before, the belted dress with the short flowy skirt made her look years younger. It really showed off her long legs.

Monica snapped her fingers. "Hey, boytoy! What was that you were saying about your girl back home?"

Heat crept up his neck and invaded his cheeks. "I beg your pardon."

She rolled her eyes and stalked out of the room. Rey hurried after her, or he tried to. Luckily his legs were longer, and he caught up with her.

"What next?" he asked.

She glanced up at him. "Did you check your new phone?"

"Not yet." He gestured at his injured side. "I can't move as fast right now as I normally do. It took me a little longer to dress."

"We've got plane tickets from here to Vancouver, British Columbia, with a layover in Japan," she said. "I'm sure it's the best Kwan Li could do on a moment's notice."

"A commercial flight?"

Monica nodded. "It's easier to blend in when you're moving with the rest of the herd."

"But security—"

"Is a joke at most airports despite what the authorities want you to think. Don't sweat it, kid. I'll get you by them."

They entered the main area of Kwan Li's . . . lair? Rey wasn't sure what else to call it. She definitely wasn't in the hero category with the frequency of her law-breaking. But neither was she evil. In fact, she reminded him a little of Tim—doing things that were technically wrong in order for the outcome to be right.

Just like he was about to do.

Monica headed for Kwan Li, who sat at a desk in the open with her staff. Damn, this may be more difficult than he thought. He'd let his sleight-of-hand skills languish over the last couple of years. He wanted to be the hero Javier, Francisco, and the other kids in their neighborhood believed he was.

He let Monica get a little ahead of him, slid his hand in his pocket, and placed the flashdrive in position for the switch. There was a coiled electrical extension cord lying part way in the aisle. This plan was going to hurt like hell.

Monica stopped behind Kwan Li, who swiveled around in her chair. Rey focused. The flashdrive could have been the only thing in the universe. It passed between the two women's hands.

He stumbled against the thick coil of plastic and wire on the floor and fell forward. His hands flailed wildly. His carryon swung towards Monica who jumped back. He knocked Kwan Li's hand. Her flashdrive flew into the air.

Time slowed. When Kwan Li's flashdrive started on its downward arc, he released the one between his third and fourth fingers and snatched hers. He rolled to his left and landed on the linoleum floor, the flashdrive secure in his palm.

Pain shot through his injuries, and he couldn't help his grunt of pain.

"Oh, no! I didn't think about your blood loss. Stay there!" Kwan Li ordered. "Don't move. I'll get some orange juice." She crouched and scooped up the blank flashdrive before she scampered off.

"Do you need some help up?" Monica approached and bent over him.

"No," he said through gritted teeth. "And would you please take a couple of steps back?"

"Why?"

He closed his eyes against the pain and embarrassment. "Because I can see up your skirt."

<hr>

Rey grimaced as he sipped his juice. He should have known he wouldn't be so lucky getting the flashdrive with the real data out. Kwan Li and Monica both insisted on checking it before he and Monica left.

But it seemed to be how his life went. Something good would happen, then everything would turn into a shit show.

Like meeting and falling for Aisha, then disappearing from her life for two months.

After the crap her ex-husband put her through, Rey knew she wouldn't cut him a whole lot of slack for not being there for her and the baby. Hell, she'd been terrified about telling him she was pregnant after she'd assured him there was no way it could happen.

"What the fuck!" That exclamation from Kwan Li was followed by several others in different languages. From the expressions on the staff around them, the additional phrases were equally profane and blistering.

"Please don't tell me I damaged it when I knocked it out of your hand?" Rey said.

"That's not the problem." Kwan Li tapped several keys. "I could recover it if that was the case. This is blank."

"That can't be," Monica murmured as she leaned over Kwan Li's shoulder and stared at the screen. "The bastards' must have inserted a virus in the data I copied."

"No, my security program would have caught that." Kwan Li looked up at Monica. "You sure you deactivated the Corvus magnetic protocols?"

"Of course, I—" Monica faltered and straightened. "Shit. I got distracted by Graceful here." She jerked her left thumb in Rey's direction.

"What are Corvus's magnetic protocols?" Rey asked.

"If anyone tries to leave one of their research facilities with unauthorized copies of data, a mini-EMP is set off inside the lab." Kwan Li shook her head. "The only way to get another copy is to go back to that lab and try to break into their Faraday vault."

"I destroyed the place before we left," Monica said mournfully.

Rey tried not to change his expression. Monica definitely didn't strike him as someone who'd forget something as important as a micro electromagnetic pulse. So what game was she really playing? Or had she seen him make the switch, and she merely bided her time until she could get it back from him?

"Well, Missy, I can't sell information for you that neither of us possess." Kwan Li pulled the flashdrive from its slot and chucked it into a trashcan.

"All right." Monica crossed her arms. "Then it's back to the drawing board. They have to be cross-checking the results from the Indonesian lab at another facility. We just need to find out where."

Rey trudged back to the alley with the huge umbrella he had been loaned. After some excellent food at a local restaurant Kwan Li recommended, he'd walked through the rain in an attempt to spread his scent as far and wide as possible. Maybe it was a totally unnecessary effort because of the rain, but he didn't want the monsters to stumble upon Kwan Li and her people. They may not be innocent, but no one deserved to be torn apart like Mama had.

No one gave him any grief during his walk, which made him wonder who Kwan Li really was here, but he knew better than to ask.

Ke and Monica waited for Rey at the same almost-blue door where they had entered Kwan Li's facility. This time Ke drove a small white car with a stenciled logo of a speeding truck. Beneath the Chinese writing, what was probably the same message in English said, "Doan's Delivery, Overnight or Else."

Rey was pretty sure something had been lost in translation.

The door opened and the elderly woman held out her hand. He handed the umbrella back to her, bowed, and said, "Xiè xie nǐ."

"Not bad for a Westerner." She grinned and closed the door.

Rey climbed into the vehicle. Once again, Ke drove like a madman through the streets of Singapore, but instead of dropping Rey and Monica off at the international terminal, Ke took the service road to the package shipping area. Several trucks and planes had the same Doan's logo on their sides. Ke pulled into a parking area in front of what looked like the company's airport office.

Monica grabbed Rey's wrist. "When we go in, follow me. Don't ask questions. Don't look around. Don't do anything to draw attention to yourself."

Rey nodded.

Sure enough, while Ke stopped to chat with the receptionist, Monica marched through the entrance and several other doors like she owned the place. In fact, several people held the doors open for them and bowed. No one made eye contact.

A cart for ferrying passengers waited for them outside of the sixth door. Monica climbed in and issued orders to the driver in Mandarin. Once Rey sat in the back, the cart darted forward on its high-pitched electric engine. The sound of the cart was tolerable compared to the portable ultrasound Tim had invented.

The thought of the inventor dropped another stone of guilt on Rey's load. Harri and Tim seemed to be on the verge of admitting their feelings to each other two months ago. Would Harri forgive Rey for his doppelgänger's actions? He blinked away the burning in his eyes and focused on his surroundings. From the occasional signs in English, they were headed toward the international terminal.

The driver brought the cart to a halt in front of a staircase. Monica got out and thanked him while Rey climbed out. The driver performed a three-point turn and raced back down the corridor.

From the noise level, the area above them was the terminal's main concourse. Rey followed Monica up the staircase. She gracefully joined the mass of people heading for their gates. However, several people in the crowd gave Rey odd looks because he towered over them.

They reached their gate and took a couple of seats in a corner with their backs against the wall. Some of their fellow passengers dozed in their own chairs.

"I'm a little surprised you're not flying first class," he murmured.

"Who says we're not," she whispered back.

"Then why are we in the coach waiting area?"

Monica smiled. "I thought your mentor was teaching you these things."

Rey grimaced. Of course. She was varying her routine, doing the unexpect-ed. Tim said one of the worst places to get yourself trapped was the first class lounges when one is dressed as a civilian. It was a good way to blow your secret identity.

Monica pulled the same magazine she'd been reading earlier out of her car-ryon and began flipping through the pages.

Rey stood.

Monica looked up at him. "Where are you going?"

He glared at her. "After all that orange juice and tea, I need to use the little boys' room."

She grinned and returned to perusing her fashion magazine.

He strode towards the bathrooms for this concourse. A quick glance told him Monica wasn't paying any attention to him. He darted into the room re-served for cell phone recharging and pulled the new phone out of his pocket.

He hesitated at punching in Aisha's number. The device was probably bugged despite Kwan Li's assurance it was clean.

"May I help you, sir?" A young man, probably about Rey's own age, ap-proached him. The other guy had a pleasant demeanor without being servile and he spoke a language Rey knew.

"I'm having an issue with my new phone." Rey shrugged helplessly. "I'm trying to make a call to the States, but it's not going through. Do you happen to have a payphone somewhere?"

"Better." The guy grinned. "Voice-over IP program. Just use one of our courtesy computers."

Rey followed him to a row of monitors and keyboards against the far wall. Only a couple were in use this late in the evening. The guy brought up the program and pointed out Rey could use his own headset and microphone, or he could provide a sanitized headset for a small rental fee.

Rey payed the man, including a generous tip, for the headset and sat before the monitor. He checked the time before he followed the English directions for placing an international call. It was the middle of the day back in Can-yon Pointe. If Aisha was with a client, she wouldn't answer her cell phone. He punched in the law firm's main number.

And he prayed someone at the office picked up.

CHAPTER 11

Susan stood and stretched. This was the first time any short-term contract left her totally alone in the office on her first day. On the other hand, she was playing receptionist despite having a JD, an LLM, and state certifications in contracts and superhero law because this was the smallest firm she'd contracted with.

She wasn't going to complain due to the benefits. It would be nice to have her own place for a while, instead of living out of her suitcase and eating the same room service menu over and over again.

What she needed was caffeine though. She headed for the break room and rummaged around until she found some tea bags. Not her decent loose leaf, but it would do until a terrible thought occurred. A quick check of the expiration date assured her the bags were fresh. It was a wonder Winters & Franklin had tea at all. These people had a fetish for coffee that went beyond the pale considering their expensive espresso machine in such a small firm. She filled a clean mug with hot water, steeled herself, and dipped the tea bag into the steaming liquid.

The phone out on Patty's desk trilled, and Susan tapped the button on the headset she wore. "Winters & Franklin, attorneys at law. How may I help you?"

Static crackled along the line, and she was sure she heard someone breathing.

"Hello? Can you speak up? I can't hear you if you're talking."

There was a little gasp at the other end before the signal went dead.

She tapped the button to close the line on the headset. It took all kinds in this world, but dammit, it would be nice if for once, someone simply said, "Sorry. Wrong number."

Whistling, she grabbed her mug and headed back to Patty's desk. Since Harri hadn't expected her until next week, her desk was still in its box from IKEA. Arthur assured her he would have it put together by tomorrow morning. He was so damn shy and sweet when he wasn't pointing a weapon at her. Susan was sure he would assemble the desk even if he had to stay up all night to complete it.

She sat back down and continued reading the endorsement contract for the superhero Cobblestone from a tire manufacturer. It was a test, but that was to be expected. Aisha only knew her from her rather short stay at Dewey & Cheatham, and from Aisha's reputation, she'd independently corroborate anything despite what her partner might say.

Susan took a sip of her tea and grimaced. Yep, she definitely needed to bring in her own stock.

A clause caught her eye, and she re-read it. Maybe this test wasn't as irritating as she thought. Aisha had cleverly slipped a morality clause for the tire corporation itself, in which Cobblestone could cancel the contract if the company or any of the execs were even implicated in questionable activities.

She flipped back to reread the company's indemnity clause when the phone rang. A tap on the headset again. "Winters & Franklin, attorneys at law. How may I help you?" Her voice echoed in the cavernous area.

"Who the hell is this?" Harri's throaty growl in Susan's ear was unmistakable.

"Someone you hired, Ms. Winters," she shot back.

"Susan? Why are you answering the phones?"

"The extension on my previous contract ended earlier than I expected, and you said you really needed me as soon as possible." She looked around the quiet first floor. "With all your personnel issues, I can see why."

"What's going on? Where is everyone?" Harri said.

"Manuel—I'm sorry—Miguel and his two oldest have an interior finish job at a new medical clinic that's going in on your street." Susan ticked off the remaining items on her fingers even though Harri couldn't see her. "Aisha and Francisco took Tim to his PT appointment. And Arthur went with Patty to Grace's well-baby checkup. Meanwhile I'm manning phones and awaiting Javier's return from school. I swear I'll get your family's names right before the week's out."

"I totally forgot about those," Harri said. She ignored the "family" comment as Susan expected she would. For someone who thought "family" was *the* F-word, Harri Winters managed to surround herself with a self-made one for as long as Susan had known her.

"We've got it covered here." Susan smiled to herself. "Do you want Aisha to call you when she gets back?"

"No," Harri said. "Our flight to Canyon Pointe should be taking off any minute. Please let Tim know we have bio-samples that will need a secure freezer."

"Bio-samples?"

"Didn't Aisha give you the orientation talk?" Harri sounded worried.

Susan laughed. "She started to before Grace and your heads of security and IT threatened to tase me."

Her overblown statement got the reaction she'd aimed for. Harri launched into a blistering obscenity-filled tirade.

When she paused for a breath, Susan added, "Though in all fairness the baby wasn't actually armed."

"I can't deal with your sense of humor, Kennedy. Not today." That wasn't the usual Harri attitude. Normally, she'd call someone teasing her a choice epithet before moving to the real reason for the call. This was more than simple worry over the firm with her name on the marquee.

"Sorry." For once, Susan actually meant it. "Tim. Bio-samples. Secure freezer. Are you going to need an escort from the airport?"

"I've got . . . muscle with me," Harri said. "If anything goes wrong, I'll send him ahead."

Was that her subtle indication a super was with her? The phone line for the firm was probably secure, but Susan knew better than to ask. "All right. Anything else?"

"No." There was a slight hesitation before Harri added, "I'm sorry for snapping at you, Susan. I appreciate you coming in early."

Wow. Harriet Mathilda Winters apologizing? Maybe the apocalypse was right around the corner.

Susan bit her tongue before she said any of those thoughts aloud. "You're welcome."

They said their goodbyes, and Susan tapped the headset to end the call. She turned back to her reading of the contract when the main door buzzed. A man stood in the entryway, dressed in business casual. He impatiently poked the buzzer again and waved at her.

Neither Aisha or Harri had any appointments until tomorrow according to Patty's calendar. After Harri's weird call, Susan became acutely aware she was the only one in the office. At all her previous contract jobs, there was always someone there, no matter the time of day, even if it was a security guard.

She pressed the comm button on Patty's phone set. "I'm sorry. Do you have an appointment?"

"No, but I was hoping to talk to one of the attorneys." The man had the most intensely blue eyes of anyone Susan had ever seen.

"I'm sorry, sir. Both Ms. Winters and Ms. Franklin are currently dealing with client matters outside of the office." She made a show of checking the calendar. "Ms. Franklin has an opening Monday at ten a.m. Would that be all right?"

"Not really." The man peered at her. "Um, this is a little awkward, but I need a lawyer who can be discreet. When I saw your ad that said you represent superheroes, I was hoping I could talk your firm into representing me."

Despite his innocent expression, some instinct tickled Susan's hindbrain. "Do you have powers?"

"Me?" He spread his hands in a defensive gesture. "No, but the people I want to sue do."

"Why do you want to sue them?"

The man sagged. "Look, I had to come during my lunch hour. If you won't represent me, please just say so."

"If you can give me the gist of your situation, I can have one of them call you back."

"I really don't like standing out here and spilling my guts. It's too dangerous."

Susan tried to hold her exasperation in check, but in dealing with supers, one needed to take any potential threat seriously. "Sir, for all I know, you're the archenemy of one of the firm's clients in disguise. The sooner you give me your story, the sooner I can help you."

He looked away and exhaled. When he turned back, worry lines creased his forehead. "My ex-girlfriend is living with a supervillain. I don't think that's a good atmosphere for our daughter."

Well, that put a different spin on things. "I take it your ex has full custody?"

"Yes, ma'am. I didn't know she was even pregnant. I was out of the country on business. When I got home a few months ago, not only did I find out I had a daughter, but she's living with a freakin' supervillain!"

"One moment." Susan pulled out her own phone and thumbed through her contacts list. She scribbled down the info on a blank page of her legal pad and ripped off the sheet.

The man's face brightened when he saw her approach the bulletproof window. Damn, he had some intensely blue eyes. And they weren't altered by colored contacts.

She slid the paper through the slot and pressed the comm button. "Regardless of what your ex's boyfriend is, your situation is still a child custody matter. I recommend Lisa Ashcraft. She's the best family law attorney in the state, and she does have experience where one of the adults involved is a super."

His expression faltered. "Oh. I thought since you dealt with superheroes…"

Susan shook her head. "Winters & Franklin mainly deal with their public side, not their personal lives. If you were a superhero in this same situation, even if you were one of our clients, I'd still send you to Lisa. She's who I'd call if I needed someone to save my child."

He took a deep breath and inclined his head to her. "Thank you for your assistance, Ms. Kennedy. I appreciate it."

She breathed her own sigh of relief when he departed. He jogged down the steps to the street, climbed into a tan Honda, the same make as Harri's white one, and sped off.

The security system beeped, and she heard the side door open and close. A boy in his early teens raced into the reception area.

"Did you talk to that guy who just left, Ms. Kennedy?"

"You're Javier?"

He nodded, but his fierce expression didn't abate. "Did you talk to him?"

"He needed an attorney." Why was the kid was overreacting over a simple inquiry?

Javier pulled out his phone and texted someone. "Did you let him in here?"

"No, give me a little bit of credit . . ." She swallowed hard. "How do you know who I am?"

"Mr. Tim and Dad both texted me you'd be the only one here when I got home from school." Javier glanced up at her. "Aisha's five minutes out by car. You did good not letting that guy in. He's a Corvus assassin."

Her blood froze when she remembered she hadn't given the man her name either.

After repeating Harri's message, Susan blinked as she stared at Aisha across the conference room table. The other attorney had described her visitor to a T. "Yeah, white man, gorgeous blue eyes. He was hoping you would represent him. Supposedly, his ex has taken up with a supervillain, and the guy wanted custody of his daughter if the ex is displaying such piss-poor judgment. I referred him to Lisa Ashcraft." Susan turned back to Tim. "I swear I didn't let him into the building."

He opened the lid of his laptop and turned it around so she could see the screen. "Is this the guy?"

The frozen picture showed the stranger peering up at the security camera from the street. He was wearing a different outfit.

"Yes." She looked up at Tim. "What's going on? Javier tried to tell me he was an assassin."

Tim ignored her question. "Did you see the car he was driving?"

She nodded. "A tan version of Harri's ancient Honda."

Aisha covered her face with her hands. "Two freaking months. Black Death hasn't been around for two freaking months."

"Black Death?" Susan looked at Aisha and then Tim. They couldn't be serious. Black Death along with the Ghost Owl were the supers' version of boogeymen.

Aisha dropped her hands to the tabletop. "This can't be a coincidence."

"There's never a coincidence when it comes to Trubble," Tim said in a grim, growly voice. The one that promised pain to anyone who stepped out of line.

Susan wondered how dangerous the man would be when he wasn't in a wheelchair. He was a disgraced, former billionaire, inventor. Her musing disappeared when Aisha floated toward the ceiling, her arms wrapped around her own middle.

"Aisha!" Tim yelled an instant before her head hit the ceiling.

"Dammit." Aisha grimaced and looked down. She took a deep breath and screwed her features into an expression of concentration. She drifted back to the floor.

Susan realized her mouth was hanging open and closed it. She never would have guessed old Snake in the Grass had powers.

"It's been a while since you lost control," Tim commented.

"Yeah, control of my powers will be handy when Patty comes after me with one of your gadgets after she loses her daughter," Aisha muttered. She buried her face in her hands again. "You have no idea how good Lisa is and how screwed we all are."

"Wait a minute," Susan yelled. "Are you two saying Arthur isn't Grace's father?"

Aisha peered between her fingers. "A little louder, Kennedy. There's some people in Thailand who didn't hear you."

"Black Death is a real person?" Susan said a little more quietly.

"Yes," Tim said. "And he's Grace's biological father."

"And Black Death's claim that his ex is living with a supervillain refers to Arthur?"

Aisha lowered her hands, and she and Tim exchanged looks.

He shrugged. "If she's going to be working here, she needs to know everything for her own safety."

"I know." Aisha groaned. "I just thought I'd have one afternoon of respite without Harri here to stir the hornet's nest."

Over the next half hour, Susan got what she was pretty sure was the *Reader's Digest* version of events since the birth of the law firm, including their tangles with a secret organization they knew as Corvus.

"Any questions?" From the look in Aisha's eyes, she was afraid Susan would bolt any second.

"Just one," Susan said. "How the hell did you hide your powers in law school?"

Aisha sighed. "Because I didn't have them." She shrugged and rubbed her baby bump. "I've got HRSP."

"Please tell me Black Death isn't also your baby daddy?" Susan leaned back in her chair and stared at the decorative plaster rosettes on the ceiling. "I'm getting a job writing a soap opera if he is."

"That is an unequivocal no." Aisha chuckled.

Susan lowered her head. "But he is a super, isn't he?"

Aisha stared at her manicure. "He's not in the picture."

Susan grimaced and straightened as the pieces clicked together. Shit, she'd unknowingly shoved her other foot into her mouth. "I'm sorry for your loss, Aisha."

She blinked rapidly, trying to hide her tears. "I don't know what you mean."

"The only client this firm has lost is Captain Justice." Susan reached over and laid her right hand over Aisha's. Whether Aisha had breached ethics by sleeping with a client was a moot point with Captain Justice's death. Susan couldn't imagine losing her romantic partner, much less raising a baby by herself. "It won't leave this room if that's what you're afraid of. I swear."

Aisha nodded. "Thanks."

"I guess I need to get downstairs and make sure there's space in bio storage before Harri gets here," Tim muttered before he rolled out of the conference room.

Susan pushed herself to her feet. "If it's okay, I'll use Harri's office to finish looking at that contract."

"If you want to run screaming from Canyon Pointe, none of us would blame you," Aisha said softly.

"Are you joking?" Susan grinned at her. "Now that I know everything, this place is going to be a blast to work at."

"Not everything yet." Aisha had an odd smile on her face. "How do you feel about vigilante superheroes?"

Susan sat back down. This was turning into one hell of a first day.

Chapter 12

Harri watched as Tim transferred the vials from the cooler she'd brought back from Colorado to a much larger industrial refrigerator. She'd never been inside this particular room of his lab before. It looked more like what she expected a lab to be, with test tubes, beakers, and Bunsen burners. It also had the smell of hospital-level antiseptic, which made her nose twitch and her nerves itch.

The odor reminded her too much of Grandma Harri's death, but she clamped down on the urge to race out into the night. She couldn't run anymore. Too many people depended on her to keep her act together, especially the three kids under the age of eighteen and one on the way currently living inside the Lechuza Building. Despite her dislike for rugrats in general, she couldn't let these kids, or their parents, down.

"Why do you have a huge refrigerator for body bits, and an itty-bitty fridge for your beer?"

"Because I can drink warm beer in a pinch." He placed the last set of vials inside, rolled back his wheelchair, and shut the refrigerator door. "Body bits spoil a lot faster." He pivoted his chair to face her and shot her a mischievous grin. "And if you keep talking lovingly about beer like your ex-husband does, it's going to cause a major dent in our relationship."

"How many times has Eddie served you your favorite scotch?" She grinned back.

"Never," Tim admitted as he headed for the main door. "However, you having a roommate is going to be inconvenient for the next few nights."

"Get a bigger bed." She closed the door behind them and punched in the security code.

"And how am I supposed to get a king-sized bed down here?" he retorted. He aimed his chair towards the elevator and zipped down the hallway.

"Put Steve to use," she said when she caught up to him. "I'd volunteer Aisha, but she has super-pregnancy hormone issues on top of superstrength. Your new bed might not make it down here intact." The antique elevator wheezed and groaned its way down the shaft.

"Take it easy on her." Tim stared at the elevator gate, but his gaze had that distant, disturbed quality. Of course, he understood how Aisha felt. His wife and son had been murdered by Seismic Shift, the superhero-in-name-only who tried to frame Tim for their deaths. Even if it had been twenty years ago, the incident had left scars on his soul. Scars that had birthed Jatz'om Kuh, the Ghost Owl.

"I don't want Aisha to fall in the same abyss you did," Harri said softly.

"Neither do I." He looked up at her. "She has you, her family, all of us here, but you can't control her grief or how long it lasts either. You're pushing her too hard. Especially when it comes to Steve."

"She's going down to Atlanta for her parents vow renewal in a few days." Harri shrugged. "If Arthur's software trick with my phone worked, Steve and I will be able to track Professor Paranoia." The elevator moaned and squealed to a stop, and she pulled open the two gates. "We'll be gone by the time she gets back."

"Harri Winters chasing a supervillain when it's not about money." Tim rolled his eyes as he wheeled past her. "You know you've really let the one time you were the Ghost Owl go to your head."

"And I fabulously fucked that up." Harri stepped inside the car. Somehow, she kept herself from slamming each gate shut as hard as she could. She jabbed the button for the top floor, and the elevator wheezed into motion. "All of you don't have to keep reminding me." She folded her arms over her chest. Taking on a mind-controlled Steve by herself hadn't been one of her better ideas. If it weren't for Aisha, she would have drowned at the bottom of Lake Del Oro.

"Yet, you keep telling me I take too many chances for all the wrong reasons," he said dryly.

"You do, but that's not the point!"

"So, what is the point of you dragging Steve around the country?"

Emotions swirled through her. So many she wasn't sure where the old anger and guilt about her father ended and the new anger and guilt over Rey began. And that was in addition to her heartache for Aisha. Her best friend was finally pregnant with the baby she'd wanted for years, only for her second chance at love to be ripped away from her.

Harri forced herself to take a deep breath and release her tension. "I need to find out what happened to Rey for my own sake. Steve . . . is still trying to understand his past. The kid has had a ton of crap thrown at him recently. Since his opportunity with the Peace Corps was supposed to be his time to figure out his life, and that has been taken from him, he's helping me in order to determine his own path."

"He can't replace Rey as Captain Justice."

"I know that!" When Tim didn't react, she swallowed her anger. "He knows that, too," she said more softly. "We had a long talk about Rey on the drive back to the airport. I discouraged Steve from registering, and he—" She couldn't help a chuckle. "Steve bluntly told me it's not my decision. Anymore than it was my fault Rey made the choices he did."

"He's right, you know," Tim said.

"I know, but we need to find out exactly what happened to Rey in order for Steve to protect himself and his parents, and for the rest of us to help Aisha protect the baby."

"And you think you brought back part of Rey in those tubes?"

"Honestly?"

"Yeah."

She shook her head. "No, I don't. Trubble likes messing with us. I think the questionable DNA is Steve's. Whatever Paranoia was up to, I don't think he took Rey to the Corvus facility in Colorado. The samples were a love note from Trubble to the Ghost Owl."

"Love note?"

"Yeah, it's about how bad he wants to recruit the Owl. Or maybe he looks at the Owl as an equal."

The elevator ground to a halt. Harri unlocked each gate and pushed them back. The rubber tires on Tim's wheelchair whispered on the hardwood as he rolled toward Harri's loft. She closed the elevator gates and followed him.

Her loft door hung open, and voices echoed down the hallway. At least, no one sounded pissed off like they were in the basement yesterday morning.

When they entered the loft, Patty sprawled on Harri's turquoise couch, her eyes closed and her lower legs on top of Arthur's thighs. The former supervillain sat at the end of the couch, his attention focused on a phone in his hands as his thumbs moved with damn-near superspeed.

Qiang commanded Harri's ancient futon from law school, her injured leg propped on a cushion. Steve sat on a stool next to her, talking quietly with the superhero.

Aisha stood at Harri's refrigerator filling glasses with ice and pouring water and soda, the furthest from Steve as she could get and still be in the same room. Susan ferried the refreshments to the guests.

Meanwhile, Molly Reinhold, AKA Nix, helped Miguel retrieve plates, napkins, and silverware in the kitchen. As if Harri couldn't tell by the delicious smell of cilantro, onions and roasted meats, a series of bags displaying the Marta's logo were lined up on the island.

"Corvus tagged Ms. Kennedy all right." Arthur's voice silenced everyone. "It's also using the voice assistant to listen to her non-phone conversations."

Tim scooted closer to the couch. "Do you know when?"

"Yesterday, the timestamp is nine-forty-one a.m."

Susan launched into a series of obscenities that made Harri's potty mouth sound like perfectly acceptable etiquette. She paused for a breath and raised her hands in the air. "How? That phone was never out of my possession!"

"Wi-fi," Arthur and Tim said at the same time.

"Don't sweat it, Susan." Harri shook her head. "They gotten all of us at one time or another."

The redhead scowled. "That was about the time Mother Defiant cut me loose, but she did it in person. Is she part of these Corvus assholes, too?"

Harri glanced at Tim, who shook his head, before she turned back to Susan. "That doesn't discount she may have been extorted by them. We also know someone at Dewey & Cheatham is in league with them. They could have infected Mother Defiant's devices as well without her knowledge." She waved in Arthur's direction. "The spyware was how Black Death knew you were alone at the office this afternoon."

"Speaking of which," Arthur said. "Do one of you supers want to do the honors, or shall we let Harri take a sledgehammer to the phone?"

"Wait!" Susan waved her hands and raced around the island. "You can't! I haven't finished paying it off yet!"

Arthur handed the phone to Tim and started massaging Patty's bare feet.

Tim looked at the screen and sighed. "He's right. They've improved their techniques. This thing is so firmly in the kernel we'd brick your phone trying to dig it out."

"We'll replace it," Harri said to Susan.

"But my contacts and my photos . . ." The redhead stared forlornly at the device in Tim's hand.

"Did you make a backup?" Arthur asked over his shoulder.

Susan shook her head. She looked like she was on the verge of tears.

"Here." Arthur held out his hand to Tim who returned the phone. "I can print out your contacts to Harri's ancient printer, but we'll have to manually re-enter them on the new phone."

"Hey! Language! My so-called ancient printer has saved your butt on more than one occasion." Harri waggled her index finger, but Arthur ignored her. He disappeared behind the partition where she kept her personal files. A whirring sound followed a *ka-chunk* from the printer.

Susan leaned closer to Harri. "What's the big deal about your printer?"

Harri chuckled. "It's so old there isn't enough room on the memory card for Corvus's virus."

"It's not a virus," Tim and Arthur said at the same time as Arthur returned to the main living area.

"Excuse me for not being a genius," Harri shot back. "By the way, do you smart guys have a replacement for her?"

"I don't have any of this particular model." Arthur looked at Susan as he headed back to the couch. "If you would prefer the same type, I can pick it up for you in the morning."

She nodded. "Please."

Patty lifted her legs, and Arthur resumed his seat.

"Want me to kill the phone now?" Molly asked.

"Hey, I wanted to do it," Qiang protested.

Harri pointed at Molly. "You are not shattering all the glass in my loft." She turned to Qiang. "And you're not electrocuting all of my appliances."

Arthur held the phone behind his head. When Harri took it, he went back to massaging Patty's feet.

"Aisha?"

Her partner set down the bottle of rum she'd been pouring into the blender. Harri tossed her the phone. Aisha caught it and pulled out the waste can.

Plastic cracked and glass tinkled against the other trash as she crushed the device.

"Powder the chip," Miguel suggested.

If Harri wasn't watching, she would have assumed the grinding sound was Aisha dipping margarita glasses in salt.

Aisha brushed her hand over the receptacle. "Good enough?"

Miguel nodded and continued unloading food from the bag he'd been working on. Aisha shoved the waste can back into place.

Susan gawked at Aisha. "You have superstrength on top of levitation?"

"Technically, it's flight." She retrieved a quart box of strawberries from the refrigerator. "My default is floating if I don't concentrate on remaining on the ground."

"You, too?" Steve exclaimed. "I swear staying on the floor in high school was harder than keeping my dick down in a stiff breeze—" His face glowed crimson when he realized everyone was staring at him. Even Patty had opened her eyes.

"Umm, TMI?" he said sheepishly.

"A bit," Harri answered.

"Harri has all rights to being this group's big mouth," Qiang offered, patting his arm.

Aisha turned away and began washing the strawberries. Harri wanted to stalk over to her partner and wring her neck. Couldn't she see the kid was trying? Dammit, she gave Arthur plenty of chances, and he had a criminal record.

"So what's really going on?" Molly asked as she passed around the silverware and napkins. "Aisha said she'll be out of town for a few days on family business." She nodded toward Steve. "I'm assuming CJ's clone here is the reason Corvus is on the warpath again?"

"Evil twin," Patty corrected.

"Hey, I'm sitting right here," Steve protested. "And I'm not evil."

"Everyone simmer down," Harri ordered. "We all know what went down two months ago. It's ancient news as far as I'm concerned. The problems we have right now are what we need to focus on."

She held up her index finger. "One, as far as we know, Professor Paranoia is still on the loose."

"But you sicced the parrot-lizards on him," Qiang said.

"You know the rules of the supervillain game." Harri glared at the superhero. "No body, no death. He's already put Steve under his control once. While Steve and Rey's biological mother has taken steps to prevent it from happening again, Paranoia may still be after him."

"Stool's behind you." Miguel shoved a plate in her hands.

"Thanks." Despite the delicious odors wafting to her nose, her stomach turned into writhing knots at the thought of eating. She sat and set her plate on the TV tray Molly had placed between her and Tim.

"Second, while Paranoia was working for Corvus, no one there knows what his real agenda is. He faked his death and killed a lot of Corvus personnel to cover it up. Trubble, through Crazy Jim, has made a job offer to the Ghost Owl to help them track Paranoia down."

"Which one?" Tim chuckled.

"Which ever one wants to take the job." Harri grinned at him. "Besides, Crazy Jim was insane enough to think we'd take the samples straight to the Owl's Nest." She and Steve had made a point of leaving the four trackers at various places around Canyon Pointe. If they'd had more time, she would have left them all at the park bench she and Trubble had used as a rendezvous in the past.

Everyone laughed except Steve and Susan.

"The third problem is I may have been the one who murdered those people," Steve said as he stared at his plate.

The laughter abruptly died.

"You didn't," Aisha said fiercely. She handed a strawberry daiquiri to Harri before she faced him again. "You may not have any memory of what Paranoia did to you, but you were fighting his influence."

"What makes you so sure?" he asked softly. The bleak look in his eyes made Harri want to hug him and tell him everything would be alright. She'd done the same with Rey once or twice.

And look how that turned out, her conscience chided.

"During the battle over the lake, you could have snapped Harri's neck any time. You didn't." Aisha took a step closer to him. "And when we fought in Westerville Park, none of your punches came anywhere near the baby."

"But—" He swallowed hard. "Look at what I did to Tim."

"True." Tim shrugged. "You pretty much shattered my left leg. You could have just as easily shattered my rib cage or my skull. You didn't. And I needed the knee replacement anyway."

"You're a lot stronger than you realize," Aisha said. "Here." She tapped the spot on his chest over his heart before she marched back to the kitchen. Maybe there was some hope for a change in her attitude after all.

"So why does Corvus want the Ghost Owl?" Susan asked.

"Besides wanting to control all the supers in the world?" Harri said sarcastically.

"The Ghost Owl is an unknown," Tim interjected. "Trubble doesn't like unknowns. Like the fact some of the DNA found in the Corvus lab where Paranoia worked wasn't human."

"Our real third problem is tracking where Paranoia took Rey." Harri glanced over at Arthur.

"Decryption estimate is still the same," Arthur said around a mouthful of burrito. "Around noon tomorrow at the soonest. Even after the info is decrypted, we don't know if there's going to be anything useful."

"We need to be just as worried about Paranoia gaining control of any super, not just Steve." Qiang twirled her forked through her refried beans. "You saw what he did to me at Westerville Park."

"But we also know what disrupts his control." Molly sat on the floor in front of the TV with her plate and daiquiri. "So is he a real problem? Or are you worried that Rey's still alive and under Paranoia's thumb?"

Harri glanced at Aisha, but her partner was studiously ignoring her. "It's crossed our minds, but Paranoia launched Steve at us a couple of weeks after nabbing him. Why wait if he already has Rey?"

"Or the parrot-lizards killed Professor Paranoia and Rey's languishing in a prison he can't break out of," Molly said.

Qiang reached over and smacked the back of the younger super's head. "Shut it." She lifted her chin in the direction of the kitchen and Aisha.

"Oh," Molly mouthed. She turned back to Harri. "Sorry."

"Fourth problem, Black Death is back in the picture," Harri said, deliberating ignoring Molly's faux pas as her law partner was obviously doing. "Lisa jumped all over my divorce, but I didn't file first. Susan, how soon do you think she could file his custody dispute?"

"If he's paying her retainer in cash, she would file them tomorrow afternoon at the latest," the redhead said grimly.

"Harri, we can't let Black Death distract us." Patty pushed herself upright. "You know this bullshit about Grace is a smokescreen so Corvus can find Rey first."

"Or his body," Aisha added with a faint tremor in her voice.

Harri wanted to kick everyone out on Aisha's behalf, but they'd only end up in another fight about Harri trying too hard to make everything all right for everyone. And she could count on her fingers the number of times Aisha let anyone see her cry.

And one of the times was with Arthur in Aisha's defunct BMW after her ex-husband threw the fact he and his new wife were expecting twins.

"Even though Harri tried to insinuate I was Rey, I don't think the Corvus guys bought it," Steve said.

"That was a delaying tactic," Patty said. "Cade is just being an asshole."

"Don't underestimate your ex's intentions, Patty," Susan said. "From what Aisha told me this afternoon, he's been stalking you for a while now. And I am so sorry for my part in this. We need to find you a good family law attorney."

"No!"

Arthur managed to grab Patty's plate before it hit the floor when she jumped to her feet.

"Patty," Harri said gently. "You need someone who is an expert—"

"All of you, shut up and listen to me!" Patty slashed her hand through the air. When everyone remained quiet, she drew a deep breath. "If we can keep Cade's attention on Grace, the more time we buy for Harri and Steve to find Rey. Let's face it. Cade's probably the only one who could really hurt him besides Aisha."

Harri opened her mouth.

Patty held up a hand. "I'm not done yet."

Harri relaxed and waited for Patty to finish.

"You guys are not going to find another attorney who cares as much about Grace's welfare as you do." She jabbed a thumb in her own chest. "I'm not going to find one either. You guys know superhero law, and you know the truth about my ex. No one else is going to believe me when I say Cade is a paid assassin because we have no real proof." She smiled at Arthur and Tim. "Sorry, guys, that's not a slam on your efforts."

Patty sucked in a deep breath and continued. "I have no problem doing all the research you need for this custody hearing. Frankly, I've been expecting this after you spotted him, and I already started. The only reason Trubble hasn't dropped the hammer on us is he wants both Captain Justice and the Ghost Owl."

She frowned at Steve. "I'm sorry, but you're the next best thing to your brother. I know Harri's probably talked you out of registering because of her own guilt over Rey. You might want to rethink your decision. Hiding in plain sight might be the better course of action."

Patty turned to Aisha. "Finally, I know you've given up, sweetie, but I believe with all my heart he's still alive. I know he wouldn't stop trying to find you if your positions were reversed. Please, Aisha, you got to have faith, if not for your sake, then your baby's."

Patty's cheeks glowed bright pink from her tirade. "Okay, I'm done." She sat back on the couch, and Arthur handed her plate back to her. The expression of pride on his face made her blush even harder.

Harri cleared her throat. "Okay, that brings me to problem five. We all still have our civilian lives to live. I want suggestions on how to watch each other's backs. For example, Aisha will be in Atlanta for a few days. Her parents are renewing their vows."

"Maybe we don't," Tim said.

"You've got to be kidding me." Harri stared at him.

"Hostages and murder were Seismic Shift's main plays." Tim shrugged. "Going about our regular business will drive Trubble and his crew insane, trying to figure out what your next move will be."

"My next move?" A tickle of worry wormed its way up Harri's spine.

"You've replaced me as Trubble's primary concern." Frown lines crinkled Tim's forehead. "Not only have you made some serious dents in the government's protection of supers, you outed Seismic Shift's plots, you know far too much about Trubble's own dealings, you've stolen a few of his operatives, and as far as he knows, you have the Ghost Owl in your back pocket. To him, the Mouse with the Mouth is way more dangerous than ole' Snake in the Grass."

Aisha zoomed over to them with the pitcher in her hand and hovered a foot above the hardwood. "If you call either of us those names again, I'll fly you up ten thousand feet and drop you." The pitcher tilted precariously toward Tim's head.

"Girl, don't waste good rum," Harri protested. She held up her nearly empty glass for a refill. Last one, she promised herself. She had too much research to do tonight regarding superhero parental rights.

CHAPTER 13

Rey settled back in his business class seat on the jet and tried not to let his nerves show. He wasn't sure what bothered him more—someone else in control of the flight or the strange woman who answered the phone at the law office.

He didn't have the chance to try Aisha's cell number before the PA boomed with the announcement boarding had commenced on his flight to Japan. Maybe he'd have a chance to pick up another phone in Tokyo.

And maybe he was lying to himself when he said Monica's admission she was Miss Purrception didn't bother him.

"You need something to settle your nerves?" she murmured in his ear.

"No," he growled. Her flirtatious attitude sawed away at the one nerve not freaking out about the flight or Aisha and their son.

Monica ignored his answer and smiled up at the flight attendant. "Two champagnes, please."

"I said I didn't need anything." He glared at Monica.

"Quit acting like a baby," she whispered back. The attendant handed her two flutes of what looked like ginger ale but smelled like the alley between River Street and Canyon Avenue, the one homeless alcoholics used as a bathroom.

"You should stop acting like a spoiled brat who always has to have her way," he retorted.

She downed the contents of one of the glasses in two swallows.

"And while I dislike alcohol, I know champagne should be sipped," he added.

"Well, la-dee-da," she said with a sneer. "Maybe I didn't grow up with all your advantages."

Rey faced her. "You had more advantages than I did, and you threw them away."

"And how would you know that?"

He waited until she lifted the second glass to her lips. "Kerry told me."

As he expected, Monica choked on the champagne. Once she finished wiping up the mess, she looked at him, her gaze analytical. "So you knew who I was the whole time."

"No," he admitted. "Not until you told me your nom de plume."

"And how do you know my daughter? Are you dating her?"

"One of my attorney's clients has been introducing me to other folks in our line of work." Rey shrugged. "Kerry mentioned her mother's moniker and how rough it was living down other people's expectations of her."

"What?" Monica's left eyebrow arched. "You were comparing parents?"

"Neither of us knew our fathers, and in a sense, we both lost our mothers at a young age."

Monica drained the second glass of champagne in two gulps and licked her lips. "In other words, you think you're better than me."

The attendant collected the empty flutes and reminded them to turn off any electronic devices.

"I don't think either of us is better or worse than anyone else," Rey murmured.

"Don't get your tighty-whities in a bunch," she snapped.

"I'm not—" He clenched his jaw at the old insult. She couldn't possibly know Cobblestone's favorite jibe. Not unless she really worked for Corvus, but from what Kerry Reinhold, AKA Sourpuss, had said about her mother, Monica only sought personal gain.

Instead, he turned and stared out the tiny window. She was deliberately picking a fight. He had obviously touched a nerve. According to Kerry, Monica had abandoned her twin daughters to their grandmother when they were very young.

Kerry's version of her mother was very different from the Monica he had observed in the lab and with the people in Singapore. But as both Harri and Aisha had reminded him, there was always more than one side to a story.

Men with orange lights were waving signals out on the tarmac. The jet lurched into motion and backed away from the terminal.

Rey forced his fingers to relax as the jet rolled toward the runway. The last thing he needed was to attract too much attention by leaving fingerprints in the metal. Monica ignored him and continued flipping through her magazine as the nose of the jet tilted upward. The familiar sensation of leaving the earth behind pushed Rey deeper into his seat.

It still sucked compared to flying all by himself.

The attendants had turned down the cabin's lighting. Most people were asleep though a few scattered overhead lamps said passengers were working or reading.

In fact, Rey assumed Monica was one of those napping. She had asked for a blanket shortly after takeoff and huddled under it for the last two hours.

"Why'd you switch the flashdrives?" she murmured.

"What?"

"Don't give me those innocent puppy dog eyes." Monica peered over the edge of her blanket and smirked at him. "That act may work with your baby momma, but don't try that shit with me."

"Why were you trying to sell my personal information to outside parties?"

She opened her mouth for a retort, then closed it. Her fingernails tapped a rapid-fire rhythm on the armrest. "You could have said something before now."

"Now who's acting innocent?"

"So you have a twin brother?"

He shrugged. "Not that I know of. The project could refer to my doppelgänger."

"Doppelgänger?"

"Don't know what else to call him." Rey rubbed his chin. Damn, he needed to shave. Kwan Li's groomer had trimmed his hair and beard so he no longer looked like the many homeless men wandering the streets of Canyon Pointe, but he'd always kept clean-shaven since puberty. He didn't look as scary to other people when his face was bare. His height intimidated them enough.

"So, who was this guy?" Monica persisted. "A clone? A robot?"

"He definitely wasn't a robot," Rey murmured. "He may be a clone, but I don't know how they would have gotten a DNA sample."

Monica pursed her lips in thought. "Stem cells would be preferable, but they could have used a hair sample."

"Crap." Rey wiped both hands down his face. "Corvus has been going through our trash then."

"Or it could have been as simple as someone with similar bone structure and a really good plastic surgeon," she muttered. "Was he trying to infiltrate the supers back home?"

"I don't know what his endgame was," Rey said bitterly.

"Oh, shit," she breathed. "Your girl and your baby. No wonder you've been a pain in the ass." Her head dropped back against her headrest. "I don't have any contacts in Canyon Pointe anymore, no one left except . . ." She audibly gulped. "You so owe me one for this, kid."

"What do you mean?"

"I'm going to call my mother when we get to Japan."

CHAPTER 14

Rey followed Monica through the Tokyo terminal. They had roughly two hours before their connecting flight to Vancouver, British Columbia. She claimed there was a phone kiosk in the custom-free shopping area.

Instead, she abruptly swerved to her right into a restaurant.

"What's wrong?" he murmured.

Monica didn't answer. Like she had at the Singapore shipping terminal, she strode through the dining area as if she owned the place and made a beeline for the swinging door that absorbed waiters laden only with bare trays.

The kitchen was noisy. No one gave them a second look except for a couple of bussers.

Rey glanced over his shoulder. A flick of the swinging door revealed three men at the entrance of the restaurant. Tattoos edged past the collars of their suits. Their manner reminded him too much of the cartel-related gangs who tried to infiltrate the northside of Canyon Pointe. They preyed on those who could least afford their drugs and pulled the unwilling into their orbit out of fear.

The odds were these men were after Monica for a reason. She charged through another door, and Rey found they were in a back hallway of the terminal.

With absolutely no cover whatsoever.

"Run," he growled. He grabbed her hand. Panic at their vulnerability kept the pain in his side at bay.

Together, they raced for the next door. Locked. As was the second and third.

A shout echoed behind them. Rey looked over his shoulder. All three men pointed guns at him and Monica. He whirled, pulled Monica against his chest and ducked.

Bullets pinged off his back. The impacts stung, but that was nothing compared to what they would do to Monica's delicate flesh.

The shooting slowed, then stopped. Leaving his carryon on the floor, Rey rose to his full height. The three men hesitated in the middle of reloading their weapons, their eyes wide with disbelief. Rey charged up the hallway.

He had to give them credit. They stood their ground against an obvious super.

Considering none of them were supers.

In less than three heartbeats, all three men were sprawled on the linoleum tiles, two unconscious and one with a definite concussion from the way his eyes crossed. Rey ignored the ache in his side and bent the barrels of their guns to make them useless.

One of the doors that had been locked opened. A young waitress from her outfit peered around the doorjamb. She looked at Rey, the men on the floor, then back at Rey. Her mouth formed a perfect "o" before she slammed the door shut.

He stalked down the corridor to Monica, who took a step backward. Wariness lay in her eyes as her attention flicked to their assailants and back to him.

"Want to tell me what that was about?" he demanded.

Her chin lifted slightly. "An old misunderstanding."

"They knew we were here in Tokyo," he ground out. "Our flight landed less than an hour ago."

"I know." Worry replaced her wariness. A vertical crease appeared in the middle of her forehead.

"And you expect me to keep you alive for the next few hours?"

"Yes." She released a deep breath. "I told you I deal in favors when it comes to friends. I'll owe you one." She reached inside the neckline, pulled a familiar flashdrive from her brassiere, and held it out to him. "Here's the original flashdrive. The one you have, the one I gave to Kwan Li is a fake."

"But Kwan Li is also your friend," Rey pointed out.

Behind them, the semi-conscious assailant groaned.

"Come on." Rey took the flashdrive from her outstretched hand. He winced as he bent to pick up his carryon. "We need to find someplace safer to make our calls."

They found a side corridor that led back to the main section of the international terminal. He spotted restrooms nearby.

"I need to use the facilities," he murmured. "Get rid of the phone Kwan Li gave you."

She slid the phone into the suit pocket of a passing business man. Rey rolled his eyes and headed for the men's room. Thankfully, the facility was empty except for one bald gentleman washing his hands.

Rey stepped into a stall, lifted his shirt and checked his wounds. The middle slice had torn open. Blood seeped from the tear, but the blood hadn't penetrated the light gauze over the injuries. He patted at the blood with a tissue before he fished out the wound bonding glue from his carryon. The patch job would have to do. He only hoped he wouldn't run into any more of Monica's so-called friends.

He pulled out the phone Kwan Li had given him, dropped it into the toilet, and pissed on it for good measure. It took him a couple of flushes before the phone disappeared down the drain.

When he stepped out of the stall, the bald man was still in the restroom, leaning against the wall nearest to the entrance.

"Thanks for the courtesy flush," the stranger said in perfect English. He added a mocking grin. "And before you do something stupid, you might want to look at my badge."

"What have I done?" Rey said. "I flushed too many times?"

"It's more the accessory to theft, fraud, and possible murder in addition to assault, assuming the Yakuza idiots who tried to shoot you press charges." The bald man reached into his jacket and produced his badge. "I doubt if you have to worry about them though."

"I can't read Japanese," Rey protested.

"Captain Takashi Takeda of Japan's Superhuman Enforcement Bureau, Mr. Davis." He slid his badge back in his suit jacket's inner pocket. "Your associate Miss Purrception is already in custody. It would be best if you came quietly."

"And if I don't?" Rey didn't like his options. Attacking an officer of the law wouldn't be his first choice, but the Japanese authorities weren't about to let him quietly board the plane for home.

"Well," Captain Takeda drawled. His eyes shifted from brown to a fiery red, and not just the iris but the entire orb. "We could have a smackdown, destroy a good piece of the international terminal, and hurt a lot of innocent people." His grinned widened. "Or my associates can seal the door and pump in knockout gas that will have you flat on your back in the time it takes me to explain while I breathe from an oxygen tank already hidden in this room." He shrugged. "Your choice, Mr. Davis."

Rey sighed. Harri and Tim always said to avoid the fight if he could find another way out of a situation, though they each had a different reason for their advice. "I'll come quietly."

"Thank you for making my job easier." The red of Captain Takeda's eyes faded. "And as long as you cooperate, I won't cuff you. However—" The officer cleared his throat. "You might want to change your clothes before we step outside. You've got a large number of bullet holes in your shirt and pants."

CHAPTER 15

Two days later, Aisha strode through the crowded terminal. Atlanta was definitely earning its reputation as one of the U.S.'s busiest airports. The Labor Day crowds only added to the normal chaos. She just prayed LaShun waited for her in baggage claim like she said she would. Her sister had been sketchy when Aisha texted her the plane from Canyon Pointe had landed.

When Aisha reached the correct carousel, all two hundred people from her flight jostled for position. She spotted her purple hardshell luggage as it slid down the chute.

"Excuse me." She tried to worm between a large group of twenty-somethings and an equally large man in a custom-tailored suit without accidentally knocking all of them over with her superstrength. "That's my bag."

"I got it, baby girl." Like a knight in shining armor, Dad pushed past the twenty-somethings and snagged her luggage.

"Well, you definitely learned to buy suitcases that stand out. I don't know how any times I grabbed the wrong bag when I did summer field work—" Dad's amused tone abruptly died, and he stared at her. No, not at her.

At her baby bump.

"I think there's something you left out of your phone call, Aisha Claudette Franklin."

Oh, shit. Not the middle name. "Can we not talk about this here?"

"You just want to spring this on your mother?" His eyes glittered behind his glasses, except she wasn't sure what emotion he was trying to hold in check.

"Dad, this wasn't how I wanted you to find out."

"I know I need surgery for my cataracts, but your belly is a little hard to miss, young lady."

Aisha sagged at the anger and disappointment in his voice. "I didn't think it was right to tell you and Mom over the phone."

"So, when were you going to tell us? When the kid graduates from high school?"

"No, Dad—"

"Is this why LaShun was so adamant about coming to pick you up?" Her father continued to stare at her as if he was seeing her for the first time. "LaShun can know, but not me or your mother?"

"LaShun doesn't know yet." Aisha blinked in an effort to keep the waterworks under control. Damn hormones. "You're the first."

"Well, hallelujah for that," Dad answered sarcastically.

"Dad, please let me explain—"

"Let's go. I want to beat the traffic." Dad stomped through the crowd, dragging her purple suitcase behind him.

For a split-second, she considered marching back to the ticketing desk and going home. But dealing with Steve was far more painful than facing her family, even though none of this mess was his fault. It just hurt so damn much to look at him. She swallowed her pride and her agony and followed her father.

⌘

The inside of Dad's sedan was utterly silent during the drive through the city. Dad's mouth was an angry slash every time Aisha glanced at him. She sighed and settled for staring out the passenger window.

She hadn't been to Atlanta since Grams' funeral five years ago. Part of her expected Mom and Dad to move back to Canyon Pointe after both Grams and PawPaw had passed, but they decided to keep the huge old house. Dad claimed his enjoyed his position teaching history here, and he did have tenure. More likely, he expected Martin to move into the old homestead once he and Renata were married so the house would stay in the family, though Dad probably hadn't said a darn thing to Martin about it.

Dad pulled into what had been the carriage drive when the house had been built at the end of the 19th century. The minivan with rental plates already parked in the drive must LaShun and her brood's.

Without a word, Dad climbed out, retrieved her luggage from the trunk and stomped up the back porch steps. Aisha counted to twenty in an effort to get her emotions under control. The last thing either her family or the neighbors needed to see was her new powers.

She unlatched the door of the sedan and climbed out. The walk up the steps took forever and sped by at the same time. She forced herself to turn the cut glass knob and walk inside.

Dad, Mom and LaShun stood in the kitchen. Shock was written all over Mom and LaShun's faces while Dad refused to look at her.

Mom stared at her for an instant before she bustled across the kitchen and wrapped Aisha in a huge hug. "Glad you could come, honey."

"Thanks, Mom." Aisha carefully hugged her back.

Mom released her and stepped back to examine her baby bump before she eyed Aisha again. "I take it this is the real reason Harri, Jeremy, and Leo couldn't come to Atlanta."

"Wouldn't come, you mean? Yeah." Aisha rubbed her abdomen. "I'm sorry I didn't tell y'all. It's just things have been . . . a little crazy at work since Captain Justice died."

LaShun stepped forward and gave her a hug as well. "Considering Jeremy didn't invite any of us to his and Leo's wedding, he can just stay in Canyon Pointe." She loosened her hold and eyed Aisha. "Please tell us you aren't carrying their baby."

"No." Aisha gave a weak chuckle. "It's mine. It's just that—" She shook her head. "All the doctors said I'd never get pregnant—"

"So you just decided a rubber wasn't worth it?" Dad snapped. "Aisha Claudette Franklin, you are old enough to know better! You want HIV or some other disease? A lot of today's STDs are penicillin-resistant!"

"Marvin! Out!" Mom's entire right arm pointed at the back door.

"You think this isn't my business?" He glared at Mom.

"Not when you're acting like a prehistoric dick." LaShun crossed her arms and added her own glare into the mix. "Go out to the shed and cool off, Daddy."

It was the first time Aisha could remember her mom and sister ganging up on Dad on her behalf. Had she stepped into an alternate universe?

Dad mumbled something under his breath. Her superhearing could only pick up "outnumbered" and "crazy" before he pivoted and stomped out of the house. She watched through the huge Florida windows as his lanky form continued stomping across the grass to the antique horse barn they all had referred to as "the shed" back when Grams and PawPaw lived here.

"Maybe I should leave," Aisha murmured. Her heart ached with the added weight of Dad's disappointment.

"No, you are not going anywhere, young lady. Have a seat." Mom jabbed a finger in the direction of the kitchen table before she turned to LaShun. "Take your sister's suitcase up to the rose room for her. I'll make tea."

Aisha obeyed. Maybe she did fall into an alternate universe.

Mom filled the tea kettle while LaShun dragged the purple suitcase down the hall. Once Mom set the water on the burner, and the gas flame danced bright blue beneath the white kettle, she sat down at the table and took Aisha's hands.

"You have an OB lined up?" Concern shown in her hazel eyes.

"Yes, ma'am."

"And they have you on pre-natal vitamins?"

Aisha smiled at Mom's fussing. "As soon as we realized I was pregnant."

"How far along?"

"According to the ultrasounds, around thirteen weeks."

Mom paused, looking distinctly uncomfortable. "Are you going to do an amniocentesis?"

Aisha faltered. Considering her age, Serena's friend Doctor O'Brien wanted to, but neither she nor any of her medical colleagues knew how to insert a needle into someone with impenetrable skin.

"There's been a little complication, Mom."

"The baby?"

"No, the baby is fine"

Her son kicked as if to reassure her he was quite all right.

"Oh my god." Mom covered her mouth for a moment as realization dawned. "You have HRSP."

"Yeah." Relief rushed through Aisha at the admission. "In my case, my skin's impenetrable. My doctor can't take blood samples, much less do an amniocentesis."

"Oh, crap!" LaShun sauntered back into the kitchen and plopped down across the table from Aisha. She'd obviously heard the last bit of their conversation. "That means any painkillers during delivery are out, too."

"Tell me about it." Aisha rolled her eyes. "But you can't tell anybody." She looked at Mom and LaShun in turn. "Please. I've been wanting a baby for so long. This is my only chance." The last word ended on a choked sob. She didn't know what she would do if the government took away hers and Rey's child. It was the last little bit of him she had.

Mom's throat bobbed, and she squeezed Aisha's hands. "Of course, honey."

LaShun laid her hands on top of theirs. "You've got it, baby sis." She cleared her throat. "What do you plan to tell Daddy? Because you know his beef about men who don't take responsibility."

"Why are you assuming there's no father involved?" Aisha shot her sister a dirty look.

"Because you would have brought him." LaShun reached across the table and whacked the back of Aisha's head. "Ow!" She drew back and shook her hand.

"Invulnerable, remember?" Aisha muttered. "Serves you right if you broke a bone."

"Mom!" LaShun whined.

"You were the one dumb enough to hit an invulnerable woman," Mom said dryly.

The switch was so startling Aisha couldn't find the words. Mom always took LaShun's side.

"LaShun, help me finish up dinner before everybody else gets back from their tour of the Coca-Cola plant." Mom released Aisha's hands with a final squeeze. She stood and arranged her chair in front of Aisha. "Now, you put up your feet, baby girl, and tell me all the latest gossip back in Canyon Pointe."

CHAPTER 16

Harri sat on the same bench in Founder's Green as she had every other time. These meetings were getting on her nerves.

This time, there was no pre-meeting with one of the Corvus lackeys. Byron Trubble, general, retired, had a newspaper in his hand when he sat down next to her. His white hair seemed a bit thin on top, and his clothes seemed looser. She hoped the pressure of his stupid illegal bullshit was getting to him. It would serve the bastard right.

"Crazy Jim still doing clean-up duty in Colorado?" She smirked.

"Would you enjoy it if I said he was?"

"Definitely," Harri answered.

"Where's your bodyguard?" Trubble inclined his head in the direction of another park bench down the sidewalk to their left. "I can't see Rue Liberty passing up a chance to give me the evil eye."

"She had shuffleboard at the senior center this afternoon." Harri had to admit the elderly superhero was right. Getting into a routine against any organization wasn't smart. But she wasn't about to tell the head of Corvus the lady at the sno-cone vendor whose legs he was admiring wasn't a woman.

Trubble finally tore his attention away from Jeremy's fake rack. "You asked for this meeting, Winters."

She cocked an eyebrow. "I thought you wanted the Ghost Owl's help."

"I don't see why you have to be the middleman."

"Middlewoman," she corrected.

"Look, if you going to throw around your PC, feminist agenda—"

"The Ghost Owl can't identify the DNA your people preserved," she interjected before Trubble stomped off in a huff. "But he did trace where Professor Paranoia sent supplies, including prisoners he was experimenting on."

Trubble's eyes narrowed. "I'm not going to beg, Winters."

"Wasn't asking you to." She handed him a sealed manila envelope.

He stared at it as if he expected it to bite him.

"Unlike your Corvus minions, the Ghost Owl didn't stick tracking devices on anything meant for you." Harri enjoyed his unease far more than she should.

"Doesn't mean you didn't," Trubble shot back.

"I've got two genius employees and a load of clients who don't like you," Harri answered dryly. "None of whom would bother with a tracking device. Rue Liberty may despise you, but you won't have any mysterious accidents with her either."

Trubble grunted and took the envelope. "Do you know what's in it?"

"The coordinates for a supposedly abandoned oil platform in the Java Sea. Corvus has been renting it from the Indonesian government through one of its shell companies." She watched for his reaction. Once again, his face went perfectly still. Only his cold, reptilian eyes glittered.

Did Trubble know they'd hacked the Corvus computers in Colorado? Did he realize Tim and Arthur had been watching Corvus and learning everything the quasi-legal black ops organization did? From their communications, those asshats had already tracked Professor Paranoia to Indonesia and found a scene similar to the one at the lab in Colorado. Or did Trubble merely think she'd gotten the information from the Ghost Owl.

Which she had. In a way.

Trubble pulled out a penknife and sliced open the envelope. His eyes darted back and forth as he read the contents. The guys had used her ancient printer for the report so only her fingerprints were on the two pages and the envelope.

Finally, Trubble exhaled. "Villanova, Gonzalez-Estes, whatever name he's using now, did a better job of cleaning up this time. He set the platform on fire."

Harri blinked. "Shit. He must have slagged the computers because he figured out you knew he was still alive."

"That was the frosting," Trubble said sourly. "He made a point of smashing all the hard drives first."

"And a Faraday vault isn't going to protect anything from a fire," Harri added.

Trubble stared at her with the first sign of surprise she'd ever seen on his rough features. "The Owl's already been there, hasn't he?"

None of her people had been there, but no sense revealing that to Trubble. "What exactly were you expecting from Jatz'om Kuh if you already knew where Paranoia had gone?"

"Who was the guy you brought to Colorado?" Trubble said instead of answering her question.

Harri considered whether to respond. Trubble must know Steve wasn't Rey. It was an old litigation trick to ask the witness questions the attorney already knew the answers to.

She glanced across the park. Jeremy flirted with the vendor while eating his sno-cone.

"How did you know?" she murmured.

"Fingerprints." Trubble chuckled. "The kid had to turn them in for his passport. What's his relationship with Garcia?"

"You go after him, and you'll be asking for more trouble than you realize," Harri warned. "He isn't some street urchin."

"And I'm not a Dickens villain." His amusement faded. "Another super under my nose with that power set, and he just waltzes through life on his trust fund." The bitterness in his voice gave her the first indication of what bubbled underneath his lizard skin.

"Is that why you targeted me?" she asked softly. "Another trust fund baby in your way?"

Her question jolted him out of his reverie, and the reptilian mask slipped back into place. "You're a boil on my backside. The fact your daddy took the rest of the Winters fortune off a cliff with him is just the cocaine on top."

The obvious low blow was expected, but it didn't stop the wave of pain that rolled through her. She forced a smile. "And if Seismic Shit had half a brain, he would have framed me for possession instead of burning down City Hall."

She waved in the direction of the steel and brick skeleton. The portions damaged by acid and the resulting fire had been replaced, and the surviving walls had been cleaned of soot. Sparkling new windows on the lower floors were open to catch any breath of air. Hammering echoed across Founder's Green as workmen carried sheet after sheet of drywall into the building.

"The only mistake I made regarding him was not hiring you to head up the southwest division," Trubble muttered.

Harri turned to stare at him and place her hand on her chest in mock dismay. "Why, Byron, that almost sounded like a compliment."

"Don't push it, Winters." He stood. "If your buddy picks up the trail again, let me know. He'll have any help from me he needs."

"I'll relay the message," she said, but Trubble was already sauntering in the direction of the sno-cone stand.

Harri shook her head, rose, and headed for the coffee shop. Maybe one of Aisha's mocha concoctions would take the edge off her unease.

⁂

It was a half hour before Jeremy waltzed into Java Joe's. He was still dressed as Lady Jaye, his queen persona, but he'd changed from the blond wig, the tight cream dress and seamed stockings to a frilly turquoise summer dress topped by a red wig.

He slid into the seat across from Harri. "Your boy doesn't take no for an answer."

She couldn't help laughing. "I'm sure you found a language he understood."

"Leo says I can still look now that we're hitched. I just can't touch." Worry creased Jeremy's perfect makeup. "I'm more concerned your buddy knew who I was."

"He probably did." She sighed. "It's not like the jerk doesn't have a dossier on all my known associates."

Jeremy leaned closer. "Girl, that jerk had no problem ordering Seismic Shift's death. Do not underestimate him. If he decides you or any of us aren't worth the trouble, he'll do the same to us."

Harri cleared her throat. "Speaking of trouble, Aisha should have heard about your wedding from you, not LaShun."

"Is she that pissed at me?" Jeremy actually looked crestfallen. "We didn't want to rub it in her face with Rey . . ."

Harri covered Jeremy's hand. "Come on, you were in both of our weddings. We kind of expected to be bridesmaids at yours."

Jeremy rolled his eyes. "I would have made you both wear tuxes."

"No one outshines Lady Jaye." Harri grinned. "I get it. But maybe she and I both needed a little celebration with all the shit that's been happening."

"Like the welcome to the world party for Gracie that you so rudely canceled?" One of his perfectly drawn eyebrows climbed his forehead.

"Black Death was stalking us at the time," Harri hissed. "I think everyone living takes precedence over a damn party."

"Gingersnap said he's back."

If the situation wasn't so worrisome, she would have smiled at Jeremy's nickname for Tim. "Unfortunately." She sighed. "He's suing for custody of Grace."

"Fuck me with a cactus. Poor Patty." Jeremy sipped the chai tea she'd bought for him and grimaced. "It's cold."

"I didn't think it would take you that long to get here. You change faster than this during your shows." She grinned over the rim of her own cup.

"If you're going to be a bitch, you can pay for the materials on the dress I made for Betty for their ceremony." Jeremy pulled a pen and pad from his beige macramé purse and jotted down a figure before he ripped off the sheet and handed it to Harri.

She sucked in her breath at the number. "What the hell did you make it out of? Diamonds?"

Jeremy sniffed. "Honey, if you want to pay for my time and I pay for the materials, that's all right with me. I know damn well you haven't sent them a gift."

"Never mind." Harri swallowed her irritation with him and her guilt over forgetting the society manners Grandma Harri tried to instill in her. Considering what her clients paid for Jeremy's design and construction of their superhero outfits, she was getting a damn good deal. "Can I get you the check next week?"

"I know you're good." Jeremy waved off the money issue with a flick of his wrist. "However, you should have gone to Atlanta with Aisha."

"You should have gone, too."

"She needed to tell her parents her situation. Leo and I being in the middle of that wouldn't have helped."

"So you *do* feel a little guilty over not inviting any of us, including Betty and Marvin, to you wedding."

"We have businesses to run," Jeremy said primly.

Harri watched the crowd on the sidewalk passing by the window. "Well, one of us needs to be here to run our practice, too."

"You sure that's the real reason you didn't go?" Jeremy muttered.

From the edge in his words, Harri could hear the trouble coming. She turned to stare at Jeremy. "Oh my god, what the hell did you tell Betty?"

"You will be getting a call from Mrs. Franklin about your new beau." Jeremy made the Cheshire Cat look like someone with chronic depression.

Harri buried her face in her hands. "Why didn't Trubble kill me when he had the chance?" She dropped her hands to her lap and looked up at Jeremy. "What did they say about Tim?"

"Oh, I didn't tell her it was Gingersnap. I'm leaving that up to you." He took another sip of the chai tea. "I can't handle this. I need them to nuke my cup." He rose and sashayed to the counter. More than one male's gaze followed Jeremy's ass.

Well, crap. Harri rested her elbow on the table and stared at the pedestrians. She owed Betty and Marvin Franklin. Aisha's parents had gotten both her and Jeremy out of the foster system when they were teens.

However, the reason they loved Aisha's ex-husband so damn much was due to Calvin entering the DA's office. Betty and Marvin were only two of the thousands of citizens in Canyon Pointe who thought Tim Canyon had gotten away with murder. They really believed their former son-in-law would clean up the city. And their opinion still meant the world to Harri.

It would be a damn hard slog to convince them Tim had been wrongly accused in the first place.

Ironically, Calvin ended up becoming the acting DA, thanks to his boss's corruption and conspiracy with Seismic Shift. At least until the November election. How much crap were they giving Aisha about not being with a man? Especially with her pregnancy?

Jeremy returned with warm tea and resumed his seat, but something was definitely wrong. His smile didn't reach his eyes. "Don't turn around, girl. Get out your compact and powder your nose. Blue Eyes is behind you."

Harri reached into her own bag and palmed her makeup clamshell. Her heart hammered as she lifted the mirror. Sure enough, Cade Wilson, AKA Black Death, sat two tables behind them.

"How the hell did he get in here without us seeing him?" she whispered.

"Didn't you check the place when you came in?" Jeremy whispered back.

"Of course, I did." And she had. Wilson must have slipped in through the delivery entrance in the alley. This is what Rue Liberty meant about altering her routine. Harri always visited Java Joe's when she came downtown. As she watched Wilson's reflection, he rose and walked toward them. "He's coming this way."

Jeremy's eyes narrowed. He pulled his purse onto his lap and reached inside. Both he and Leo possessed and practiced with an array of Tim's non-lethal weapons, which was the whole point of bringing him as her backup.

She pulled her keyring from her pocket and palmed the mini-pepper spray canister.

Wilson stopped at their table. "Ms. Winters, may I speak to you privately?"

Harri looked up at him. "Does your attorney know you're here?"

His jaw worked before he bit out, "No."

"Mr. Wilson, I can't speak to you without Ms. Ashcraft present," she said firmly. "Now, if your boss sent you to deliver a message . . ."

Wilson deliberately jammed his hands into his jeans pockets, but his gesture didn't relieve Harri. "Grace is my daughter, too," he said.

So Trubble didn't know he was here either.

"I can call your attorney or your boss, Cade," she said softly. "It's your choice."

He turned on his heel and stalked out of the café. The tension poured out of her, and she started shaking.

"So that's Patty's baby daddy." Jeremy pivoted his chair to keep an eye on Trubble's pet assassin.

"Unfortunately," Harri muttered. She pulled out her phone and hit the speed dial for Lisa's office number. The phone rang once. Twice.

"Ashcraft and Associates," her receptionist said. "How can I help you?"

"Hi, Fern. It's Harri Winters. I need to talk to Lisa now. One of her clients just confronted me and a friend at the Java Joe's across from Founder's Green."

CHAPTER 17

"Well, I'd say we missed our flight," Rey said dryly two days later. He lay on his bunk at the Japanese's supervillain short-term detention center and stared at the ceiling. His feet didn't just hang off the thin mattress and frame. His knees bent and his heels rested on the reinforced concrete floor.

The too small bed wasn't the worst part. The authorities had taken his jade amulet when they had processed him. His nerves twitched with the worry that the monsters could show up any minute.

"Are you always such a sarcastic jerk?" Monica asked. Her voice echoed from a cell above and to his right.

"Not always." He grinned. Aisha often remarked Harri had totally corrupted his sweet nature. Of course, Harri muttered the same complaint about Aisha once they started sleeping together. "I blame it on my foster mom."

"You were in the system?" Monica sounded genuinely curious.

"Not exactly." How did he explain the complicated mess his life had become since May? "It's just kind of the role she played in my life. I saved her from a mugger in Founder's Green. She took me in when she found out I was living on the streets."

There. That was the simplest story he could tell and stay within the bounds of truth. After Tim told him the guy who tried to strangle Harri was a Corvus assassin, he didn't feel quite so bad about throwing the asshole into a parked car. Harri, Tim, and Miguel were the closest things he had to parents since his mom had been murdered.

"She sounds like a saint," Monica said. Was that a tinge of jealousy in her voice? "Did she know you're a super?"

"Yeah. She does. She's the one who helped me find a lawyer to get registered."

"How's your injuries doing?" Monica asked.

"Better." Which was true. The pain was down to a dull ache, and he didn't feel like he would rip the slices open by taking a deep breath anymore.

Captain Takeda had questioned Rey about the wounds after a doctor checked him over. Rey said he didn't know the little bald man who kidnapped him while he was away from home on business. All he knew was the man had weapons sharper than steel. Rey left out the part about the monsters. Japanese law enforcement already thought he was a bit nuts, hanging out with Miss Purrception. Rey stuck to the story that she found him injured and had helped him get medical aid.

"You know the only reason they locked us in this wing by ourselves?" Monica asked, abruptly changing the subject.

"They're recording us, hoping we say something incriminating," he replied. "Japanese authorities don't normally allow inmates to converse."

"Aren't you the smartest superhero in his class?"

"I'm not the one with a record," he shot back. Yet. The longer they stayed here, the sooner his fake identity would come to light. Carrying Monica for eighteen hours across the Pacific Ocean wasn't the issue. He simply wasn't sure he could fly that far. Trying to stop at Hawaii or Alaska without contacting the U.S. authorities ahead of time could get Monica killed. NORAD got rather pissy about unknown supers flying into their jurisdiction and had been known to fire first.

And heaven help any super who acted in self-defense against any nation's military.

Captain Takeda had finally let him make a phone call after a third session of questioning. Rey had tried Aisha's cell phone twice. Knowing the Japanese authorities would be recording from his end, he kept his message brief.

Rey chuckled at Monica's original question. "It's also why I haven't asked you what you did to tick off both the Yakuza and the SEB."

From the opposite end of the aisle, titanium and steel doors rattled and clanged. It was too early for breakfast.

"Great," Monica muttered. "Another round of interrogation."

Two guards stopped in front of Rey's cell. One of the men ordered him to stand in Japanese. It was one of the few words he'd picked up in the last couple of days.

Rey climbed to his feet and clasped his hands behind his head. The guard who had spoken unlocked his cell door. Once he stepped into the aisle, they quickly and efficiently shackled his wrists and his ankles.

He found it a little hard to trust in the system, no matter what Harri said. But he owed Monica for her help. He might still be trapped on that abandoned drilling platform if she hadn't come along. He couldn't leave her here. He just wished Harri or Aisha would do something soon, but that was assuming Aisha had received his message.

The guards escorted him to the same interrogation room. From Arthur's description of the one in the downtown Canyon Pointe police station, the facilities were much cleaner in Japan, than in the United States.

But all the bleach in the world couldn't mask some odors.

The guards pointed to one of the chairs. Once Rey was seated, they locked the shackles on his wrists to the table. Despite his good behavior, the Japanese authorities weren't taking any chances. Considering Miss Purrception's reputation for escaping custody, he didn't blame them.

A few minutes later, Captain Takeda walked in with a manila folder. He didn't have his "good cop" smile this time.

"We seem to have a slight problem, Mr. Davis." Takeda didn't bother to sit down. He flipped open the folder and tossed stapled papers in front of Rey.

He looked at the top sheet. A scanned copy of a face smiled back at him. A face that was his, but wasn't his.

"Facial recognition says you're Stephen K. Connors of Seattle, Washington." Takeda tapped the paper. "Mr. Connors suddenly returned home two weeks ago after he disappeared from his hostel in Honduras back in May. He claimed he was kidnapped according to the United States FBI."

He tossed the second set of papers on top of the first. "But the more interesting call came from the U.S. National Superhero Bureau. According to them, your fingerprints belong to the recently deceased Captain Justice. They confirmed Stephen K. Conners is not Captain Justice's civilian identity. So, let's start from the beginning. What is your name, and why are you in Japan?"

CHAPTER 18

Jada and Devon attacked Aisha with hugs as soon as they ran in the back door. The three adults followed at a more sedate pace.

Any hope Aisha had of anyone pretending her pregnancy didn't exist were dashed when Devon turned to Eric and yelled, "Check out Aisha, Dad! We're getting a cousin!"

Martin's fiancée Renata moved first and embraced Aisha. "Congratulations!"

Eric and Martin got over their initial shock and followed suit.

"Does Dad know yet?" Martin whispered in her ear.

"Yeah." Aisha grinned at her baby brother. "That's why Mom banished him to the shed."

He rolled his eyes. "Dinner's going to be fun tonight." From his expression of curiosity though, he was dying to ask what was going on, but he had the sense to wait until their parents went to bed.

"That is the understatement of the century," Eric grumbled under his breath.

The formal dining room had never been this silent. Not since the Franklin family had been taking their meals in here back when PawPaw's dad first built this house.

Aisha sighed when Dad threw the spoon into the mashed potatoes hard enough to make a sound. Eric hadn't been wrong about how uncomfortable this dinner would be. Any attempts at small talk died under Dad's withering gaze.

"This roast beef is great, Mom," she said.

"Still living on take-out?" Mom raised an eyebrow.

Aisha passed the sweet corn to Devon. So much for thinking she'd escape any of Mom's criticism whatsoever. "If you tasted Marta's food, you'd understand why I go there so much."

"Marta?" LaShun asked.

"She owns a Latin cuisine restaurant five blocks from our building." Aisha sliced off another bite from her slab of roast. "She has the best chicken taquitos and guacamole—"

"Really?" Dad threw his silverware. The knife and fork landed on Mom's good china with a loud clatter. "We're going to pretend the elephant isn't in the room?"

"Marvin," Mom hissed under her breath.

Aisha couldn't ever remember being angry with her father. Even during her rebellious teenage years, Mom had been the disciplinarian, not Dad. But copping a horrible attitude at a family dinner was out of bounds.

"You will not call your future grandson an elephant, Dad," Aisha said coolly.

"I can know the baby's a boy, but I can't know who the father is and why you haven't married him?"

She wasn't sure if Dad was hurt or angry. It didn't matter. Not when it dredged up her own pain. The agony she kept stuffed inside of her when she was with other people.

Aisha laid down her own utensils. "This isn't the time or place to discuss this."

"Tell me who's the father, and I'll drop it." Definitely anger in Dad's voice. "And don't tell me it's Calvin Johnson. If that little asshole—"

"Stop it, Marvin!" Mom snapped. She turned to Aisha and took her hand. "Does the father make you happy, honey? That's all that matters."

"Kids, take your plates and go watch TV," LaShun ordered.

Jada and Devon exchanged looks before Devon blurted, "Are you kidding? This is better than *Real Housewives*!"

"Go. Now," Eric growled.

With some muttering under their breath, Jada and Devon grabbed their plates, glasses, and utensils, and they headed for the family room.

"Maybe I should go with them," Renata whispered to Martin, though it was so quiet around the dining room table everyone could hear her.

He shook his head, his eyes sparkling in barely repressed humor at Aisha's situation. "We're just having a grown-up conversation about grown-up things. Aren't we, Aisha?"

"Shut up, Martin." She jerked her hand from Mom's grasp and clenched her fists on her lap. The light-headed feeling swept through her. She couldn't lose it. Not here. Not now. Not when another power could spring to life. She hooked her feet around the legs of her own chair.

"Don't talk to your brother that way, young lady," Dad barked. "And I want to know who the father is and whether he's going to step up?"

"Dad, this isn't your business—"

"It damn well is my business!" He threw his napkin on the table, all pretense of a civil dinner gone. "Especially if you end up having to move here!"

"I'm not moving to Atlanta," she said hotly. "And I sure as hell don't expect you and Mom to take care of me!"

"Baby girl—" Mom patted her shoulder. "You're going to need help with a newborn, especially if the father's out of the picture."

"He's not out." The words felt like glass across her vocal cords. She couldn't deal with Rey being gone. Not until she saw a body. And that's what she was sure she would eventually find. A corpse. It didn't matter what his so-called mother said. If he were still alive, he would have busted his ass to come home.

"Who is he?" Dad asked. "Are you that ashamed of him?"

"I'm not ashamed of him!" She couldn't break attorney-client confidentiality either. Not now. Not ever.

"Then who is he?" Dad roared.

"Tim Canyon!"

A glass shattered in the family room, quickly followed by Devon's voice. "Awesome! We're going to have a murderer in the family!"

CHAPTER 19

"That son of a bitch?" Dad roared. He stood, shoving back his chair so hard it crashed to the floor.

Oh, god. Aisha wanted to sink into the floor. What had she just said? Tim would kill her.

No, Harri would beat him to the punch, even if he hadn't just got out of rehab.

Her chair wiggled, and the front started to rise. The antique wood was too light to keep her grounded. Her fingers latched around the nearest table leg to keep from floating to the ceiling. Wood splintered under her grip, but no one in the family seemed to hear the sound.

"Dad, this isn't your business," Aisha said as calmly as she could.

"You're carrying my grandson. It damn well is my business!"

Dammit. She couldn't leave the room. Not without flying out. But if she stayed here, she would definitely lose her temper. Time to quit treating him like her father, and treat him more like a hostile witness.

"So, were you lying to me in May, Dad?"

"What are you talking about?" He honestly appeared perplexed.

"When you said you never had to worry about me. That I made good choices." Her anger drained out of her, and the grief she'd been struggling to keep at bay flowed into the empty space of her soul. The front legs of her chair settled back on the hardwood floor of the dining room.

"It-it's different when you've got someone else to think about," he spluttered.

"I know this is different." She released the table leg and rubbed her abdomen. "The doctors said I'd never have a child after I lost—I lost—" The lump in her throat threatened to choke her, and she swallowed hard. "This child is a miracle for me. Maybe the circumstances aren't what I imagined, but I will do right by him regardless of—of anything or anyone."

Dad stared at his plate. He'd never been this quiet, but then he'd never been this angry either.

"It's been a long day for me." A flutter underneath her skin seemed like agreement. "I'm going upstairs to lie down."

Aisha stood, set her napkin on her chair, and carefully walked toward the staircase. The kids peered around the corner of the family room doorway, their dinner forgotten. Jada rushed forward and wrapped her arms around Aisha's waist.

"If you need me to come down and babysit next summer, I just need the plane ticket," Jada whispered. "I got my CPR and first aid certifications."

"Thank you for the offer, sweetie." Aisha kissed the top of her niece's head.

Devon ran over and hugged her, too. "I can help. Just not with the diapers."

Aisha laughed and kissed him as well. "You two go finish your dinner. We'll discuss this later."

Devon walked back to his TV tray, but Jada looked over her shoulder, as if unsure whether to leave. Aisha made a shooing motion, and her niece nodded before she headed back into the family room.

Aisha made her way up to what the entire family called the rose room because of the antique cabbage rose wallpaper. She and LaShun slept in here when they stayed with Grams and PawPaw. Once Aisha closed the door, she collapsed on the bed.

The last thing she wanted was to fight with Dad. He'd be the first person to admit he believed in old-fashioned ideals. She had expected a measure of disappointment from him because she wasn't married.

Married.

Miguel had let it slip Rey had dragged him to a jewelry shop to look at rings before Rey disappeared. He wanted a family so bad. And so had she.

But she couldn't tell her family the truth. Not without giving away Rey's secret identity. It was bad enough Mom had figured out she had HRSP. She couldn't chance the government taking her son.

A tear slipped down her temple. She swiped it away. No, she'd been crying enough.

She rolled over and unplugged her phone from its charger. There were probably five messages from Harri because Aisha hadn't called to let her partner know she'd arrived safely in Atlanta. She tapped in her security password.

And frowned at the screen. The darn thing was still on airplane mode. She tapped the icon to switch off the safety feature. Her phone pinged repeatedly as texts, e-mails, and voice messages loaded.

She swiped through the list. A couple of calls from clients. Four calls and three texts from Harri. One text from Qiang saying to *please* call Harri before the superhero electrocuted her law partner. Two calls from an international number she didn't recognize. She tapped on the second call since it showed a voice message.

Japan? She played the message.

"Aisha, it's me. I was on my way home when I was picked up by Japan's Superhuman Enforcement Bureau at the Tokyo airport. The officer in charge of my case is Captain Takashi Takeda. I know you're keeping an eye on Mom, Uncle, and the kids, but I really need an attorney ASAP. I-I will tell you the rest when I see you. Watch out for the crow that likes to hang out in the front yard."

Her breath hitched in her throat. She sat up and hit replay. It definitely sounded like Rey. She wanted to believe it was him.

Reality came crashing down. She needed to check this out carefully. Was it all a trick to get her out of the country? Or worse, a trick by someone to get their hands on her son?

Aisha hit the speed dial for Arthur's apartment.

"Hello, Aisha. How was your flight?" Something clattered in the background that sound more like pots and lids than computer equipment.

"Arthur, can you remote access my phone?"

"Give me a minute to get on my computer." The clattering stopped.

"Did I interrupt something?"

"I'm making lasagna for dinner. Patty and Qiang took the children to the park. What's going on?"

"I got a voice message from someone in Japan who sounds a lot like Rey."

Static crackled through the receiver for what seemed like forever. Aisha stood and paced, waiting for Arthur to tell her something. Anything.

Finally, he said, "The message and envelope information are stored on our server here. Give me another minute."

"Okay." Aisha released a shaky breath. He hadn't called her crazy.

In the background, she could hear keys clicking, then the message. More keys clicking.

"I can confirm the call was placed from the Superhuman Enforcement Bureau in Tokyo at four-forty-eight p.m. local time which was—"

"When Harri was driving me to the airport this morning." Aisha wanted to scream. She'd missed Rey's call by minutes. "I set my phone to airplane mode in the car on the way so I wouldn't forget."

Think, Aisha, think!

"Arthur, tell Harri what's going on," Aisha ordered. "I'll text her once I have my return flight to Canyon Pointe. Also, ask her to call the SEB in Tokyo once they open in a couple hours."

"And get you a ticket to Tokyo?"

"Let's confirm he's there first." The possibility Rey might still be alive made her giddy, and she laughed. "Last minute international tickets are expensive as hell."

"Be careful coming home. I'll see what I can find on Corvus operations in Japan."

"Thanks, Arthur. I—" Her emotions did a one-eighty, and she was on the verge of tears again. Damn hormones. "I really owe you for this."

"You don't owe me," he said softly. "I owe Rey."

Aisha ended the call. It only took a couple of minutes to book a seat on the red eye to Canyon Pointe.

Thankfully, she hadn't unpacked yet. She stowed her phone in her slacks pocket, unplugged the recharging cord, and tossed it in her suitcase as well. She needed to retrieve her toiletry bag from the bathroom.

Aisha grabbed her suitcase and carryon, yanked the bedroom door open and jumped back with a start at the shadowy figure in the hall. "Dad?"

"Can we talk, baby girl?" He looked haggard. Mom must have given him a good tongue-lashing.

"Not for long. I've got a flight home." As soon as the words left her mouth, she realized how snappish they sounded.

"Aisha, please don't leave like this." It wasn't like Dad to beg. "Your mom and I want you here for the ceremony."

Crap. The presents were still in her suitcase.

She whirled and tossed the suitcase on the bed. "Dad, there's an emergency back at the office."

"You don't have to make excuses." He shuffled into the bedroom. "I'm trying to apologize here."

Aisha forced herself to slow down before she accidentally did something at superspeed. "I know you are, Dad. And I'm sorry, too, for not telling you and Mom earlier about the baby." She rested her palms on his shoulders. "I swear I'm not leaving because of our fight. One of my clients is in really big trouble, and I'm not failing . . ." Her throat closed as she fought to get the words out. If there was even a remote chance Rey was still alive, she had to find out.

"Baby girl, you didn't fail." Dad pulled her in a tight embrace. "I did."

"No, you didn't. I'll come back and explain everything." His aftershave filled her head, a warm, comforting scent. "I promise, but I've got to leave now." She patted his back.

"Okay." He released his hold on her as someone knocked on the door.

LaShun stood there with Aisha's toiletry bag. "Sorry for eavesdropping. Thought you might need this if you're leaving."

"Thanks." She took the bag from LaShun's outstretched hand, opened her suitcase, and exchanged the toiletries with the two wrapped presents. "Here. One is for Mom and Dad. The other is for Martin and Renata. Don't let any of them open the packages early."

"No worries." LaShun's expression was terribly serious. She set the two wrapped boxes on the dresser before she pulled Aisha in a tight hug. "Whatever you're doing, be careful," she whispered.

"I will." Aisha patted LaShun's back. "Now, get off me. I gotta go!" She grabbed her suitcase and carryon and stalked out of the bedroom.

"You shouldn't be carrying luggage in your condition," Dad yelled as he followed her down the stairs.

"The old man's right," LaShun hollered from behind Dad.

"I'll drive you to the airport," he added. "And I'm not old."

"No!" The entire family shouted at the same time. Everyone gathered in the main entryway.

"You know you can't drive at night with your cataracts." Mom shook her finger at Dad.

"It's summer," Dad snapped. "There's still daylight outside!"

"Renata and I will take her," Martin said. "We'll see the rest of you tomorrow afternoon at the restaurant."

Eric grabbed for Aisha's bags. "Your father's right. You don't need to be carrying them in your condition."

She decided it was better to give in rather than trash her luggage or injure her brother-in-law. There was another quick round of hugs ending with Mom.

"I expect an explanation at some point, young lady." Mom squeezed her hard and kissed her cheek.

"I will."

"Now, go save your man." Mom winked.

For a second, Aisha was frozen in place. How did Mom know? Then Renata was tugging on Aisha's arm.

They rushed out the front door. Eric and Martin spoke quietly in front of a silver SUV.

"You want me to drive?" Martin asked.

Renata glared at him. "You are not dinging my precious."

"Oh, my god!" Martin shook his head. "You are worse than Aisha is about her vehicles." But he climbed into the passenger seat.

Eric hugged Aisha and made sure she was secure in the back seat before he slammed the passenger door shut.

Martin peered around the headrest of his seat as Reneta accelerated down the street. "You going to tell us what's really going?"

"There's an emergency with one of my clients—"

"I'm not Mom or Dad," Martin said dryly. "And I'm sure as hell not as deliberately ignorant as LaShun pretends to be. Does this have something to do with Captain Justice?"

She took refuge in attorney-client privilege. "You know I can't tell you who my client is."

"Yeah," Martin drawled. "That's what I thought." He smirked.

"Besides, Captain Justice is dead," she said softly.

Martin's smile faded. "Then what's the rush, A? Harri's just as good as you are, and there's nothing you can't handle."

"We're still getting the new attorney up to speed."

Renata glanced at Aisha in the rearview mirror. "You've already hired someone? That's great!"

"Yeah, because my sister's going to be a little busy in six months." Martin chuckled.

Yes, she would have her hands full when the baby made his debut. But would Rey be by her side? It was almost too much to hope for.

She pulled out her phone and tapped out a text to Harri.

Chapter 20

Harri read Aisha's text with her arrival time and thumbed, *I'll be there.*

"When does she get back?" Tim shuffled over to her couch with his walker.

"Flight's supposed to land at eleven-oh-seven." Harri frowned at him. "I know your orthopedic surgeon gave you the all clear, but don't you think you're pushing it?"

"You haven't been trapped on your ass for the last two months," he grumbled.

"I'm surprised you haven't headed back down to the basement to supervise Arthur." It took all of her willpower not to smirk at him.

The line between Tim's eyebrows creased. "You don't think he can handle the cross-check of that message Aisha received?"

"I think he can handle it." Her smile broke loose. "The real question is can my control-freak boyfriend handle letting my IT guy do the work by himself."

"Har-dee-har-har." Tim glowered at her for a moment, but his expression shifted to worry. "I'm more concerned about my control-freak girlfriend getting her hopes up that message really was from Rey."

"It's not me we need to worry about." Harri shook her head. "For all of Aisha's claims that she thinks he's dead, she's all over this damn call."

Harri's phone vibrated, and she jumped. Tim's snicker earned him a dirty look before she saw the ID and pressed the answer icon. "This is Harri."

"I'm sorry to call so late, my dear," Rue Liberty's voice quavered through the phone.

"Never apologize, ma'am," Harri said. "What's wrong?"

"M-my daughter called the house today."

Shit. "Give me a second, ma'am." Harri stood. "Client business."

"I can clear out—" Tim started.

"Take a seat, and watch tonight's baseball game or something." Harri pointed at the couch. "I'll be in the bedroom for a bit."

She snagged her laptop and headed toward the partitions for the sleeping and bath areas. Behind her came the voice of the local announcer for the Canyon Pointe Copperheads. While there weren't any real walls in her loft, the noise from the TV would mask her conversation. She climbed onto the bed and sat cross-legged.

"I'm alone," Harri said. "What happened? Did you talk to her?"

"No, she left a message on my answering machine. I was out all day helping a friend deal with her husband's funeral." The normally imperturbably Rue Liberty sounded totally shaken. "Monica said she's being held in Japan by their version of the NSB, but that wasn't why she called me. She asked for me to give you a message."

"Me?" All the muscles in Harri's back stiffened. Why the hell would a supervillain she'd never dealt directly with want to send her a message? What the hell kind of a supervillain calls her mom to pass a message?

Or worse, what if Tim was wrong about Miss Purrception not knowing his secret identity, and she didn't like Harri living with her former stress relief playmate?

"Yes, you." There was a quivering inhalation through the speaker before Rue Liberty said, "'Tell Harri Winters her housemate's BF isn't who they think he is. The real one is here with me.'"

Holy shit! Harri couldn't breathe. Rey was still alive.

"Monica also said to ask for James Davis when you call Japan," Rue Liberty added.

The non sequitur threw Harri for a second. "The cartoonist?"

"No." Obvious exasperation sounded through the receiver. "That's probably the name on the fake passport Monica dredged up for him."

"Ma'am, I so owe you for this."

Rue Liberty cleared her throat. "Harri, I know it's a lot to ask, but is there any way you could help Monica get out of there?"

"Ma'am, I—"

"I'll pay whatever retainer you want in cash." A sound suspiciously like a sob came from the other end of the call.

"Ma'am, it's not a matter of money." Harri latched onto the deep, calming tone she used for settling a client's emotional state. "Until I call Japan, I don't know what they've been charged with, and—" She exhaled trying to release the tension that drove a spike of pain down her spine. "Given Monica's past, there may not be much I can do if there's an outstanding warrant for her arrest in that country."

Rue Liberty sniffed loudly. "If you could check on her, I'd appreciate it. And I'll still bring by the money for your retainer since you'll be going to Japan. Won't you?" Her question ended with a quiver.

"I'll do my best, but I can't promise anything."

Once they ended the call, Harri checked the time difference between Canyon Pointe and Tokyo. Crap. Eleven hours meant Japan's SEB didn't open until ten her time.

Right about when she needed to head out in order to pick up Aisha at the airport.

She shut the clamshell lid of her laptop and headed back to the main living area.

Tim muted the Copperheads game. "Everything okay?"

"I think I just got independent confirmation Rey's still alive." She dropped next to Tim on the couch.

"That's great!" Tim's excited expression immediately fell. "And you're not ecstatic about this why?"

"You're not going to like this next part," she muttered.

He pinched the bridge of his nose. "Please don't tell me he ran out on Aisha."

"It's worse than that. When he was picked up in Tokyo, he wasn't alone."

Tim released his nose and stared at her in confusion.

"He was with Miss Purrception."

The blood drained from Tim's face, making his freckles stand out like beacons. "No."

"Apparently, she called her mom—"

Tim snorted. "I hope it wasn't for bail money."

"Actually, she was trying to get a warning to me about Rey's duplicate."

Tim shook his head. "Two months too late for that."

Harri rolled around the facts she knew. Some insight felt right on the edge of her consciousness if she could only figure out how the pieces fit together.

She took Tim's hand in hers. "You said Miss Purrception hated Corvus almost as much as you did. Do you know why?"

Blood rushed back to his face. "We didn't exactly have a real sharing type of relationship, Harri."

"I know you don't like talking about that period of your life, but this is important," she murmured.

"I really can't help there." He paused. "I take it Rue Liberty doesn't want to talk about her either."

Something about the way Tim said the last words and his red ears clued her to what was really bothering him. She started laughing. "You-you're worried Sourpuss and Nix are your kids."

"It's not funny, Harri," he growled, but so much blood flushed his face, neck, and ears they were nearly purple.

"Yes, it is," she said before another round of hysterical mirth. "Leave it to vigilantes to be paranoid about their one rooftop stands."

"It wasn't one rooftop—" He must have realized he was digging himself a deeper hole and grimaced.

"Oh, god, I'm never going to be able to fly again without wondering how many rooftops you've scored on." Harri swiped at her tears and tried to catch her breath.

The intercom buzzed and saved her from whatever Tim might do as revenge. She jumped up, strode to the unit, and pressed the reply button.

"Yeah?" she said, still chuckling.

"Harri, I found something, and I'm not sure how to handle it." Arthur's voice rasped through the speaker.

His worried tone sobered her quickly. "What did you find?"

"I know you weren't here on Ms. Kennedy's first day." Arthur gulped. "But we were all out of the building on appointments for a couple of hours and left her here by herself."

"Yeah?" Harri wasn't sure where he was going, but she already had a bad feeling.

"I've been double-checking the firm's phone records, and there was an incoming call from Singapore that day." He sucked in a deep breath and rushed on. "It lasted thirty-seven seconds, and Ms. Kennedy was the only one here to answer it."

She glanced at Tim. His mouth was set in a grim line.

"We'll take care of it, Arthur," Harri said. "Was there anything else?"

"No, that was the only anomaly I found." He almost sounded relieved that she took him seriously.

"You and Patty get some sleep," she said. "Tomorrow is going to be a very busy day." She thumbed the intercom button when she really wanted to put her fist through the wall.

Harri looked over at Tim, but he was already in his wheelchair. She glanced at his walker and back at him.

He shrugged. "The wheels are faster if there's a fight."

Resignation filled Harri. "Corvus could be holding a hostage over Susan's head, just like they did with Qiang, Cobblestone, and Miguel."

Tim cocked his head. "Do you want to debate this, or do something about it?"

"How will we know for sure?" She folded her arms over her chest.

"Serena."

⁕

The second Susan entered the firm's conference room, Harri closed the door and locked it. Their new associate was dressed in a t-shirt, yoga pants, and slippers, her red hair pulled back in a messy bun, no makeup. Even during law school, she never appeared this unkempt in public.

But then, the Lechuza Building was more home than work.

Susan stared at Harri before her gaze shifted to Tim across the table and finally Serena, leaning against the window sill. "What's going on?" Her attention turned back to Harri. "You said a client emergency had come up."

Tim slid the printout of the phone records across the table toward Susan. "We need to ask you about a few phone calls on your first day here."

"Look—" Susan held up her hands with her fingers spread. "—if this is about Black Death—"

"Let us ask the questions, Susan." Harri gestured toward chair. "Have a seat. Our nurse here is going to monitor your vitals while we talk."

"How? She doesn't have any equipment—" Realization dawned on Susan's face. "Of course. The green hair. You're a super."

Serena smiled and twirled her braid around her right index finger. "Among other things. I won't hurt you unless you try to lie or kill one of us."

Susan's eyes slowly blinked. "A living lie detector." She turned to Harri. "Does this have something to do with Corvus?"

"Yes," Harri said a little more sharply than she meant to.

"All right." Susan took the seat Harri had indicated. "Let's get this over with. What do I need to do?"

Serena pushed away from the window sill. "Which is your dominant hand?"

"My right."

Serena took the chair on that side of Susan and held out her palm. After a split second of hesitation, Susan clasped Serena's hand. Harri had to give the lawyer credit. It took guts to jump into an unknown situation with both feet.

Susan gasped. "Whoa! Serious head rush there."

"Interesting," Serena murmured. The soon-to-be physician's assistant cocked her head and examined Susan. "Did you know you are a super yourself?"

"What?" Susan's eyes turned into two huge hazel circles on her pale, pale face. "No. That can't be."

"I can't tell what your ability is." Serena cocked her head. "I've never felt something so . . . vague before."

Harri looked at Tim.

He mouthed, "Did you know?"

She shook her head. It didn't make sense. Susan had been in the top ten percent of their class, but there had never been anything to set her apart from any other student than hard work. There hadn't been any rumors unless Harri counted Susan's drunken make-out session with Trey Wild at the post-bar exam party. No weird absences.

"Great." Harri threw up her hands. "I'm the only non-super attorney here. Therefore, my name stays first on the marquee."

Susan shot Harri a sour look. "You said you had some questions."

"Which of these incoming calls did you take on your first day here?" Tim tapped the sheet on the table. He'd deliberately left off the location of each call.

Susan picked up the page with her free hand and examined it. A slight frown twisted her mouth. "I gave Aisha the messages from Luxman Manufacturing, Redwood, and Costumes, Etc. This one though—"

She laid down the sheet and pointed to the fourth line. "This was the next to last one I answered before Patty got back from Grace's well baby appointment. The last one was Harri herself." She made a face. "I could hear someone breathing at the other end, but they never said anything. I chalked it up to a wrong number, or possibly Black Death because he showed up a little bit after."

Harri looked at Serena who nodded and released Susan's hand. "Thanks for cooperating, Susan. I appreciate it."

The attorney looked up at her. "What has Corvus done to compromise your people so I know what to watch for?"

"They like going after our kids," Tim said bitterly.

As much as Harri wanted to comfort him, she knew better than to do it in front of other people. Hell, they were too much alike in that regard.

Susan sucked in a harsh breath as she put the pieces together. "I'm so sorry, Tim."

Time to change the subject. Harri tapped the paper. "What if Rey was on the abandoned rig Corvus had been using? If he escaped, the next closest country to the Indonesian territorial waters where it's located would be Singapore."

Tim nodded. "If it was Rey who called, he wouldn't have recognized Susan's voice. As an unauthorized super in a foreign country, he would have hit up the supers' underground."

"You make it sound like the old Underground Railroad," Harri commented.

"It pretty much is," Serena said. "You see the bright and shiny side of supers. You don't see the heartbreak. Children ripped from parents on the flimsiest of excuses—"

"Shit." Harri abruptly sat down in a free chair. "That's why the Reinhold ladies hate Corvus so much."

And Trubble had already threatened to take Aisha's baby. Winters & Franklin would never survive if Aisha and her baby had to disappear in order to be safe.

CHAPTER 21

Rey stared at the paperwork Captain Takeda had slapped in front of him. He pushed aside the set with his fingerprints and examined the other set. A chill stole through him at the picture that looked like him but wasn't.

"May I please talk to someone at the U.S. embassy?"

"They've already confirmed your passport is fake." Captain Takeda watched Rey. "You're not James Davis, and I really doubt you can draw a cat. So, who do I tell the United States ambassador is asking for her?"

Harri was right. There were times when withholding the truth was the more prudent course of action, but Rey was so far beyond that point it didn't matter anymore. His gut said Takeda was a lot like Harri's ex-husband Eddie, someone who would do the right thing, but he wouldn't let Rey try to call Harri or Aisha again, not without good cause. Rey didn't have anything left to lose.

He pushed the set of sheets with a copy of his fingerprints toward Captain Takeda. "Tell her it's Captain Justice."

The SEB official pursed his lips before he said, "You look very healthy for a dead man, Captain Justice. Why did you fake your death?"

"I didn't."

"Then why did the U.S. NSB tell me you were dead?"

Rey sagged in his chair. "They must have presumed I was dead. I was abducted approximately two months ago."

"Interesting." Captain Takeda tapped the stapled sheets that probably contained the personal information of the man from Seattle. "Very similar to the story Mr. Connors gave your FBI."

"When was I proclaimed dead?"

"The end of July."

"I was captured around the fifth of July." Rey stared at the photo again. "I don't know who this Connors guy is, but he may have been the person I saw when I was abducted. I received an alarm call from the NSB about an emergency. There was someone at the site who looked like me when I arrived."

Takeda pursed his mouth before he asked, "And how did anyone kidnap a super with your power set?"

"Grenades with some kind of anesthetic gas." At the captain's disbelieving look, he shrugged. "Despite my power set, as you put it, I still have to breathe like anyone else."

Takeda frowned at him. "Just one problem with your story. Captain Justice was spotted in the Canyon Pointe area several times between when you claim you were kidnaped and the announcement of his death."

Rey leaned over the table. "For me to prove my identity, and for you to know the truth, we both need to contact the embassy. Or does the truth mean nothing in this country."

"Regardless of the truth, you still entered my country illegally." The SEB official almost sounded amused. "And you were caught with a known supervillain."

"Who ironically rescued me from someone who in all probability was another supervillain pretending to be a superhero. I'll pay whatever debt to your nation I have to, but right now, we both need to get to the bottom of this mystery."

"All right, Captain Justice, one more question—"

"On one condition."

Takeda's right eyebrow tried to repopulate his shaved scalp.

"I need my amulet back."

"And why should I do that?" Takeda folded his hands on the table.

"Because I'm asking nicely," Rey said. "And because it's the last thing I have of my mother's." It would be best not to speak of monsters. In this case, Harri was absolutely right about withholding some information. Takeda would never believe in monsters.

"You know our lab will have to check it out first before my superior will clear it."

Rey nodded. "I figured your lab would have already examined it and told you it is composed of Central American jade."

The amused look crossed Takeda's face again. "That only leaves my supervisor, so you'd better give me a compelling reason to return your amulet."

It was the best deal Rey could get under the circumstances. "Ask your question."

"Who did you call yesterday? You had the chance to contact the embassy or your attorney in the U.S. at that time, and you didn't."

Given Takeda's thoroughness, he probably already knew who Rey had phoned. After he compromised her cell, he hoped Aisha would be smart about getting a clean phone from Arthur.

"I did call my attorney. At her private cell number." Rey leaned back in his chair. "I tried to call the firm's main number from Singapore. When I didn't recognize the voice of the woman who answered, I hung up."

"That's the first smart thing I've heard either you or Miss Purrception say," Takeda muttered.

<hr>

The Japanese authorities escorted Rey back to the block where he'd been held for the last two days. He caught a glimpse of Monica peering between the bars of her second story accommodations. Once the guards had locked him in his cell and the main doors clanged shut, Monica asked, "You okay, kid?"

"Yeah." Rey sat on his cot. "Captain Takeda wanted to prove he knew my real identity."

"How?"

"I told you I'd started the registration process." Rey leaned back against the concrete block wall. "All they had to do was compare my fingerprints."

"I'm so sorry, Rey." Her cot squeaked. "I never dreamed we'd get delayed here. Getting you back into the U.S. should have been our real challenge." After a long pause, she said, "Has your attorney called back?"

"If she has, I doubt if the authorities here would tell me."

"True," Monica said. "But certainly, being Captain Justice carries some weight, even here."

Rey's blood froze inside of him. "What did you say?"

"I've known since the oil rig. Your hero moniker popped up as one of the file names." She sighed, a long, drawn out, tired sound. "I was hoping you'd trust me enough to be straight with me. Then I assumed your reticence was because I hadn't been equally truthful, which was why I revealed my identity."

"Guess we both have trust issues." He stared at a dent in the ceiling. From the shape, someone's head had made it. "I just want you to know I didn't kill Jatz'om Kuh, the original Ghost Owl."

"I kind of figured it was this mysterious twin of yours." She went silent again, but it felt like the pause was from Monica working out the puzzle in her mind. Finally, she said, "You know who the original is, don't you?"

If Tim were dead, it shouldn't matter who knew. But Rey couldn't betray Tim any more than he could Miguel or Dom or most especially Aisha. So he settled on the best truth he could.

"He was my mentor. He encouraged me to go legit instead of becoming a vigilante like him. He really believed I could make a difference in Canyon Pointe."

"Does the NSB know about your relationship?"

"No. He was trying to get out of the game. Retire, you know." The hard truth, the one Rey's mind had been avoiding since Monica got him off that damn oil rig, kicked him in the head. "Both you and Takeda said my double was running around Canyon Pointe. If he was not behaving as I would, Jatz'om Kuh would have confronted him. That's probably what got him killed."

Far, far away from their friends and family living in the Lechuza Building. Tim would have died alone. Did Aisha and Harri even know what had happened to him?

No, there had to be more. "You mentioned there was a woman dressed as the Ghost Owl who took down my double?"

"According to the FBI reports I could access. The internal NSB data always referred back to the FBI because they were the only law on site during the beat down."

FBI. Aisha and Harri knew Tim's attacker wasn't him. Despite Harri's protests, Aisha would have called Eddie. He was the only law enforcement person she trusted.

Rey stood and started pacing, which amounted to two whole steps in his cell. The picture of what really happened a couple of months ago began to coalesce.

"What was this new Ghost Owl's power set, and who was with her?" he asked

"According to the reports, she could fly, had superstrength and superspeed…

she basically had your power set." Monica was silent for a long moment. "She would have figured out it wasn't you right away."

Mother Mary, thank you for telling Monica not to say Aisha's identity out loud.

"She's very smart. I doubt my doppelgänger was aware he'd been made right away."

Monica cleared her throat. "The other three supers with her that night were Sparx . . . Sourpuss, and a new woman called Nix."

Rey would have laid good money she was about to say "my daughters."

"I've sparred with all three of them. They are very smart and talented ladies." He chuckled. "I almost feel sorry for my double."

"They knew the Ghost Owl, too?" From Monica's tone, she had wanted to ask about Kerry and Molly for some time, and she'd been afraid to.

"Yes. He's . . . been like a father to all of us."

She sighed. "There was a time when every superhero in Canyon Pointe was after him."

"I believe the Sheriff of Nottingham felt the same way about Robin Hood."

"Did Captain Mojave give up, too?" Her bed squeaked again. "That man is relentless in almost everything except personal responsibility."

"You sound bitter."

"Old grievance," she snapped. "Let it go."

"All right," Rey said.

He dropped on his cot and curled on his side. Tomorrow would be the third day without his amulet. The nightmares could show up any minute. He prayed Takeda wouldn't put his people in danger out of pride. But no one ever believed him about the monsters.

Not until they appeared and ripped out the throats of the people around him.

CHAPTER 22

Stalking through the doors of the Canyon Pointe International Airport's arrival pickup, Aisha thought her day couldn't get any worse. However, her hackles rose as soon as she saw the hulking shadow in the front passenger seat of Harri's vehicle. Both front doors opened.

"Get back in the damn car!" Aisha shouted at Harri and Steve.

For once, her law partner didn't argue. Steve looked like he was about to, but there must have been something in Aisha's expression. Or maybe he really did remember part of the beat down she'd inflicted on him two months ago. She tossed her bags in the trunk of Harri's older white Honda before she climbed into the back seat.

"What did the SEB say when you talked with them?"

"You need to buckle up first. I'm not going to be responsible for killing my godson."

Okay, maybe she did deserve that from Harri. Aisha reached for the seatbelt. The straps were already squishing her tender breasts and the latch barely stretched beneath her baby bump to lock.

Once that was done, she took a deep breath and released it. "What did the authorities in Japan say?"

"Before you start screaming at me, I haven't called them yet." Harri flicked a look at Aisha in the rearview mirror before she checked traffic and pulled away from the curb.

Aisha dug her fingernails into her jeans. The heavy material sliced beneath her natural keratin, which was now super sharp. She forced her hands to relax.

"May I ask why?"

"Have you calculated the time difference between here and Tokyo?"

Aisha opened her mouth to snap back when she realized she was back on Canyon Pointe time, and she'd calculated based on Atlanta time because her phone had automatically adjusted to Eastern Daylight Time from this morning's flight.

"Sorry I'm acting so pissy, Harri." The tension she'd carried all the way back from her parents fell away, and she leaned against the seat back. "That message shocked the shit out of me."

"You aren't the only one, girl, but I thought it best we do this call together."

Thankfully, Steve had kept his mouth shut through their entire exchange. Even better, he hadn't so much as twitched in Aisha's direction. Maybe there was hope for the kid after all.

And how could she think of Rey as a man, and his twin brother as a boy? Maybe her attitude lay in the way they acted. Rey was Mr. Super-responsible. Steve reminded her of the trust-fund brats in law school. The rich kids with places guaranteed at their mommies and daddies' firms.

She looked at her law partner and best friend. Harri might have been just like the other rich kids if her mom or her dad or even her grandmother had survived and taught her what it was really like to lord power over others.

Aisha rubbed her baby bump. On the other hand, she didn't want her son to be as bitter and closed off as Harri could be at times. That's why it was necessary to get Rey back.

Harri reached for her phone mounted on the dashboard and hit a speed dial number and the speaker icon. She'd planned ahead.

The line rang once. Twice.

Someone rattled off a greeting in Japanese.

"This is Harri Winters of the Law Firm of Winters & Franklin. One of our clients is being held at your detention facility."

The person at the other end said something that definitely sounded like a question.

"Is there anyone available who can speak English?"

"Harri, would you mind if I tried?" Steve spoke for the first time.

"If this is a sexist thing—" Harri growled.

"It's not. Konnichiwa—" The rest of what Steve said beyond "hello" devolved into gibberish in Aisha's tired brain.

The person in Japan asked a question.

"I've explained to them I'm your translator," Steve said softly. "Who am I asking for?"

"James Davis," Harri replied.

Steve repeated the name. There was a long pause before the person at the other end said something. The voice was followed by a click and elevator music.

"What happened?" Harri asked. She flipped the turn signal for the entrance ramp of the freeway though no one else was around them this time of night.

"They're transferring me to the officer in charge of the James Davis case," Steve murmured.

"What I want to know is why you can miraculously speak Japanese at this moment?" Aisha snapped.

Steve looked over his left shoulder. "My grandparents insisted all the grandkids learn, even though they were Nisei and spoke perfect English."

"Nisei?" Harri shot Aisha a glance in the rearview mirror.

"Second generation Japanese-American," Aisha answered. She looked at Steve. "How many other languages can you speak?"

He shrugged as he stared out the windshield. "Just Spanish and a little bit of K'iché for my position with the Peace Corps. I never really had a chance to practice it."

Aisha switched to the K'iché dialect her father's associates had spoken at a couple of digs. "K'iché is spoken in Guatemala, not Honduras."

Steve's head whipped around, his eyes wide, then he grinned. "I was supposed to go to Guatemala originally. There was some . . ." He frowned as he obviously struggled to find the right word.

Aisha switched back to English. "It's okay." She leaned forward and patted his shoulder. "I'm surprised I still know as much as I do."

Steve switched back as well. "As I was trying to say, there was some last-minute shuffling because one of the folks heading for Honduras didn't have all their vaccinations. They asked if I would mind trading positions since I'd be teaching the same subject, and it would be at a Spanish-language school."

The music emanating from the speaker of Harri's phone disappeared. "Ms. Winters, this is Captain Takeda of the SEB. I do speak English. I've been told you are inquiring about a man in custody named James Davis."

"Yes, Captain—"

"Do you realize your client was apprehended coming into Japan with forged identification documents?"

"I was made aware of the arrest a few hours ago by Miss Purrception's mother," Harri said coldly. "I had to wait until your main office opened in order to talk to someone from your bureau."

"She called her . . . mother?"

"Yes, Captain," Harri snapped. "Has Mr. Davis been harmed, or is he showing signs of mental incompetence?"

"He has some massive slices on his right side that were treated prior to his arrival here. He claims he obtained medical care in Singapore. Otherwise, he seems to understand how much trouble he is in."

The fear smothering Aisha for the last couple of months seemed to want to complete the job.

Harri hit the turn signal and pulled over to the berm. "Captain, we have reason to believe the man you're holding might be one of our clients, a superhero registered here in the States. He goes by the moniker of Captain Justice."

"That's the identity the prisoner claimed, but according to your own government's records, Captain Justice is dead."

Aisha leaned forward. "Did he have a jade amulet on him when he was arrested?"

"I'm sorry, but who am I speaking to?" the captain asked.

"Aisha Franklin, Harri Winter's legal partner." She sucked in a deep breath. "Please answer my question."

"He was wearing an amulet similar to what you describe."

"What color of streak was on the stone?" Aisha asked.

"I'm sorry?"

"What color was the streak?" Aisha clenched her fists at how long this was taking. "If it was red, he's been compromised by a supervillain called Professor Paranoia. If it's blue, you need to give it back to him."

"Why?"

"Because it hides him from the people Professor Paranoia work for, enemies of his biological parents."

"This contradicts the story he gave me," Takeda said in a cold voice.

Aisha willed herself not to shout at the Japanese official. "Did he tell you it was the only thing left of his mother's?"

After a long pause, Takeda said, "Yes."

"That was the truth. Red or blue?" Aisha asked.

"Blue."

"Praise Jesus," she murmured. She wasn't as religious as Grams had been, but a little prayer of thanks seemed to be appropriate in this circumstance.

"Please, may we speak to him, Captain Takeda?" Leave it to Harri to take control of the situation.

"I'd have to clear that with my superior." He hesitated for a moment. "It would be helpful if you had someone here in person whether it's someone from your firm or local counsel. Your client is in some serious trouble."

"We understand." Harri glanced at Steve. Aisha recognized that look, but before she could stop Harri, her partner blurted, "Whichever one of us comes, we will be bringing a super with us. It'll be Captain Justice's twin brother. Is that going to be a problem?"

"Twin?" Again, Takeda hesitated. "His name wouldn't happen to be Stephen Connors, would it?"

"How did you know that?" Aisha snapped.

"His was the only facial recognition match," Takeda answered. "Is that why Mr. Connors was abducted two months ago? His relationship with your client?"

"Yes," Aisha said. "Please don't tell Captain Justice. He doesn't know he has surviving family yet, and it would be better if I or my partner break the news."

"Very well."

"As I said, will bringing Mr. Connors to Japan be a problem?" Harri inserted herself back in the conversation.

"No, I can understand wanting . . . backup. I'll do what I can to expedite your visas," Takeda said.

Aisha breathed a sigh of relief. This conversation could have gone much worse.

"Can you please give Captain Justice a message so he knows you actually talked to us?" She tried to keep her voice level. If it weren't for the seatbelt, she'd be bouncing all over the car's interior due to her out-of-control emotions and equally out-of-control powers.

"Of course."

"Tell him we need him to sit tight until one of us gets to Tokyo. Black Death is after Patty's baby, and we don't need Captain Justice making things worse."

"All right," Takeda drawled, obviously confused by the message. "I will tell him. Once you have your flight arrangements, please let me know, and I can start the paperwork."

"Thank you, Captain Takeda," Harri said. "We appreciate your assistance." She tapped her phone, and she turned to look at Aisha. "Think it's a trap?"

"It could be," she answered at the same time Steve muttered, "Of course it is."

"But if it is, we can't send Susan," Aisha added.

Harri slumped back against her seat. "I don't like the idea of you going either."

"Can we discuss this after I get something to eat? They didn't feed me on the plane." A butterfly movement from her son seconded her motion. Aisha smiled and rubbed her abdomen.

Harri shift her Honda back into gear and checked her mirrors. "What are you and my godson craving?"

"Burger Chateau." Aisha leaned back in her seat as well. Rey was alive.

Just stay that way until I can get to you, baby.

CHAPTER 23

"Who else do we know who handles both family law and supers?" Harri dragged a fry through ketchup and popped it into her mouth before she stared at her fellow attorneys and Steve gathered at the firm's conference room table.

Luckily, the kid stayed quiet and focused on his food.

Susan dragged her attention away from Aisha plowing through her second double cheeseburger with the works. "We need someone who'd be sympathetic to a reformed supervillain as the new boyfriend." She shook her head. "No one I know is going to stake their reputation on someone with a record."

Their new associate was merely saying what Harri knew deep in her gut. Even if Arthur was essentially harmless, no lawyer would want the reputation of standing up for a supervillain, even a former one, in a child custody battle.

"What about you?" Harri said. "You going to bail?"

"Just because things are rough?" Susan grinned. "Hell, no." She sobered as she played with the straw of her chocolate milkshake. "But the case has been assigned to Judge Barrowman's court. The fact that Patty didn't tell Wilson about the pregnancy is going to be an issue with her."

"I heard she can be a hardass," Aisha mumbled around a mouthful of double cheeseburger.

Harri rolled her eyes and shoved more napkins in her partner's direction. "That means you're taking point on this one, Kennedy."

"I'm not a partner."

For the first time Harri could remember, Susan looked unsure of herself.

"But you've been in front of Judge Barrowman." Harri waved her thumb between herself and Aisha. "Neither of us have. And you know family law procedure. I haven't looked at that crap since taking the bar. You and Aisha—"

"No." Aisha laid her burger on its wrapper and wiped her fingers on a napkin. "I'm going to Japan. You're helping Susan with Patty's case. She's trusting you to look out for Grace since you're her godmother."

"That doesn't mean you should go to Japan." Harri pointedly looked at

Aisha's baby bump before returning her attention to her partner. "There's more at stake for you—"

"Than losing control of my powers in open court?" Aisha tilted her head, daring Harri to argue.

"If we go for a jury trial—" Harri started.

"We can't," Susan interjected. "Not with Arthur involved. The public's bias against supervillains will counteract any sympathy garnered by Aisha's condition."

"So you trust Judge Barrowman not to hold his past against him?" The last thing Harri wanted was to destroy the budding relationship between Patty and Arthur, but if her assistant had to choose between her daughter and her boyfriend, Harri already knew who Patty would choose. And the result would destroy Arthur.

Susan pushed aside her remaining onion rings and leaned her elbows on the table. "She's tough, but fair. Arthur's stepped into the daddy role, and Wilson didn't come clean to Patty he was a super. The question is how far are you willing to go in court."

"What do you mean?"

"The only way to keep Grace completely out of her biological father's hands is to expose him as an assassin."

Harri leaned back in her chair. It wasn't like the same thought hadn't crossed her mind.

"If we do, you know Trubble will declare open season on us," Aisha said. "Seismic Shift was a pawn he was willing to sacrifice. He'll go nuclear before losing Black Death."

Which was the other issue troubling Harri. She rubbed at her scratchy eyes. Twenty hours without sleep was not the best condition to make any decisions, but one of them needed to be on the next flight to Tokyo.

"All right, Aisha." Harri glared at her partner. "If you insist on going to Japan, you're taking Steve here as backup. No arguments."

"Do I have any say in this?" Steve blurted.

"No," Harri, Aisha, and Susan answered at the same time. The kid sat back with an odd expression on his face, but he stayed quiet.

"I'll get our tickets." Aisha pushed to her feet.

If Harri was tired, her partner had to be exhausted. But if she said a word, it would only piss Aisha off.

Once the door closed behind her, Steve turned to Susan. "May I have the rest of your onion rings?"

The redhead nudged the carton to him, and he dug into the leftovers. His appetite reminded Harri of Rey's.

"How did your parents keep you fed?" she asked.

He shrugged and swallowed. "They both worked, and Dad chalked it up to my size and puberty." A rueful smile crossed Steve's face. "He also said to remember my metabolism would slow down once I hit thirty."

"Unless you need anything else, Harri, I've got to get some sleep," Susan shoved back her chair and stood.

Harri shook her head. "We'll hit the research in the morning after we've both had coffee."

"Or tea." Susan flashed a tired smile. "And lots of it." She left them, closing the conference room door behind her, too.

The silence stretched until Steve finally cleared his throat. "Are you sure it's a good idea for me to accompany Aisha to Tokyo?"

"You've got the power." Harri pushed the rest of her fries over to him. The way he fell on them reminded her of Rey the first time she bought him dinner at Marta's. Of course, Rey had been living on the streets then, barely eking out an existence. Yet, he still tried to help people in danger.

God, was that only four months ago? It seemed like a lifetime.

"But I'm not official," Steve objected before he shoved more fries into his mouth.

"The SEB captain knows you're coming, and—" Her mouth went dry at what she was about to admit. "I went ahead and put together the paperwork for your application for foreign travel. You need to sign it. I've got a friend at the NSB who can push it through so you have the temp paperwork and visa in order to act as Aisha's bodyguard."

Steve wiped his mouth with an extra napkin and leaned back in his chair. "Were you this manipulative with my brother?"

Harri exhaled. It was a fair question given everything that had happened to Steve.

"I'd like to think I wasn't. Rey might have a different opinion." Harri leaned her elbows on the table. "The only thing we ever really argued about was Aisha's pregnancy."

Steve's eyes widened. "He didn't take advantage of her—"

"Oh, god, no!" Harri waved her hands. "Nothing like that. It's just . . ." She stared at the wood laminate surface of the table, trying to find the words to explain. "It's the fact you two are young enough to be my sons, and that's how I regard Rey. A street kid who needed help."

She looked up at Steve. "I let my own crappy childhood affect my thinking. That wasn't really fair to him either."

"Come on." A smirk appeared on Steve. "Even I'm smart enough to use a condom."

"Aisha and her doctors believed she couldn't have kids."

Steve played with a french fry. "So this wasn't just an oops?"

"This baby is a freakin' miracle." Harri sighed and scrubbed at her eyes. "But even more, Aisha and Rey really do love each other."

"Um, I didn't, uh, with Aisha when Professor Paranoia . . ." Steve dropped the french fry and stared at Harri, pleading plain in his golden irises.

This would be terribly funny if it weren't for the circumstances.

"No." Harri shook her head. "You didn't. She would have done more than beat you over the head with a tree trunk if you'd tried."

"I have no doubt about that." Steve slurped the rest of his soda. "I need to call my parents, then I'd better get some sleep."

"Use the conference room for your phone call. Just let me—" She reached for a bag to stuff empty wrappers and cartons into.

"Harri." Steve gently wrapped his fingers around her wrist. "I'll clean up. Go to bed."

She nodded. "Thank you." She stepped out of the conference room.

As she closed the door behind her, Steve said, "Hey, Mom."

The light in Aisha's office was still on, and Harri frowned. Why hadn't her partner gone upstairs and hit the sack?

Harri crossed the reception area to Aisha's door and knocked lightly. Aisha stared at the screen of her laptop, but Harri wasn't sure she was actually seeing whatever was on the display.

"You okay?" Harri murmured.

"No." Aisha looked up at her. "I've got the tickets. The expense will come out of my share."

"Who pays for the damn tickets is the last thing I'm worried about." Harri crossed to one of the visitor chairs and sat. "How are you dealing with the news?"

"Trying not to get my hopes up, but I think it's too late." A weak smile tilted Aisha's mouth. "I'm just praying the guy the Japanese authorities are holding isn't Rey and Steve's triplet brother."

Exhaustion finally took its toll on Harri's mind. Her giggle slipped out before she could stop it. "Let's hope Xquic didn't have a whole freakin' litter of them."

Aisha laughed. A real one. "A dozen of them would be one hell of a superhero calendar."

The image was so ridiculous Harri couldn't stop herself. She howled until tears ran down her face.

Once she and Aisha could collect themselves, she asked the more serious question. "What do we do about Miss Purrception? Rue Liberty wants us to try to get her out, too. She's willing to pay us an obscene amount of money."

Aisha leaned back in her chair and brushed her dreds from her face. "It really depends on whether she has outstanding charges in Japan and who has applied to extradite her. My guess is Japan does, or they wouldn't still be holding her. Otherwise, the U.S. embassy would already be involved."

"So what do I tell Rue Liberty?"

Aisha shrugged. "That I'll do my best, but I can't guarantee anything. Our flight doesn't leave until—" She glanced at her screen. "—this afternoon. I can start making phone calls, do some research, before we have to be at the airport."

"That sounds like a plan." Harri pushed to her feet. Her forty-year-old muscles reminded her she couldn't do all-nighters like she used to in law school. "Get to bed. You're sleeping for two these days."

"I will," Aisha murmured.

No, she wouldn't, but Harri didn't have the energy to argue. Nor did she have the energy to climb the staircase to the fifth floor. She stabbed the elevator button, and the antique device groaned to life.

The last thing she would admit to Aisha was her own fears. While she hoped

Professor Paranoia had been poked to death by his parrot-lizards months ago, odds were the bastard was already on his way to Tokyo, if not already there. He wanted Rey and Steve too bad to give up now. She prayed the SEB was ready for whatever Paranoia threw at them.

CHAPTER 24

The next morning, Aisha managed not to slam the receiver of her phone down in frustration. It wasn't Eddie's fault his hands were tied. Nor should it have been a surprise. His new supervisor, Special Agent Howard Dreyfuss of the FBI, was a tool for Corvus.

The last thing she wanted to do was tip off Trubble that Rey was alive and trapped in Japan. The head of Corvus would try to beat her to Tokyo.

No, he would beat her to Tokyo.

Her pregnancy had killed any desire for cigarettes, but her hormones had done nothing to quell her desire for chocolate. In fact, they seemed to amplify her craving for it. And she really needed some after her phone call with Eddie.

Oh, screw it! The baby could handle one peppermint mocha. She pushed back from her new desk.

And floated to her office doorway.

Damn it! She squeezed her eyes shut and concentrated on the carpet. Fibers tickled the tips of her toes, and she dared to open her eyes. Yep, her Louis Vuitton Nomad Sandals were firmly on the floor. She took mincing steps on the reception area tiles toward the breakroom.

Patty looked up from her desk and frowned. "Forget your rubber bands again?"

Aisha glared at the younger woman. She'd resorted to a rubber band chain to stay in her office chair when she first became pregnant. "Girl, do not start with me. I'm one peppermint mocha away from becoming a supervillain."

Patty glanced at Harri's office door to make sure it was still closed. Harri and Susan had been ensconced in there all morning, working on strategy for Grace's custody case.

"I had a one-shot mocha nearly every morning I was pregnant. Harri thought it was hot chocolate, and if you narc on me—" Patty waggled her index finger at Aisha. "—I'll return the favor."

Aisha made the cross sign over her heart. "She'll never hear it from me."

Then she realized what the oddity was. "Why are you down here on a Saturday morning?"

A bleak look appeared in Patty's eyes. "Research to keep my daughter."

"Harri and Susan will find a way to stop this." Aisha just wished she felt as confident as she sounded. "You know Harri's not going to let any supervillain get his hands on her goddaughter."

"Damn straight." Patty nodded and returned to whatever she was reading online.

Aisha headed into the breakroom. In less than a minute, espresso dripped into her cup, and steam bubbled through the milk. This day needed a couple of squirts of regular peppermint syrup instead of sugar-free. She stared at the mixture in her cup. Screw it. No sense worrying about calories right now. She reached into the fridge for the can of whip cream and squirted a healthy dollop on the surface of her mocha.

Aisha sauntered back into the reception area. Tim stood next to Patty, talking with her as she waved at something on her screen. He sniffed in Aisha's direction.

"That does not smell like your usual brew." He grinned at her.

The second oddity finally clicked in her tired brain. Tim . . . was standing.

"When did you start walking?" Aisha stared at him. Was she that out of it from the flight to the east coast and back on top of the news Rey was alive? She glanced at the basement door. "You didn't come up the stairs, did you?"

Tim shrugged. "I'm just doing a little bit every day, and no, I'm not ready for the stairs yet. I'm using the elevator."

"Besides Harri would kill him if he tried to do too much," Patty added.

The intercom buzzed, and all three of them turned toward the front doors. Aisha blinked. Was she really that tired, or was she hallucinating?

"Mom and Dad?" First Tim being upright, now her parents at her door? Maybe she was having a stroke. It was a rare, but not unknown, event in pregnancies. And God knew her pregnancy was anything but normal.

Before she could say another word, the front door lock hummed and released, and her parents waltzed right into the building, dragging their luggage behind them. She shot Patty a nasty look, but their assistant merely shrugged.

Aisha turned back to her parents. "Wh-what are you doing here?"

"We cancelled our vow renewal." Mom waved her hand blithely. "It didn't make sense to do it when you, Harri, and Jeremy can't be there."

"But LaShun, Eric, and the kids flew all the way from Portland to Atlanta for your ceremony!" Aisha couldn't stop staring at her parents.

"LaShun and them are staying in Atlanta and enjoying the rest of their vacation." Dad was eyeing Tim in a way that made Aisha nervous. "We'll do the renewal next year when all of our grandchildren can attend."

Aisha ignored his pointed jab about her condition. "That still doesn't explain why you're here."

"You needed us, and we weren't the best parents earlier this year." Mom raised her chin as if daring Aisha to argue. "So we are here now."

Aisha blinked again, trying to wrap her mind around Mom's words. Of all the times for her to decide to take an interest in their middle child, why now?

"Mom, Dad, I appreciate you being here, but I'm leaving for Japan in a couple of hours." A wild idea occurred to her. Okay, it was partly revenge. "If you want to practice your grandparenting skills, why don't you stay in my loft upstairs and spoil Patty's daughter Grace?"

"Who's Patty?" Mom's eyebrows formed a "V".

"Me." Patty raised her right hand and waggled her fingers.

"Patty Ames is our legal assistant and all around Girl Friday." She gestured toward Tim. "And Tim Canyon handles our security—"

Tim held out his palm to shake Dad's hand.

Dad moved faster than Aisha would have believed possible. He cocked his fist back and clocked Tim in the jaw. She grabbed Dad as Tim crumpled to the tile.

The main alarm started ringing before Patty rushed around her desk and knelt by Tim. Harri and Susan raced out of Harri's office. Arthur charged into the reception area from his office with Grace slung in his tactical baby carrier. The infant screamed in counterpoint to the alarm. Harri slapped the alarm control just as Steve flew down from the third floor balcony.

On the other hand, Mom clapped her hands, an expression of delight on her face. "Baby girl! You left out the part about being able to fly!"

Only then did Aisha realize she was holding her father a good six feet from the floor.

In the conference room, Aisha breathed a sigh of relief when Serena proclaimed Tim fine other than the nasty bruise Dad left on his jaw. Steve came back from the break room and handed Tim an ice pack.

However, Dad and Harri weren't quite so forgiving.

"You lied to your dad?" Harri screeched. "What the hell were you thinking?"

Funny how Patty and Susan decided to escort Betty and the luggage upstairs to Aisha's loft when Harri started yelling.

"And why'd you decide to start now?" Dad growled. "You were the one child of mine I didn't have to worry about doing stupid shit."

"Since when did you start punching random men?" Aisha threw up her hands. Which was a big mistake. She started rising into the air.

"Watch the breathing, girl," Serena said.

Their student physician's assistant/healer had started Aisha on a combination of Lamaze and meditation breathing techniques in an attempt to keep her emotional equilibrium under control.

Aisha focused on a deep breath through her nose and out through her mouth. After three breaths, she could focus enough to land. But Serena's methods was barely keeping her feet on the carpet.

"I wouldn't have decked him if you hadn't lied to me about who my grandson's daddy was!" Dad roared.

"And why did you pick me of all people?" Tim stared at her in disbelief.

"I didn't expect him to fly to Canyon Pointe so he could deck you!" Aisha drifted upward again.

"Yay! One mess that isn't my fault." Steve waved his hands in the air and grinned.

"This isn't funny," Aisha snapped.

"Oh, on the level of crazy relative stories, I'm going to have everyone beat at Thanksgiving this year." With a rather pleased expression, Steve dropped in the seat next to Tim and folded his arms.

Aisha glared at Steve. Too bad she hadn't developed telekinesis to keep his mouth shut.

"Crazy relative stories?" Dad said.

Steve mustered an innocent expression. "I'm adopted, but I recently found out my twin brother is Captain Justice, and he's the one who knocked up your daughter, sir."

"Shut up," Aisha growled.

Dad looked at her and then Steve again. "How old are you, son?"

"Twenty-one, sir," Steve said earnestly. "I'll be twenty-two next March."

Dad's head slowly swung around to face Aisha again. "You're having a baby with a baby?"

"We're both adults," Aisha ground out.

"That's debatable," Harri muttered.

Aisha clenched her fists. "Stay out of it."

"You're the one who dragged me in by blaming my boyfriend for your condition," Harri shot back. "And would you please land before someone sees you through the windows?"

"You want some popcorn?" Steve pseudo-whispered to Tim. "This might take a while."

"Don't you have a flight to catch?" Tim said dryly as he held the blue gel-pack to his jaw.

"Wait a minute." Dad turned to Harri. "Why the hell are you dating that murdering—"

"Dad!" Aisha shrieked right before she shot upward and her head hit the ceiling.

"—son-of-a-bitch?" Dad finished, totally ignoring the fact she was bouncing against the plaster medallion over the conference room table. Thank god, she hadn't worn a skirt or dress today.

Harri propped her hands on her hips. "That was uncalled for, Marvin, and get Aisha down from the ceiling before she hurts herself, Steve."

"She's invulnerable," Steve muttered.

The nasty look Harri gave the super would have been funny if Aisha wasn't the one bobbing against the ornate plasterwork. She closed her eyes, concentrated on her breathing, and pushed off of the ceiling. Aisha opened her eyes and landed gently on the carpet.

"See?" Steve cocked an eyebrow as he looked at Harri. "She didn't need me."

"I don't need you to go with me to Japan either," Aisha grumbled.

"You need a translator," Steve and Harri said at the same time.

"Going back to the original insults," Tim interjected. "I'm not a murderer. Nor do I appreciate being accused of impregnating a woman I've never slept with."

Dad shook his finger at Tim. "Your money may have kept you out of the electric chair, but Harri here is one of my girls. You're not doing to her what you did to your wife and boy."

Tim's face grew redder than his hair. "I didn't kill anyone. And if you consider Harri your daughter, then where were you when the man who murdered my family was trying to kill her?"

"You mean someone you hired to scare the poor girl so she'd run to you?" Dad shot back.

"Marvin!" Harri threw her hands in the air this time, but she didn't float up to the ceiling. "I'm standing right here, and I don't appreciate the insults either."

"He's a big boy." Dad sneered at Tim. "He can handle it."

"She's talking about you insulting her, Dad," Aisha said.

"I didn't insult her!"

"Yes, you did, Marvin." Harri crossed her arms, probably to keep from whacking Dad in the head. "You just stated I have no judgment when it comes to men."

"Well, neither of you seem to," Dad muttered with a nervous glance at Aisha.

"And on that reassuring note from my father, I'm heading to Tokyo." She headed for the door, willing herself to stay on the floor.

"Aw, come on, baby girl. Don't walk out mad."

She whirled to face Dad. "You're the one bitching because my baby's father wasn't in the picture. If I want him to know his son, I need to go to Japan and rescue him."

"But you're pregnant!" Dad pushed to his feet. "After all the problems you went through before trying to have a baby, you need to take it easy. Can't someone else go?"

"No, Daddy, they can't." She shook her head sadly.

"Why not?"

"Because rescuing people is what superheroes do. Even when we're pregnant."

CHAPTER 25

Late the next afternoon, Rey was a little surprised when the block doors opened and Captain Takeda strolled down to his cell with shackles in his hands.

"If I let you out for a talk, you promise not to fly away?"

Rey sat up. "I haven't yet."

"Because you gave me your word?" Takeda smiled.

"How can we expect citizens to obey the laws if we don't?"

Takeda chuckled. "What's the American expression—you're too good to be true?"

"You hit the nail on the head," Monica called out from above them.

"You still have to wear these." Takeda held up the shackles.

"You're still afraid of me?" Rey stood.

"Me? No." Takeda signaled toward the security camera. "But you scare my people. And we both know you could have broken these at any time."

Which was true, but Aisha and Harri had said multiple times he needed to cooperate with the authorities and let them handle any mess as his attorneys, as long as he or a civilian weren't in imminent danger.

Rey held out his hands. The cell door hummed and slid back. Takeda cuffed Rey's wrists before he knelt and locked the manacles around Rey's ankles.

Walking in the stupid things was a pain in the ass. The shackles were designed to keep a prisoner from running. Rey had to take short, mincing steps to keep from snapping the chains. The whole situation was incredibly stupid, but the expressions on the non-super agents, and even a few of the obvious supers, as he and Takeda exited the block and headed for the interrogation rooms said Aisha and Harri were right.

He followed the captain into a different interrogation room than the last time. This one was even cleaner. Even though the SEB was meticulous, their janitors couldn't eliminate all the odors, but it would be terribly rude to point this out. Besides, other supers with his level of senses would already know how bad it smelled.

A young woman handed a folder to the captain before he entered the room. He laid the manila folder on the table. The door locked behind them, and Takeda waived for Rey to take the opposing chair. This time, the SEB didn't secure his wrists to the table.

Once they were both settled, Takeda said, "One of your attorneys and her translator are on their way here."

Rey frowned. "They're in Japan already?"

"Their flight gets here in a few hours." Takeda flipped open the folder.

"Then why are we talking again?"

"You Americans would say I'm crossing my 't's and dotting my 'i's." Takeda picked up the photo on top of the pile of documents inside, turned it around and shoved it in Rey's direction. "Do you recognize this man?"

A chill ran down Rey's spine. The man was a decade or two younger in this photo, and he had more hair, but the eyes were unmistakable. "Yes. He's the one in charge when I was drugged and abducted. I don't know his name."

Takeda pushed another photo across the table. "What about this one?"

This photo was much older than the other one, easily taken two or three decades before the first photo. Instead of street clothes, the man wore a super costume. But even with the mask, his kidnapper's eyes were unmistakable. Cold. Alien. As if the creature looking through them wasn't quite human.

"I never saw him in this outfit." Rey looked up at Takeda. "I'm assuming you've identified him."

"Hector Gonzalez-Estes, AKA Professor Paranoia." The captain seemed to expect Rey to know who he was talking about.

"I've never run into him before the morning in July when I was kidnapped." Rey shrugged and slid the photos back to Takeda. "And I don't remember his name from the active supervillains in the U.S. federal database."

"That's because he's Honduran."

The chill in Rey's spine settled into a frigid ball in his gut. "Does this have something to do with my mother?"

"That's what your attorneys said." Takeda tapped the folder against the table top. "Ms. Franklin asked that I give you a message to assure you I did talk to her and Ms. Winters. You are supposed to sit tight until she arrives in Tokyo. Black Death wants Patty's baby, and they can't have Captain Justice making the situation worse."

Rey stood and glared at the captain. "Patty and Grace are in danger?"

"You're missing the point of sit tight—" Takeda started.

A scream echoed down the corridor and penetrated the walls of the interrogation room. Overhead, the lights flickered.

"Do not move," Takeda ordered as he jumped to his feet. He whirled, took a step, and banged on the steel door.

A crash came from outside the interrogation room followed by weapons' fire. No one unlocked the door for Takeda.

Rey closed his eyes. Some of the SEB officers were supers. It wouldn't be the slaughter it had been on the oil platform, but these people didn't need to die because of him. It wasn't right.

"Unlock my shackles," Rey said. "Your fellow officers are being attacked by monsters that are after me."

Takeda looked over his shoulder. "What makes you say that?"

"You took my amulet. It hides me from them. They're under Professor Paranoia's control." Rey rattled his chains. "I need the amulet back, or they will kill everyone in this building trying to get to me."

Finally, Takeda nodded. "Just one problem." He inclined his head toward the corridor. "The key to the interrogation room is out there, and your amulet is in my office."

"Do you have an issue with me breaking government property?"

Takeda chuckled. "Well, we do have a betting pool on when you'd try to make a run for it."

"Not one on Miss Purrception?" Rey yanked his arms straight up. The chain between the cuffs on his wrists and the ones on his ankles snapped, but pain seared his right side, a reminder he was still healing.

"Purrception escaping was a given, but she's stayed. We've been trying to figure out her game." Takeda waited until Rey broke the two chains between his wrists and his ankles before he added, "You know if you try to make a run for it, I'll have to take you down."

Rey ran through his options. None of them were good. "It's not my first choice, but what if me running is the only thing that saves your colleagues?"

More shouting and cries of pain filtered down the corridor along with stranger sounds. Sounds he remembered all too well from the platform. Sounds of razor-sharp talons ripping through delicate flesh.

"Just make sure it's your last option—" Takeda hesitated.

"My real name is Rey." He smiled.

"Or I'm going to have to charge you with escaping, Rey." Takeda smirked in return.

"Get behind me, and I'll bust the door open."

"How about you let me take care of the door?" A wry expression twisted Takeda's mouth, and he held up his right hand.

His glowing right hand.

"I'm not injured," the captain added.

"You're also not invulnerable."

"If you're telling me the truth, neither are you against what's out there." Takeda inclined his head toward Rey's side. "I know how to use my abilities. I simply prefer a suit to spandex."

He turned and grasped the door jamb where the latch was located. The metal softened like putty under his grip and he pulled it away from the latch and bolt. The door swung open as another scream rent the air.

Takeda pointed to the right, and Rey nodded. He followed the captain to a cross hallway, but a quick peek showed several SEB agents in a battle for their lives. The monkey-wolves' claws and teeth flashed as they attacked the humans. A couple of people lay bleeding. One wasn't breathing.

"What are those things?" Takeda whispered. He stank of fear though his expression only showed mild surprise.

"Like I said, monsters," Rey muttered. "Don't use conventional firearms. These things will gut you before bullets can take them down." The Corvus goons on the oil platform had to die to learn that lesson. "Use your powers on the monsters. Tell your colleagues to drop to the floor."

Takeda yelled a Japanese phrase. Rey snatched up a discarded riot shield and flew down the corridor before the last syllable left the captain's lips. The SEB agents responded to Takeda's command and flattened themselves along the linoleum tiles.

The glee in the eyes of the first monster turned to alarm as Rey plowed through the creatures. His shield groaned under the stress, but the polycarbonate didn't crack. He slowed and pivoted in midair at the end of the corridor.

As he expected, the monsters turned their full attention toward him. Takeda picked up Rey's hint. He and two other SEB supers launched their counterattack at the creatures' backs. In addition to the captain's plasma bolts, acid spit and ice knives sliced through their opponents. Howls and cries filled the air.

Rey used the confusion and struck out with his riot shield. He smashed the throat of the closest wolf-monkey. The second one ducked beneath the edge of the polycarbonate and swiped at Rey's legs.

He somersaulted in mid-air and kicked the head of the creature. It crashed through the plasterboard wall. A third wolf-monkey leapt at him. He raised the shield barely in time. An ice knife ripped through the monster, and the tip pierced the polycarbonate.

Rey lowered the riot shield. The hallway was silent other than the moans of the human wounded. The non-super SEB agents rose from the floor. At the other end of the hallway, Takeda and his two compatriots breathed heavily from the battle.

"Is this all of them?" the SEB captain asked.

A bird-like shriek nearby rose in pitch before it abruptly cut off.

"I think that answers your question." Rey landed on the linoleum. The ice spear melted enough that it slid out of the hole it had made in the shield. The body of the wolf-monkey landed with a thump.

The cuts on his side ached, but he couldn't just stand here while people died around him. "Where's your office?"

"To the left." Takeda pointed in the same direction. He turned to the lady with the ice powers and rattled off what sounded like instructions before he waved Rey to follow him.

"You should stay here with your people." Rey shook his head. "These things are here for me."

More gunfire echoed through the building, coming from three different directions.

"And it's my fault SEB agents are dying." Takeda's eyes glowed almost as bright as his hands. "I should have listened to you." He charged around the corner.

Rey had no choice but to follow the captain. He'd recognized the look of guilt on Takeda's face. The guilt that came from someone you cared about dying because you did something very stupid.

Bang! Bang!

Rey whirled at the gunshots and shifted between the monster behind him and Takeda. This creature was something he'd seen on the oil platform, a weird combination of a lizard with a parrot's beak and colorful feathers along its legs and tail. Bright red blood trickled from the holes in its head. It slowly toppled over revealing Monica behind it, guns in both of her fists, wearing street clothes and a sly smile on her face.

"Need some help, boys?"

CHAPTER 26

Rey blinked. "How did you get out of your cell?"

"These things." Monica gestured at the dead parrot-lizard. "One of these is what cut you up, right, kid?"

"Yeah," he muttered.

She turned to Takeda. "Watch the claws and beaks. These things can slice through steel like it's butter. The other ones look like a monkey had rage sex with a German Shepard with claws and teeth just as sharp as the feathered lizards. Double tap to the head is the only way to take any of them down besides superpowers. We need to get the kid out of here before they kill your entire bureau."

"If we can get to the captain's office, there's something that can help us," Rey said.

She cocked an eyebrow. "Don't tell me. Your man jewelry is really a magic amulet?"

Rey frowned. "How did you know about it?"

Monica only smirked.

"I should arrest you for escaping," Takeda muttered.

Her expression transformed into sheer boredom. "I haven't left the building yet, and I saved your men's asses down in holding."

"Why didn't you escape while you had the chance?" Rey asked.

"You hired me to get you back to the States, and you won't pay me until I do so. Also, you won't leave until we save a bunch of civilians from your monsters." Monica pushed past the two men. "So c'mon boys. Let's go save the day."

Rey and Takeda looked at each other. The captain matched Rey's shrug, and they trotted after Monica.

At the next left junction, a parrot-lizard screamed and tore at what was left of a closed door. The hallway looked like someone had overturned an industrial-sized shredder. The paper bits were waist-high around the monster. Double headshots from Monica dropped the parrot-lizard.

Rey swallowed the disapproving remark on the tip of his tongue. Her casual violence bothered him, but she was saving people's lives. It wasn't like he could do anything other than get ripped to bits like the two bodies they had passed.

Takeda waded through the white pieces of paper, calling out in Japanese. A muffled female voice answered him. He shoved at something, but couldn't budge it.

"Kid." Takeda gestured for him to join him.

Rey flew over and saw the problem. The door was gone, but the remnants of some kind of machine blocked the lower half of the doorway while layers of cardboard and paper did the same for the top half.

"Tell the people inside to stay back," Rey said.

Takeda called out in Japanese, and again a female voice answered him. He turned to Rey and nodded.

Black toner leaked from a plastic canister amidst the gears. Rey bent, braced his left shoulder on the frame of the machine and pushed. The paper and cardboard stacked on the copier quivered, but the material stayed in place on top of the machine as he pushed the makeshift barricade inward. His right side burned by the time he'd created a space large enough for the trapped ladies to escape.

Takeda directed the survivors back toward the interrogation rooms. The ladies ran once they got past the paper drifts, though they each gave Monica a wide-eyed stare as they passed her.

Without another word, Rey and his compatriots continued on their way. After two rights, the noise amped up. In front of them was a room full of cubicles. Wolf-monkeys chased workers around and through the flimsy walls. Some folks tried to seek shelter in glass offices around the edges of the room. Those provided even less protection than the cardboard and aluminum cubicles.

Monica took a running start and bounced from a chair to a desk to the top of the metal framework of the cubicles. Somehow, she balanced on the waving structure and shot one of the monsters. Its momentum carried it into the water dispenser in the closest corner.

The huge bottle on top wavered, then in slow motion, it fell over. Water spilled out of the spout and soaked papers scattered across the linoleum floor.

The noise of Monica's gun got the attention of the other wolf-monkeys. Beady black eyes peered over the tops of the cubicles. Rey's stomach clenched.

Even though Monica had been the one who shot their companion, every single creature focused on him.

"I count four of them," Takeda muttered.

Another head popped over a partition.

"Five," he amended.

The one Monica shot stirred.

"Six," Rey said, but she fired into the beast's head again. It collapsed into
the puddle, and red tainted the clear water spreading across the floor. It didn't
move again.

"You're right," Rey said. "Five."

"I'll keep 'em busy!" Monica yelled. "You two get the civilians out!" True
to her word she danced, tumbled, and balanced on the top framework of the
cubicles, all while firing at the monsters if one showed his head. Like some
bizarre version of whack-a-mole.

Rey would have laughed if people weren't dying.

Takeda ran to the first office, yelling the same phrase over and over again
while pointing at another doorway. The pictogram on the wall next to the
door looked like stairs.

Rey repeated the phrase to the survivors in the next office with its glass
smashed. He wasn't getting the pronunciation right from the odd looks he was
getting, but the members of the SEB got the gist. They helped their injured
companions toward the stairwell.

At the growl behind him, Rey shot to the ceiling. Takeda incinerated the
wolf-monkey in mid-leap with a plasma bolt.

The elevator chimed and its doors parted. A parrot-lizard bolted out of the
car. It spotted Rey. Repeating Monica's stunt, it bounded from floor to chair to
desk. It leapt for Rey, using its rear feet to push off of the top of the aluminum
frame.

All of Tim's combat lessons took over. Rey spun and kicked in mid-air. His
foot caught the beast in its feathery chest. The parrot-lizard crashed through
the closing elevator doors. The machine whirred to life and sank below their
floor.

Unfortunately, being in midair, he was in full view of the remaining three
wolf-monkeys. Monica had taken down a second beast, and one of their

compatriots realized she was a danger to them. It slammed into the cubicle partition she balanced upon, and the blow sent her flying—

Straight through the gaping maw of the ruined elevator doors.

Rey darted for the opening and dived down the shaft. Thank god for his super-vision, else he couldn't see the woman falling. And the parrot-lizard gave a weak cry as it waited for her to reach it at the bottom. It had literally torn its way out of the car.

Monica bounced from side to side in the shaft. Only when Rey caught up with her did he realize she was in control and attempting to slow her plummet. And she still managed to retain both guns.

The parrot-lizard shrieked in fury when Rey caught Monica outside of its range. Lethal talons from its two unbroken legs scrabbled against the steel and concrete in the monster's desperate attempt to reach them.

"Hang on tight, and keep swallowing to equalize the pressure in your ears," he muttered.

"Why—"

The rest of Monica's question stayed at the bottom of the shaft with the parrot-lizard as Rey arrowed up the elevator shaft. One of the wolf-monkeys poked its snout through the opening accidentally created by Rey. Monica kicked it as they passed.

"That's a good way to lose your foot," Rey said.

She grinned like a crazy person.

They reached the top set of doors in the shaft. She tucked one of her weapons in the waistband of her pants.

"Set me on the ledge," she said. "No sense pissing off the SEB further by ripping apart another set of elevator doors."

Somehow, she managed to balance on four inches of steel framework while he carefully pushed the doors apart. The sound of nails on metal echoed up the shaft. Rey glanced down. Two of the wolf-monkeys were climbing toward them.

Monica scrambled through the opening he created. He followed and let the doors slide shut. The walls here were the same industrial off-white as the floors below. There was no damage indicating monsters were in this floor. Red and white lights flashed in the wide corridor, but no audible alarm blared. The elevator doors wouldn't give them much protection, but he didn't plan on waiting for the monsters to reach them.

"What about getting Takeda and the rest of those people away from your monsters?" she said.

"They know I came up the shaft. The surviving wolf-monkeys will follow me. Are following me." Rey examined the signs. All of them were in Japanese with no pictograms to explain them.

"This way." Monica grabbed his palm with her free hand and tugged.

"We're not escaping," Rey warned.

"Kid, those damn monkey things are climbing up the shaft. We need to someplace defensible and I need more ammo." She pulled on his hand again.

They jogged down the corridor. When it dead-ended at a cross hallway, Monica turned left.

Rey hesitated. "Why that way?"

"Fresher air." At his suspicious look, she rolled her eyes. "The SEB's head honcho will want to make sure these creatures don't run wild through Tokyo. In case you hadn't noticed, the only way out of the holding and interrogation section was the elevator or the stairs. That means he or she will be using the main entrance for coordination and containment."

What Monica was saying seemed to make sense. Reluctantly, he went down the side corridor with her.

This one had a series of doors. Without a word, they separated and started twisting the door levers. Some were locked. Others entered into abandoned offices.

Deep scratches marred the last door Rey checked, and it was partly open. The man who worked in this office didn't make it out. Rey silently pulled the door shut and scratched an "X" in the wood composite. He turned to find Monica, all humor gone from her expression and her complexion greenish.

"Mark this one, too," she whispered.

That's when he knew her entire dossier in the NSB database back home was a lie. Murderers didn't get sick at the sight of dead bodies.

He scratched an "X" in the surface of the door she'd closed.

A scream echoed down the hallway from the direction they'd been heading. Gunshots followed, along with sounds Rey couldn't identify. Last was the cry of a parrot-lizard monster.

The squeal of claws on steel and growling came from behind them. The wolf-monkeys had reached the top of the elevator shaft.

He pulled Monica behind him and headed for the gunfire.

"What do you think you're doing?" She tugged at the grip he had on her free wrist. "You're as vulnerable as I am to those creatures."

Rey looked over his shoulder. "But you're vulnerable to bullets. I'm not."

Behind them came the screech of tearing metal.

"Fine. Let me go so I can watch our six." She shook the arm he held.

Reluctantly, he released her. Not because he didn't trust Monica to watch his back, but these things had ripped Mama apart before his eyes.

And he had run.

He couldn't run. Not this time. He couldn't go home and face Kerry and Molly if he got their mom killed, too.

Monica drew the other gun from her waistband. "Let's go."

Rey stalked down the hallway. The corridor turned to his right. The building opened into a very modern atrium. Glass panels and stainless steel railing guarded the edge of the floor from the air.

Below them, metal security doors covered what was obviously the main entrance. SEB agents had six of the parrot-lizards pinned down behind a glass panel with an etched scene of Mount Fuji. The glass must be bulletproof because the agents only shot if one of the monsters poked its head out.

"Rey! Move!" Monica deliberately elbowed him in his rib injuries.

He flew backward out of the pain reflex. She fired at the first wolf-monkey. On the fourth bullet, it tumbled and dropped a few feet from her. The other one dived back around the corner. Every time it poked its head out, she fired.

Until the chambers on both of her guns merely clicked.

The second wolf-monkey charged Monica. She spun low to evade its talons and delivered a solid kick in its groin. The monster grunted, but it was too fast. It lunged for her. Talons caught the super, and it threw her through the second story glass.

Gritting his teeth against the pain, Rey smashed through another glass panel and caught her a few feet from the floor. He landed gently and bowed over Monica to protect her fragile flesh as the glass that had followed them rained down.

Then they were skidding involuntarily along the wooden floor.

Rey looked up, but an invisible force had a tight grip on his body.

No. A woman about his age held out her left hand. She used telekinesis to push him towards the other SEB agents. However, her main focus was on the glass.

Above them, the wolf-monkey howled its frustration and leapt through the empty space caused by Monica's body. The woman flung her right arm in the direction of the monster. The shards rose as one and impaled the wolf-monkey. It screamed right before it landed with a thump on the floor boards.

The parrot-lizards screamed their fury, but a round of well-placed shots kept them behind the image of Mount Fuji.

A couple of people tried to pull Monica away from Rey. He released his grip on her once he realized they were checking her for wounds.

"I'm fine," he repeated over and over as another man tried to examine him.

"I can't believe you two are still alive." Captain Takeda stood over them. Blood oozed from an ugly slash on his upper arm and soaked his dress shirt. His tie had been used as a makeshift tourniquet.

A silver-haired older man joined Takeda. From their expressions and gestures, the captain was making his report to his superior.

One of the parrot-lizards dodged around the etched glass and raced for the humans. The woman with the ice powers from downstairs froze the monster in mid-stride. It teetered before it fell over and shattered. Icy bits slid across the floor.

"The monsters followed you into the elevator shaft," Takeda said, returning his attention to Rey. The captain shook his head. "I'm sorry. I tried, but I couldn't find your amulet in what's left of my office."

"It doesn't matter. We won." Monica grinned at him while another agent bandaged the handful of nicks and cuts on her face and arms.

An ominous growl came from above them. Everyone looked up at the gallery. At least, twenty monsters crouched up there, eyeing the human smorgasbord below.

"I think you jinxed us, Missy," Rey murmured, using the Singapore underground's nickname for Monica. He slowly stood.

The remaining five parrots-lizards cackled from behind their hiding spot. Rey had the distinct impression they were laughing at the humans.

"I'm sorry, Captain Takeda," he said, taking a step backward.

"Our supers can protect you," Takeda hissed.

"And how many more people will die?" Rey shook his head and looked at the captain. His expression carried the same bleakness Rey felt. "I don't want to break my word to you, but it's the only way to save everyone here." Rey rose into the air and shouted, "Here I am!"

The attention of every monster scattered through the atrium immediately fixated on him.

"Rey, don't!" Monica cried out.

He whirled and plowed through one of the security gates. A handful of stars twinkled against the darkening sky. He looked over his shoulder as he flew. Thirty or so monsters poured out of the SEB headquarters. More converged from the artfully placed foliage.

On the southern horizon, a bright glow signified the city. All he had to do was lead them away from the populated areas.

And hope he came up with a plan to deal with the monsters before they killed him.

Staying just above the tree line, he flew into the twilight.

CHAPTER 27

To Aisha's surprise and consternation, the pilot ordered everyone to remain in their seats once the commercial airliner pulled up to the gate. An attendant came to her and Steve and said they needed to disembark first because their government party was waiting.

Aisha and Steve exchanged looks. From the inclination of his head, he wasn't going to argue with her call. So, they gathered their things and followed the attendant to the jetway.

At the other end, four people stood calmly. The fact no other passengers were in this section of Tokyo's international terminal was eerie as hell though.

The only woman stepped forward and bowed. Her sleek black hair had a pink streak running through it, and she wore a skirt instead of black dress pants like her three compatriots. Otherwise, she looked as severe and uncompromising as her fellows.

"Welcome to Japan, Ms. Franklin," she said. "I am SEB Agent Nakamura. Captain Takeda sent us to escort you and Mr. Connors to our destination."

Aisha frowned. "May I see some ID first?"

"Of course." The woman pulled a wallet out of her jacket pocket and handed it to Aisha.

She examined it. The seal was correct, and the holographic image on the ID looked appropriate, but she couldn't understand a damn word. In turn, she handed it to Steve.

"Reads legit," he murmured and handed the wallet back to the agent. "Thank you for your cooperation, Agent Nakamura." He bowed to the woman.

"This way please." Agent Nakamura gestured for them to follow her. "We must depart so the other passengers can disembark." She and one of the male agents set off at a brisk pace down the concourse.

Aisha hiked her carryon over her shoulder and strode after the agents. Steve fell in step beside her. The last two agents brought up the rear.

Steve was uncharacteristically quiet as they walked. Aisha looked up at him, but he wasn't doing the sulking thing. In fact, he seemed hyperalert.

"What is it?" she whispered.

He shook his head. "Sorry. Tim and Harri have me a little paranoid."

"You sure it's not your own encounter in Honduras that's bugging you?"

"That's part of it," he admitted. "But I also have no doubt Tim would devise a thingamabob Harri could use to flay me alive if anything happens to you."

Agent Nakamura led them to what was obviously a private elevator. They all climbed on board, and the doors slid shut. The baby chose that moment to practice his World Cup moves on Aisha's bladder.

"Agent Nakamura, may I visit a restroom before we head to SEB headquarters?" Aisha asked.

The agent looked a little flustered and bowed again, which was awkward in the tight confines. "Yes. My apologies."

"No worries." She smiled at the woman. "It was a long flight."

Nakamura appeared confused until Steve translated the idiom. She nodded and bowed to Aisha for a third time.

She nudged Steve in the ribs. "Can you get her to stop that?"

"No," he said through gritted teeth. "And you're being rude."

"You don't have someone dribbling one of your organs for the winning goal."

The elevator ground to a halt, and the doors slid open. Agent Nakamura charged out of the car and stopped abruptly.

They were surrounded by ten men, all dressed in black and heavily tattooed. The leader growled something to them.

Aisha looked up at Steve who scowled. "Yakuza. They know you're here for Miss Purrception. They plan to trade us for her."

Agent Nakamura shook head and replied forcefully.

Aisha held up her hand. "I don't need the translation for that." The baby fluttered. The movements tickled her bladder some more.

Some of the Yakuza drew weapons. At least one of them was a super. The quills sprouting through the t-shirt of the biggest thug was a dead giveaway.

"Translate for me," she whispered to Steve. She stepped beside Agent Nakamura.

"What are you doing?" the SEB agent hissed.

Aisha ignored the younger woman. "Gentlemen, this is not the time or place to have this discussion." Steve repeated her words in their language.

Their leader snickered before he spoke.

"What makes you think you can stop us?" Steve translated.

"I've been on a plane for twenty hours, I'm exhausted, and I have to pee," she said.

The Yakuza leader's expression indicated he wasn't sure if she were crazy or an ignorant American.

"You'll be leaking more than piss," Steve translated. "We want the foreigner working with Miss Purrception as well."

"Why?"

"He put three of my men in the hospital."

Rey. It had to be. Only he could drive the bad guys this insane.

It took all of Aisha's will not to laugh at the gangsters. She took another step toward their leader.

"Do you know the only thing more dangerous than a superhero?"

"What?"

"His attorney when she's pregnant and she has to pee."

With Steve's last syllable in Japanese, she shoved the Yakuza leader into his fellows. If the gangsters were bowling pins, she would've had a seven-ten split.

Unfortunately, Quillman was in the ten position. He launched his barbs at her.

The projectiles stopped a foot from Aisha's face before they dropped to the floor. Steve's right cross put the quill-throwing super out of commission.

The guy in the seven-pin position slowly crouched and laid his gun on the floor before he straightened and held up his hands.

Aisha turned to Agent Nakamura. The woman from the SEB lowered her right hand. So, she was the one who stopped the quills.

"Thank you for the save, Agent Nakamura." Aisha bowed. "Now, could you please tell me where the ladies' room is?"

⁂

When Aisha returned from using the facilities, she had to swallow her impatience. Agent Nakamura insisted they hand over their attackers to the Tokyo police. It didn't make sense considering Quillman was a super.

When the SEB van pulled into the parking lot of their headquarters over an hour later, Aisha's stomach did a slow, queasy roll as she stared out the window. The place looked worse than the Canyon Pointe City Hall after a supervillain attack. No wonder the SEB handed the Yakuza thugs off to the local police. Things didn't look any better without the van's tinted windows in the way when she climbed out of the vehicle.

She turned to Agent Nakamura. "What happened?"

"We were attacked last night." A frown pinched the agent's face. "Some kind of strange beasts."

Bile stung the back of Aisha's throat. "Did they look like a weird combination of a parrot and a lizard?"

Agent Nakamura slowly nodded. "How did you know?"

"We . . . encountered them back in the States." Her knees wobbled and threatened to give, which only triggered the damn lightheadedness. Steve gripped her elbow and kept her on the ground. For the first time, she was thankful for his presence. To come all this way and lose Rey . . .

"The wolf-monkeys as well?" Nakamura asked.

"I haven't, but one of my clients has." Aisha sucked in a deep breath while she and Steve followed Nakamura. Dust and the tang of blood filled the air. "They disintegrated roughly ten minutes after you killed them, didn't they?"

"Yes," Nakamura said.

"Have I seen these things?" Steve whispered to Aisha.

She looked up at him. The worry in his eyes reminded her of Rey. She nodded. "We'll discuss it later."

He took the hint and dropped the subject.

Nakamura led them to a bald man wearing wire-rim glasses. He wore a pristine white dress shirt, but his left arm hung in a black sling. Dust decorated his dark slacks. He was in an earnest conversation with a gentleman in a hard hat.

"Captain Takeda," Nakamura murmured when he turned to her. "Ms. Franklin and Mr. Connors."

"Good that you made it here, Ms. Franklin—" His double-take as he took in Steve's features would have been comical if the situation wasn't so dire. "You weren't joking."

"No, Captain. I wasn't." Aisha gaze swept the scene. "Is there somewhere we can talk privately? Then I'd like to see my clients."

Takeda motioned for them to follow. The fact he didn't say a word about Rey or Miss Purrception froze the acid in Aisha's throat.

The Japanese official led them to what appeared to be a conference room on the first floor. Inside, a very attractive white woman with brunette hair paced along the windows. She whirled to face them, and her frown transformed into a wide grin.

"Rey! You're—" Her grin disappeared, and her eyes narrowed. "You!" She leapt on top of the table and launched herself at Steve.

Aisha managed to catch her in mid-air. The woman struggled, but super-strength came in handy. Part of Aisha wondered how she'd cope with a superb-aby if her HRSP disappeared after delivery and she didn't have Rey.

Captain Takeda closed the door before he looked up at the women, an amused expression on his face. "Are you sure you want to represent Miss Purr-ception, Ms. Franklin?"

"Franklin?" Miss Purrception twisted to see Aisha's face. "You're Captain Justice's attorney, right?"

"Yes. Can you behave yourself if I set you down?"

"Yes."

From everything Aisha had read about Miss Purrception, she didn't expect such rapid capitulation. "How do I know you'll keep your word?"

"Because I promised Rey I wouldn't try to escape." Well, that wasn't the answer Aisha expected, but then Rey's friendship with the former Professor Venom kept the latter on the straight and narrow.

"You got out of your cell," Takeda pointed out as Aisha floated back to the floor with the supervillain.

"You're welcome for saving your ass," Miss Purrception snapped. "Or would you have preferred to be in the morgue with those other SEB agents who were sliced to ribbons?"

Aisha asked the question she wasn't sure she wanted to know the answer to. "Where's Captain Justice?"

Captain Takeda waved at a chair. "Please take a seat, Ms. Franklin."

"Stop avoiding my question." Aisha's voice dropped an octave, her don't-mess-with-me voice. "Where is he?"

Takeda's expression looked as bleak as Aisha felt in her soul. "We don't know."

She forced her lungs to work again. "I think it's time we laid our cards on the table. If the parrot-lizards and the wolf-monkeys attacked your facility, that means Professor Paranoia is somewhere on this island. Where is Captain Justice?"

"He flew off to lure the monsters away from here." A rueful smile crossed Takeda's face. "Your Captain Justice even apologized for breaking his word."

"Breaking his word?" Aisha cocked her head.

"He could have escaped here at anytime, Ms. Franklin." Takeda shook his head. "But he listened to his attorney's advice. At least until innocent non-supers were at risk."

Aisha's emotions split between wanting to scream in frustration and shouting from the rooftops Rey was alive. "That means Paranoia's hunting Captain Justice. Assuming he hasn't already been captured. Why didn't you give him back his mother's amulet?"

"I was checking out your story about both Professor Paranoia and the jewelry." Takeda pulled a familiar piece of carved jade from his pocket. "I was about to go to my office to retrieve the piece when the monsters hit us. When your Captain Justice distracted them, I went to my office, but I couldn't find it." He handed the amulet to Aisha. "It was found in the debris of the office next door to mine. My people can't figure out what's so special about it. May I ask?"

"Would you believe magic?" she said.

"Then let us hope he has other magic tricks up his sleeve."

Aisha's heart sank as she stared at the amulet. Rey was out there, somewhere, alone and unprotected.

That was assuming he wasn't dead yet. And Aisha knew if she had to mourn him a second time, she would totally lose her soul.

<h1 style="text-align:center">Chapter 28</h1>

"Damn, Lisa was thorough!"

Harri looked up from the counterclaim she was in the process of drafting. Susan stomped across Harri's office and threw herself facedown on the couch.

At least, she didn't leave stiletto holes in Harri's brand new carpet the way Aisha did, but the new associate's bare feet when clients weren't around was beginning to drive her insane. There was casual, then there was beach bum.

"I told you Corvus has dossiers on all of us." Harri revised a sentence before she glanced at Susan. "I'm sure Black Death handed over nearly everything they had on poor Arthur."

Susan rolled to her side and propped her head on her palm. "This isn't one of those cases where the mediator can gently tell the parties how they're hurting their own kids to get them to be reasonable."

"Actually, it's exactly like that," Harri said and frowned at her monitor. "Masqueraded" was a much better verb than "pretended" in order to show how dangerous Black Death was.

"Harri, are you listening to me?" Susan sat upright. "Never mind the misdemeanor record. They pulled every shitty thing every supervisor has said about the guy."

"You're the one who sent Black Death to Lisa," Harri murmured. Her fingers flew across the keyboard as she added her standard relief closing to the counterclaim.

"Harri! This is serious!"

She tapped the "Save" icon and looked up from her monitor. "I know just how serious this is. Grace can't go with her dad. God help me, I never thought there could be a father worse than my own in this world. That's why I need you on this case with me, Susan. I can't be objective. This is my goddaughter we're talking about, and I'll be damned if I let an assassin get his hands on her."

"So when I say we out Black Death in court, are you going to fight me on it?" Susan's expression was cold. Dispassionate.

Was that the real problem? Harri leaned back in her office chair. Was her fear for her chosen family affecting her more than she realized?

"Let me ask you something." She reached for her coffee. "Is your family's life worth outing Black Death? Because if we do, you and anyone close to you will be in the firing line, too."

"Well, if we're just talking about my baby sister, I'm all for it." Susan grinned.

Harri swallowed her sip. "But your parents?"

Susan's grin faded. "My mom's in the beginning stages of dementia. From what you're told me, Corvus would kill Dad and Cindy in order to make me Mom's sole caretaker, and probably wipe out my parents' retirement funds in the process." Her eyes unfocused as she considered the problem. "I can call in a few favors to protect Cindy and her family. We can hide Mom and Dad's funds like Tim did with the little he had left."

"But what about your parents' personal security?" Harri protested.

Susan sat up and shrugged. "Mom's been wanting to go to Mal Paraíso for ages."

Harri's jaw dropped. It took her a couple of seconds to work her mouth. "You can't be serious! Are you trying to get them killed?"

"Actually, it's the safest place to stash Mom and Dad." A sly smile spread across Susan's face. "An island owned by supervillains is a place even Corvus would think twice about invading. Does this mean you're onboard with outing Black Death?"

"We'll save it as our last resort," Harri muttered. "But yeah, I'm onboard."

⁕⊱⊰⁕

"Are you insane?" Tim stared at her like she had lost her last marble after she told him, Arthur, and Patty the plan over dinner at Arthur's apartment.

Thankfully, the guys cooked so the pasta, chicken, and vegetables were remotely edible.

"I'm a Winters. I thought that was a given." Harri sipped her diet cola. "But this is totally up to my client."

Patty twirled her fork in her fettucine while she considered Susan's idea. "She's right. The judge needs to understand Grace's biological father is more of a villain than Arthur ever was. He could have contacted me directly if he really wanted to be a parent to Grace instead of stalking us. Not to mention, I couldn't have contacted Cade if I changed my mind about telling him I was pregnant even if I wanted to."

She sniffed and blinked rapidly to keep her tears from falling, and Arthur laid his right hand over her left.

"You don't have to make a decision right this minute," Harri said. "Susan's looking at all the possibilities."

"Not all of them," Arthur said quietly. His dismal look ripped at Harri's heart.

"No," Patty growled. "You are not leaving our home. We've both already given up our old apartments."

Arthur laid down his own fork. "If I move out, he can't use me against you and Grace."

"He won't stop there," Harri said. "Hell, Lisa won't either, even though she knows she's being used. She *needs* to win. It's one of the reasons I hired her as my divorce attorney, but we can't let her win this one. You'd have to leave your job with the firm, and I need you both here."

"Tim can handle—" Arthur started.

"No." Harri raised her fist, but if she struck the table, she'd upset Grace who cooed contentedly in her bassinet next to Patty. Harri forced her fist to rest in her lap. No one needed both her and her goddaughter ugly-crying.

"I need you both to help me run this firm," Harri finished more quietly. "Especially with Aisha going on maternity leave."

"Patty was back to work a few days after she gave birth," Arthur said innocently.

"That's because she's a stubborn—"

Patty jerked her hand from Arthur's grip and held up her index finger. "What did I say about who gets to teach Grace swear words?"

Harri rolled her eyes. "I was going to say 'woman'. A stubborn woman who cancelled the temp contract without asking the senior partners, I might add."

"And not every lady can recover from childbirth that quickly," Tim inserted. "Rebecca had a rough time, even with a nanny and a housekeeper. And I hate to point out Patty's a year younger than my Shane should be. Grace could be my granddaughter."

The baby burbled cheerfully though she shouldn't be old enough to recognize her name.

"I would be very careful about saying Aisha's too old to have her baby in front of her." Harri grinned at him. "She can kick you to the moon right now."

"Thank you." Tim made a face at her. "Both Rey and Steve already made that point abundantly clear."

His statement sobered their little dinner party. No one wanted to talk about the possibility Aisha couldn't get Rey released from Japanese custody. Arthur, bless his heart, started talking about the Copperheads' chances of making it to the baseball play-offs.

⁂

Later that evening, Harri read through the employment offer Aisha proposed for Qiang on her laptop screen. Tim sat beside her on the couch watching the Copperheads with his legs propped on a storage ottoman she bought for her new loft. The game had started later than usual since the baseball team was playing in San Francisco.

"Argh." Harri leaned back and closed her eyes.

Tim muted the audio. "What's wrong?"

She opened her eyes and rolled her head to look at him. "We can't keep hiring our clients. And I'm sure Aisha dumped this on me right before she left so she didn't have to hear me bitch."

"I thought you were the head of the Winters' save-a-stray program," Tim teased.

"So did I, but—" She waved at the screen. "Qiang's getting some blowback from her boss about all the time she's been taking off recently. I have to admit a lot of that time has been helping us with the Seismic Shift and Corvus problems."

"So what's the issue?"

"Money for one thing." She closed the laptop lid, set the machine aside, and curled up next to Tim, who wrapped his arm around her. "We don't have enough work to justify her salary, not to mention we're stretched thin on providing medical insurance already."

"And you're freaking out about my hospital bills," he murmured.

"You're the one who insisted on being an independent contractor." She sighed. "I don't want to fight about money with you tonight."

"What if—and this is my only suggestion, then I'll drop the subject—Qiang opens her own accounting firm? She's a licensed CPA. How many supers could use decent tax and money advice from someone who's in the same boat as them?"

Harri straightened and looked at him. "That's actually not a bad idea. Let me guess, we also rent office space to her and her clients?"

"Well, I'd need to talk to my building co-owners—"

"*My* building—"

The ringing of her phone saved Tim from further mocking. She checked the caller ID. "It's Aisha." She tapped the icon to answer. "Hey, girl! How's he doing?"

Nothing came over the receiver for a long moment. "He's not here."

"What do you mean Rey's not there?" Harri bolted upright.

"What's wrong?" The super-serious superhero expression replaced Tim's teasing grin.

"Shush!" she ordered as she stood. "What happened?"

Aisha sighed. "SEB headquarters where he and Miss Purrception were being held was attacked by Professor Paranoia's parrot-lizards. They brought friends with them this time. Some kind of canine-ape hybrids."

"Like the ones he described as killing his mom?" Harri started pacing across the loft. The nice thing about her new living quarters was the space to walk more than three steps without hitting a wall.

"Yeah." Aisha sounded really tired.

"Are you, Steve, and the baby okay?"

"We're fine," Aisha said. "The attack happened a few hours before our plane landed. He flew off to draw the creatures away from the SEB agents, so we have no idea where he is. And he doesn't have his amulet with him."

Harri's heart splashed all over the floor. She couldn't say her worst fear. Not to Aisha. Not now.

She cleared her throat and resumed her pacing. "Anything else go wrong?"

"Our only problem was some Yakuza thugs attempting to kidnap me at the airport as leverage to exchange for Miss Purrception."

Harri paused in mid-stride. "Excuse me?"

"Like I said, we're fine." Aisha chuckled. "They shouldn't have gotten between me and the ladies' room with the baby practicing his goal kicks on my bladder."

"What about Miss Purrception?"

"She was still at SEB headquarters because, get this, she promised Rey she wouldn't try to escape and she'd wait for me to get here."

"That doesn't sound like her." Harri glanced at Tim. Of course, he was listening to her side of the conversation.

"I swear he has this weird affect on everyone he meets. However, it's working in our favor. The SEB is willing to drop all charges against her for her assistance during the attack and rescuing survivors on two conditions—she never returns to Japan and she gives back the empress's jewels. She's already abided by the jewelry return. However, if she ever comes back once she leaves with me, they'll reinstate all charges."

"It sounds like you've been a busy lawyer."

Something that sounded suspiciously like a yawn came over the receiver. "Our next step is to track him if we can. Captain Takeda's superiors gave us three more days, local time, before I have to get Miss Purrception off the island."

"All right. I'll wait for your next call." Harri resisted the urge to tell her partner to get some sleep. Aisha wouldn't respond well to the mothering, especially with Rey being in more danger.

"What about Patty's custody case?" Aisha asked.

Now wasn't the time to get into Susan's plan. "You know how it is. Pre-trial paperwork up the ying-yang. I'm sure you'll be back in time for the actual fireworks."

There was a sharp intake of breath from the other end of the line, but whatever Aisha was about to say, she changed her mind. "I'll call once I know something concrete."

Once they said their good-byes, Harri thumbed the icon to end the call.

"Well?" Tim's eyes glittered with worried anticipation.

She relayed the events in Japan. "I don't like being stuck here and not able to help."

"You think I do?" he said with a quirk of his eyebrow.

Harri crossed back to the couch and dropped beside him. Once again, he wrapped his arms around her.

"I think this is the real reason I didn't want kids," she whispered. "I can't handle not being able to do something to fix the situation."

For once, Tim didn't say anything. He merely held her tight, but she was pretty sure he worried about their friends right along with her.

CHAPTER 29

Rey's breath came in huge puffing gasps as he aimed for the summit of Mount Fuji. Exhaustion was a new concept to him. Flying at this altitude didn't help.

The monsters hadn't given up chasing him. In fact, every time he took one out, two more seemed to join the pursuit. Any doubts regarding his ability to fly non-stop across the Pacific Ocean had definitely been answered. His old friend hunger gnawed on his belly as well.

Any time he tried to land and rest on an uninhabited islet dotting the sea surrounding the main Japanese islands, the damn creatures would show up five to ten minutes later. What he wouldn't give for a pizza and a half-hour nap right now.

Takeda must have passed the word to any of his fellow citizens to stay out of the American's way. Rey hadn't seen any Japanese superheroes since he left the SEB headquarters.

He hadn't dared flying to another country either. Showing up on Russia, China, or even North Korea's radar would be a good way to start a war. He was just too damn tired after nearly two days with no sleep to think of any idea to get rid of his pursuers.

He landed on a rocky outcropping near the summit of the dormant volcano. As fast as the monsters were, it should take them a few minutes to climb the mountain.

Unless they teleported again. Teleportation was the only answer for how fast they reached the islets he'd rested on.

He laid back and closed his eyes. The cold rock actually felt good against his overheated skin.

Had Aisha or Harri reached Japan yet? Takeda hadn't been specific about the time of their arrival. Or had they gotten into a fight over who came to fetch him?

He chuckled at the image in his mind. Aisha may have picked up his superpowers because of their baby, but he'd bet one of his endorsement advances that Harri could fight dirty when it mattered.

Dios, he missed everyone at home.

A squawk below him said he'd run out of time. The call was followed by the sound of flesh hitting flesh.

He opened his eyes and sat up. Sure enough, monsters climbed through the snow below him. He rolled off the rock and flew a circle around the summit. They'd planned to surround him if the parrot-lizard hadn't alerted him.

Despite their part-lizard appearance, the cold didn't seem to affect them. Rey frowned. Maybe he was looking at the problem from the wrong direction. He visualized the map in the article he'd read at the library concerning the earthquake and tsunami a few years ago. The dual disasters had damaged a nuclear power plant. The Japanese government was still trying to clean up the area.

Checking the position of Tokyo and the sun, Rey turned and shot toward the damaged power plant.

CHAPTER 30

Aisha ended the call with Harri and yawned again. Despite a nap, the time difference took its toll.

"Harri's not pissed, is she?" Steve asked.

"About what?"

"Us losing Rey again." Worry flickered in his eyes. "I swear I didn't tell anyone where he was."

She smiled at him and patted his arm. "Don't worry. This isn't on you, but it's a reminder to keep your amulet on at all times." She gestured at the side pockets on her unitard. "I brought some insurance in case you or Rey are possessed again."

Jeremy, bless him, had scrounged together two lightly armored supersuits for her and Steve. Or maybe scrounged wasn't the right word. Jeremy claimed she needed something while she was pregnant in case she decided to be the Ghost Owl again while Tim was out of commission.

Which was why she had thigh pockets on her outfit instead of a belt.

Steve's outfit was the original one Jeremy had started designing when Tim planned to recruit Rey as the new Ghost Owl. Neither outfit had masks. It wasn't their identities Aisha worried about protecting in this situation.

They walked out of the quarters the SEB had assigned to her and headed for Miss Purrception's room. Aisha had no trouble picturing the flamboyant supervillain as Nix's mother, but the disconnect in behavior between her and Rue Liberty was truly disconcerting.

Aisha knocked on the open door. Miss Purrception stood on her head in some kind of yoga position. She twisted and tumbled to her feet so smoothly she appeared unreal. Like Aisha and Steve, Miss Purrception wore a unitard, but hers was a brilliant blue instead of utilitarian gray.

"We ready to head out and search for Rey?" she asked.

"There's a couple of things we need to discuss," Aisha replied. "Mind if I come in and sit down?"

Miss Purrception waved at the single chair in her room before she started braiding her hair. Steve followed Aisha into the room, closed the door behind him, and leaned against the closest wall.

"What happened to attorney-client privilege?" Miss Purrception asked sarcastically.

"It went the same place as Ms. Franklin's safety," he shot back.

"Enough you two," Aisha snapped. She pulled Tim's jammer out of her upper left pocket and pressed it to the wall before she took the offered chair.

Miss Purrception's eyes narrowed. "Where did you get that device?"

"From a friend," Aisha coolly replied. "If the SEB broke their word and have any bugs in your room, this will interrupt their signal."

"I know what it does." Miss Purrception stared wonderingly at Aisha. "You're the one who took down Captain Justice Two-point-oh. He killed your predecessor as the Ghost Owl—" Miss Purrception waved at Steve. "—and you're comfortable working with him?"

How the hell did she know all of that? The only place that held a modified record of the events in Canyon Pointe was . . .

Aisha stared at her incredulously. "You broke into the FBI database?"

"Actually, I hacked the information from Corvus who stole it from the FBI." Miss Purrception frowned. "Speaking of which, Corvus has a buttload of data on your boys. Rey had the flashdrive on him when we were arrested. It contained everything they had on their Gemini Project. We might want to make sure we get that back before we leave. I don't know if Takeda has actually looked at the information yet, but you should assume he has."

Aisha fought the urge to put her fist through the wall. Gemini was the Greek astrological sign for the Hero Twins. Wonderful. Odds were Trubble had known exactly what Professor Paranoia was up to the whole time he worked for Corvus. What else had Trubble lied to Harri about?

However, she needed to focus on the immediate problem. "Speaking of leaving, as your attorney, I think it's in your best interest to return to the U.S. on an earlier flight."

Miss Purrception placed an elastic band around the end of her braid. "No." She flipped her hair back over her shoulder. "Anything else?"

Aisha forced a placating smile on her face. "I'm thankful for your offer of assistance. I truly am. But it may take longer than the three days Takeda's superiors gave us—"

"I'm not leaving without Rey." Miss Purrception folded her arms over her chest. "I promised the kid I'd get him home, and I don't break my promises."

"As my client, your wellbeing is just as important—" Aisha began again.

"And the most important thing to Rey was yours and the baby's safety." Miss Purrception shook her head. "If anyone should be leaving early, it's you. You shouldn't have come here, especially not with Captain Justice Two-point-oh here." She waved a dismissive hand toward Steve. "Rey's going to freak when he sees you two together. Your partner should have been the one to come to Japan."

Aisha opened her mouth to refute Miss Purrception, but the supervillain held up her hand.

"Despite everything, I understand why you came, but I'm still helping you find Rey whether you like it or not." Miss Purrception shrugged. "And let's face it, you wouldn't have taken me on for a client if it weren't for my mother."

Aisha could appreciate the other woman's brutal honesty. "You're right. I wouldn't have. But I respect Rue Liberty. She's stepped out of retirement to help my partner and my clients when Corvus had contracts out on us. She didn't have to do that, but she did it because it was the right thing to do.

"And I'm trying to do the right thing by you here because you helped Rey. I don't want you to lose your freedom based on some misguided sense of obligation."

"That's just it," Miss Purrception said softly. "If I don't keep my promise to Rey, I'm just as bad as they say I am."

Her confession sent a wave of shock through Aisha. There was more to her story than probably even her mother and daughters knew.

"Then answer me this," Aisha said. "Why did you steal the empress's jewels?"

"To keep them out of one of the Yakuza clan's hands." Miss Purrception shrugged. "They were going to use me to get the jewels, and then use them to frame another clan. This has been my first opportunity to get them back to the Japanese government."

"Without you serving time for the theft," Aisha said wryly.

Miss Purrception grinned. "I would have escaped." Which, if everything Aisha had read about the alleged supervillain was true, she would have done.

"All right." Aisha stood. "You can come with us to look for Rey, but don't argue with me about leaving in three days if we don't find him before then."

"Deal." Miss Purrception held out her hand.

Aisha shook it. "Let's go find our boy."

"I have an idea about that," Steve offered.

"I'll take any suggestion at this point," Aisha said.

"We find an open area with no civilians, and I take off my amulet—"

"No." Aisha shook her head fiercely. "Absolutely not."

"Hear me out." Steve held up a hand. "You're nearby with it. Once these things get my scent or whatever it is they use to track us, you give me back my amulet. Once they lose me, they'll head straight back in Rey's direction, right? We follow them," he finished with a shrug.

Aisha blinked. His plan was so amazingly simple she wanted to kick herself for not thinking of it. But it wasn't without risks.

"But Professor Paranoia has some kind of mind control that affects everyone, not just you and Rey," she protested.

"You said you had something to disrupt it." A suspicious expression clouded his face. It was almost as if he dared her to lie to him.

"All right," she said finally. "It's the best idea we've got so far." She waggled her finger at him. "Don't make me beat you over the head with trees again."

"Wait! What?" Miss Purrception swiveled as she looked at Aisha, then Steve, and back again. "The FBI report was true?"

"I have HRSP," Aisha stated. "It's not just the flying."

"Then let's go get your man before you lose those powers!" Miss Purrception practically skipped past them and out of her room.

"I'm beginning to understand Kerry and Molly a little more," Steve murmured in Aisha's ear as they followed the supervillain.

Miss Purrception leaned around the doorway and glared at Steve. "You'd better steer clear of my daughters, or we'll find out just how invulnerable you are."

CHAPTER 31

People milled around the third floor of the new Lake County Courthouse as Harri and Susan headed for Family Court #1. Most of the parties had an air of sad inevitability, but a few seemed furious to having their personal tragedy play out in public. Their attorneys alternated between playing pit bull and therapist.

A part of Harri wondered if her parents would have ended up here. How many of her earliest memories were a child's perspective of happiness? Did Dad have emotional problems before Mom died in that skiing accident? Would she have made sure he got help for his addictions? It seemed like Mom's death triggered Dad's problems, but was that really what happened? Had losing her only made Dad's mental health issues worse?

To distract herself from her maudlin thoughts, Harri compared the sleek modern building to the stone hulk of the old one. The new courthouse was built in an effort to preserve the original from supervillain shenanigans. Its historical value as the former capitol building of the state was deemed a priority by some rich folks and their pet politicians. So, this allegedly super-proof monstrosity was built two blocks north of City Hall and police headquarters. Eventually, all the courts would be moved here, but the family courts had been moved first. Its sterile atmosphere didn't seem conducive to family harmony. The city jail had a homier atmosphere.

"Kennedy! Winters!"

Harri and Susan turned to see Lisa Ashcraft striding toward them, one of her junior associates practically running to keep up. Like Aisha, Lisa had run track in high school. She still cut a lithe figure in her tailored suit and sensible pumps. If anything nasty could be said about her, it was her love of being a blond. According to Leo, she was in Jeremy's shop every two weeks on the dot to deal with her roots.

It kind of made Harri glad she relented to Jeremy and Aisha's demands for highlights in her own hair so the grays didn't stick out.

"Good morning, Lisa," Harri said.

"Morning. Can we talk privately?" Lisa inclined her head toward one of the unoccupied consulting rooms.

"Sure." Susan made a point of taking the lead.

A little chunk of Harri's ego protested, but she slapped it down and followed the other two women into the consulting room. Instead of coming in, Lisa's associate headed into the courtroom.

"I've heard you two are hanging out with the Ghost Owl." Lisa laid her case on the table.

"And where did you hear that?" Susan asked.

"My client said the Ghost Owl confronted his boss in front of your office." Lisa's bright blue eyes bore into them.

The bitch had to be wearing tinted contacts now. Contacts paid for with Harri's retainer for the damn divorce. At least, Lisa made sure Harri walked away with something. Aisha should have consulted with Lisa in her split from Cal.

"You know better than to believe every bullshit story a client tells you," Susan said in a bored voice.

"My contact in the FBI confirmed the Ghost Owl has used your office to pass tips to your clients," Lisa replied coolly.

"Your contact wouldn't happen to be Special Agent Dreyfuss, would it?" Harri asked.

"You know I won't divulge my source." However, Lisa's left eyebrow twitched, meaning Harri had hit her mark.

"He's my ex-husband's boss, and he's been trying to cause trouble for both me and the asshole." Harri shook her head. "I'm saying this as a friend and a colleague, Lisa—you should drop this case."

Lisa laughed. "I can't believe you of all people are representing supervillains and vigilantes. C'mon, Harri! You wrote the book regarding financial seizures on supers!"

"And your client is very good at conning people." Harri shook her head. "Did he tell you he was a super?"

Lisa froze like a deer in headlights.

"That's what we thought." Susan rested her hand on the doorknob. "He lied to me when I straight-up asked him if he were one, or I wouldn't have sent him to you. You want to delay this hearing?"

"No." God help Wilson from the icy glare on Lisa's face. "This doesn't change the fact that our clients' infant daughter is living with a supervillain."

"Arthur Drallhickey isn't a supervillain any more than I am," Harri replied hotly.

"You may be stupid enough to hire him after he threatened you." Lisa shook her forefinger at Harri. "But the judge's concern will be the health and safety of my client's daughter."

"Guess we're done here." Susan shoved the door open and stalked out of the room.

"Grace is my goddaughter, Lisa," Harri said. "Her health and safety is my priority." She turned and followed Susan.

Maybe Tim's original plan to fake his death and lay low on some tropical island needed to be resurrected and used for Arthur, Patty, and Grace. It may be the only way to keep them safe.

But Black Death would not be happy no matter how he lost Grace. And the idea he might take his anger out on Lisa chilled Harri to the bone.

Chapter 32

Rey circled high above the damaged power plant. However, the creatures wouldn't approach closer than a half-mile to the leaking nuclear reactor no matter how low he dipped. He didn't want to get too close either. Maybe the radiation couldn't penetrate his skin, and that was a huge maybe, but it still tainted the air. Like he'd told Captain Takeda, he had to breathe just like everyone else.

Well, if the monsters wouldn't enter an area contaminated by radiation, time to try another tactic.

Rey flew straight toward the creatures. At the last second, he veered left and slowed a bit. The agitated monsters shrilled and howled and galloped after him. Unfortunately, pretending to be tired prey wasn't much of an act on his part.

He flew straight toward a sea cliff. Screams of outrage met his ears. He spun one hundred-eighty degrees.

The ones at the head of the pack stopped in time, but their fellows in the back crashed into them. A handful of parrot-lizards and two wolf-monkeys were pushed over the edge. Unfortunately, one of the wolf-monkeys managed to grab an overhang. It climbed up the volcanic rock face, turned toward Rey, and screeched its fury.

Rey's stomach gurgled as if in answer. He needed to find something to eat and soon. Otherwise . . .

No. He'd do what he had to in order to see Aisha and his son again. He had to stay alive for them.

An hour later, Ray had stolen a change of clothing and some food from an unoccupied house. The residents left the rear door unlocked. He'd left a note telling them to contact Harri for repayment. He landed in the top of an evergreen in a forest on the incline of Mount Fuji. The tree was at least seven stories high, which should give him plenty of warning when the monsters found him again.

While the shorts and t-shirt sort of fit, he needed to find some sandals or flip-flops. Japanese people seemed to have much smaller feet than he did. He straddled a limb and leaned against the trunk.

He resorted to stabbing the fish and vegetables with the chopsticks he found with the take-out container in the refrigerator. For the rice, he tipped the plastic and scooped the grains into his mouth.

Did Aisha know how to eat with chopsticks? She probably did. He was a little glad she didn't witness his uncouth manners. Maybe he could get Tim or Jeremy to show him how to use chopsticks properly, then he could surprise Aisha when he took her out to a Japanese restaurant. He dared to close his eyes.

Howls echoed through the forest, and Rey's eyes popped open. So much for his respite. The food and catnap helped though.

"There you are."

Rey jumped and nearly fell off the tree limb he sat on. A wizened bald man stood next to him, perched precariously on another branch. It was the creepy guy who'd abducted him. The odder thing was the man hadn't spoken either English or Spanish this time, but Rey understood him.

A red stone glowed at the old man's throat and seemed to throw off an equally red fog. Too late, Rey realized the red fog had already encircled his legs. He threw the plastic food container at the old man's head like a frisbee. His abductor ducked.

Rey used his hands to heave his paralyzed left leg over the tree limb. Instead of rising into the air, he plummeted through the branches and sharp needles to land hard on the forest floor.

He pushed up on his arms. A mix of blue and green plumage and black fur surrounded him. He was at the monster's mercy. They parted to show the old man.

"No, you're not escaping this time, Xbalanque," he said with a cackle.

The old man's words made no sense. Red mist flowed up from Rey's legs and surrounded him. His last thought was he'd never have a chance to teach his son how to use chopsticks.

CHAPTER 33

Aisha shook her head. Steve's idea worked like a charm. Luckily, they were faster than the parrot-lizards, and they could fly. It wasn't hard to keep up with them as they bolted through orchards and rice paddies.

The comm unit in her ear crackled to life. "They seem to be headed for Aokigahara," Takeda reported. The captain sounded worried.

He and Miss Purrception followed in one chase vehicle. Nakamura and another SEB agent introduced as Ito followed in the second vehicle. Ito's powers involved freezing things from her chilly handshake.

The three Japanese officials had been involved in the battle at SEB headquarters, so they had a clue of what they were up against when it came to the monsters. And none of them even blinked when Steve started into Mayan magic and mythology during the briefing session.

"What's so special about this place?" Aisha asked.

"It's also known as the Sea of Trees or the Suicide Forest," Steve replied. "It's haunted."

She waited for Takeda to refute him, but the comm remained silent.

"Seriously?" She risked a glance at Steve despite the speed at which they were flying.

"Yes, he's very serious, Ms. Franklin," Takeda said. "Given your involvement with men who are considered a fable, perhaps we should be cautious approaching Captain Justice."

"Understood." She glanced at Steve again and couldn't help grinning. "One of my boys has already been possessed by a ghost of their father's past. We'll be careful. How far to this forest?"

"For you, about forty kilometers," Takeda reported. "It's going to take us another half hour to reach the entrance. I'm calling ahead to clear the national park." Though he muted his comm, Aisha could hear him speaking to someone else in Japanese.

"National park?"

"Yes, it's part of the Fuji-Hakone-Izu National Park." Steve grinned at her.

"My grandparents brought us here once when I was a kid. It's the Japanese version of the family trip to Yellowstone."

Damn, that meant civilians were present. This could be worse than the fight at Westerville Park.

"Steve, drop back," she said. "Let me distract Professor Paranoia."

"I'm not going to put you and the baby at risk," he growled back. For an instant, she would have thought Rey flew beside her.

"Paranoia already tried to nab me once before," Aisha said. "I'm a more tempting target than you since I'm a two-fer. I'm hoping he thinks I'm the one who distracted his creatures."

"That is a huge gamble on your part," Miss Purrception said over the comm.

"That's why I'm trusting the rest of you to watch my back," Aisha replied. "Let me know the instant one of you spots Captain Justice."

"You're *loca*," Steve muttered.

"So your brother keeps telling me," Aisha answered. "But I'm not suicidal. Trust me and drop back."

Hopefully, Paranoia didn't have anything that interfered with the trackers Jeremy had sewn into her and Steve's suits. If Paranoia did his mind control shtick on her like he had on Sparx, the SEB should be able to track her.

Steve didn't argue with her anymore. He dropped out of her peripheral vision. She kept her attention locked on the parrot-lizards.

Or she did until they entered some thick brush, and she had to arch upward to avoid the trees. The parrot-lizards may have disappeared from her sight, but she could definitely hear them as they crashed through the dense thicket below.

"I've lost direct visual," she reported. "But I still have audible."

"Back off," Takeda barked. "The forest would be an excellent place to spring a trap—"

As if on cue, a black, furry form with a tail launched itself at her from the top of a tree. Aisha evaded it, only to have another one leap for her.

I need some altitude.

That was her last thought when fire raked her calf, and she plummeted from the extra weight on her left boot.

CHAPTER 34

Harri had the distinct impression Judge Barrowman had her under a microscope. Thankfully, they were one of the last cases to be called. The judge peered over her reading glasses at Harri.

"Ms. Winters?" The judge looked at the pleadings in front of her and back at Harri. "Aren't you with the city attorney's office?"

"I left that job back in May, Your Honor."

"Made enough enemies of the super community you can only get supervillains as clients?"

"My client Patricia Ames is not a super, ma'am," Harri said tersely.

"I don't brook any shenanigans in my court, Winters." Barrowman took off her glasses and laid them on top of the file. "You'd better know your family law if you're going to practice in my court."

"Yes, ma'am."

The judge turned to Lisa. "Ms. Ashcraft, I don't see a thing in your pleadings to justify a temporary order removing a two-month-old infant from her mother's care. Do you wish to add anything else to the record?"

"Your Honor, the mother is cohabitating with a supervillain," Lisa bit out. "That, in and of itself, constitutes a dangerous home environment to the child."

"Your Honor, Arthur Drallhickey has only one conviction, served his community service, is gainfully employed, and has had no trouble with the law over the last year and a half," Susan interjected.

"Mr. Drallhickey and Ms. Ames are not married—"

"Really?" Judge Barrowman cut off Lisa in midstream. "You're going to go there? This is the twenty-first century, counselor."

Lisa's face didn't show any reaction to the reprimand. "Mr. Wilson is concerned about the example Ms. Ames's actions set for his daughter."

"You're really going to argue your client's hurt feelings because he didn't bother to put a ring on it?" Harri blurted.

"My client and Ms. Ames's relationship is not the issue here," Lisa snapped back.

"It is because he was the one who broke off the relationship and ensured Ms. Ames had no method of contacting him," Susan replied. "By his own admission in his affidavit, he was out of the country for the majority of Ms. Ames's pregnancy. He made no effort to contact her once he returned to the United States, nor did he bother to until he learned of my client's living situation though he already knew of the pregnancy when he came back to Canyon Pointe. And then, it was by this custody lawsuit, rather than contacting our client directly."

"Ashcraft, is your client a super?" Judge Barrowman frowned at Lisa.

"I have reason to believe he is though he hasn't admitted such to me."

Harri had to give Lisa credit for saying that with a straight face. If a client had lied to her, she would have used one of Tim's Tasers on the bastard.

Including Tim himself.

"Winters, does Mr. Drallhickey have any archenemies?"

"No, ma'am. Shortly after he began, he realized trying to be a supervillain was a mistake. He quit before he targeted any particular superhero. In fact, Captain Justice had been mentoring Mr. Drallhickey until Captain Justice was declared killed in action by the feds."

"For all we know, Drallhickey was responsible for Captain Justice's death," Lisa snapped.

Harri's mouth opened to deliver a blistering tirade, but Susan nudged her in the arm.

Instead, their new associate said, "If Ms. Ashcraft truly believed that, she would have subpoenaed the FBI file regarding Captain Justice's death. Lord knows she dredged up every other piece of dirt she could find on Mr. Drallhickey."

"Enough, counselors." Judge Barrowman sat back in her chair, her right index knuckle pressed against her lips. Her gaze flicked between the three attorneys. Finally, her hand lowered.

"I'm denying Mr. Wilson's motion for a temporary order to remove the child from the mother's home."

Lisa opened her mouth, but the judge held up her index finger. "I haven't finished yet." She turned to Harri and Susan. "Both parents have equal rights to their child under the law. A court's child advocate will be assigned to Grace Harriet Ames. When the advocate calls to schedule a home visit, I strongly suggest both Ms. Ames and Mr. Drallhickey be there for a full assessment."

Judge Barrowman looked to Lisa. "As will Mr. Wilson. Also, your client will submit to DNA testing to prove he is in fact the child's father and whether or not he's a super. And all attorneys will emphasize with their clients I do not appreciate a pseudo-super battle in my court."

"Yes, Your Honor," Harri said. The other two attorneys nodded.

However, the judge wasn't finish by a long shot. "Ms. Kennedy, was the child DNA-tested at birth?"

"Yes, ma'am," Susan answered confidently. "The results are attached to our answer along with the hospital's affidavit."

The judge put her glasses back on and flipped through the folder until she found the paperwork Susan had filed with the court. "Good, the child's not a super. The feds won't be involved."

Even Harri had to agree with that assessment. If Grace had tested positive for super attributes, the National Superhero Bureau would already be trying to take her away from Patty.

Barrowman looked over her glasses at Lisa. "Unless you are planning to subpoena the records on Captain Justice?"

The opposing attorney shot Harri a calculated look. "I agree with the court that it's not in the best interest of Grace to involve the feds."

Judge Barrowman glared at all three attorneys in turn. "On the other hand, while our state recognizes the paramount rights of the biological parents, I will have no trouble removing the child from both parties if I believe it's in her best interest. Is that understood, counselors?"

"Yes, ma'am," they all murmured.

"Good." The judge pulled out the draft of Harri's order and scribbled something on the paper. "My clerk will schedule an evidentiary hearing once the home evaluations and the presumed father's DNA testing have been done." She looked up from what she was writing. "This will be a priority on both mine and the advocate's schedule."

"Understood, Your Honor," Susan said firmly.

Once the court clerk provided copies of Judge Barrowman's order, the three attorneys retreated to the corridor. It was much quieter now that parties and their counselors were in their respective courtrooms or had left after their own hearings. Quiet except for a young woman on a bench at the other end of the hallway, weeping as an older man tried to console her.

God, Harri wouldn't be able to deal if Black Death got his hands on Grace and Patty cried like that.

"Any chance we can work out some kind of deal?" Lisa asked.

"We could have if your client hadn't been a dick and stalked both Harri and Ms. Ames," Susan answered.

"If this guy is such bad news, why'd you send him to me?" Lisa shook her head in disbelief.

"Like I told you, I was played," Susan said. "Are you planning to withdraw from the case?"

"No." Lisa grinned. "It'd be a nice feather in my cap to beat the infamous Harri Winters on a super matter."

As much as her ego wanted to drop Black Death's identity in front of an audience, Harri couldn't let an opposing attorney, much less someone she actually liked and respected, to blithely walk into danger. "This isn't about winning or losing." She looked at Susan, who nodded before Harri turned back to Lisa. "Can we talk privately?"

Her grin faltered. "You know my client's identity, don't you?"

"Do you?" Harri asked.

Genuine curiosity crossed Lisa's face. "Why didn't you slap me with this in front of Judge Barrowman?"

Harri gestured toward the same consultation room they had used before the hearing. Lisa sat, stunned, as Harri laid out everything that had happened since the City Hall fire back in May.

Well, the pertinent details involving Seismic Shift, Corvus, and most especially, Black Death.

"Please don't blame Susan," Harri said. "She had no idea what was going on because we hadn't had a chance to warn her. I was out of town, and Aisha never dreamed Black Death would approach Susan like that. We should have anticipated this. I'm so sorry."

Lisa swallowed hard. "Black Death is just the supers' version of the boogey-man. Like the Ghost Owl. Or are you going to tell me the bullshit my client fed me about his boss, you, and the Ghost Owl is true?"

"Yes, it's true." Harri grimaced. There were some secrets she didn't dare reveal. "He's dead."

"A client of yours?" Lisa cocked her head.

"Not exactly," Harri said. "As Dreyfuss told you, the Owl called in tips for situations that needed one of our client's skill sets."

"You sure the Owl wasn't creating these situations—" Lisa made air quotes with her index fingers. "—for some other reason."

Harri's lips quirked. "I'm pretty sure causing metal fatigue in a jet engine at forty-thousand feet three hundred miles away from Canyon Pointe was beyond even the Owl's skill set."

Lisa stared at the ceiling a moment before she blew out a deep breath and looked at Harri again. "Regardless of what Wilson has allegedly done, he still has the right to see his daughter."

"The man can kill with a touch," Susan said. "How can you guarantee to my client he won't kill Grace out of spite during visitation?"

"Dammit, Susan." Lisa threw up her hands. "You know I can't offer that kind of a guarantee."

Harri leaned forward and rested her elbows on the table. "Honestly, Lisa, I'm more worried about your safety when you lose this case. Seismic Shift—"

"*When* I lose?" Lisa laughed, but immediately sobered. "Look, Shift screwed over a lot of people." Lisa shook her head. "How many other people wanted him dead? I heard the autopsy was inconclusive. His death could have been stress-related. Or wrongful death from assault injuries." She shot a pointed look at Harri. "You can't prove my client killed him, or you would have done it."

Harri's jaw dropped.

Susan chuckled. "Seriously? You're blaming Harri for Shift's death after the FBI cleared her?"

Lisa shrugged. "If the concrete wall fits."

"Out of professional courtesy, my respect for you, and our friendship, I warned you about your client." Harri stood and slung her case over her shoulder. "Remember that when an aneurysm explodes in your brain." She headed for the door, but paused with her hand on the latch and looked back at Lisa. "Give your client a message for me. I'm doing exactly what he asked me to do the night he was ordered to kill me in my jail cell. I'm protecting Patty and Grace, even if it means from him, too."

CHAPTER 35

Rey was trapped in a red-shrouded nightmare. He shouted in rage at his helplessness, but no sound came out of his mouth. All he could do was watch as Aisha fell. Torn apart by monsters just like Mama.

The old man chuckled. "Corvus was wrong. She does not carry your child. However, my pets can protect us from the usurpers, see? Those fools that pretend to be gods."

Aisha and the wolf-monkey shredding her leg disappeared behind the thick foliage. Rey tried to move, to go to her aid. He couldn't even force himself to blink.

"One more victim sacrificed to the Forest of Sorrows." The old man turned to Rey with a sly smile. "Make sure she's dead. Kill her."

Rey felt his body launch skyward and arrow for the spot he'd seen Aisha go down.

And there wasn't a damn thing he could do to stop himself.

CHAPTER 36

After the initial pain and shock, Aisha whirled in midair as if she were trying to throw a discus. Except she was using her feet, and the object she was attempting to dislodge was a very alive monster.

The wolf-monkey clung to her left boot by a couple of talons. It couldn't deny all the laws of physics though. She twirled too fast for it to grab her with its other hand. The sole of her boot ripped off from the centrifugal force, taking the wolf-monkey with it.

"Aisha!" Steve's panicked voice in her ear. "Incoming!"

Something slammed into her side and brought her spin to an abrupt halt. The sudden stop almost brought up the rice she had for breakfast as well. She landed hard on her ass. Dirt and pine needles flew in all directions.

The dust made it hard to breathe. She painfully climbed to her feet and launched herself skyward.

Aisha cleared the cloud of debris. A man hovered in midair above and ahead of her, highlighted by the morning sun. Her heart leapt.

Rey.

He wore a navy t-shirt a size too small and athletic shorts that were also too tight. His hair was cut differently, and he sported a beard and moustache. His feet were bare. But the look on his face wasn't her boyfriend's.

It reminded her too much of the crazed look on Steve's face the night she fought him. The same night Professor Paranoia also put some kind of spell on Sparx to turn her against Aisha, except there was no red nimbus around Rey.

He dived for her.

"Steve, Paranoia is controlling Rey. No red nimbus. Probably an amulet on him." For the first time, she was glad Steve insisted on knowing what had happened the night they fought in Westerville Park. He'd know what to look for.

She sucked in a deep breath and dropped back into the dust cloud. Once inside, she floated to her left.

It probably wasn't her best idea. Paranoia's creatures could be hiding in here as well. However, it would limit both the creatures and Rey's visibility until

Steve caught up with her. Aisha found herself wishing she'd brought all of the Ghost Owl gear with her, even if it never would have made it through security back in the States.

Something whooshed by her through the dust cloud. She was as blind in here as her opponents.

"Your plan worked a little too well," Steve grumbled in her ear.

She didn't dare answer him. If she took a breath, she'd start coughing and alert Rey to where she was.

"Monsters are closing in on your position," Steve added.

Not to mention the dust was starting to settle. She'd be visible in a few seconds. She flew straight up and pulled out Tim's sonic device from her unitard's thigh pocket. Below her, the bright plumage of the parrot-lizards stood out against the forest floor. There had to be dozens of the damn things.

Steve flew over to meet her. Scratches rent his suit, but only a couple were deep enough to score his skin. "Did you see him in there?"

"No, just felt him fly past me. You okay?"

A self-deprecating laugh poured out of Steve. "Nothing a few bandages can't handle, but the wolf-monkeys are no longer a problem. What about you?"

The slices on her calf burned, and a little blood dribbled down her unitard to drip from her heel. She shook her head. "I've done worse while shaving my legs."

Steve's expression shifted. "Here he comes."

Aisha turned. Rey was heading straight for them. "Get back." She raised Tim's device. "This thing hurts." She pressed the button. The high frequency sliced through her brain like an ice pick, but she kept the device aimed at Rey.

Except he wasn't stopping.

He grabbed her right arm with both hands and tried to wrench the sonic emitter from her hand. Her thumb slipped from the button, and the ice pick sensation disappeared. So she resorted to Harri's favorite tactic. She slammed her knee into his crotch.

Her maneuver didn't faze him. Rey squeezed her hand. Bones snapped, and Aisha cried out. Her nerveless fingers dropped the damaged emitter.

A high-pitched hum pierced her eardrums, but it was nothing like before.

"It's not working!" Steve apparently had caught the device.

Rey seized her throat. She couldn't answer if she wanted to. Her lungs burned, and black spots appeared in her vision.

God, help her. She couldn't kill her baby's father. But if she didn't do something fast, she and their baby were dead. With her left hand, she yanked at the neckline of his shirt. The fabric ripped away from his chest.

He wasn't wearing a version of the amulet Paranoia used to control Steve.

Rey cried out, and the pressure on her throat disappeared. She started to fall.

"Gotcha." Strong arms caught her.

"I'm okay," she choked out.

"Yeah, I can tell by the broken hand," Steve growled. "How do we stop him? Tim's gadget didn't work, and I didn't see anything hanging around his neck when you ripped his shirt off."

"I don't know." Aisha tested her ability to swallow. It hurt like hell, but she managed. "How'd you get him off me?"

"Looked like there were healing claw marks along his right side." Steve's laugh sounded a little self-deprecating. "So I hit him there. Did you try the knee-to-the-groin stunt with me?"

"You tell me." She smirked.

The comm crackled to life in Aisha's ear. "Are you keeping an eye on Rey?" Miss Purrception snapped.

"Yes," Steve shot back. "He's heading our way again." He released Aisha.

Ignoring the agony in her hand, she darted to her right to put some space between her and Steve. Rey altered course straight for her.

"Go!" Steve roared.

But she had already spun and sped away. A glance back said Rey was tight on her tail. "Folks, we're gonna need a little help here."

"We're passing the park entrance now," Takeda reported. "Bring him this way."

"One problem," Steve said. "Those damn parrot-lizards are following Aisha and Rey."

"Take out as many of the bastards as you can from behind before they reach us," Miss Purrception ordered. Funny thing was Takeda and the other two SEB agents weren't questioning the supervillain's lead.

Aisha considered her next course of action. If dealing with Evil Rey was anything like Evil Steve, he had the strength, but she was faster and more maneuverable. But beating Rey until he was nearly dead wasn't an option she liked. And there was also the baby to consider.

She zigged and zagged using the trees as cover. Rey merely plowed through the trunks like they were nothing.

Why didn't the sonic emitter work if he wasn't wearing an amulet? Harri had cut off Paranoia's amulet that controlled the parrot-lizards. Aisha had ripped the amulet off of Steve that controlled him

What if Paranoia had learned from their previous battle? His creatures could cut through hers and the twins' nearly invulnerable skin.

"Purrception, when did you say Rey was hurt at the illegal lab?" Aisha asked. She dived through some thick underbrush. The branches caught her dreds, but her hair just snapped the wood and brought it along for the ride.

"Almost a week. Why?"

"That can't be," Steve interjected. "The cuts where I hit him looked pretty damn fresh."

"The amulet's inside his body!" Aisha and Takeda yelled at the same time.

Chapter 37

For the first time since she and Aisha opened their little boutique firm, Harri wished she didn't have to walk through the reception area to reach her office.

Patty looked up expectantly as Harri and Susan entered the building. "Well? How did it go?"

"We won on the temporary order." Harri shook her head. "But it's going to be an uphill battle to deny Cade dual custody."

"And even though Harri warned Lisa about who he really is, Lisa's going to be swinging for the fences, and she's using Arthur as the bat," Susan added.

"Then I need to leave," their IT guru said as he came out of his office. Grace cooed happily in the harness strapped to his chest.

"No." Harri shook her head fiercely. "In fact, we're going to do the exact opposite. Grace's child advocate will be coming to do a home study. We're going to show you're a much better father to Grace than Black Death."

"How the hell am I going to prove Arthur's a good dad?" Harri poured a healthy serving of café zinfandel into her wine glass. She couldn't do scotch. Not tonight. Not when she needed to brainstorm.

Thankfully, Jeremy and Leonardo were keeping Betty and Marvin entertained for her this week when Aisha's parents weren't visiting old friends. The Franklins refused to leave Canyon Pointe until their daughter returned from Japan.

"You and Susan will figure something out." Tim glanced up from the pasta and veggies he tossed in her frying pan and smiled. "When Aisha gets home, she'll pitch in. Given the notorious slowness of the courts, you've got a few months, right?"

"I'm not sure we do," Harri said. She sipped her wine before she continued. "Judge Barrowman has put a priority on this case."

"Isn't that a good thing?" He turned off the burner.

"Not necessarily." Harri stared at the bottle of wine. Tim wasn't going to drink any, so why had she even bothered with a glass?

For the same reason you don't need to drown your worry in whiskey, her inner voice muttered.

"Walk me through it," Tim said as he filled their plates.

"Assigning a child advocate is standard procedure, but there's a huge backlog in the family courts." She carried the plates to her kitchen table. "The fact that she is putting Grace to the front of the list—"

She turned in time to see Tim's left leg start to buckle. He grabbed the counter and fridge door to stay upright. She dragged his walker over to him.

"I'll get your water." She jabbed a finger at the table. "Go sit down before you fall. I don't have Aisha's superstrength to haul your ass over there."

"What? No lecture about overdoing it?" He grabbed hold of the walker as if it were a lifeline.

"Would it do any good?"

"Nope."

She smiled and shook her head as he shuffled past her. "Then why waste my breath?" She retrieved the bottle of water he had been reaching for and grabbed her wine glass before heading for the table herself.

Something bugged her as she sat. The scene was a little too . . . domestic. Just as it had been the other night with Patty, Arthur, and Grace.

This is what she told herself she wanted, but then, she'd said the same thing when she was with Eddie. So why was she fighting this so hard?

Because you're afraid you're going to lose your made-up family any minute now.

"You okay?"

Harri blinked at Tim's question. Did she tell him the truth? Well, they'd already had one major fight over her insecurities, but she had been trying too hard to hide them. She'd taken so many chances over the last four months, what was one more with her pride and her heart?

"No, I've been on pins and needles since Rey disappeared." She sighed and took another sip of wine.

Tim said nothing. He merely twirled his fork in his linguine and waited for her to continue talking.

"And I'm worried about Aisha." Harri stabbed a broccoli floret. "She's handled clients who've gotten into trouble in other countries plenty of times in the past, but . . ." She shoved the bite in her mouth.

"But it's never been personal?" he asked.

She chewed and swallowed the bite in her mouth before she answered. "No, it hasn't. And we still have no idea where Professor Paranoia is."

"So in other words, you're going to stay up all night waiting for her phone call again, aren't you?"

"It's been nearly twenty-four hours since their plane landed—" She jabbed her fork into a carrot slice. "I'm being stupid and controlling, aren't I?"

"Oh, good, I don't have to point it out." He smiled to take the edge off his sarcastic teasing."

"Jerk," she muttered before she popped the carrot slice into her mouth.

"You need to focus on Grace." His eyes darkened, and the faraway expression took over his face. The one that said he was reliving his own son's death.

"Susan still wants to out Black Death in court."

That definitely yanked Tim back to the present day. "Aisha filled her in on all the crap we've had with Corvus. What the hell is Susan thinking?"

"That melting paint off some park benches is nothing compared to killing people for an illegal government agency when it comes to raising a child."

Tim shook his head. "Didn't you already tell Susan that's a good way for her to end up dead? Trubble was willing to let us take down Seismic Shift because he'd become more trouble than he was worth. Black Death is way too valuable to him."

Harri considered their options. She didn't like the fact that she circled back to their original plan, but this wasn't just her decision. "Remember when you first approached me about the tell-all book about Corvus?"

Tim paused in mid-bite and laid his fork back on his plate. "You can't be serious."

"If the original Ghost Owl is dead, what would it hurt?"

"But Trubble knows someone has taken my place," he protested.

"No." Harri waggled her index finger. "He knows someone has taken the Ghost Owl's place. It's no secret the original Ghost Owl has been calling in tips to the firm for us to pass on to our clients. What if the new Ghost Owl wants to clear the air in return for her hanging up her cowl?"

"How's that going to convince Black Death—" The change in Tim's expression when he pieced together her plan was almost comical. "That might actually work. With the added benefit of embarrassing Trubble, and possibly putting him in jail, at the same time."

"We'd have to alter your manuscript or whatever you've already put together," Harri said. "I'd still want to run this by Aisha before we launch Project Screw Corvus to save Grace."

"We might want to tell Susan, too, since her ass is now on the line." He forked his bit of pasta into his mouth.

"Then I think we have a plan, Mr. Canyon." Harri held up her glass. Tim clinked his water bottle against it.

She really wished Aisha would call soon. Harri needed the reassurance her idea wasn't totally insane. Getting her little family all killed wasn't a good start for a legal godmother.

CHAPTER 38

"Oh, god, we'd have to cut him open to get it out." Aisha's stomach threatened to rebel.

"How?" Nakamura's accent was thick over the comm. "Nothing we have can cut through his skin."

"Those creatures can," Miss Purrception stated.

"The monsters disintegrate within a few minutes of killing them," Takeda said. "Harvesting a claw would be difficult."

"If it's just under his skin, why couldn't we break it with a well-placed punch?" Steve asked.

"Paranoia wouldn't be that stupid," Miss Purrception said. "He knows you're on the loose. If he figured out a way to re-open those cuts along Rey's ribs, he would have forced the stone between the bones so it's protected."

"Then I hope one of you brainiacs know a way to hold Rey still long enough to operate on him," Aisha snarled. She'd gotten far enough ahead of him she wasn't at immediate risk, but she'd be at the park entrance in seconds. Her right hand had gone numb from the broken bones. She'd be a sitting duck if she slowed or stopped flying.

Ito said something in Japanese.

"Stay on course for the park entrance," Steve translated. "Nakamura can hold him long enough for Ito to encase him in ice."

You hope. But Aisha didn't give voice to her thought. Instead, she said, "I'm almost there."

She spotted a road below her. Cars headed in the same direction she flew. Shit. Evacuees.

Their little super team were going to need extra space between the civilians and a place to spring their trap on Rey. Time to pour on the speed. She hugged her broken hand tight against her chest and swooped in the direction of the lake on the north side of the forest.

"Aisha?" Steve hissed through the comm.

"Look down," she said. "The park isn't clear yet. You know the language.

Get down there and help. I'll play Ring-Around-the-Rosie with my possessed boyfriend while you get the civilians to safety."

She ignored Takeda and Miss Purrception's protests. Surprisingly. Steve took Aisha's side, saying, "She's right, and you know it."

The rest of what the two men said was lost to her as they resorted to Japanese—Takeda barking orders at the local park security and law enforcement and Steve soothing tourists from their respective tones.

She risked a glance behind her. Rey had dropped even further behind her. If Takeda was right, and Rey had been on the run for the last couple of days, he had to be exhausted. She slowed a bit.

"Aisha, what's wrong?" Worry laced Miss Purrception's voice.

"I'm fine," she replied. "Rey must have been on his last legs when Paranoia caught up with him. He's lagging behind, and I don't want to lose him."

"Understood."

Minutes ticked by as Aisha flew across the lake, but Rey wasn't any closer to catching her. The north shore was coming up quick. She didn't want to circle around Mount Fuji, but she prepared to make the turn.

"Park's clear," Takeda reported. "There's a stand of trees on the east side. Can you come back?"

"No problem." Aisha slowed more. Another glance. Rey had the same ugly hate-face Steve had worn when she battled him back home. She couldn't cross her fingers with a broken hand, so she settled with a silent prayer. *Please, God, let Ito's plan work. I can't lose Rey again.*

Her third glance over her shoulder. Rey reached for her injured leg. She dived down and twisted as if she were swimming laps at the Grandma Harri's pool before she zipped in the direction she had come from.

The flight back across the lake seemed to take less time even though she was flying slower. Bright plumage gathered on the southeastern shore of the lake, well away from the public docks.

"Aisha, fly a little more to your left," Takeda said.

"Why?"

"Because then I'll be right below you," Steve said. "I can bring him down for the others to restrain."

"I hope you're right," she muttered as she altered course.

"Purrception?" Takeda asked.

"I'm in position." The supervillain's voice crackled on the comm.

Ahead of Aisha was a clearing. Charred trunks circled the area though the forest worked hard to reclaim the site. Fire from a lightning strike?

Behind her, Rey cried out in pain. By the time she turned around, Steve was diving after his falling brother. Takeda, Nakamura, and Ito ran into the clearing from three separate directions.

Steve caught Rey, only to have Rey deck him. The blow must have stunned Steve because Rey broke his brother's grip on him. Aisha dived for Rey, but he dropped to the ground.

Or started to. Something caught his body in midair. Not something. Nakamura held out her left hand toward him, but she kept glancing over her right shoulder. Her right hand aimed behind her.

Blood oozed down Rey's side from the reopened cuts. That must have been where Steve hit him. Aisha blinked to clear the tears that threatened to fall because they had to resort to hurting the man she loved.

Meanwhile, Ito waved her hands in an odd manner. Ice started coating Rey's body. She added layer on layer until he was nearly as wide as he was tall.

Takeda stood to the side with a gas grenade launcher in case Rey managed to get loose. But the ladies had him well in hand. Ito nodded to Nakamura who lowered the ice-encased Rey to the ground.

Steve landed beside Takeda, and Aisha drifted to the ground next to Rey. He yelled something at her that sounded a bit like K'iché, but not quite.

Aisha looked up at Steve. "Do you understand what he's saying?"

Steve cocked his head. "It sounds like the dialect our mother uses." He shook his head. "Unfortunately, I never picked up more than 'water', 'food', and 'bathroom.'"

Aisha peered closer. Something orange was inside one of Rey's ears. She pulled out the dense foam and held it up. "Earplugs. No wonder the sonic emitter didn't work on him."

"Apparently, Professor Paranoia learned from using me as his freakin' guinea pig," Steve said sourly while Aisha pulled the second one from Rey's other ear.

Bird shrieks and calls came from the forest right before the parrot-lizards erupted from the foliage. Nakamura frowned as she concentrated. The monsters ran headfirst into her telekinetic wall. They circled the clearing, but she held them back.

Takeda touched his right ear. "He's secured, Purrception. Where are you?"

"Coming." The supervillain appeared the edge of the clearing, a parrot-lizard slung over her shoulders like a big game trophy. Had Miss Purrception managed to knock it out? She eyed the circling monsters, who ignored her, before she started running for Nakamura's telekinetic wall.

Purrception leapt on the back of another parrot-lizard and heaved the one she carried toward the center of their circle. Steve darted up and caught it before it hit the ground. Purrception jumped and danced from back to back on the monsters until Steve was out of the way. Using a monster head as her stepping stone, she gracefully launched herself up and somersaulted over the telekinetic wall. Her landing would have earned a perfect score if supers were allowed to enter the Olympics.

Ito handed her backpack to Steve. Takeda slung his grenade launcher off his shoulder and handed it to Ito while Purrception dragged the parrot-lizard closer to Rey's frozen form. He was still yelling in his strange language.

The SEB captain knelt beside Rey. He waited until Steve pulled the emergency medical kit out of Ito's backpack. Then his hands and eyes glowed red. He touched the ice covering Rey's injuries, and water ran down the block and soaked into the volcanic soil.

When blood started to mix with the water, Takeda stopped melting the ice and rose. He turned and used a plasma bolt to slice off one of the parrot-lizard's talons.

Purrception wrapped the severed talon in a cloth Steve handed her. She crouched beside Rey and sliced along the injury.

Rey howled what was probably obscenities in the odd dialect he was speaking. Aisha concentrated on the ache in her right hand to keep from going to his aid. He wouldn't be her Rey again until they got that damn stone out of him.

"I need those long tweezers." Purrception traded the talon for the steel instrument Steve handed her.

She inserted the tip into the cut along Rey's lowest ribs. He howled again, one not of words but sheer anguish. She pushed it in a little further and was rewarded with a metal on rock sound.

Thankfully, Rey passed out from the pain. Even the parrot-lizards became silent.

"Got you, you little sucker," Purrception muttered. She pulled out a bloody stone.

Aisha didn't have to think twice. She stalked forward, snatch the amulet from Purrception's instrument, and crushed it with her left hand. The dust that didn't stick to her skin as mud trickled between her fingers to mix with the puddle of bloody water at her feet.

The parrot-lizards started screeching and squawking again. Thank goodness, Nakamura's telekinetic wall insulated the noise somewhat. Otherwise, the creatures' noise would have driven her insane.

"I need you to thaw him so I can seal the wound," Purrception said to Takeda.

"Are you sure it's safe?" Steve asked.

"One way to find out." Aisha nodded toward the backpack he still held. "You have smelling salts in there?"

He pulled out a white capsule. Takeda took it from Steve, broke it open, and held it under Rey's nose, who woke with a jerk of his head.

"Aaagh! Get that away from my face."

Aisha knelt beside his head and wiped her filthy hand on her unitard leg before she cupped his cheek. "You with me again, baby?"

He closed his eyes and whispered her name. "I never thought I'd see you again." His eyelids fluttered. "Why am I so cold?"

"You're in a block of ice."

"Our son?"

Aisha smiled. "He's just fine, baby."

"You colored your hair red?"

"Yep."

He smiled. "I like the dreds."

"Baby, there's something I need to tell you before Captain Takeda lets you loose."

"What's that?"

"You have a twin brother."

CHAPTER 39

Someone who looked just like Rey stepped into his view. Actually, the stranger looked just like him when he was clean-shaven.

"He's a fake! A trick by Corvus!" Rey struggled to free himself. The ice crackled, but he couldn't get loose. "Aisha, run!"

"Stop," she said gently. She squeezed his chin and forced him to look at her. When did she get so strong? "Steve was under Professor Paranoia's control. Just like you were."

"She's telling you truth, kid." Monica crouched beside Aisha. "Do you remember the last five minutes?"

"I—she—the old man—" He sucked in as deep a breath as he could manage. His right side hurt like a mother again. "The old man who originally captured me showed up . . . in this forest, I think. He tried to tell me Aisha's baby wasn't mine, then he . . ." He shook his head. "Sorry, but everything's rather fuzzy."

"Sounds about like me after Aisha broke Professor Paranoia's hold," Steve murmured.

"I'll release you." The amusement was back in Captain Takeda's eyes. "But if you don't behave yourself, you will be encased in ice for the entire trip back to the United States."

"I'll behave myself."

"You broke your last promise to me," Takeda teased.

"You can have my attorney draw up the contract, but you'd still need to unfreeze my arm to sign it." Rey grinned at the SEB captain despite the agony in his side.

It only took a couple of minutes for Takeda's plasma bursts to melt the ice enough for Aisha and the other man to break Rey free. He jerked his arm out of his lookalike's grip. He still wasn't quite ready to call him family no matter what Aisha said.

A body with brilliant plumage and only three feet lay behind Aisha. He shoved her behind him and yelled, "Monster!"

Monica glanced at the still form before she grinned at him. "Don't worry, kid. That one isn't going anywhere for a while. I conked it pretty good on the head."

"Here." Aisha unsnapped a pocket on her outfit. An outfit that was the same color as the Ghost Owl's. She pulled out his amulet. A metal chain ran through the hole carved in the top. "Put this on. It should shut up the rest of the damn monsters."

"You sure about that?" Rey eyed the parrot-lizards.

"Yeah, those things only come after us when we're not wearing protection," Aisha quipped. Her smile relieved him to no end.

Rey took the amulet and unscrewed the clasp, but when he raised his arms to put it on, fire shot through his right side. He looked down to see blood oozing from his cuts, except the middle cut looked even deeper than before.

"Can you put this on for me?" He held the amulet out to Aisha.

"I can't right now." She turned to the lookalike. "Steve?"

"Why him?" Rey glared at his so-called twin.

"Because she can't." Steve snatch the amulet out of Rey's grip and stepped behind him. "You broke her hand, dude."

Rey's gut churned as he looked at Aisha. "You said you and the baby were okay."

"I am," she said.

"Not if I hurt you—"

"Quit whining, kid." Monica took the med kit from Steve. "We need to get you patched up and figure a way to take care of the monsters before they decide to chomp on the locals."

Dios! How did everything go so wrong? No, this was normal for him. The two months with Aisha were the exception in his life.

As soon as the amulet rested on his chest, the parrot-lizards quieted. They chittered to each other and wandered aimlessly around the clearing.

Monica wiped his cut with antiseptic pads, and he hissed at the burning sensation.

"Quit acting like a baby," she muttered. "Changing diapers in a few months is going to be a hell of a lot worse."

He gritted his teeth as she pressed the wound edges together as Kwan Li had back in Singapore. It felt like that had taken place years ago.

"What are you putting on him?" Aisha demanded.

"Relax," Monica said as she spread the contents of the tube along the seam of his cut. "It's a special wound glue." She glanced at Aisha with a smirk. "Unless you've got something that will penetrate his indestructible hide to sew up the incision I had to make."

"Don't worry," Rey murmured in Spanish. "Molly's mom knows what she's doing."

Aisha visibly relaxed. Did she really think he was that stupid? He simply hadn't any choice on who to trust during his escape from Corvus.

"Any of you have an idea on how to deal with these creatures?" Takeda asked once Monica taped Rey's wound with gauze as a precaution.

A red glow appeared around the SEB agent with the short, spiky white hair. The one with the freezing powers who'd fought the monsters inside the holding and interrogation section of their headquarters. She aimed the grenade launcher at Aisha.

Rey rushed her and knocked the launcher upward as she fired. She punched him in his wounds. He gritted his teeth against the pain and yanked the weapon from her hands.

The grenade arched up and over Nakamura's telekinetic wall. It exploded and gas poured across the clearing.

Takeda shouted an order in Japanese as the cloud floated toward them. The parrot-lizards closest to the burst of gas keeled over. The ground shivered as roughly a quarter of them collapsed. Amid squawks and a flurry of feathers, the rest darted for the surrounding trees.

The gas floated over and around the dome Nakamura created. Sweat poured down the poor super's face at the strain of keeping them safe.

Rey had his hands full, trying to restrain the lady with the ice powers without hurting her or letting her injure him any further. Steve wrapped his arms around the agent with the ice powers and pulled her off Rey.

"Would your sonic weapon free her from Paranoia's influence?" Takeda asked.

Aisha shook her head. "It's damaged." Her face lit up with an idea. "Rey, whistle!"

He cocked his head. "You sure you want me to do that in this enclosed space?"

She nodded and slapped her hands over her ears. So did Takeda and Monica. Rey shifted so Nakamura was behind him.

Steve rolled his eyes.

"Payback's a bitch," Aisha taunted.

Rey raised his fingers to his lips, sucked in as deep a breath as he could manage, and whistled.

Steve winced, but the SEB agent sagged in his arms. She blinked as if she was coming out of a deep sleep and said something in Japanese. He answered her in kind. She nodded, and he released her.

"I don't suppose you three have any more of those handy dandy amulets," Monica said.

Aisha stared at the surrounding forest. "Dammit, one of us will have to take ours off to get the conscious parrot-lizards back here."

"But how do we control or subdue them once we get them back here?" Takeda said. "They are not stupid. They learned to avoid the knockout gas when they invaded our headquarters. Paranoia's attempt to incapacitate us through Ito caught them by surprise"

"There's a way to kill two birds with one stone." Steve reached beneath the neckline of his unitard and lifted his amulet over his head.

Rey couldn't help but notice the bastard made a point of handing it to Aisha.

The screeches of the parrot-lizards sounded through the forest. The crashing in the underbrush came closer. Steve waved the rest of the group toward the opposite side of the telekinetic dome. Once they complied, he said, "Mother, I found Xbalanque."

Light burst in the clearing, whiter and brighter than the sun. Rey lifted his hand to shade his eyes. It wasn't just him. Everyone, even Steve, had to do the same.

The conscious parrot-lizards ran back to the clearing and bowed before the light. One by one, the monsters knocked out of the anesthetic gas woke and hobbled over to their companions. Even the three-footed one inside Nakamura's invisible wall blinked blearily in the direction of the light.

A woman stepped from the light, or maybe she was the source of the light. Rey wasn't sure.

Aisha's left hand folded around his right. "That's Xquic, your birth mother."

"Maria Garcia—" Rey started.

"Was the mortal name your nurse Ixq'anil took when I sent her away with you." The woman of light looked around her. "Seven Macaw's pets are still on the loose, I see."

"We're not exactly sure how to get them away from civilians without killing them, ma'am," Aisha said.

The woman of light chuckled. "That's the real reason Hunahpu summoned me, isn't it?"

"Well, I was hoping you'd have some tips." Steve gestured at his cuts and scratches. "Those claws of theirs are pretty wicked."

She whistled an odd little tune. A black spot appeared next to her and grew larger. It was a doorway or a tunnel or some kind of swirling vortex. Rey's mind couldn't quite decide how to decipher the optical impulses. Or maybe it was a black hole.

Then she said something in the strange language the old man who had captured him had used. The parrot-lizards rose and trotted or stumbled through the black hole. The one inside with him and Aisha tried to follow its kin, but it kept bumping its head against Nakamura's telekinetic sphere.

At Takeda's nod, the Japanese super lowered her hands. The parrot-lizard headed for the black hole in a three-legged skipping motion and disappeared along with the rest.

"Noooooo!" The angry cry came from their right. The old man hobbled into the clearing. "You have no right to take them!"

"They belong in Xibalba," the woman said gently.

"They were mine to command!" he shouted.

She shook her head sadly. "And you used them to try to kill my sons and daughter-in-law."

"I had a deal—"

"Yes, I know who you have bargained with." She stalked toward the old man and gestured sharply. "And the power was never yours to keep."

The old man dropped to the ground like a puppet with its strings cut. Something black oozed out of the old man and crawled over to her. She picked it up and cradled it. Two eyes peered at them from over her arm. She whispered to it. The thing leapt down and crawled into the black hole as well. She whistled her odd little tune once again, and the black hole collapsed on itself until nothing was left.

"You're not taking him with you?" Takeda asked, gesturing at the old man.

"He is mortal, and it is not his time." She knelt beside him, ripped an amulet from his neck, and crushed the stone in her hand before she crossed the clearing to their small group. "He is yours to do with as you see fit."

"We know him as Professor Paranoia," Aisha said. "He has his own gift, as small as you might consider it. How can we be sure he won't control the minds of those who guard him in our plane?"

Xquic leaned close to Aisha. "Have your friend the tinker devise something like the machine in Hunahpu's pocket." Xquic winked before she kissed Aisha on the cheek. "Take good care of my grandson."

Rey wasn't sure what to say to this strange woman when she turned to him. Aisha had thrown a lot of information at him in the short minutes they'd been reunited.

Xquic cupped his face. "You don't have to say anything to me." Had she read his mind? "I have no right to claim you. Not after I had to send you away to save your life. Ixq'anil was the mother you knew, and I will honor her gift and her sacrifice for you. She will always be your mama."

The events of the last several months caught up with him with his foremost fear landing on top of the pile. "I don't know how to be a father."

"Of course you do. Love and patience, both of which you have in abundance." She wrapped her arms around him, but she didn't squeeze too hard. Almost as if she were afraid to break him. He couldn't help himself. He hugged her as fiercely as the cuts on his side allowed.

There were so many questions running through his head when they parted.

Xquic lay a finger on his lips. "There will be a time to ask your questions, but now is not it. You need to go to your home." She glanced at the old man lying on the ground. "The mortals he allied himself will be after your family, Xbalanque. They will need your help."

She moved to Steve and hugged him as well. "Thank you for finding your brother. Watch each other's backs. Paranoia is not the only danger in this world."

Xquic released Steve and walked into the light. It flashed even brighter, then she and the light disappeared.

Rey simply stared at the spot where she had been despite the dark purple afterimages flashing in his vision. He thought his world changed when Mama died. He thought his world changed when Harri took him in. He thought his life changed when he fell in love with Aisha.

But this?

His whole universe changed, and he didn't have a damn clue on how to fly through this one.

CHAPTER 40

The melody to "Brick House" woke Harri out of a sound sleep. She grabbed her phone as Tim jerked upright beside her. Three-oh-one shone above the "Answer" and "Reject" icons.

"Chill. It's Aisha." She tapped the icon. "About time you called."

Tim groaned before he turned on the bedside light and flipped back the covers. Harri blinked at the sudden brightness.

Aisha chuckled over the faint static on the line. "I hope you weren't waiting for me to call the entire time. I was going to wait until you were awake, but our plane leaves soon."

Tim swung his legs over the side of the bed, grabbed his walker and headed for the bathroom.

"And?" Harri prompted.

"Rey's alive, we're all safe, and Professor Paranoia is currently in custody for his attack on the SEB headquarters," Aisha reported.

"What about Miss Purrception?" Harri crossed her fingers.

"I've negotiated her release." From Aisha's hesitation, another problem had cropped up. "She's banned from Japan for life, but she doesn't want to come back to the U.S. with us."

"Rue Liberty will be disappointed." Harri didn't relish telling the elderly superhero her daughter wasn't coming home, but even Rue Liberty admitted Miss Purrception had several outstanding warrants in the States.

"I can't blame Miss Purrception. It's too risky for her. However, Rey's insisting we escort her to a safe place." Aisha sighed. "It's going to be an extra day before the boys and I are home. Also, as part of getting Rey released, we need to deliver a sonic emitter to the SEB to keep Paranoia in check. Mine got broken in the scuffle."

"I'll let Tim know. Tell Captain Takeda I'll overnight it once it's built. How did Rey take the news about Steve?" Harri winced at the sound of the toilet flushing from her bathroom. Maybe a loft wasn't such a great idea.

If Aisha heard with her superhearing, she decided to ignore it. "Skeptical at first, but he's warming up to the idea."

"Meaning they haven't killed each other yet?" Harri laughed.

"Still feeling each other out," Aisha said. "The sibling rivalry will come. Don't worry. How's things with our custody case?"

"Judge denied the emergency motion and temporary orders." Harri sighed as Tim shuffled back into the bedroom. "The child advocate is doing the in-house study here tomorrow."

"This soon?" Aisha asked.

"Today," Tim whispered as he climbed back into bed.

"Yeah, Barrowman put a rush on our case. Sorry, Tim reminded me the visit's today," Harri amended. "This is what happens when you wake me out of a sound sleep."

"Hey, you're the one who always claims she's a morning person." Aisha laughed, but it sounded forced. "That's way too fast. Judge Barrowman give you a reason?"

"I'm worried about the rush, too," Harri admitted. "So is Susan. Barrowman claims she doesn't want a pseudo-super battle in her court."

"You two outed Black Death already?"

Harri sighed. "Only to Lisa because I don't want her to die when she loses in court. Barrowman asked her point blank if Wilson was a super. Lisa said she suspects he is, but he hadn't admitted it to her. I'd love to be a fly on the wall when she confronts him."

"Let's hope he doesn't kill Lisa for confronting him because she won't let something like a client lying to her slide." Leave it to Aisha to voice Harri's own fear.

"He'll just hire another attorney," she muttered.

"Well, he can't kill them all without raising suspicion," Aisha said sourly. "That's a plus in our column."

"Tell me about it." Harri nodded when Tim pointed at the lamp. He turned it off, and darkness swallowed the loft again. "Susan's already feeling guilty as hell for sending him to Lisa."

"We can only play the hand we're dealt," Aisha said.

"And try to make sure our opponent isn't cheating," Harri finished.

Someone called Aisha's name in the background. "My ride to the airport is leaving. I'll give you a call at our next stop."

They said their good-byes. Harri ended the call and laid her phone on the nightstand. Her eyesight had adjusted. She curled up against Tim.

"What have I been volunteered for?" Tim murmured sleepily.

"The SEB needs an industrial-strength version of your sonic emitter in return for Rey's release." Harri yawned. "Aisha and the boys captured Professor Paranoia. The bastard's remaining in Japan's custody, which means he's out of our hair."

"How much do you want to bet your buddy Lisa asks for a delay if Black Death heads to Tokyo?"

With Tim's comment, Harri was wide awake again. "You really think Trubble would order Paranoia's death?"

"He was desperate enough to ask the Ghost Owl for help to find the bastard. Why else would Trubble want to know his location?"

Shit. Harri stared at the shadowed ductwork overhead. Of course, that was Trubble's ultimate goal. Paranoia had stolen Rey and Steve out from under the retired general's nose. He wouldn't take that betrayal lightly. Seismic Shift had merely inconvenienced him. With Paranoia, any punishment would be purely personal.

And if she told Trubble where Paranoia was, she'd be an accomplice to a murder.

⋯⋯⋯

Later that morning in her office, Harri gave a rundown of Aisha's phone call to Susan. "What do you think Lisa will do if Black Death takes off in the middle of the home audits? How do you think Barrowman will take it?"

The other attorney leaned against the back of the couch and sipped her tea while she considered Harri's questions. "Lisa will try to cover her client's ass. Barrowman will throw a fit. You want to twist this to our advantage?"

"Yep."

Susan's right eyebrow lifted. "So, you want the asshole to fly to another continent to murder someone in order to win a case?"

"No. What I want is a hat trick." Harri grinned. "I want Rey back, I want

Black Death to lose custody, and I want Trubble and his thugs arrested, tried, and sentenced to a very long time in prison." She sobered. "What I don't want is for anyone to die in the process."

"Don't want much do you?" Susan raised her cup of tea. "Here's to shooting for that hat trick."

⁂

Mrs. Hartmann, the child advocate, arrived at the Lechuza Building ten minutes early. Thankfully, Susan prepared Patty and Arthur for that contingency.

The child advocate could have played Miss Hannigan in a Broadway production of *Annie*. Her gray hair was teased and sprayed. She wore a jacket and skirt that was stylish when Grandma Harri was Grace's age. But her pursed lips and sour expression didn't indicate a kindly grandmother.

She glared at poor Patty who sat behind her desk. "Why are you living in the same building where you work, Ms. Ames?"

"She moved in here because her ex was stalking her," Harri bit out as she charged out of her office.

Hartmann turned her ugly glare on Harri. "This interview is between me, the parent, and her partner."

"And I'm Grace Ames's godmother." Harri matched the advocate's glare.

Mrs. Hartmann's face softened a hair. "Let me speak with Ms. Ames and, ur . . ." She had to look at her notes. "Mr. Drallhickey." She looked at Harri again. "I'll speak with you after I've seen their home situation."

"Then you won't have a problem if my chief of security scans you and I escort you to their apartment. For Grace's protection, of course." Harri attempted to sound as reasonable as she could. But her statement still seemed to take Mrs. Hartmann by surprise.

"Is all this really necessary?"

"Yes, ma'am." Tim rolled from Arthur's office right up to the advocate. "It is."

"What's really going on, Ms. Winters?" Mrs. Hartmann's sour expression was back.

"In the last four months, there's been numerous attempts on my life, including two by Seismic Shift. At least three attempts on my law partner's life. My legal assistant has been stalked by her ex. My head of security was mugged. My head of IT was framed for arson at City Hall." Harri ticked off each person on a finger. "And finally, one of my clients, Captain Justice, was declared dead a couple of months ago. As the saying goes, it's not paranoia when someone really is out to get you. So, with not only Grace, but all the other children who live here, we do take security rather seriously."

While Harri spoke, Tim waved the wand of one of his devices over Mrs. Hartmann's body. "She's clean," he announced.

"And your name is?" she said archly.

"Timothy Mitchell Canyon."

Harri bit her bottom lip to keep from laughing at the shock on the child advocate's face. She and Patty would be hearing about his presence from her on the ride up to the apartment.

He tucked the device into the left pouch on his wheelchair before he rolled over to Patty. "You are relieved, my lady."

"Hit the hashtag and the extension to transfer a call," Patty ordered.

"I know how it works." Tim made a face at her. "Who do you think installed the phone system?"

"Arthur did," she shot back.

"I helped." Tim flashed a grin.

Patty merely shook her head and gestured toward their antique elevator. "This way, Mrs. Hartmann."

The child advocate followed Patty, and Harri brought up the rear. Patty opened the first and second gates and entered the car.

Mrs. Hartmann sniffed when she reluctantly stepped aboard. "When was the last time this device was inspected?"

"Last month." Patty tapped the framed placard that hung on the back wall.

Harri focused on closing the two gates to keep from laughing at the older woman. She punched the button for the fourth floor, and the elevator groaned to life. "How long have you been a child advocate for the courts, Mrs. Hartmann?"

She looked up from whatever she was writing in her notebook. "How does my employment history have any bearing on Ms. Ames's case?"

Tension tightened Harri's neck and shoulder muscles. So, that was how things were going to be.

"Like I said downstairs, I want to make sure my goddaughter doesn't get the shaft."

"Yet, you are representing one of her parents, are you not?" A drawn eyebrow rose above Hartmann's wire rim spectacles. "What happens if your goddaughter's interests and your client's interests do not coincide?"

"They do," Harri said coolly. "Or I wouldn't have taken the case."

Hartmann sniffed again, but she didn't say another word.

Thank god, she stayed silent. Harri wasn't sure she could keep her temper in check with the self-righteous bitch.

The elevator shuddered to a halt at the fourth floor. The women exited. Once again, Patty took the lead and headed straight for the apartment she shared with Arthur. She opened the door and halted abruptly.

Harri caught a whiff of the stench before she saw the disaster. If Grace weren't burbling happily, wrapped in Arthur's shirt, Harri would have thought the baby had exploded.

Poo covered a good portion of the kitchen counter and the backsplash. Brown tainted the bubbles in Grace's baby tub sitting in the sink. More brown flecks spotted Arthur's face and hair, but none were on his blindingly white chest.

He looked ready to cry when he said, "I don't think the formula supplement agreed with her digestive system."

CHAPTER 41

Rey felt half-way normal after a shower and getting dressed in the spare street clothes he had on when he was officially booked. Even better, Aisha had brought his real passport and wallet with her.

He ran a hand over his beard. He'd planned to shave it off, especially after Aisha complained it tickled once he had the chance to give her a proper kiss. But if he did so, he'd look like the other guy.

Steve. Hunahpu.

His brother.

He wasn't sure he could get used to the idea after all these years.

But Steve wasn't the one who broke Aisha's hand. Rey wasn't sure how she could even stand him touching her. Letting him feel their baby move inside of her.

A polite knock echoed on the door of the quarters the SEB let him use to clean up. He opened the door to find Captain Takeda.

The agent bowed and said, "May we speak?"

Rey nodded and stepped out of the way. In the few days he'd known Takeda, he didn't recall seeing him nervous. Not like this. He closed the door and waited.

"The flashdrive you had on you with your amulet?"

Rey nodded.

"Standard procedure here is to look at it and make a copy." Takeda sucked on his cheeks. "Do you know what's on it?"

Rey nodded slowly. "Information Paranoia and his minions collected about us. Me and my brother, I mean."

"This is not information that should spread." Takeda pulled out a familiar flashdrive from his pocket and held it out to Rey. "I would suggest you destroy it and drop the fragments in the Mariana Trench."

Rey accepted the flashdrive. "What about the copy you made?"

"Unfortunately, I hadn't made a copy before Paranoia's monsters destroyed the flashdrive when they attacked us." Takeda smiled. "My superiors were most disappointed."

His gesture touched Rey. Since Mama died, no one had really stuck up for him. Now he had a whole new family in Canyon Pointe, and a brother he needed to know before he made any decisions about rebuilding his life, other than doing right by Aisha and his son. But Taneka had no reason to stick his neck out for Rey.

Other than he believed in doing the right thing.

"Thank you, Captain." Rey held out his palm. "For everything."

Takeda shook his hand.

Rey grabbed his bag and followed the SEB captain to the reception area of their building. The space had been cleaned and repainted. New glass had been installed. A person wouldn't know a battle had taken place a few days ago unless they'd been here at the time.

Steve and Monica waited near the doors. Behind them, a dark sedan sat in the drive.

Rey spotted a familiar lithe form in an alcove, a phone to her ear. His heart thrummed at seeing her again. After the last couple of months, it felt like he was seeing her for the first time.

"Aisha!"

She held up an index finger in his general direction and continued talking. Probably to Harri.

As much as he missed her, too, he didn't want to interrupt their discussion. With Black Death suing Patty for custody of Grace, the ladies had more important things to talk about besides his homesickness.

Aisha ended her call and strode over to him. "Sorry about that." She rose on her toes and pecked him on the lips.

"Everything okay?"

"No." She made a face and turned to Captain Takeda. "To let you know, we suspect a super by the codename of Black Death may be on his way here to kill Professor Paranoia. Currently in the States, he's using the civilian name of Cade Wilson."

Takeda nodded thoughtfully. "Thank you for the information, Ms. Franklin. He has a reputation even here. We shall take precautions." His gaze swept the rest of their little group. "It has been a pleasure meeting you. However—" His attention settled on Monica.

She held up her hands. "I know, I know. If I set foot in any Japanese territory again, you'll throw the book at me."

"As long as we understand each other." Takeda smiled.

The four exited the building and climbed into the vehicle. Ito was in the driver seat. She grinned at Steve, who had taken the front passenger seat, and said something in Japanese. Steve answered in kind. The ice-powered superhero gunned the engine, and they zipped down the road.

To make sure Monica left the country, the SEB put them on a chartered flight back to Singapore.

A few hours later as the plane taxied toward Singapore's private terminals, Rey leaned over to look at Monica. "You sure it's safe for you to come back here?"

"Safer than the U.S." She grinned, but the humor didn't reach her eyes.

"I still owe you a favor."

She shook her head. "No, you don't. I didn't fulfill my part of the bargain. I didn't get you home."

Rey looked at Aisha. He reached over and squeezed her hand. "Maybe you did after all."

"Do this for me then." Monica took a deep breath. "Tell Kerry and Molly I miss them and I love them. Tell my mother—" She looked at Aisha. "Tell her she has damn good taste in attorneys."

"Let me have your phone." Aisha held out her hand.

Monica's eyes narrowed. "Why?"

Aisha raised one eyebrow, and Monica relented. She handed over her device. Aisha's thumbs darted over the letters and numbers before she handed it back to Monica, who frowned.

"Who's this?"

"A friend who specializes in supervillain criminal defense. When you decide to come home, give him a call. He may not be able to keep you from doing some jail time, but he's your best chance of keeping it to a minimum."

Monica clutched her phone like it was a lifeline. "Thank you, Aisha."

Warmth washed through Rey. Maybe, just maybe, some good would come out of this horrible experience after all if Monica could some day see her daughters again.

CHAPTER 42

Taking shallow breaths at the unbelievable smell, Harri swallowed hard to keep her breakfast down. She brushed past Patty and Mrs. Hartmann and charged over to poor Arthur. "I'll hold Grace while you empty and clean her baby tub. Then you take a shower while I give her a quick bath."

Arthur handed the two-month-old over with a grateful smile.

Patty crossed to the kitchen island. "I'll hold her—"

"No, you're free of baby poo." Harri shook her head. "Go open a few windows to air out the place while I give Grace her bath."

"But the rest of the kitchen—"

"Arthur and I have it." Harri hoped Patty would pick up the hint she needed to play nice with Mrs. Hartmann, or she might lose her daughter.

Patty grimaced, but she opened a couple of the living room windows before she darted off to the bedrooms to get a cross breeze going.

Mrs. Hartmann marched over to the island that separated the kitchen and living room. Thankfully, she stayed on the other side while Arthur quickly cleaned the counters and backsplash with antibiotic wipes.

She peered over her glasses at Harri. "Do you always have to instruct Ms. Ames in infant care?"

Harri smiled and shook her head. "Nah. Patty's just a little frazzled over the custody suit. She's normally very loving and efficient when it comes to Grace."

"And do you have any background in childcare, Mr. Drallhickey?"

"I was Gaia Johnson's nanny for four years." There was a slight tremor to his voice, but he performed just like Harri and Susan had practiced with him. "I have her reference on file if you'd like to see it."

Mrs. Hartmann blinked owlishly. She obviously recognized the name of the tennis pro. "Actually, I'd like a copy of that and Ms. Johnson's contact information."

"I'll get it for you." He started to head for the nook that served as his home office.

Harri grabbed his arm. "Grace's tub and a shower first, Arthur."

"Oh, yes, of course." He dumped the polluted bath water, cleaned the baby tub, and rinsed it well. He helped Harri unwrap Grace from his shirt before he took off for his bedroom.

"Do you have any questions for me, Mrs. Hartmann?" Harri said as cheerfully as she could manage with her goddaughter's atrocious smell. She double-checked the water temperature before she carefully set Grace in the special tub and lathered the bath mitt. The lavender scented bath gel abolished most of the odor within seconds.

"You said other children live here in you building?"

Harri could hear scribbling on paper behind her as she gently wiped the filth from poor Grace. "Yes, our building manager Miguel Esperanza has four boys. They live in the big apartment on this floor. Well, I can't really call Dom and Emilio kids any more since they are both over eighteen, but Javier is thirteen and Francisco turns eight soon.

Patty rushed back into the kitchen. "I can take over now."

"Let me rinse her, and you can have her right back." Harri reached for the sink sprayer, checked the temperature of the water on her wrist, and splashed clean water over Grace's soapy body. "Can't she, Gracie-poo?"

The baby laughed and tried to grab the water as it shot from the nozzle. Once she was rinsed, Harri wrapped her in a clean towel and handed her to Patty.

While she dried and diapered her daughter, Harri drained the tub and rinsed it out. With the final clean-up, she realized it smelled a lot better in the apartment.

"Would you like something to drink, Mrs. Hartmann?" she said as she dried her hands on some paper towels.

"Water, please." Her tone was slightly less acidic than it had been downstairs. Maybe this interview would go better than Harri had feared.

She retrieved bottles of water for the ladies and an energy drink for Arthur from the refrigerator. Patty gave her a grateful smile as she and Mrs. Hartmann took seats in the living room with a diapered and dressed Grace.

"I'll take the trash with me." Harri snatched up the bag from the receptacle, tied it shut, and headed for the door. "Buzz us when Mrs. Hartmann is ready to come back downstairs."

With the smell wafting from the bag, her choice to do this simple chore for Patty was probably the smartest thing Harri had done all year. Maybe they needed a special hazmat dumpster if this was going to be Grace's reaction every time something new was introduced to her little digestive system. Once she tossed the trash in the dumpster and reset the alarm, she headed for her office.

"Please tell me the odor that came down with the elevator was Grace's diapers and not you," Tim called out.

Harri changed directions and strolled over to the receptionist desk. "Really? You're going to insult your girlfriend like that?"

"From now on all odd smells shall be blamed on tenants under the age of eighteen." He grinned.

She told him what had happened upstairs, and he burst out laughing.

"Glad to know it's not just my kid," he said between chuckles. "Rebecca had hand-painted Shane's nursery. A very detailed woodland scene. One day, I was changing him, and I thought he was done. He was not."

Harri laughed as well. "Ate the paint off the wall?"

"No, he had carrots for lunch. Everything was stained orange, including the carpet."

Harri laughed even harder.

"Rebecca started to get mad," Tim continued. "Until I pointed out if I had Shane pointed the other way, we would have had to destroy all of his stuffed animals."

Tears rolled down Harri's face as she howled.

"I'm so glad I'm only the godmother," she said once she got her mirth under control. "I can always give the kid back." She noticed something else. It was the first time Tim had spoken of his wife and son without the haunted expression on his face.

"Do you want some coffee?" he said.

"Taking this legal assistant thing seriously, huh?" She grinned.

"No, I'm being polite because I'm getting myself some," he said archly.

"Well, then, thank you. I would love some."

⸎

Two cups of coffee and an hour and a half later, Tim buzzed Harri that Mrs. Hartmann was done interviewing Patty and Arthur. When she reached their apartment door, Mrs. Hartmann was the most relaxed she'd seen the advocate today.

"I have to admit when I speak to a parent in this type of situation, they have a tendency to paint a terrible picture of the other parent," Mrs. Hartmann said in the elevator.

"I don't think Patty could be deliberately mean if her life depended on it."

"What if it does?" Mrs. Hartmann's voice could barely be heard over the whine of the elevator's pulleys.

A chill ran through Harri. "What do you mean?"

"Could she defend her life and her child's if the father used his powers against them?"

Time to play stupid. "Is Wilson a super?"

"Ms. Ames believes he is."

"And what do you believe?" Harri prodded.

"I don't like bullies," Mrs. Hartmann said.

"Neither do I." The elevator ground to a halt, and the women walked to the reception area.

"Would you like something to drink before we talk privately?" Harri gestured toward her office.

Mrs. Hartmann took a long look at Tim before she turned back to Harri. "Any parent seriously concerned about their child's welfare would have mentioned a notorious accused murderer's presence in the child's life in addition to a former supervillain's. Especially since most people don't know Seismic Shift admitted to murdering the Canyon family." She pursed her lips. "That means Mr. Wilson knows who your chief of security is and doesn't care, or he knows more about all of you than he's told his attorney, and he's playing her."

Harri wasn't sure what to say about Mrs. Hartmann's suspicions. Family law wasn't her forte.

Before she could formulate a reply, Mrs. Hartmann said, "Grace is an adorable child. Tell your assistant to watch her back."

Harri held up her right index finger. "Can I ask one favor?"

"If I can."

"If Mr. Wilson or Ms. Ashcraft reschedule your appointment with him, would you please let me or Susan Kennedy know?"

"Why?"

"I can't go into details because it involves another client, but I can guarantee you people's lives depend on it." Harri prayed the child advocate would take her hint.

From the gleam in Mrs. Hartmann's eyes, she understood. "Of course. Have a good day, Ms. Winters."

Tim buzzed Mrs. Hartmann out of the building before he asked, "What was that about?"

Harri merely smiled. "How many times have I told you? The only thing more dangerous than an ex-supervillain is his attorney."

CHAPTER 43

Aisha breathed a sigh of relief when thankfully, Rey and Steve decided to get a beer before their flight left Singapore. Maybe the two could work through some of their issues without her playing middlewoman.

Guilt immediately speared her. The guys had a lot dumped on them over the last four months. The birth family thing was bad enough. Plus, both were probably suffering from PTSD after what Professor Paranoia had done to them. She'd be a little pissy with that much stress, too.

She found a quiet corner and punched in Harri's cell number. It rang once before Harri blurted, "Please tell me nothing's happened to you and the boys."

Aisha laughed. "We're fine. Miss Purrception left the airplane without incident. I'm taking a mental break while Rey and Steve try to work out some things."

"Just tell me it doesn't involve property damage."

Aisha could almost hear her partner rolling her eyes. "Only to their livers. How'd the child advocate's visit go?"

"Better than expected." Harri laid out her private conversation with Mrs. Hartmann and her plan for taking down Black Death and Corvus.

"I already warned Takeda of the possibility of Trubble sending Black Death after Professor Paranoia," Aisha said.

"Good." Harri hesitated for a moment before she added, "Speaking of which, Delante left for Honolulu this morning."

Aisha cursed under her breath. "I wanted to be home before we set your plan in motion."

"You folks are the ones who decided to catch the commercial flight under your own names, which alerted Corvus. We're getting extra help from the Canyon Pointe FBI office. Dreyfuss has managed to piss off everyone there, not just Eddie." Harri chuckled. "I had him file charges for Delante's two attempts on my life."

"You sure that's what you want to do?"

"I look at it as more of a delaying tactic." Harri slurped something. Given the time of day, it was probably coffee, but it made Aisha wish she'd gone for a beer with the guys. Anything to settle her nerves, but she couldn't.

At least not for another five months.

"Speaking of my ex," Harri continued. "He's already spoken to Jimmy."

"Damn, I hope he gets to us before Delante does," Aisha muttered. "You know that asshat will bring muscle with him."

"I'm sorry, but there's no way for any of us to get to you guys before Delante," Harri said. "Make sure you stay in public places."

"I just hope we don't get delayed meeting our connecting flight." Aisha blew out a deep breath. "I'd really like to sleep in my own bed with the right person."

Harri laughed. "Don't forget to call me when you reach Honolulu."

"I won't."

But after Aisha hung up, worry scratched at her nerves. Harri's plan was ambitious, but it assumed too much about Trubble's ego and not enough about Black Death's. Aisha had first-hand experience when it came to the male weirdness involving children.

If her ex-husband Cal was so desperate for his own progeny, what would Black Death do to gain control of his daughter?

⁘⸎⁘

Aisha groaned and stretched when the pilot announced the plane's arrival in Honolulu. As uncomfortable as she was in the tight confines of coach, the guys' joints had to be killing them. Even worse, she had to sit between them the entire flight. She could feel Rey tense up every time Steve spoke. Apparently, their little talk at the bar hadn't gone as well as she had hoped.

"Too bad we can't stay a few days," Rey murmured as the jet rolled toward the terminal. He'd obviously wanted to stay in Singapore, too, from the way he had been peering through the windows the entire layover.

"If Patty didn't face losing Grace, I'd agree." She smiled at him.

"The surfing is awesome on O'ahu's North Shore." At the dirty look Rey shot Steve, he shrugged. "I mean when you two come back after the baby's born."

Once the jet parked, they unbuckled seatbelts, gathered their carry-ons, and joined the crush of tourists heading for customs. None of the officials said anything about Rey or Steve's passports. For a brief instant, Aisha believed they'd make their connecting flight to the mainland.

Until a balding man in a black suit stepped in front of her.

"Ms. Franklin, would you and your companions come with me, please."

"And you are?" She looked around them and counted five other men dressed the same way. Lord only knew how many of the civilians belonged to him.

He reached into his inner jacket pocket and held up his ID. The blue, white and red shield of the National Superhero Bureau glimmered next to his name.

Crap. Where the hell was Jimmy?

"What's this about, Agent Willis?"

He folded his ID wallet, slid it back in his pocket, and glanced around at the crowd. Everyone around them was preoccupied with their own business.

"It concerns one of your clients, Ms. Franklin. May we please escort you to a facility where we can talk? I don't think you wish to out a client in public."

"No, I wouldn't." She regarded the agent for another moment, but he wasn't nervous or excited. He seemed like just another government stooge doing his job. She released her breath. "As long as you understand my legal partner will be expecting my call before we are scheduled to board our connecting flight. Any delay, and she will raise holy hell with your boss."

"Understood, ma'am." He gestured to his right. "This way."

Rey shot her a questioning look, and she shook her head. Fighting their way out of this situation in public wasn't their best option. But after everything that had been done to him, she couldn't blame him for his distrust of the government agency. Thankfully, Steve followed her cue, too.

Agent Willis led them to a secure section of the airport. Or what the government deemed secure. Their locks made the Lechuza Building's security look like Fort Knox. He escorted them to a small room and left.

A folding table and four cheap plastic and aluminum chairs were the only things in the holding area. Well, if Aisha didn't count the camera in the ceiling and the two-way mirror.

"What the hell is going on?" Steve muttered.

Aisha cocked her head. "No clues after what happened to you in Honduras?"

"You're blaming this on me?"

"Watch your tone when you speak to her," Rey snapped.

"I was kidnapped and brainwashed," Steve retorted. "I think I have a right to be pissed."

"So was I!"

"Stop it! Both of you!" Aisha glared at them. The twins looked everywhere else in the room besides her and each other. "I need everybody's cooperation because I want to go home as much as the two of you do."

The door opened, and a different agent entered the room. Salt and pepper hair and deep-set brown eyes were the only things that truly distinguished him from the NSB agent who had approached them in the international terminal.

"Ms. Franklin? I'm Agent Smith. Why don't you and your clients have a seat?" He gestured at the chairs.

Aisha crossed her arms. "Not until you tell me why we're being detained."

"It's standard procedure to debrief a registered superhero who has been declared dead."

"First—" She stepped into Smith's personal space. "You will tell me who authorized the alert to Captain Justice's pager on the morning of July 5th."

Smith blinked. "I don't know what you are talking about."

"That's a lie!"

Aisha held up her hand, but she didn't look at Rey. He didn't say anything more after the initial outburst. She also remained silent and waited for Smith to make the first move.

Pink crawled up the agent's neck. "I can't give you that information, ma'am."

"Then tell Byron Trubble to be careful where he walks because there's snakes in the grass."

"I-I don't know what you're talking about." Smith tugged at the knot of his tie.

She swallowed her own fury at his bald-faced lie. "My client is still well within the time frame to make his official statement. If you're not willing to play nice, there's no reason for me and my clients to remain here." She headed for the door.

The agent darted between her and the exit. "I can't let you, urp—"

Steve picked Smith up by the waist. "You heard the lady."

"Don't hurt him," Aisha ordered before she walked out the door.

"Yes, ma'am."

"You sure that was wise?" Rey whispered.

"It is if they're trying to detain us until Corvus gets here," she whispered back. "Harri said Delante's on his way."

Steve jogged up to them as they strode toward the exit to the main terminal. "Don't worry. I set down Mr. Smith gently."

The other NSB agents merely watched the three of them as they walked past. Aisha watched everyone from her peripheral vision. It couldn't be this easy. If the NSB wanted to restrain them, they would have brought local supers, but no one made a move toward them.

Aisha reached for the main door's lever when it swung open. Her breath froze in her lungs. She'd never seen the man walking in except through photos Tim and Arthur had hacked from the Corvus servers.

Valentine Delante, AKA Crazy Jim, Corvus's top wetworks man after Black Death.

And he'd brought back-up with him.

CHAPTER 44

Rey yanked Aisha behind his back, and Steve moved to stand shoulder-to-shoulder with him. At least, the idiot was keeping his priorities straight.

Delante's face twisted into a sick grin. "So, there really are two of you."

"You're the guy who tried to strangle Harri," Rey growled. "Twice."

Delante rolled his eyes. "You threw me into a car. I was in traction for a month. I think that makes us even." He looked at Steve. "Or was that you who tossed me around?"

Rey scanned the three men standing behind Delante. He'd bet his entire book collection all three were supers, but none of them were familiar.

"If you gentlemen are finished posturing, we have a flight to catch." Aisha ducked under Rey's arm.

His hands twitched, but yanking her behind him again was liable to result in Aisha pulling Harri's favorite trick. With her HRSP, Aisha could actually hurt him. And he'd like to have a couple of more kids.

"Whoa, there!" Delante eyed her hot pink cast. "Did the boys get a little too frisky with you, Miss Aisha?"

"You have no authority here, Delante. You don't exist, remember?" she said coolly.

"I'm just here to collect a dead man." He smirked. "Smith, why didn't you restrain these assholes?"

Rey looked over his shoulder. The NSB agent propped a hip on the closest desk.

Smith shrugged. "Based on what? Superheroes come back from the dead all the time. His attorney has already told him he's got to make a statement to the NSB about his absence within three days of returning to the United States. He doesn't have to make it here if he doesn't want to."

Rey gritted his teeth. Damn, what he wouldn't give for one of his powers being telepathy to ask Aisha what the hell was going on. A slight smile played across her mouth while Delante looked positively pissed.

A fifth man strolled down the corridor toward them. Delante and his team split and hugged the walls to keep their eyes on everyone.

The newcomer filled out his navy blue suit with muscle, and his demeanor reminded Rey of Harri's ex-husband Eddie. He pushed back the edges of his jacket to display an FBI badge on his belt as he approached and grinned, his teeth white against his dark skin.

"Am I too late to the party, Agent Smith?"

"Nah," Smith said. "What's your interest in our visitors, Special Agent Thompson?"

"We gotta report some unauthorized yahoos pretending to be federal agents were harassing the staff and clients of a law firm back on the mainland." The FBI agent sucked on his teeth. Behind him, two of Honolulu's supers appeared at the end of the hallway—Typhoon Mary and Iolani.

Now, Rey understood why Harri, Aisha, and Tim constantly quizzed him about the public identities and powers of known supers. He and Steve would have a hard time getting past these two ladies using brute strength even if they didn't take Delante's side. And he hated the glimmer of doubt in the back of his mind that said Aisha may be in over her head.

Delante's expression flickered as he analyzed the situation. "I'm trying to make a citizen's arrest." He jabbed a finger in Rey's direction. "He assaulted me in May in the city of Canyon Pointe."

Aisha strangely said nothing.

"You a super?" Thompson looked at Rey.

At Aisha's nod, he replied, "Yes, sir."

Thompson waved casually toward the NSB agent. "That's the guy you need to file a complaint with. What's the turnaround time for restitution these days, Smith?"

"Depends on what the Canyon Pointe Police Department and local hospital reports say." Smith shrugged. "A couple of weeks if you've got copies with you. Do you have copies, Mr.—?"

Delante kept his mouth shut.

"I'm going to need to see some ID, gentlemen," Smith said as he walked toward them. "You see, I have a warrant for the arrest of a Mr. Valentine Delante for impersonating an NSB agent."

"Really?" Thompson said. "I need to see IDs, too. I have a warrant for Valentine Delante for two counts of attempted murder."

The Corvus assassin smirked. "Of course, we'll show you our IDs. Won't we, boys?"

Thompson checked the photo IDs of the three men accompanying Delante first. When he got to the Corvus assassin, he took a very long look at the passport. Finally, he shook his head.

"You know, Mr. Delante, if you hadn't handed me a fake passport, things would have gone so much better for you." His gaze swept the other three men. "And now, I have to assume you gentlemen also showed me fake identification. The question is whether Agent Smith or I get to add charges of assault and destruction of public property."

"There hasn't been any assault or property damage," Delante said through gritted teeth.

"Yet." Smith said. "You see, both the FBI and the NSB requested Typhoon Mary and Iolani's presence in order to serve their respective warrants." He indicated the two women behind him. "Are you four gentlemen planning to resist arrest?"

Part of Rey wished they would just so he could pound someone.

The three men with Delante looked at Rey and Steve, then the superheroes at the other end of the hallway, and finally at each other. They turned to Special Agent Thompson and shook their heads.

However, a nervous tic had Delante eyes and mouth twitching. "You'll both lose your jobs for this."

Thompson ignored him. "Smith, you want to book him for your charges while I escort Ms. Franklin and her party to their gate?"

"Sure," Smith drawled. "Thank you for cooperation in this manner, Ms. Franklin."

"Thank you for yours, Agent Smith."

Steve lifted an eyebrow, the confused expression terribly familiar.

Rey shrugged and followed Aisha and Agent Thompson. Steve matched his pace.

They crossed into the domestic terminal before Agent Thompson said, "Lemme guess. I'm the first one to meet your baby daddy."

"Shit," Aisha muttered. "Does everyone in the family know?"

"You do know LaShun, don't you?"

Aisha and the FBI agent burst out laughing. They paused and turned to face Rey.

"Honey, this is my cousin Jim Thompson." She gestured toward him with her uninjured hand. "Jim, this is Rey Garcia and his twin brother Steve Connors."

Everyone shook hands politely before they continued walking.

"Are you really an FBI agent?" Steve frowned at the man.

"Yes, I really am." Jimmy turned to Aisha and tapped her upper arm with the back of his hand. "Tried to recruit Aisha here, but she wanted the big-time law firm corner office. By the way, why didn't you tell me Eddie and Harri had gotten divorced?"

"Because I'm not LaShun," Aisha said with a grin. Her smile faded. "How'd Aunt Queenie deal with the news about me not being married?"

Jim chuckled. "Grandma dealt with it better than Marvin from what I hear. Did he really deck one of your employees, thinking he was the father?"

Aisha grimaced. "Unfortunately."

"Wait a minute." Rey's attention flicked between the two. "Your dad hit Arthur?"

She sighed. "No, Tim. I'll explain it to you later. I promise."

Where the hell would Aisha's dad get the idea Tim was the father of her baby? Rey tried to squelch the ugly whisper of jealousy inside his head. What exactly had he missed over the last two months that Aisha hadn't mentioned on the flight from Singapore? Well, there was one thing he could ask about.

"That doesn't explain what happened back there." Rey jabbed his thumb in the direction they'd come from. "Or the warrants for Crazy Jim's arrest."

Aisha rolled her eyes. "How many times have Harri and I told you? Behave yourself and let us do the legal lifting."

"You two set him up?"

"Actually Harri and Susan came up with the plan." Aisha shrugged. "And let's not discuss this anymore in public. I'll tell you everything later."

"You've been saying you'll explain it later for the last two days," he growled.

"Do you know how many Corvus agents are here in the Honolulu airport?" she murmured.

He shook his head. "Do you?"

"No, and that's what worries me." She looked up at him. "They've already threatened to take our baby. So, would you please do this my way for now? That's all I'm asking."

Her big brown eyes begged him. And Aisha Franklin was not a woman who begged.

He nodded and remained silent.

The one thing Aisha had wanted most in her life was to have a baby of her own. This wasn't about her treating him as incompetent because of their age difference. This was her protecting their son.

The question that really bothered Rey was whether Aisha still wanted him in her life now that she had the child she'd always wanted.

CHAPTER 45

Harri jumped when her cell phone vibrated across her desk, then breathed a sigh of relief when she saw it was Aisha. She tapped the answer icon.

"Please tell me you and the boys are in Honolulu."

"We're at the gate." Aisha chuckled. "Rey and Jimmy both say hi. Now I'm getting the ugly glare that I should have added Steve in that greeting.

"So did your cousin get to meet our old friend from the park?"

"Yep. You know Uncle Crow's gonna have a fit about this."

Harri stifled a yawn. "He shouldn't have threatened the babies if he didn't want us to retaliate. By the way, Baby Daddy tried to cancel his appointment this afternoon."

"And?" Aisha asked breathlessly.

Harri leaned back in her office chair. "The child advocate refused, so our buddies in Asia shouldn't have any problems before the next court hearing."

"That's great. It means I'll be home in time for the fireworks. How's our present for our overseas buddies coming?"

"He's working on it as we speak."

A sigh that could only be called relief whistled through the receiver. "That'll be a load off the captain's mind. How's she doing?"

Harri didn't have to ask if Aisha meant Patty. "Calm thanks to a certain person. You were right to bring him aboard."

After a pause long enough Harri thought she lost the signal, Aisha said, "Can I get that in writing?"

"No, you cannot. You were the one who taught me never give documentation to another attorney if we can possibly help it."

Aisha laughed. "Glad you learned something from that fiasco in moot court."

Harri didn't want to hang up yet. Emotion clogged her throat. "C-can I talk to him?"

"Sure."

It almost sounded like her law partner understood. Maybe she did. Harri sure wouldn't have kept it together half as well as Aisha had if Tim disappeared for two months.

"Hey, Harri."

Her eyes watered at Rey's voice. "Hey, kid. Sorry we didn't find you right away."

"It's not your fault, Harri—"

"If I hadn't pushed you into registering—"

"No one would have given a shit when I disappeared," Rey interjected. "And I hate to say this in front of him, but Steve's family doesn't have the resources mine does to get us out of trouble."

A voice in the background protested, and there was the sound of flesh striking flesh.

Rey laughed, and that sound made two tears roll down her cheeks. "Mo-o-om, Steve's hitting me."

More rustling over the phone before Aisha came back on. "Stop it, you two. I'm not missing my plane home if you get hauled off by the air marshal." Apologies murmured in the background. "Hey, girl! *I'll* see you in the morning."

Harri laughed amidst her tears. "I'll be there to pick you up."

She hung up and grabbed a couple of tissues to wipe the moisture from her face. But the few trickles turned into a torrent as the pent-up fear and rage and relief poured out of her. She curled up on the nearest corner of her office couch and stayed there until Tim came to find her hours later.

⁂

Miguel generously allowed Harri to borrow his minivan to collect her way-wards at the airport at six a.m. Tim came along, claiming to keep her company. She would have believed him if his pockets weren't full of Ghost Owl gadgets.

Thankfully, he didn't try any other superhero shit and insist he drive.

"You know, we should really think about buying one of these," Tim said as Harri merged onto the freeway.

"Why?" She shot him a suspicious glance. Traffic was fairly heavy, but she was heading out of the downtown area. The outbound lanes weren't at a crawl like the inbound ones.

"At the rate we have to keep borrowing Miguel's for airport drop-offs and pick-ups alone?" Tim offered. "Not to mention superhero shenanigans, it'd pay for itself in taxi and Uber savings alone."

The tension along Harri's shoulders and neck eased. "I suppose you're right."

"You were that worried I'd bring up us having kids?"

She shrugged. "It's not like you can't go out and find some young thing…"

Tim laughed, long and loud. Something she hadn't heard much of over the last couple of months. When he finished, he shook his head and said, "I'd much rather spoil everyone else's rugrats rotten before we send them home. Besides, you're the only one who can put up with me."

"Besides Miss Purrception, you mean?" She shouldn't have gone there, and she knew the minute the words left her lips.

Tim was silent, but she could feel his attention on her.

"Is that what's bothering you?" he asked softly. "You were afraid she'd come back to the states with Aisha and the twins, and I'd dump you for her?"

Harri blew out a deep breath. "A little."

"Harri, Monica Reinhold is older than you, so technically, you're the pretty, young thing in my life."

"You knew who she was?" Harri couldn't keep the accusatory tone out of her voice.

"I didn't look her up until we found out she'd been picked up with Rey in Tokyo," he said.

"You sound terribly defensive for someone who said it was only a rooftop fling."

For a long time, the interior of the minivan remained silent. It wasn't until she pulled onto the exit for the airport that Tim cleared his throat.

"What have I said about taking your anger out on me?"

"I'm not taking anything out on you," she protested. She'd gotten everything out of her system on her office couch last night.

Hadn't she?

"I've noticed you do it more when things are going well, like Rey coming home."

She glanced at Tim. False dawn and the flicker of oncoming headlights formed weird patterns on his features.

And he was totally right. Again. A fact that sent a wave of old familiar anger through her. She opened her mouth to yell, but that's exactly what she would have done with Eddie. And look how that turned out.

She released another deep breath. "You're right. I'm sorry for taking my guilt over Rey out on you."

"I don't suppose I can get that in writing," Tim teased.

"I'm not stupid enough to give you anything in writing." she shot back. "Unless you're calling me stupid?"

"Of course not, counselor."

When Harri pulled into the pickup lane, she spotted her crew, and her heart leapt in her throat. Rey's hair was even shaggier than the day she'd met him. A short beard and moustache didn't hide his gaunt appearance. If it wasn't for the way those golden eyes kept looking at Aisha, Harri wouldn't believe he was the same man.

And her partner sported a bright pink cast on her right arm.

Harri threw the transmission into park, jumped out of the minivan, and ran around the vehicle.

"Did you forget something in your phone calls?" She stared pointedly at Aisha's arm.

"This is my own stupidity," Aisha growled. She pulled Harri into a one-armed hug that threatened to crack ribs. "We're just glad to be home."

They parted, and Harri hesitated, but Rey swept her into a bear hug.

"Really glad to be home," he murmured in her ear.

"I don't move as fast as the boss does, but I wouldn't mind one of those hugs," Tim said.

Rey released Harri and turned to Tim. She half-expected them to do the manly clasp of the forearms, shoulder bump, and two slaps on the back. Nope, the two men actually hugged. When they parted, they both ducked their heads, thinking that would hide their emotions.

Harri shot a look at Aisha, and her partner grinned back.

"Did Mom and Dad stay out of trouble?" she asked. "Or did you convince them to go home?"

"No such luck," Harri said. "And I wasn't about to send them to a hotel, considering the plan. Jeremy and Leonardo have been babysitting for me." She turned to Steve. "You're going to be my houseguest since Betty and Marvin are still in town."

"You know, I'm really feeling like a fifth wheel here," Steve complained.

"C'mere," Harri ordered. She hugged the super, and he carefully returned it. When she let go, she grinned up at him. "You did good over there, kid."

"Thank you." His mouth twisted before he added, "Once you get through Patty's hearing, can I pick your brain for some career advice?"

She blinked. "Of-of course."

"Speaking of which," Aisha said as she loaded her bag in the back of the mini-van. "Has Judge Barrowman set the evidentiary hearing yet?"

"Next Monday," Harri said. A policeman was starting to eye their group. She headed for the driver's seat.

Everyone piled into the minivan. Steve even graciously took the rear seat so Rey and Aisha could sit together in the second row.

"How's the prep coming?" Aisha asked as Harri pulled into the traffic flow departing from the terminal.

"Get caught up on the other work first, and then we'll do a walk-thru with you and Patty in two days." Despite her lapse in religion after her grandmother's death, Harri prayed they would pull off a miracle in court. Otherwise, she just might kidnap her own goddaughter to keep Grace out of Black Death's, and especially Trubble's, hands.

CHAPTER 46

Aisha stared at the mound of envelopes in her in-tray. It didn't feel like she'd been gone long enough to accumulate that much mail. Harri claimed she and Susan had taken care of anything that had been time sensitive. If Aisha hadn't spent so many hours on a plane and hadn't had so many time changes during her whirlwind tour of the Pacific Rim, maybe she'd feel differently. She'd been to places she'd dreamed of visiting, but she didn't have one damn moment to enjoy any of it.

But dealing with her mail was a much better alternative than dealing with her parents this morning. She grabbed the first envelope.

A soft knock preceded Rey entering her office and closing the door. She still couldn't quite get used to the facial hair. It made him look . . . older.

Maybe Harri was right about her cradle-robbing. Not that Aisha would ever admit it to her best friend.

"I thought you were going to visit with Arthur, Patty, and Grace for a while," she said softly.

"I did." He walked across the room, his steps tentative, and took a seat across from her desk. His hesitancy sent a trill of alarm through her.

"Are your wounds bothering you?" Aisha reached for her desk phone. "I can get Serena over here—"

"No, that's not . . ."

Something else rippled through her. This was the first time they'd really been alone since the morning he disappeared. Was he about to break up . . .

Air froze in her lungs. He'd spent time alone with Miss Purrception. Just the two of them. Monica rescued him after Aisha had given up on finding him. Could she really blame him if he left her?

"There's something you need to know." Rey reached into his pocket and pulled out a small jewelry box. "I bought this for you before Professor Paranoia, before . . ." He set the navy blue velvet-covered cube on her desk. "I understand if you don't want it. Don't want me."

Her lungs burned, demanding she release the carbon dioxide. She exhaled as she picked up the box, too scared to lift the lid.

She looked up at Rey. "After you disappeared, Miguel told me you'd taken him with you to ring shop." She swallowed hard. "He didn't want me to think you'd left on purpose."

"I'm not Cal." Hurt lay in Rey's golden eyes. "And I don't understand why you told your parents Tim was the father of your baby."

"Because I didn't want them to think I was so starstruck by you, by Captain Justice, that I'd do something stupid." She shook her head sadly. "And I wanted to hurt my dad because he got all self-righteous about me being a single mother. Because I thought you were dead, and Trubble threatened to take our baby if we outed him."

"I wouldn't leave you, and I wouldn't leave any child of mine." His voice carried the low, throaty growl of a jaguar. "Not by choice."

"I know. Deep down, I know that," she said softly. "Can you forgive me for not finding you sooner?"

"Can you forgive me for disappearing for a couple of months?" A wry smile tilted his facial hair.

The odd murmur in the reception area penetrated Aisha's swirling emotions. "Why is everyone crowded around my office door?" she whispered.

"Because when I retrieved the ring I'd planned to give you from Arthur, Patty was a little miffed." Rey grinned. "Apparently, she'd found it a few weeks ago and thought Arthur had bought it for her."

Aisha covered her mouth, but it was no use. She burst out laughing. "Please tell me he's still alive."

"He is." Rey shrugged. "He planned to ask her to marry him, but Susan told him to not even think about it until the custody case was settled. That seemed to mollify Patty."

Aisha rubbed her left temple. "Until she decides to give Susan a hard time about interfering with her life."

"You mean Harri doesn't interfere enough?"

Aisha laughed again. Outside her door, Harri hissed at everyone to shut up because she couldn't hear what was going on.

"If there's something you want to ask me, you might want to hurry," she whispered as she stood and circled around her desk. "The natives are getting restless." She sat on Rey's lap and handed the box to him.

He lifted the lid. Inside, a plain gold band with a solitaire diamond nestled in black velvet. It was perfect.

"Aisha Franklin, would you marry me?"

She smiled and cupped his cheek. "I would be honored to, Reyes Garcia."

He plucked the ring from the box, placed the box on her desk, and drew her hand from his face before he slid the ring on the appropriate finger. His kiss sent tingles all the way down to her toes.

"I missed you," she murmured.

"*Dios*, you have no idea how much I missed you, too."

More voices came from the other side of her office door. Two of them she knew too well. She sighed.

"You ready to meet the future in-laws?"

Rey eyed her. "Is your dad the one threatening to bust open the door?"

"Yep."

"Then we'd better go out there before he belts Tim out of frustration." Rey grinned.

Hand in hand, they stood and headed toward her office door. And their future.

CHAPTER 47

Three days later, Harri tensed when Lisa and Black Death entered the court-room. The lovesick look he shot in Patty's direction almost made Harri feel sorry for the super. Any sentiment was quickly quashed when Black Death's expression turned hateful toward Arthur.

Lisa lifted a questioning eyebrow. Harri nodded. She and Susan joined the opposing attorney by the empty jury box.

"My client verified what you told me," Lisa said softly. Most people wouldn't be able to hear their conversation, but Harri knew Aisha and Rey listened from the intent look on their faces. Steve leaned over, his lips close to Tim's ear. No doubt the super repeated everything to Tim. He insisted on bringing his wheelchair so he could hide weapons that would pass security in case Black Death made the stupid decision of taking Grace by force.

Harri just wished Betty and Marvin had stayed locked up in the Lechuza Building where they would be safe. But since Rey popped the question to their daughter, they'd spent nearly every waking minute with him, which includ-ed following him to the courthouse. Though Harri expected a little of Betty's motivation was hero worship once he verified his former superhero moniker to them.

"Look, he's doing this by the book, regardless of what you think." Lisa ran the tip of her tongue over her upper lip, a nervous gesture from long before law school. "If Professor Venom can clean up his act, why can't your client give that same consideration to Mr. Wilson?"

"Did he threaten you?" Harri breathed the words more than said them.

"Not him." Lisa glanced at her client.

Harri looked at Black Death. He was far too confident-looking. It ex-plained Lisa's nerves.

"Who?"

"Someone trying to pretend she was one of your supers. Said if I didn't throw the case, I'd be sorry."

Shit. That certainly explained Black Death's smug attitude. An incident like that would normally make Lisa dig in even more on a case. Harri had to give Corvus credit for finding out which buttons to push, but they'd underestimated her law school classmate.

"What happened?" Susan asked.

"I called her on her bullcrap." Lisa shook her head. "Said she was probably one of the heroes you forced to pay restitution, and if she was a friend of Black Death's, she wasn't doing him any favors by pulling this stunt." From the sly expression on Lisa's face, she'd called Wilson immediately afterward and chewed him a new one.

"Any chance your client would be willing to mediate?" Susan asked.

"You're the one who was adamant about not negotiating." Lisa shook her head. "I tried when I pointed out you knew more about him than I did. However, the Professor Venom thing is his deal-breaker."

"Then I guess it's pistols at five paces in ten minutes," Harri murmured. The attorneys dispersed to their separate tables. Harri took a good look at the three people sitting behind the plaintiff's table. Compared to the legion of superheroes and neighbors who came to testify on Patty and Arthur's behalf and the dirt Harri found on Cade Wilson, this may be easier than she thought.

Assuming their judge wasn't compromised. Corvus could be threatening Barrowman like they tried with Lisa.

"Well?" Patty whispered when Harri and Susan took their seats.

"He's not backing down," Harri replied.

Susan scribbled on her legal pad and nudged it to where Harri could read it.

Barrowman comp?

So their new associate was thinking the same thing—Wilson was a smug bastard because he or someone else from Corvus had gotten to the judge after their stupid stunt with Lisa didn't work.

Harri leaned forward and scribbled on the pad.

She may already be part of the flock.

Susan read Harri's answer and pursed her lips. There wasn't a damn thing they could do at this point if Barrowman was compromised. They would need proof, and by the time they had it, Black Death could whisk Grace out of the country.

Harri clenched her left fist and pressed it against the top of her thigh. Too bad neither she or Tim still had their family fortunes. They could have taken Patty's little family someplace else. Hidden them from Corvus. But in both their cases, the money was long gone. And they'd be guilty of the same shit she accused the supers of—using their power to get out of doing their fair share.

Deep down, Harri knew she should be grateful. They'd managed to score one and a half of her desired hat trick. Rey was home, even if his superhero career was in tatters. Valentine Delante and his cronies had been denied bail in Federal court, according to Aisha's cousin Jimmy. And the last Tim had heard, Eddie's boss was on administrative leave pending an investigation into his illegal wiretapping of his own employees.

But this was the goal she really needed to score for Grace's sake.

The bailiff rose to his feet. "All rise. Judge Joanna Barrowman presiding."

Everyone in the courtroom stood as she strode to the bench and took her chair.

"Be seated."

The crowd resumed their seats while Barrowman put on her reading glasses and examined the case paperwork in front of her.

"This is an evidentiary hearing on In Re Grace Harriet Ames." The judge looked up from the file. "Does the plaintiff have any preliminary motions before we begin?"

Lisa rose to her feet. "Your Honor, plaintiff once again objects to the superheroes listed on defendant's witness list. They have no direct knowledge of the Ames household. Any testimony would be hearsay."

Susan jumped up like the proverbial jackrabbit. "Your Honor, since the entire sum of plaintiff's reason for him to have sole custody of Grace Ames lies on the character of my client and her boyfriend, any and all character witnesses are appropriate in this circumstance."

"Objection overruled." Barrowman eyed Susan and Harri. "Any preliminary motions from the defendant?"

"No, ma'am." Susan resumed her seat.

Harri resisted the urge to sigh. She was used to being on the plaintiff's side and having some control. The only good thing was Aisha held Grace behind the defendant's table. If things degenerated into a free-for-all, she would get the baby to safety while the guys and their superhero clients dealt with Black Death.

Lisa called Black Death to the witness stand. He kept to the same sob story he'd given Harri in the hospital garage elevator the day Grace was born. This time, he added how his parents were looking forward to meeting their new granddaughter, how his sister offered to help raise the baby, and of course, how he'd already fixed up a room at his house for Grace.

The saccharin-sweet tale made Harri want to vomit more than Aisha's favorite coffee concoction did.

Lisa turned to the defendant's table with a smile worse than Aisha's pixie barf. "Your witness."

Harri made a point of adjusting her reading glasses before she stood, the notes for this hearing in her hand though she had them memorized.

"What did you say your profession was again, Mr. Wilson?"

"I'm a software project manager for Netware Technologies." Wariness narrowed his eyes.

"By your own admission, this position involves a lot of travel. How do you plan to take care of Grace while jetsetting around the world?"

"She would be afforded an education Ms. Ames can't provide by visiting the countries I travel to."

Harri had to give the judge credit. She managed to quell the expression of surprise that started to crawl across her face at Wilson's admission he intended to take Grace out of the U.S. However, he glared daggers at Harri.

She took a couple of steps toward the witness stand, an old ploy she used to prove she wasn't afraid of the supers whose assets she went after as restitution for the city. "Don't you mean you want to keep Grace away from her mother?"

"Objection, leading the witness," Lisa said.

"Sustained," the judge answered. But Harri's question had gotten under Black Death's skin.

"She's sleeping with a supervillain!" Wilson jabbed a forefinger in Arthur's direction.

"Mr. Drallhickey was honest with her about his genetic history before they began their relationship. Were you?"

"Objection! Rule 51." Lisa's strident voice echoed off the courtroom's high ceiling.

Harri looked up at the bench. "Rule 51 only protects registered superheroes in public matters, ma'am. It does not apply to private matters, especially when a civilian's health and welfare are at stake."

"Sustained." The judge was trying very hard to keep a straight face.

Harri turned back to Wilson. "Did you tell Ms. Ames you were a super prior to engaging in intercourse with her?"

Both Wilson and Lisa remained silent.

"Must I remind you that you are under oath, Mr. Wilson?" The judge gave him the stink-eye. The not-so-subtle warning they were about to slap a contempt charge on you was the same regardless of the particular official's age, race, or gender.

"No, I did not," Wilson bit out.

"Why didn't you tell her? No birth control is one-hundred percent effective."

"Because she made me feel normal." Heartbreak replaced Wilson's fury. "I wanted to marry her, but . . ."

"But what?" Harri asked gently.

"Seismic Shift threatened to kill Patty if I didn't do what he told me to do."

An actual admission wasn't what Harri expected, but Wilson continued on in a rush.

"I went to the authorities. About the same time, I really was sent overseas by my employer for seven months. Both I and the feds thought Patty would be safe as long as I stayed away. While I was gone, they built their case against Shift."

Harri ground her teeth. Dammit, he actually had her until he went overboard about Seismic Shit. Wilson's woe-is-me was just another con job.

"Once I learned he was in jail, I came straight back to Canyon Pointe, hoping Patty would forgive me and want to be a family, but she was already living with Professor Venom," he finished with a sneer.

Out of the corner of her eye, Harri noticed Lisa flinch. Her attempts to woodshed Wilson had failed. It always sucked when a client went offscript during their testimony under oath. The ugly expression may not be in the court reporter's record, but judges never forgot that shit.

"If you were that concerned about Patty's well-being, why didn't you tell her you are a super?" Harri said

"I was scared."

"Mr. Wilson, do you know what HRSP is?" She stared into his intensely blue eyes.

He blinked before he shot a furtive look at Patty. "I-I . . ."

"Do you know what HRSP is?" Harri repeated.

He swallowed hard and whispered, "Yes."

"Mr. Wilson, you need to speak up so the court reporter can hear you," the judge instructed.

"Y-yes, I know what HRSP is."

"You claim you wanted to marry Patty, but you didn't tell her you are a super." Harri made a show of consulting her notes, but she'd memorized the stats the minute she found out Aisha was pregnant. "Are you aware a non-super woman is ninety-nine times more likely to have a super baby if the father is a super?"

"Yes."

"Are you aware that one in ten thousand non-super women develop hormone-related super powers when they are carrying a super baby?"

"Yes."

"Your Honor—" Lisa stood. "Is there a point to Ms. Winters' questioning besides reciting facts every junior high student knows?"

"Move it along, counselor," Judge Barrowman ordered Harri.

"Yes, ma'am." She turned back to Black Death. "If you failed to take Ms. Ames' safety into consideration prior to your break-up, Mr. Wilson, how can Ms. Ames, Judge Barrowman, or anyone in this courtroom be assured you will not disregard Grace's safety?"

"She's my daughter," Wilson growled. "She's family."

"So were your biological mother and your sister," Harri replied.

From the stricken look on his face, he hadn't expected her to dig up any facts about him other than the carefully prepared documents he'd given to Lisa based on the fake information Corvus had planted in various government and financial databases. But Corvus had to layer in some truth to make the fakes look believable. And Harri knew what to look for.

Hell, she'd practically written the book on digging up a super's assets despite federal protections for the registered supers. Except this time, there was far more at stake than replacing public buildings, highways, and bridges from damages caused by these spandex-wearing bozos. And she hadn't needed her hacking team to find Wilson's dirt.

"The woman sitting here in court today is not your biological mother, is she, Mr. Wilson?"

He glanced at the spectators on the plaintiffs' side. "No, she isn't, but she was my mother in all the ways that counted. She adopted me."

"What happened to your biological mother on the day you were born, Mr. Wilson?"

Pink flooded his face. He couldn't meet her gaze. "She died in childbirth."

Harri steeled herself for the next part. "In fact, the trauma of your birth was so great to you, it triggered your powers, and you gave your mother a heart attack."

Wilson's head jerked up. "It was an accident."

"But what if your child had your powers?" Harri waved in Patty's direction. "Ms. Ames could have taken precautions if you had warned her you were a super."

"Grace doesn't have powers," Wilson snarled.

"But what if she did?" Harri glared back.

"Objection," Lisa called. "Counsel is asking witness to speculate about facts not in evidence."

"Sustained."

Harri took a deep breath. Her next line of questioning wasn't any more pleasant.

"You said your mother's death was an accident, but the brain aneurysm you gave your sister after losing a game of hide-and-seek wasn't," she said. A single sob came from behind her. "What about the various injuries and diseases you caused in your schoolmates who made you angry?"

"I was bullied in school."

"Yes, there's documented incidents between you and Blake Nolan." Harri glanced at her notes. "He suffered repeated nose bleeds until his corrective surgery. But what about Billy Loomis's leukemia after he asked the girl you liked to the junior high Spring Fling? Or Christine White's perforated stomach after she said no to going with you to the dance after all? And then there's

Glenn Larkin's odd anaphylactic reaction to nothing after he topped you on the honor roll."

"Those happened before I had control of my powers," Wilson growled.

Harri eyed Wilson. "What happens when you can't get Grace to stop crying? How many babies have been shaken to death by non-super parents? How can you guarantee you won't slip when you're lacking sleep the night before you have a big assignment and you lose control of your powers with Grace?"

"That's why I have my family to help."

Wilson's confidence was starting to return. Time for the coup de grace.

"What do you plan to do if Grace does develop powers when she hits puberty? Are you going to send her to a government facility like the one your parents sent you to?" Harri leaned closer to Wilson. "You know what happens to kids there, Cade. Are you going to put Grace through that?"

If they weren't in a very public courtroom, Harri had no question Black Death would have gleefully stopped her heart.

He jumped to his feet and faced Patty. "You would send Grace away, too! You know it, Patty! That's why I didn't tell you. I knew how you'd react—"

Whatever else he said was lost under the hammering of the gavel, Judge Barrowman calling for order, and Lisa pleading loudly for a short recess.

CHAPTER 48

Lisa and Wilson's family managed to hustle him out of the courtroom upon the judge's granting of a ten-minute break. Patty leaned against the nearest wall and hugged herself as Arthur tried to soothe her. Somehow, Grace managed to sleep through the shouting.

"You are going to need a twenty-four-hour guard after this," Susan murmured. "Preferably of the super variety."

"That's why I wanted to handle the cross," Harri said. "I didn't want you and your family in his crosshairs."

Aisha handed Grace to Betty and walked over to join them. "Normally, after that kind of performance, I'd present a settlement offer."

"Not going to work in this case." Susan shook her head.

"No shit." Aisha's lips twisted into a wry smile. "You two did everything but actually say the name 'Black Death.'"

"This isn't a contract dispute over licensing percentages," Harri said. "This is my goddaughter's life."

"No one's questioning that," Aisha replied. "But he's treading the super-villain line with that screaming soliloquy. I hope we didn't push him over the edge."

Lisa and her party re-entered the courtroom. Both Wilson's stepmother and sister had obviously been crying. Unfortunately, Wilson himself appeared calm. Too calm.

Dammit, he was planning something. Harri would bet her law license on it. What could he do to Patty and Arthur that he hadn't already done?

Besides kill them?

Harri repressed a shudder that threatened to vibrate her apart. She'd do whatever she had to in order to keep Grace even if it meant going to jail herself.

The bailiff rose to his feet once again. "All rise."

Everyone scrambled to stand before their chairs or benches.

Judge Barrowman re-entered the courtroom and claimed her seat. "Next witness for the plaintiff."

Lisa called up each of Wilson's family members, trying to mitigate the damage Harri had caused. She couldn't get a good read on what effect their testimony was having on the judge. During her cross-examination, the best she could do was get the witnesses to admit Cade's powers had frightened them when he was a teenager. His parents regretted having to send him to a government training facility, but they felt they didn't have the resources to deal with his powers. All of them emphasized how responsible Cade had become since he'd been trained properly by the NSB.

When Harri resumed her seat, she scribbled another note to Susan.

Think they know about his alter ego?

She frowned and wrote beneath Harri's question.

If they do, they all should get Oscars.

Susan called Patty for their side's first witness. Harri wanted to hug her assistant. She kept calm with the right amount of steel in her replies. On cross-examination, Lisa couldn't shake Patty, even when she tried to poke holes in Patty's testimony about Wilson's weird absences. But when Lisa got to the poor, sad daddy portion of her question, Patty stepped up her game.

"You said you knew you were pregnant the last time you saw Cade." Lisa leaned forward like a girlfriend sharing a confidence. "Why didn't you tell him the truth then?"

"As I said before, it was obvious Cade didn't want to be with me." Patty lifted her chin. "I know what it's like to be a child unwanted by her own family. I didn't want that for my daughter."

"Yet, you didn't give him a chance to decide for himself," Lisa pointed out.

Patty's lower lip trembled for an instant. "He could have told me Seismic Shift threatened my life. He could have tried a long distance relationship with me. He could have even just called me once in the eight months he was gone. You keep asking why I didn't tell him. He didn't care about me or my safety. Not once. Why on earth would I assume he would care about Grace?"

"So what you're saying is you wouldn't gone out with him if you knew he was a super?"

It was a good thing Patty didn't have laser vision. "I wouldn't have gone out with him at all if I'd known he was a lying, cowardly bastard."

The vehemence of her answer made Lisa take a step away from the witness chair. "No . . . further questions for this witness."

While Susan called Miguel to the stand as a character witness, Wilson passed a note to Lisa when she sat back down. She frowned and glanced at the defendant's table before she wrote an answer to him. Anger sparked in Wilson's eyes, and he scribbled furiously on the paper. Lisa sighed and slid the paper into the pocket of her folder.

Harri went back to watching Susan question Miguel before Lisa noticed her attention. Now what the hell had that been all about? Whatever Wilson wanted her to do, she wasn't happy about it. Fear crawled over the anxiety in Harri's spine. What could be more damaging to Patty's case than Arthur's past?

Susan quickly rolled through the superheroes who took the stand on Patty and Arthur's behalf. Sparx's testimony was especially compelling. She admitted she had been the superhero who'd objected to Arthur's presence the most out of all the firm's clients and how his concern for Patty and Grace's welfare when Seismic Shift targeted the law firm and its clients changed Sparx's mind.

Unlike some other judges Harri had encountered, Judge Barrowman was actually paying attention to the testimony. Maybe, just maybe, they could convince her Patty and Arthur had Grace's best interests at heart. Much more than Wilson did.

Finally, Susan called their last witness—Arthur himself. Harri, Aisha, and Susan had debated well into the night about whether to put him on the stand. As Aisha had pointed out, if they didn't control the narrative, Lisa might name him as a hostile witness.

Arthur's face was pale and his hands trembled as the bailiff swore him in, but his expression appeared determined. Harri crossed her fingers he would remember what she told him about staying calm and asking for the attorney to restate the question if he didn't understand it.

Susan quickly laid her foundation. "Mr. Drallhickey, how did you meet Ms. Ames?"

"It was the day Seismic Shift set fire to City Hall while pretending to be me. I was sitting in Java Joe's, a café halfway between City Hall and the Old Courthouse."

"What were you doing at Java Joe's?" Susan asked.

"Working on job applications." Arthur's throat bobbed. "They have free wi-fi for customers. Anyway, I heard another patron say there was smoke coming from the top floor of City Hall. All of us went outside. Captain Justice, before he was officially Captain Justice that is, rescued several people."

Anger brought some color back to Arthur's face. "I went back inside to finish the job application I was filling out when several of the other patrons came in saying they'd heard Professor Venom had started the fire, trying to kill one of the city attorneys. The only city attorney I know is, um, was Ms. Winters. I walked down to the police headquarters where the victims were being treated to see if I could find her."

"By Ms. Winters, you mean Harriet Winters, my co-counsel?" Susan gestured toward the defendant's table.

Harri gritted her teeth at the mention of her full name, but Susan needed to keep this professional.

"Yes, ma'am." Arthur nodded.

Susan cocked her head. "Why did you go looking for Harri Winters, Mr. Drallhickey?"

"When I was really stupid and tried to extort the city a couple of years ago, Ms. Winters advocated to the DA's office on my behalf and requested only time served, a fine, and community service. I could have been turned over to the federal prosecutor on domestic terrorism charges."

"Did Ms. Winters do anything else for you?"

Arthur blushed a brilliant scarlet. "She yelled at me and said if I didn't straighten up and fly right, she'd kick my ass hard enough I'd need a surgeon to get her shoe out."

Everyone in the courtroom, even Judge Barrowman, chuckled at his statement. Everyone except Cade Wilson. In fact, Arthur's testimony only seemed to make the super angrier.

Harri looked over her shoulder at Aisha. Her partner gave a slight nod. Good to know the folks behind her and Susan were keeping an eye on things.

"Was this before or after you found Ms. Winters in the crowd of victims from City Hall?" Susan continued.

"This was during my original charge," Arthur amended. "The day of the fire as I was searching through the crowd, I heard former mayor Quentin Samuels accuse Ms. Ames of being in league with Professor Venom and fire her. I knew it was a lie because I'd never met her before that day.

"After the mayor walked away from Ms. Ames, I went up to her and introduced myself. She was rather upset. In addition to being terminated, she'd lost her purse, phone, and all her keys in the fire. I offered to take her wherever she needed to go, let her use my phone, and bought her some dinner."

"Why would you do that for someone you just met?" Susan asked.

"Because she was pregnant and tired and hurt. Because she was all alone after a supervillain attack." Arthur shot a loving look at Patty. "I know what it feels like not to have anyone care about what happens to you."

"Did you have anything to do with May's fire at City Hall?" Susan prodded.

"No, ma'am." Arthur shook his head vigorously. "In fact, I tried to hire Ms. Winters to clear my name after I learned she'd lost her job, too. She said she couldn't because she was a witness to the incident at City Hall, but she referred me to Ms. Franklin who did."

"How did you come to be employed at Winters & Franklin?"

"I helped Ms. Franklin with some computer and phone issues, so she offered me a job. Technically, I worked for her before she and Ms. Winters officially formed their law firm."

"Did Ms. Ames also work for Ms. Franklin?"

Arthur licked his lips. "No, she, um, she was sort of working for Ms. Winters."

Susan gestured toward Patty. "So you and Ms. Ames were co-workers first when Ms. Winters and Ms. Franklin formed their partnership?"

"Yes, ma'am."

"When did you start seeing Ms. Ames socially?" Susan asked.

"Four weeks and three days ago," Arthur answered promptly.

"But you've been living together since—" Susan checked her notes. "—June, isn't that right?"

"I-I wouldn't call it living together in the conventional sense." Arthur turned bright scarlet. "There had been several attempts on Ms. Winters and Ms. Franklin's lives at that time. They were worried the rest of the staff would be targeted, so I spent a couple of nights on Ms. Ames's couch as a precaution. After the danger passed, I didn't stay at her apartment again until shortly before Grace was born."

"Why is that?" Susan prompted.

"First of all, I was one of Ms. Ames's birthing coaches. Then, my lease on my old apartment expired before my new apartment was ready. She asked me to stay at her place during those few days because she had been experiencing Braxton-Hicks contractions and wanted somebody to stay with her."

"On the couch?" Susan grinned.

"Oh. Yes. Definitely." Arthur's eyes grew big and round as he nodded vigorously. "I would never impose myself on her."

"When did Ms. Ames move into your apartment?"

"The morning of July 8th." Arthur's expression turned grim. "An unknown super was impersonating Captain Justice, and Ms. Franklin told me to bring Ms. Ames and Grace to the Lechuza Building for their safety. It is the most secure place we have."

"Why didn't she move back to her apartment after the danger had passed?"

Arthur shot a glance at Wilson. "Because someone, a man, was following both Ms. Ames and Ms. Winters. Several of our neighbors on Sixth Street noticed the same man in the same car as well."

"Was there any other reason?" Susan prodded.

"Ms. Ames liked the fact I had childcare experience. I worked as Gaia Johnson's nanny through college and graduate school. Plus us splitting our time for Grace's care meant Ms. Winters and Ms. Franklin weren't short-staffed."

Harri breathed a little sigh of relief when Barrowman didn't bat an eyelash on the subject of Arthur's past employment. She didn't seem like the type, but gender roles could be a tricky subject.

"Thank you, Mr. Drallhickey." Susan looked up at the judge. "No further questions at this time, but we reserve the right for redirect."

Lisa was on her feet and approaching Arthur before Susan had resumed her seat. Their new attorney frowned at Harri. She gave Susan a thumbs-up gesture behind the table. They knew Lisa's cross-examination of Arthur would be their problem spot. The rest was up to him now.

"Your threats against Ms. Winters aren't the first time you've threatened a supervisor, is it, Mr. Drallhickey?" Lisa said.

Arthur lifted his sharp chin. "I wrote the threatening letters to Ms. Winters before she employed me. As I said, I made an error in judgment, and I've paid my debt to society."

"I'm referring to Mr. Wallace Cunningham of Nile Computers. Did you or did you not tell him—" Lisa referred at her notes and smirked. "—you would drip snake venom on him for all eternity?"

Arthur sighed. "Mr. Cunningham had passed off my break-thru in quantum state computing as his own. I was so angry the only bad thing I could think of was the Norse deity Odin's punishment of Loki for betraying him."

"So you turned around and embezzled nearly three million dollars from Nile Computers. When Mr. Cunningham discovered your crime, did you attack him?"

"I didn't steal from my employer." Arthur grimaced. "I did punch Cunningham for fabricating the evidence to make it appear as if I had committed the crime. All charges were dropped in that matter."

"But Nile Computers fired you, didn't they?"

"Yes."

Harri's heart broke at Arthur's forlorn expression. It was the same look he had the first time she'd met him face-to-face. Lisa was crushing all the confidence he'd built up since May.

"When did you decide to become Professor Venom?"

"About six months after that. Nile Computers had blackballed me in the industry."

"Do you have proof of that?" Lisa snapped.

"No."

"So any reluctance for another employer to take a chance on you could be solely due to your own behavior?"

"I don't know."

"Come on, Mr. Drallhickey," Lisa drawled. "Would you want to hire someone with a history of violence?"

Susan leapt to her feet. "Objection! Asked and answered."

"Withdrawn." Lisa smiled, one that boded trouble. Harri leaned forward in her chair.

"If Grace were your child, would you want some with a history of violence around her?"

"No." Shame smeared across poor Arthur's face, but he turned and pointedly glared at Wilson. "Which is why all of us at the Lechuza Building were concerned when Mr. Wilson started stalking Ms. Ames and Ms. Winters."

"Why didn't you call the police?" Lisa asked.

"Because we weren't sure who we could trust in the police department." Arthur didn't take his eyes off Wilson.

Lisa frowned. "Are you trying to insinuate the Canyon Pointe Police Department is corrupt?"

"Not all of them."

"Or maybe you didn't call the police because you preferred to take care of Mr. Wilson yourself."

That statement jerked Arthur's attention back to Lisa. "Wh-what?"

"In fact, you turned to vigilantism after supervillainy didn't work out." Lisa's shark smile filled her face. "Isn't it true you are Jatz'om Kuh, the Ghost Owl?"

CHAPTER 49

The courthouse erupted into chaos. Harri and Susan jumped to their feet, yelling "Objection!" Arthur's mouth fell open. Judge Barrowman hammered her gavel on her podium and shouted for order.

Through it all, Lisa tried to maintain a serene expression, but her left eyebrow twitched. Harri had known Lisa would do anything for a client. Hell, that was the reason she hired Lisa when she and Eddie split. But she never believed Lisa would out-and-out lie in court.

Harri's attention flicked toward Wilson. Unless that's what Lisa and the bastard had been arguing about earlier.

"I will have silence, or I'll hold all of you in contempt!" Barrowman roared.

Everyone in the gallery shut up.

The judge eyed the defense table. "Which of you is going to make the actual objection?"

Susan immediately sat.

Harri couldn't blame their new associate for forgetting their plan. Her own heart had lurched at Lisa's accusation. She sucked in a deep breath.

"There's no foundation for such an accusation."

Lisa straightened. "Your Honor, by the witness's own testimony, he has a history of criminal acts and violence."

"I'll allow it." The judge folded her fingers together. "But I warn you, counselor, I take false accusations of criminal activity as seriously as I take actual criminal behavior."

"Understood, You Honor." Lisa turned back to Arthur. "You said a man was stalking Ms. Ames. Who was that man?"

Arthur's voice trembled as he answered, "Cade Wilson. And it wasn't just Ms. Ames—"

"And how do you know my client was following anyone currently living in the Lechuza Building?" Lisa interrupted.

"We observed him parked on the street, both visually and through security cameras," Arthur said with a little more confidence. "He was also seen in front of Ms. Ames's former residence more than once."

"Did you personally see these actions?"

"Some. Not all."

Lisa strode over to her table and pulled out several pages. "Your Honor, I'd like to enter additional evidence, marked as Exhibit F." She handed the top copy to the judge, who put on her glasses and examined the sheet. Lisa stalked over and gave the second sheet to Susan.

Harri looked over her shoulder. Her stomach threatened to crawl up her throat and flee the courtroom when she saw whose signature graced the bottom of the page.

"This is an affidavit from Mr. Wilson's employer, Byron Trubble," Lisa continued. "He was asked for some information by Ms. Winters. When he tried to deliver it, he was confronted by the Ghost Owl in front of the Lechuza building. The Owl told Mr. Trubble that if he didn't stop Mr. Wilson from following Ms. Ames, the Owl would kill both Mr. Wilson and Mr. Trubble. Is this a true and accurate statement?"

Arthur finally closed his mouth and swallowed hard. "Yes."

Harri surged to her feet. "Your Honor, we request a five-minute recess."

"Request denied." Judge Barrowman narrowed her eyes when she glared at Arthur. "Mr. Drallhickey, do you realize you have just admitted to a criminal act while under oath in open court?"

Arthur straightened in his chair and faced the judge squarely.

Shutupshutupshutup! The screaming went on and on in Harri's head, but the words froze in her throat.

"Yes, Your Honor, I do," Arthur stated. "I am the Ghost Owl."

"He's lying!" Harri broke past the paralysis freezing her muscles and jumped to her feet.

"You'll have your opportunity on redirect, Ms. Winters," the judge said.

"He's lying to protect me, Your Honor." Harri steeled herself for the admission. "I'm the Ghost Owl."

It was almost worth the comical look on Judge Barrowman's face if it didn't mean the end of her legal career.

"No, Judge, they are both lying to protect me."

Harri whirled around at Aisha's voice behind her.

Aisha ignored Harri's frantic gesture to shut up, her attention locked on the judge. "I'm the one who threatened to kill Wilson if he didn't stop stalking Patty."

"No, Your Honor." Tim struggled to his feet. "My attorneys and their staff are trying to cover for me. I'm the real Ghost Owl."

Miguel stood. "Judge Barrowman, don't listen to them! I'm Jatz'om Kuh."

"No!" Nix rose and pulled off her mask. A gasp went up from the spectators. "I'm the Ghost Owl. Harri and Aisha convinced me it was smarter to go straight."

The rest of their witnesses, both superheroes and regular folk, jumped to their feet, each of them screaming they were the notorious vigilante.

Once again, Judge Barrowman banged her gavel on the podium. "Everyone settle down now! Or you will all spend the night in the tank!"

The crowd quieted and took their seats.

Harri faced the judge. Her heart hammered, and Lisa stared at her like she'd lost her mind. Maybe she had, but she couldn't let Arthur go to jail. Not for something she'd done.

"I know what you're up to, counselor." Barrowman glared over her glasses at Harri. "You're lucky there's not a jury in here, or I'd report you to the bar for your shenanigans." The judge's nostrils flared. "I might just do it anyway for attempting to cast doubt on your own witness's testimony if you don't sit down now."

"But, Your Honor—"

"Do you really want to spend another night in jail, Winters?" Barrowman growled.

Harri looked at Wilson, and he glared back at her. In her gut, she knew he'd finish the job Seismic Shift had sent him on months ago. And she damn sure couldn't help Patty and Grace if the judge held her in contempt. Susan tugged on her arm, and Harri slowly sank into her chair.

"Continue, Ms. Ashcraft," Barrowman ordered.

Lisa tore herself away from staring at Harri and turned back to Arthur. She cleared her throat. "Mr. Drallhickey, I remind you that you're under oath. Did you personally threaten Mr. Wilson?"

Arthur bowed his head. "No, ma'am," he said in a quiet voice.

"Did you personally threaten my client's employer Mr. Trubble?"

"No, ma'am."

"Why did you say you were the Ghost Owl, Mr. Drallhickey?" Lisa appeared bewildered.

"Because all of us that live in the Canyon Block are the Ghost Owl." He straightened and faced Lisa again. "We have to be because no one else in the city cares. We watch out for each other. We're family."

Harri sniffed back the snot. Family. That's all any of them really wanted. For the worst supervillain ever, he was the greatest dad she'd ever known.

Lisa looked even more confounded. "No further questions for this witness." She returned to her table, but she shot Harri an odd look as she passed.

"Ms. Winters," the judge prompted.

Harri slowly rose to her feet and forced herself to approach the witness stand. Her eyes burned. She couldn't lose it. Not now.

"Mr. Drallhickey—" She sniffed back more snot. "Arthur, why would you say you were the Ghost Owl when you're not?"

"Because Black Death is desperate to get me out of the girls' lives." His big brown eyes watered. "If the only way for Patty to keep Grace is for me to go to prison, then that's a sacrifice I'll make."

God bless him, Arthur had given her a way out.

"Who's Black Death, Arthur?" Harri asked softly.

"Grace's father. Cade Wilson."

<hr>

After a half-hour of deliberation, Judge Barrowman took off her glasses and leaned her elbows on her podium. "The law says both biological parents have equal rights to their child unless, by a preponderance of the evidence, exercise of such rights are not in the best interest of the child."

Dread sat in the bottom of Harri's gut. Patty's grip on her left hand was damn near agonizing. She expected her bones to crack any second.

Barrowman exhaled and glanced at the papers in front of her before she resumed looking at the crowd in her court. "Taking in account today's testimony and the child advocate's reports, physical and legal custody of Grace Harriet Ames shall remain with Patricia Ames."

Harri closed her eyes and whispered, "Thank god." A whimper came from Patty at the same time as a strangled, masculine cry from the plaintiff's table.

"Furthermore, Cade Wilson will be allowed reasonable supervised visitation with Grace Harriet Ames through Mrs. Hartmann at the Lake County Children's Facility. I trust the parties can come to an agreement on this without my input, counselors?"

"Yes, ma'am," Harri said at the same time as Susan and Lisa.

"Counselors, if any one of you, your clients, or your witnesses *ever* pull a Spartacus stunt in my court again—" Barrowman pointed her pen in the direction of the defendant's side of the room. "I'll hold you all in contempt. Make sure the rest of your superhero and attorney associates know that as well."

A scattering of soft "Yes, ma'am"s and "Yes, Your Honor"s murmured through the courtroom.

"And finally, Ms. Ashcraft, if you or your clients bring in an affidavit on an unrelated matter than the one being heard before any court in Lake County, you will be charged with perjury."

"Understood, Your Honor," Lisa said crisply.

Harri quelled the urge to dance around in glee. Lisa wasn't going to get a reprimand because of Wilson and Trubble's stupidity. Barrowman hadn't blinked at Arthur's explanation of Black Death, so maybe the judge knew more about supers than she had indicated in court.

"Court is adjourned." The judge slammed down her gavel before she stood and stalked out through the door leading to her chambers.

Harri found herself enveloped in Patty's hug.

"Thank you, thank you, thank you!"

"You can't keep me from seeing my daughter, Patty."

Harri turn to find Black Death in her face. "Now's not the time, Wilson."

Lisa laid a hand on his arm. "She's not stopping you, Cade. Let me work out a visitation with Ms. Ames's attorneys—"

He whirled to face Lisa. "This is your fault. You made sure I lost."

Tim inserted his wheelchair between Wilson and Lisa and glared up at the super. "If Lisa Ashcraft shows up dead, I can guarantee the Ghost Owl will have a little talk with you, Cade."

"You really think you can threaten me, Four Wheels?" Wilson taunted.

Before Harri could make a retort, Aisha sidled next to Tim and quietly said,

"It's not a threat. Your boss calls me a snake in the grass, but you're just a little rodent who'll never hear the silent wings until the owl's talons are wrapped around you."

Even Lisa blinked at Aisha's not-so-subtle threat. She tugged on his arm. "Let's go, Cade. We don't want to make matters worse."

Harri glanced around and saw why Lisa was worried. The bailiff, the court reporter, and the court clerk watched the tableau. Harri knew from experience they'd report everything to Judge Barrowman. And if Black Death cut loose with his powers, there were too many witnesses for Lisa to keep him out of jail.

Or the whole matter could turn into a supers brawl as Rey, Steve, and the rest of the Winters & Franklin clientele circled protectively around Patty, Grace, Arthur, and Aisha's parents.

Black Death glared at Harri over Tim's head. "This isn't over, Winters. Not by a long shot."

"Cade, stop," Lisa hissed. She tugged on his arm again, and this time, he let her lead him from the courtroom.

Their group released a collective sigh when they disappeared from view. Patty laid a pretty serious kiss on Arthur before accepting Grace back from Betty.

Susan leaned close to Harri and murmured, "He's going to do something stupid."

"Right off the reservation, just like Shift," Aisha added.

Harri didn't say anything as she stared at the open door to the building's main hallway. She'd seen the same scary look in Seismic Shift's eyes every time the bastard had tried to kill her.

CHAPTER 50

Rey insisted on taking everybody living in the Lechuza Building out to dinner that night to celebrate the victory. He'd been a little surprised at what all Aisha had accomplished with the Captain Justice brand after he'd been declared dead.

As they waited for Marta and Rueben to set up the back room, he edged closer to Steve. "How soon do you have to go home?"

Steve's right eyebrow rose. "Why? Looking forward to getting me out of your life?"

Guilt twinged Rey's conscience. Steve had been used by Professor Paranoia, just like he had. And they both had a lot of personal issues to work out, not only dealing with each other, but the wider implications of what they were.

"Actually, I wanted to make sure you were staying through this weekend. I want you at my wedding."

Steve glanced over at Aisha, who was talking with her parents. "Let me ask you something first. How would you feel if I applied to the Canyon Pointe University law school?"

Rey stroked his beard to give himself some time. Part of him resented Steve's presence, but another part desperately wanted a connection. "What about the Peace Corps? Or your MBA?"

"After what happened in Honduras, getting a visa is going to be a pain in the ass, and the Corps isn't going to want someone who's more trouble than they are worth, especially the mounds of paperwork if they're a super." Steve shook his head. "Watching Harri and Susan in action today made me realize how many people need help. Patty's ex lied to her. What if she'd developed HRSP? He put both of hers and Grace's life in danger, all without the use of his powers."

He shrugged. "I want to help people, but I don't want to be wearing tights to do it."

Marvin clapped Steve on the shoulder. "Good to know one of you has the sense to wear trousers." Aisha's father turned to Rey and poked him in the chest. "I have a bone to pick with you, son."

"A bone?"

"Look, I respect that you want to make an honest woman of my daughter, but I can pay my share of this wedding."

"It's just going to be a small affair in front of a judge, sir." Rey wasn't quite sure why Aisha's father was bent out of shape about their decision. She had the big showy wedding with her ex, and she was adamant this affair would be much . . . less. "We were planning a dinner afterwards."

"And you're having it here." Marta strode up to their group with more than a dozen menus under her arm. When Rey opened his mouth to protest, she held up the index finger of her free hand. "No arguments. Everyone on the block was planning a welcome home party for you this weekend. A wedding will be so much better."

Rey looked over at Aisha who smiled and nodded. Of course, she heard the conversation with Marta.

"All right, but you are charging me for the food and labor," Rey said sternly.

"No, you are charging me for the food and labor," Marvin interjected with a glare at Rey. "And no arguments from you, young man."

"You pay for the food. The labor will be our gift to Rey and Aisha," Marta countered.

"Deal." Marvin held out his hand, and Marta shook it.

As they headed into the back dining room, Rey leaned closer to Steve and murmured, "No, I don't have a problem with you sticking around Canyon Pointe."

"You going back to your previous profession?"

That was a question Rey had been mulling. After he'd given his statement to the NSB, the agent he spoke with had asked him the same thing. Aisha told him to take his time.

"Honestly, I'm not sure yet."

"Look, I know Marvin and Betty are going to want you and Aisha at their place for Christmas—" Steve began.

"Are we still allowed to celebrate Christmas?" Rey quipped.

"I don't know, but I'd play nice with the in-laws if I were you." Steve grinned. "What I'm trying to ask is would you two like to come to Seattle for Thanksgiving?"

Aisha's warm hand enveloped Rey's as everyone claimed a chair around Marta's two largest tables pushed together to form one huge table. "We would love to, wouldn't we?"

"Are you going to be allowed to fly by the time the holidays roll around?" He looked pointedly at her baby bump.

Aisha chuckled. "Doctor O'Brien said she's cutting me off after New Year's. Me going into labor on a jet would not be good for the rest of the passengers."

"What ever you want, *azúcar*." Rey brought her hand to his lips and kissed the back.

"Hey! Get a room, you two!" Harri yelled from across the table.

Everyone laughed, including Francisco though the boy probably didn't understand the reference.

Rey looked around the room. Despite Corvus's efforts, and especially Professor Paranoia's, he was home with the people he regarded as family surrounding him.

Maybe he hadn't been wrong to hope after all.

CHAPTER 51

Saturday afternoon, Aisha sat on a kitchen chair in her bedroom and wriggled the fingers of her right hand, enjoying the freedom. The one really good effect of her HRSP was the accelerated healing of her bones. Even Serena's friend Doctor O'Brien had been amazed Aisha had only needed the cast on her arm for a little over a week. And better, the damn thing was gone in time for the wedding.

"Don't you dare smudge the polish I just applied," Jeremy snapped.

"Now, I know why you didn't invite me and Harri to your wedding," Aisha retorted. "You were afraid we'd be as bitchy as you have been at ours."

"Hold still," Leo hissed. "I should have left thorns in these roses to make you behave."

"You'd stick yourself more than me," she shot back.

But she held still while Jeremy painted the nails of her left hand and Leo arranged the flowers in her hair. Leo had pulled her hennaed dreds into a high knot. He used fresh miniature red roses and baby's breath to create a crown around her hair.

She examined the arrangement in the huge mirror the guys had brought with them. "You sure these won't wilt by the time we get to Marta's?"

"Hush, girl!" Jeremy glared at her. "Do you think we'd let you go to your own wedding looking anything less than fabulous?"

Harri burst into Aisha's bedroom. "The guys just left with Rey. You aren't even dressed yet?" She stared at the scene with an appalled look.

"What did I tell you, Leo, honey?" Jeremy rolled his eyes.

"On it." Leo poked one last bloom into Aisha's hair. The stem stabbed her scalp.

She jerked. "Ow! I may be nearly invulnerable, but that still hurts!"

With her motion, Jeremy left a trail of scarlet along her little finger. He made a derisive sound. "That's why she's not dressed yet." He set aside the bottle of nail polish and dabbed delicately at Aisha's skin with a remover pad.

Meanwhile, Leo seized Harri's arm and yanked her to the chair Patty had vacated a few minutes ago. He immediately set to work disassembling her ponytail.

"Hey!" she protested. "I was ready for the wedding."

"You are not going to any wedding trying to look twenty years younger than you are, even if you're dating the most scrumptious ginger on the face of the planet," Leo retorted.

By the time Aisha's nails finished in the nail dryer the guys had brought with them, Leo had styled Harri's hair into a chic, modern chignon. Harri made a show of coughing and choking as he sprayed the final layer into place.

Jeremy helped Aisha into the white sleeveless sheathe she'd chosen. He'd grumbled about it being off the rack when they'd gone shopping at Winters Department Store, but it didn't totally emphasize her baby bump the way the other outfits she tried on had.

Not to mention, it was too damn hot outside to wear anything more even if it were technically the first day of autumn.

"Where are you people?" Patty shouted from the living area. "Arthur's waiting for us downstairs."

"In the bedroom getting tortured!" Harri yelled back.

A clatter came from the other side of the loft. Two seconds later, Patty charged into the bedroom with the handle of Rey's new and expensive frying pan in her hands. She took in the tableau and lowered her makeshift weapon.

"Oh, you were joking," she muttered.

Harri eyed their assistant. "What were you planning to do with a frying pan?"

"Says the woman who took out an assassin with a peanut butter pie," Aisha teased.

"Given everything that's happened this year, someone could have been back here threatening you all." Patty shrugged. "But Arthur's downstairs with Miguel's minivan running with the A/C on high so our makeup doesn't melt off our faces and the flowers wilt before we get there. We need to go now."

Aisha slipped on the plain white leather pumps she'd bought to match her dress. "Then let's go."

When Arthur pulled in front of the restaurant, a large, neon-bright sign was posted in Marta's new door, stating the place was closed for a private party. The tables and chairs had been moved to the roped off parking lot. Paloma, Christina, and Anna were putting the final touches on the decorations. A few people were already gathered, talking amongst themselves until they saw the minivan, and a cheer went up.

Dad waited for them on the sidewalk. He looked distinguished in his new suit. Everyone else scrambled out of the vehicle. Harri shoved the bouquet into Aisha's grip before she followed Patty and Arthur into the building. Dad took Aisha's free hand and helped her out of the front seat.

"Don't know how it's possible, but you look more beautiful than the day you were born." He pulled her into a tight hug.

"I'm glad you're here." She blinked rapidly to keep the tears from falling and ruining her makeup.

He released her and looped her hand around his elbow. "Let's make you an honest woman."

"Da-a-ad," she groaned. But at least, he wasn't making cougar jokes like LaShun had since she and her family arrived from Portland last night.

They entered Marta's. Rueben hit the switch on the portable stereo and strains of "Here Comes the Bride" filled the dining area.

At the other end of the room, Judge Inunza stood, smiling. He'd been surprisingly pleased at being asked to officiate. But it was the man on the judge's left who kept Aisha's attention.

Rey wore the same charcoal suit he had on the first day they met. But this time, he wore a tie the same deep red as the polish on her nails and the roses in her hair. He'd trimmed his facial hair into a circle beard, their compromise because he really abhorred his resemblance to Steve.

She couldn't blame him. She'd probably would have felt the same way if she and LaShun were twins.

But Rey's smile made her toes tingle as Dad escorted her down the rough aisle formed by their friends and family. Dad placed her hand in Rey's, then he glared at the younger man.

"You mess up with my daughter, well, there's not a damn thing I can do about it." He shook his index finger at Rey. "But I know there's people in this room who can, and I'll be calling them."

Everyone laughed, including Rey.

"Dearly beloved," Judge Inunza's voice rang out. "We are gathered here today to celebrate the union of Aisha and Rey . . ."

The rest of his words disappeared in a wave of light-headedness. Aisha concentrated fiercely on keeping her feet on the floor. She couldn't float away in public no matter how happy she was.

Harri jabbed an elbow in Aisha's back. A glimmer of worry shone in Rey's eyes. She belatedly realized the judge had asked the important question.

"I-I do."

"I believe you have rings to exchange," Inunza prompted.

Miguel handed Rey the gold band, and he slid it onto her finger. Aisha did the same with the matching ring Harri handed her.

"By the power vested in me by the state, I now pronounce you husband and wife. You may now—"

Rey lifted her in his arms and kissed her soundly.

When they parted, Judge Inunza cleared his throat. "Next time, let me finish."

"There won't be a next time, Your Honor," Rey said fiercely.

"Damn straight there'd better not be," Mom blurted.

Once again, everybody broke into laughter.

"Time to get the real party started!" Jeremy yelled. He and Leo danced their way out the door.

"Ready to greet the rest of our guests, Mr. Garcia." Aisha smiled at Rey.

Rey grinned at her. "I'll follow you anywhere, Mrs. Garcia."

⁂

"You are not taking his name," Harri protested. "Do you know how much we've spent on everything that has the firm name on it?" Her eyes widened. "You're not going to quit on me now, are you?"

Aisha laughed at the expression of horror on her law partner's face. "I'm not going anywhere. There's nothing wrong with using Franklin for business and Garcia for personal affairs."

People still danced under the strings of holiday lights even though full dark had fallen. The citronella candles in the buckets placed around the parking lot turned party plaza kept the mosquitoes at bay.

Her nephew Devon was in seventh heaven with all the superheroes present. The kid currently had Cobblestone and his nurse friend Claire cornered, showing them his superhero card collection and all the autographs he'd finagled tonight. He squealed when Molly handed him a first edition Nix card.

At the table and ice chests serving as their semi-legal bar, Rey was still getting a large amount of teasing from the men, but he kept looking her way and smiling.

"You could hyphenate," Susan said. "It's not uncommon to use both names."

"It still means changing the marquee," Harri growled.

"Arthur is going to take my name when we get married," Patty said around a mouthful of chocolate mousse. "Mine's so much easier to spell."

"Have you talked to him about it?" Aisha asked.

"Of course not." Patty licked the final bit dessert from her spoon. "He's not ready for the 'm' word yet."

"Speak of the devil," Susan murmured.

Aisha looked over Harri's head to see Marta dragging Arthur in their direction. Little Grace was still firmly strapped to his chest.

Harri looked over her shoulder and turn back to the others. "Should I even ask what he did this time?"

"You sure it was him and not Grace?" Susan chuckled. "I got a whiff of what she did to his kitchen."

Marta stopped by their table. "Ladies, I want to license Arthur's mousse recipe."

"Okay, not what I was expecting," Harri murmured.

Even Arthur seemed surprised by Marta's proclamation.

"Since I handle Mr. Drallhickey's IP licensing, I'd be happy to talk to you." Aisha waved a hand nonchalantly. "But considering this is my wedding day, can we wait until Monday before I draft the paperwork?"

"I didn't mean right this minute, *tonta*." Marta made a face at Aisha. "I don't want him to forget. Even Rueben was impressed with his mousse."

"That's great, honey." Patty beamed up at him.

Instead of beaming back at her like he usually did, Arthur's face went blank.

"Arthur, you okay?" Harri asked.

Blood oozed from his nose and gleamed scarlet in the candlelight.

"Arthur?" Fear flitted across Patty's face.

Grace howled, an unearthly sound. Arthur's body convulsed, and he started to go down with the baby.

Aisha's chair flew backward as she sped around the table. She and Marta caught Arthur, and they eased him down to the concrete on his back. More blood oozed from his ears.

"Serena!" Panic filled Aisha's voice as she eased the screaming baby from her carrier.

"Arthur!" Patty knelt next to Marta on the other side of his prone body.

A crowd had formed around their table. Someone was on a phone with 9-1-1. The physician-assistant-in-training pushed her way past Miguel and Dom.

No, Rey and Steve were herding guests back to give Serena some room. Those who didn't listen got their toes stomped on by Tim and his cane.

Aisha stood and moved out of Serena's way. She tried to comfort Grace, who continued to wail. Her screams didn't sound like any baby Aisha had ever heard.

Serena crouched over Arthur and ran her hands over him. Bloody saliva bubbled in the corner of his mouth.

"Harri, take Grace. I'll get Arthur to the hospital."

"I don't think that's a good idea," Harri said, her voice shaky.

Aisha turned toward her partner. Like Arthur, blood oozed from Harri's nose. Her grip on the back of her chair slipped, and she started to go down, too. Rey zipped over and caught her.

In that space, Aisha noticed the figure on the sidewalk.

Black Death.

CHAPTER 52

Aisha whirled and shoved Grace into Patty's arms before flying toward Cade Wilson. She locked his arm in the hold Tim had shown her, and wrapped her other arm around his neck. She'd moved fast enough even the supers were caught by surprise.

So much for hiding her HRSP.

"Stop it now," Aisha hissed in Black Death's ear. "Or I will break every bone in your body."

An odd tingle ran through her body, almost like somebody tickled her from the inside.

"Wh-why doesn't my power work on you?" he choked out.

She ignored the question. Instead, she glanced over at her partner. Rey had sat the stricken attorney on an empty chair. "Harri? You okay?"

Harri swiped at the blood under her nose while Claire checked her pulse on Harri's other wrist. "Yeah." She glared at Black Death. "I thought you had to touch someone—"

Patty's scream filled the night. "Arthur?" She shook his body. Grace, cradled in Patty's arm, howled even louder at her mother's anguish.

Serena looked up at Aisha, sorrow in her expression, and shook her head.

"Fix him," she growled in Black Death's ear. "One of my friends is not dying on my wedding day."

"I-I can't."

"Can't or won't?" Harri pushed herself to her feet with Claire's help and stumbled towards Black Death, a murderous look on her face.

"Steve," Aisha ordered. Her new brother-in-law snagged Harri around the waist and pulled her back from her target.

"He just killed Arthur!" Rey's expression was almost as homicidal as Harri's.

"You're not a vigilante." Aisha shook her head. "We're going to do this properly."

Patti lay on Arthur's chest, hugging him and the baby while she wept bitterly. Oddly, Grace was now quiet. Maybe she'd worn herself out.

"How are the police or even the feds going to hold him?" Tim asked softly. He leaned heavily on his cane. While he didn't have Harri and Rey's fury or Patti's agony, something filled his eyes. Aisha finally realized it was resignation. Tim would go along if she did snap Black Death's neck. Hell, he'd dispose of the body for her.

She met Susan's gaze. "You going to throw away your ethics and common decency, too?"

The other attorney hugged herself. "I don't want to, but he's a danger, not just to everyone here, but the entire human race."

Qiang stepped forward. Static crackled along her hands and arms. "Girl, if we're going to do this, we need to make it look like an accident."

The other superheroes in the parking lot nodded

"You hear that, Cade?" Aisha murmured in his ear. "No one's on your side. All of this was for nothing."

"Patty! I just wanted us back together!" Anguish filled Black Death's voice. "I wanted the family neither of us had!"

Patty ignored him.

And for the first time, Aisha actually felt sorry for the guy. "You went about the wrong way, Cade." Her attention drifted across her husband and their friends gathered around them.

Her family.

"Is that what this is all about?" she asked. "You don't have a family of your own, so you want to destroy ours?"

"N-no!" His body trembled under her hold. "No. It's just . . . just that he . . . the thought of my daughter raised by a supervillain—"

"Arthur Drallhicky was a hundred times the man you'll ever be," Cobblestone rumbled. "You don't have to dirty your hands, Ms. Aisha. I'll kill him for ya."

"You can't do this." Dad stepped between Black Death and the rest of the wedding guests. "Listen to yourselves! This is what my parents fought against." He whirled to face Aisha. "You wouldn't have that fancy law degree if it weren't for people willing to fight for justice. Or is that just words to you all?" He turned to Rey. "Is it?"

Rey couldn't meet Dad's eyes, and his head dropped. No one in the crowd could meet Dad's fierce gaze. No one but Harri.

"Call Eddie," Dad said. "Tell him to get his people over here now."

Harri shot Aisha a questioning look.

"I'll hold him until the FBI get here," she said sourly. "I'm the only one here he can't affect."

Tim handed Harri his phone.

"Did we fall asleep on the couch again, Gracie?"

Everyone stared down at Arthur as he lifted his head and took in the tableau.

"Patty, why are you crying?"

"Arthur?" She looked up at him, mascara smeared in huge circles around her bloodshot eyes.

"Serena?" Tim said. "What did you do?"

"It wasn't me." The green-haired girl seemed as startled as the rest of the crowd.

Everyone's heads, except Grace's, swiveled to stare at Black Death.

"You said you couldn't do anything," Aisha muttered in his ear.

"I-I didn't bring him back. I-I can't." Black Death seemed as shocked as the rest of the group.

Aisha's eyes met Harri's once again. Good, her partner had the same suspicion, but they needed to play it cool until Black Death was taken care of, and they were back in the relative safety of the Lechuza Building.

⁕

It was several hours later before everyone was home. Tim and Patty insisted Harri and Arthur go to the hospital to be checked out. Susan volunteered to supervise the clean-up of Marta's parking lot.

Aisha turned her loft over to her family, though Devon ended up downstairs with Javier, Francisco, and Qiang's son Connor. The boys had bonded better than any of the parents expected. Poor Miguel would have his hands full tonight.

But Aisha didn't want any of her immediate family in their hotel. Not if Corvus decided to retaliate over Black Death's arrest. Eddie had come up with a ton of charges beyond simple assault for what Cade had done. Of course, Harri's ex being the new head of the FBI office had helped.

Aisha had smiled to herself when Steve insisted on escorting Qiang home. There was definitely more than his brother and law school keeping him in Canyon Pointe.

That left Aisha and Rey watching Grace until her parents got home from the ER.

Aisha smiled to herself as she rocked Grace. It wouldn't be much longer before she'd have her own nighttime routine with her son. The nipple slipped from the baby's mouth. Her eyes stayed closed as she licked her lips and snuggled deeper in Aisha's lap.

Yep, definitely too much excitement today for the little girl. Aisha set the nearly empty bottle on the night stand, stood and lowered Grace into her crib. The baby squirmed once before she settled into the sleep only innocents and dogs could achieve.

Aisha collected the bottle, closed the door behind her, and padded to the kitchen in her bare feet. Her knit shorts and oversized t-shirt felt normal after the way her wedding day ended.

Rey stood by the counter, staring at the teakettle. He hadn't changed yet, though his jacket and tie were slung over Arthur's couch, and his sleeves were rolled to his elbows.

"I thought you didn't have heat-ray vision," she teased.

He looked at her. "No, just waiting for the conventional variety of heat." As if on cue, the kettle whistled. He turned off the burner and poured the hot water into two waiting mugs with teabags.

Rey set down the kettle and looked at her. "Are you disappointed in me?"

"Disappointed? What are you talking about?"

"That I wanted to break Black Death's neck." He shook his head sadly. "That I wanted you to break his neck."

Aisha blew out a deep breath and wrapped her arms around his waist. "I wanted to hurt him, too. It's part of being human."

"Except I'm not human." Bleakness drew shadows on his face that weren't there before he disappeared two and a half months ago.

"Oh, baby." She hugged him tight. "I'm not sure I am anymore either. But we didn't do anything stupid tonight."

"Only because your dad stopped us."

Aisha looked up at him. "A second's temptation doesn't condemn us for eternity. We'll get through this. What I don't get is why his power didn't work on me?"

"Steve and I have a theory, but you have to promise not to laugh."

She chuckled and shook her head, but she didn't dare point out Rey was getting along better with his twin. "I can't promise that. With the insanity my life has become, laughing is the only way I can keep from crying."

"All right, but I warned you." He inhaled deeply and released his breath. "We think Xquic's kiss protected you. Like the Witch of the North's protected Dorothy in *The Wizard of Oz*."

"You are seriously invoking L. Frank Baum?"

"Is it any crazier than our grandfather being one of the Lords of Xibalba?"

His theory wasn't as funny as she hoped. "I think you guys may be right." Aisha shrugged. "We can ask Dad about it in the morning."

"This isn't how I imagined our wedding night," Rey said ruefully before he sipped his tea.

"I never imagined you coming into my life." She smiled and sipped her own tea.

Arthur's apartment door swung open. He walked in with Patty, Harri, and Tim on his heels. Both Arthur and Harri sported huge bruises around their eyes.

"You three, go sit," Patty ordered the rest of her party. "How's Grace?" she asked Aisha as she tossed her purse on the kitchen table.

"Sound asleep," Aisha assured her. "What happened at the hospital?"

"We're both fine," Harri said. She flopped on the couch next to Tim. "Doctors think the exceptional heat caused a sudden change in our blood pressure, which in turned caused us both to faint and resulted in broken capillaries in our faces."

Arthur collapsed in his recliner. "Amazing what doctors can justify to themselves." Patty crossed over to him and curled up next to him in the chair.

Aisha perched on the arm of the couch next to Harri and nodded to her.

"Well, crap," Harri muttered.

"So, Serena confirmed it?" Tim asked. Whether Harri told him of their suspicions was immaterial. The man was smart enough to have figured it out on his own anyway.

"Confirmed what?" Patty eyed them suspiciously.

"That Grace is the one who saved me," Arthur murmured.

"No!" Patty leapt out of the recliner. "She couldn't have! She's not a super!"

"Keep your voice down," Aisha hissed. "She's asleep."

"But-but—" Patty's hands flailed in the air. "She was tested."

"Serena says Grace is a lot more powerful than she is," Aisha continued. "More than even Cade."

"No." Patty hugged herself. "No, it can't be true."

"Honey, we can deal with this in the morning." Arthur patted the spot on his chair Patty had vacated. "It's been a long day." His actions said how bad Arthur felt. Normally, he'd have jumped out of his recliner and hugged Patty.

"I-I need to check on Grace and change my clothes." She rushed from the living room.

Arthur waited until his bedroom door closed before he said, "I don't want to scare Patty, but none of us are going to be safe when Corvus gets Black Death out of jail."

"He's right," Aisha said.

Harri shook her head. "Remember when Eddie told us about the FBI investigation into irregularities in the prosecutor's office and the judiciary of Canyon Pointe?"

"Yeah," Aisha drawled.

"He said he couldn't go into details—" Harri started.

"Eddie has a bead on Trubble." The excitement in Rey's voice was matched by the gleam in his eyes. "You'll have your hat trick."

"Susan blabbed about our plan," Harri replied sourly.

Rey sat on the armchair that matched Arthur's couch. "It came up when I apologized to her for hanging up on her a couple of weeks ago."

"The tell-all has the same information I delivered to Eddie in the spring," Tim said. "Do we go ahead and publish it now?"

Harri shook her head. "We wait until any arrests are made. I don't want to accidentally blow Eddie's case. He mentioned it shouldn't be much longer."

"Then let's hope Eddie really can pull this off." Aisha held up her crossed fingers. Because if Eddie and his FBI team failed at whatever they were planning, there would be hell to pay.

CHAPTER 53

Judge Joanna Barrowman had been expecting the shadowed form in her chambers for the last three mornings. She flipped the light switch. "What took you so long, Byron?"

"I asked you for one simple favor." Trubble watched her with his cold, reptilian eyes.

"You didn't tell me Jatz'om Kuh was more than one person. What did you expect?" She pulled on her robes before she turned back to him. "Now get the hell out of my chair."

"You should have had them all arrested for vigilantism."

"This is a family law court," she said as she crossed to the windows. "All I can do is pass the information to the district attorney. It's up to him to file charges. Oh, wait. Your pet DA got himself arrested for corruption, didn't he?" After she raised the blinds, she grinned at Trubble.

He didn't move. "I should have you killed for your smart mouth."

"You've tried how many times with Harri Winters?" Joanna shook her head. "You're not scary anymore. You're a washed up old man who's lost control of his black ops agents."

"I haven't lost control—"

Joanna crossed her arms. "Where's Black Death right now?"

"That's your fault!" The mask slipped, showing a glimpse of his fury.

She sighed in resignation. "If you're going to kill me, Byron, you're going to have to do it the old-fashioned way."

He pulled out a gun. "You're right, Judge Barrowman." He stood and waved at her chair with the weapon. "Have a seat."

"An assassination?" She moved to take her chair, fear tripping along her nerves. "Over a non-super baby?"

"I may have lost the Ames kid." An ugly grin replaced his scowl. "But I need someone on the bench who will make sure I get Aisha Franklin's rugrat when she gives birth. You've already proved you can't be trusted to do the job right."

She lowered herself and settled against the back of her chair. "If you insist on killing me, then get it over with."

He shoved the barrel into the loose skin beneath her chin. Joanna blinked. The gun roared, but she and her chair were on the other side of the room. Trubble was bent over her desk. Handcuffs clicked shut around his wrists.

With Trubble secure, Blue Racer looked at her. "You okay, Judge?"

She nodded at the superhero. Now, if she could only get her heartbeat to slow before the organ hammered its way through her ribs.

Men burst into her chambers. Most wore vests with "FBI" in bright yellow letters, but acting DA Calvin Johnson stalked over to her. "You sure you're uninjured, Your Honor?"

"I'm fine," she snapped as she stood. Her knees threatened to give out, but she wasn't about to show any weakness in front of Trubble. "Just tell me you recorded everything."

"Yes, ma'am, we did." The rugged FBI agent in charge of the corruption investigation wasn't a looker, but his self-assurance was comforting. "Judge Inunza has offered his chambers for you to take a minute and catch your breath. I'll be down to take your statement."

"Thank you—"

"Special Agent in Charge Edward Lewis, ma'am." He nodded to Johnson. "Take care of her, Cal."

He turned back to the handcuffed man. "I've been looking forward to this, so I hope you don't mind if I take my time. Byron Sylar Trubble, you are under arrest for the attempted murder of Judge Joanna Barrowman. You have the right to remain silent. Anything you say will be held against you in a court of law. You have the right to an attorney . . ."

The FBI agent's Miranda warning faded in the background as Joanna followed the acting DA down the back hallway to the side of the courthouse housing the criminal judges' section. Like the family law portion of the building, the doors blurred together. Johnson stopped in front of a particular door and knocked.

A muffled "Come in" came from the other side.

Pablo looked at them over his reading glasses as they entered. "You okay, Joanna?"

She nodded and sat on one of the guest chairs in front of his desk.

"Is there anything I can get you before the FBI comes down, Judge Barrowman?" Johnson asked.

"No, thank you," she answered softly.

He nodded before he closed the door behind him.

Pablo rose and poured a cup for her from his private pot. "Now that our acting district attorney is gone, how are you really?"

Joanna's hands trembled as she took the proffered mug of coffee. "I was okay until it was over."

"You had him eating out of your hand," said a familiar voice behind her. Joanna looked over her shoulder. Monica Reinhold, AKA Miss Purrception, strode into the room from Pablo's clerk's office.

Guilt tugged at Joanna's conscience. She'd only been an intern when Judge Kavanaugh took Monica's little girls from her. It had been wrong, but both she and the super had been powerless to stop it. Eavesdropping on Kavanaugh and Trubble led to her discovery of Corvus. And in an incredible breach of judicial decorum, Joanna tracked down Rue Liberty and let her know what had happened to her granddaughters.

Monica quickly pulled on jeans and a light jacket over her supervillain suit and pulled off her mask. "I don't blame you for your nerves though. Blue Racer cut it a bit close for even my comfort." She smiled at Joanna.

"Did either Blue Racer or Trubble see you?" Pablo asked.

Monica shook her head. "Both of them were too intent on their respective missions." She hesitated a moment. "Pablo, we might want to consider bringing in the new Ghost Owl on this. Corvus isn't going to stay down with Trubble's arrest, and the FBI wouldn't have their case without the information provided by her predecessor."

"No." Joanna sipped her coffee. "We should warn Aisha Franklin Corvus is after her baby."

The little smile Monica got when she knew something no one else did appeared on her face. "She already knows. The new Ghost Owl warned her."

A month later, Aisha lay next to Rey on the black sands of a secluded beach on the island of Kauai. Sun warmed her skin. This little slice of paradise was simply perfect.

Everything back home has fallen into place after Trubble's arrest. Henry Luxman, one of Aisha's superhero licensing contacts, had jumped all over the Ghost Owl book. Tim's anonymous tell-all had been rushed into production and was on target to be the bestselling book of the year. The rush of legal success was almost as good as flying.

Almost.

"Aisha, I've been thinking . . ." Rey started.

"Ack! No! No thinking on our honeymoon."

He rolled over on his side, his head propped on his fist. "I know I can't go back to being Captain Justice, but I want to go back to superheroing. I see the good Cobblestone's doing with his charity work, and well, . . ."

"You liked those aspects of the job."

"Yeah, I did."

"Hmm." She pretended to think about it. "I want an agreement with both of you that you aren't going to beat each other over the head with my appliances."

Rey made a disgusted face. "You aren't going to let the refrigerator thing go, are you?"

"Hell, no! I'll be telling our grandbabies that story until the day I die."

"Then I agree with your dad, and my new persona will wear trousers," he demanded.

Aisha laughed. "Are you trying to break Jeremy's heart?"

"No, but . . ." Rey glanced at the waves lapping the sand before he looked back at her. "I don't want to hurt Tim's feelings, but I don't want to be Jatz'om Kuh either."

"Not a problem." She grinned at him. "You know Harri will beat him up if he says one bad word about you."

Rey laughed. "Yeah, she would. So you don't think it's stupid?"

"No, definitely not." Aisha hesitated a moment. The idea had been running through her head since the night she'd donned one of Tim's spare outfits. It was insane, but considering the odds were she'd have superpowers for the rest of her life thanks to her mother-in-law . . .

"Baby, what would you say if I registered and became the Ghost Owl?"

If you're enjoying the adventures of Harri, Aisha, and the gang, drop me a line through my website (www.suzanharden.com), Twitter (twitter.com/Suzan_Harden), or Facebook (www.facebook.com/SuzanHardenWriter).

Recommending the 888-555-HERO books to your friends or writing a review would be even better.

If you like your fantasy with a cup of mystery, a teaspoon of legal drama, and a dash of thrills, check out the first chapter of *A Question of Balance*.

A Question of Balance

©2016, Suzan Harden

Since it was Rest Day, I was still in my bedclothes and breaking my fast when Duke Marco's messenger arrived. Setting aside the rich cinnamon bread, I glared at both the nervous young man and my personal assistant Sivan. "Tell me, is there a chance His Grace, his lady wife or his retainers might let me finish one morning meal in peace?"

"When the stars fall from the skies, Justice?" Humor edged Sivan's response.

My displeasure settled on the messenger. His bright scarlet face and hands quivered.

I smiled sweetly, but the boy wasn't comforted by my demeanor. My appearance discomfited nearly everyone the first time they saw me, my lover being the sole exception. "What is so important that your master could not wait for a reasonable time, like *after* Second Morning?"

"My apologies, L-Lady Justice. Duke Marco respectfully requests your presence. A-a body was found in one of the keep's wine barrels." His voice cracked on the last syllable.

Orrin was the third largest city in Issura and had the second largest seaport. While crime wasn't rampant, the city's main problem was disorderly conduct from sailors on shore leave. Or it was until I was assigned as the resident justice last summer. Even then, I was rarely called to investigate normal offenses like theft or smuggling, which the Orrin magistrate and his peacekeepers handled quite ably. It was for inconvenient things like this.

I shoved my plate away, wiped my mouth with my napkin and stood. "Thank you so very much for destroying my appetite."

The boy whimpered. From his voice and his manner, he was the highest ranking page available. No matter if he had heard the rumors many times over, my red eyes had made more than a few grown men wet their smallclothes.

"Run across the street, and request a priest from Light to accompany me."

"Y-yes, ma'am." He fled as if I'd summon demons to eat his scrawny hide.

Sivan didn't bother to hide her laughter any longer.

"You did that on purpose," I accused. According to the gossip I overheard on my way to the temple kitchen one evening, my nickname was the Red Justice. So far, no one had the effrontery to call me that to my face.

Sivan folded her hands primly in front of her. "He said he was instructed to only deliver the message to you, m'lady. Far be it for me to interfere with his duty."

I stalked over to the wardrobe in the corner of my private chamber. Inside were several sets of formal cloaks. To any one else, they looked identical, the black of the Temple of Balance from hood to ankle. But for me, I could still see the blood stains on all of them.

Various laundresses' best efforts not withstanding.

Out of some sense of perversity, I chose the set that still carried the stains of the sorcerer Samael, a distant member of the royal family whom I'd illegally executed to save Duke Marco.

And the world.

Once I'd donned leggings, boots and a silk undershirt, I tied on my robes, pulled up the hood, and added my sword to the ensemble. In the half year since Marco's parents had been found guilty of treason due to their conspiracy with Samael DiRoy, little incidents had been occurring. Small challenges to the duke's authority. Carefully crafted insults.

It didn't help that he'd married a commoner who'd been conceived during the Spring Rituals, though the Lady Katarina was a healer of no mean skill.

So far, the young man had been holding his own. But a body found on his estate would only escalate the problems with the nobility, even if the young lord and his retinue were innocent. Nothing like a good scandal to stir the masses.

I reached the stables to find High Brother Luc, chief priest of Orrin's Temple of Light, already mounted, waiting for me with two of his wardens. Cold raindrops trickled dark purple tracks down his cloak.

I had to hide my delight that he came. "Brother, please don't bother on such an ugly day. Either of your junior priests would do in this circumstance. Surely as the head of your temple, you have more important duties."

"Considering where the body was found, it seemed that our best truthspeller should accompany you, Justice." Amusement flavored his tone. Now that we were both permanently assigned to Orrin, we went through this dance of words every time we met in public since we could not often meet privately without arousing suspicions.

By the Twelve, I missed sleeping with him.

I inclined my head. "Thank you for your assistance, Brother."

Little Bear, one of my own wardens, moved to assist me on my horse. I glared at him, my foul mood spilling over once again.

Luc muffled his laugh, and the warden had the grace to say sheepishly, "My apologies, Justice. I forgot."

Reining in my temper, I said, "I understand, but this behavior must stop."

"Before she knocks someone's teeth out," Luc added. Like Sivan earlier, he didn't bother hiding his laughter.

"Yes, m'lady." Little Bear bowed and turned to his own horse.

It was habit on the warden's part, I knew. Every priestess in my order was blind.

Every single one except me.

The wardens and clerks acted as the justice's eyes. None of the staff at Orrin knew what to do with a sighted justice. Not that I saw the world as they saw it, but I had vision enough I wasn't helpless by any means.

I climbed on my precious Nassa and patted her neck. "Shall we discover what's troubling Duke DiMara today?"

Luc snorted. "I'd say it was his ruined wine."

I couldn't be angry with the page for spreading unnecessary gossip. Luc could charm the knowledge out of anyone without the need of a truthspell.

We guided our mounts through the postern gate, down the alley that separated my goddess's temple from that of Mother, and up Temple Street, the main thoroughfare of the city. The business district gave way to small shops and eateries. Orrin was rich enough that the streets were cobblestoned, but the winter rains kept most of the citizens indoors despite the absence of mud.

Small homes appeared between the merchant buildings. Gradually the shops disappeared, and the houses grew larger as we climbed the bluffs on the north side of the bay.

The DiMara estate overlooked the city and harbor, an imposing stone enclave that still bore signs of its original purpose as a fortress. A guardsman swung open the ornate wrought iron gate, a show of the family's wealth, as we approached. The duke's family controlled a majority of the Orrin harbor trade, and those ships they didn't own outright, they had invested in over the years.

Two stableboys took our horses while the guardsman led us on foot to a warehouse on the left. The dry interior was welcome after our short, wet ride.

Orrin's magistrate, Malven DiCook, was not.

"'Bout time his lordship's pet priestess got here." He coughed and spat on the floor, close enough to me to be thoroughly disgusting but intentionally missing my boot. Duke Marco wasn't the only one dealing with insults and challenges to authority, but the ones aimed at me weren't so carefully crafted.

If I had the evidence Malven was involved in the former lord and lady's treason, I'd behead the bastard without blinking. But I didn't, which meant I had to tread lightly around the duly elected city magistrate.

And tolerate the sickly sweet odor of the damn licorice-scented dye he used to disguise the effects of age in his hair and beard.

He hooked his thumbs in his belt and rocked back on his heels. "His lordship wouldn't let me examine the body until you arrived."

I brushed back the hood of my cloak and stepped closer. Being a tall woman was handy at times. I met the magistrate's glare before he turned his attention toward the floor. Sometimes, my idiotic attempt to give myself sight came in handy for unnerving my antagonist.

He muttered the Cantish word for "freak."

"No," I answered in the same language. "I was chosen by the Goddess. If you have an issue with her selection, I'm sure the Reverend Mother could arrange an audience for you." I didn't add my personal opinion of his hygiene habits.

He jerked and shuffled a step backward. I didn't know whether it was due to my knowledge of Cantish or my not-so-subtle threat. Nor did I wish to probe his thoughts to find out. Mucking out Duke Marco's horse stalls would be a far more pleasant task.

Luc's amusement at the magistrate's reaction tickled my mind, but he said nothing.

"This way m'lady." The guardsman beckoned us to follow. He marched for the opening that yawned in the floor of the storage room.

Luc faced our wardens. "Two up. Two down with us." Without a word, one of his and Little Bear moved to positions where they could watch both the main door, the passage to the underground storage rooms, and each other's backs.

Marco's guardsman lit an oil lamp and led our retinue and the magistrate down the wide wooden ramp. The air was terribly dry for such a miserable, wet day. Small bowls sat in alcoves along the wall. The bone salt in them absorbed the moisture in the air to prevent mold and rot.

At the bottom of the ramp, my desiccated airways itched from both the mineral and the sawdust coating the floor. Despite the sweet scent of mountain pine, another sickly smell met me. The guardsman gestured to the wide double doorway to our right.

I strode past the guardsmen to find Duke Marco, his wife and sister, his steward, and another household servant on one side. Facing them were three of the city's peacekeepers. A wine barrel stood upright between the two sets of observers. The tension in the wine room was more suffocating than the odor of death.

"You and your household seem rather intent on disturbing my morning meals, Your Grace." I nodded to the women. "Lady Katarina, Lady Alessa."

"Truly, I would prefer not to." Marco's grim humor matched mine. "However, the circumstances warranted your curious mind."

"Would it make you more comfortable if I provided you a knife to threaten someone with, Justice Anthea?" Lady Katarina offered with the same amusement as her husband. She rested a bright red hand over her prominent stomach.

Sometimes, the odd eyesight I'd given myself let me see things that others couldn't. Like the rise in the lady's body temperature. Knowing she was with child before she did had been entertaining.

An odd sort of friendship had sprung between Lady Katarina and myself over the last six months. Probably because we were both products of the Temple of Love's Spring Rituals. Definitely because I had saved her and her husband's lives from his deranged mother and the demons her pet sorcerer had summoned.

"That will be unnecessary, m'lady," I replied and brushed the pommel of my sword at my shoulder. "I've learned to carry bigger weapons when you two are involved."

"If you're going to do nothing but joke with His Grace, maybe you should leave." The magistrate's irritation felt like steel scraped across slate.

I turned my gaze on DiCook. "I didn't realize you had been named the Reverend Mother of Balance."

"Your predecessor had a sense of decorum in these matters," he shot back.

Sometimes, I wondered if the elderly justice who held the temple seat here before me was willfully, as well as literally blind. But that wasn't fair. None of the priest or priestesses of the eleven other temples detected so much as a whiff of trouble with Marco's parents before it was too late.

Unless I'd totally misread their allegiances.

I had gotten lucky, and I knew it. Otherwise, we'd be neck-deep in another demon war now.

"Really, Sir Magistrate? In reviewing her records, I did not come across any accounts of bodies in wine barrels. Care to enlighten me?"

He muttered another obscenity under his breath, but otherwise remained silent.

The duke and his party wisely said nothing as well while I crossed to the source of the odor and peered inside. I couldn't distinguish much in the deep green mass because the body had cooled to the same temperature as the liquid it floated in, so I inhaled deeply.

I looked up at Luc who had joined me. "He or she didn't loose their bowels in there."

"She," he corrected. At my quizzical expression, he added, "Too much hair floating at the top of the barrel."

"Could be Pagonian." I shrugged. Both men and women of Issura's neighbor to the north only cut their locks during a period of family grieving.

Luc shook his head. "No. Hair's too pale even soaked in dark red wine."

I sighed. "I suppose I should examine the timeline before we pull whoever it is out of the barrel."

Luc grunted and looked over his shoulder. "Duke Marco, when was this barrel brought onto your estate?"

The nobleman's sister Alessa was the one who answered. "Three days ago, High Brother."

"Was the wine seal intact?" I asked.

The three nobles looked at the steward who turned to the man beside him who nervously shuffled his feet before he answered. "The wax weren't broken, m'lady, but the winery stamp weren't there neither." He shrugged. "We git 'em that way sometimes, usually in the summer. The tops melt."

"But this is the middle of winter," I said softly.

"During winter cleaning, the lads at the winery set the barrels outside in the sun," the steward volunteered. "The air temperature is cold enough to keep the wine fresh, but the direct light softens the wax."

"Sounds reasonable," Luc said.

Luc turned back to me. *We can always confirm with the priests at Vintner.* Out loud, he said, "With her being dead, I won't be able to track her."

I grinned at him. "Afraid the Wilding priests might show you up?"

DiCook stomped over to the barrel. "If you two are finished making light of someone's murder, maybe you'll get around to finding the culprit."

"Murder? Who said anything about murder?" I couldn't resist needling the magistrate.

His face turned a brilliant scarlet. "So this poor woman decided to take a swim in a barrel of his lordship's wine?"

"We cannot assume anything at this point." My Luc, ever the voice of reason. "What do you need, Anthea?" His question was for the benefit of everyone else in the room.

"Just some quiet," I murmured. I pulled off my gloves and settled cross-legged on the cold flagstone floor. With one hand on the barrel and one on a shard of decorative onyx embedded next to the slate, I concentrated.

The stone quivered beneath my palm, eager to tell its story. It paid more attention to the vagaries of the mobile beings than its slate brothers.

I tugged the strings of time with the stone's assistance, unwinding back to four days ago. Luc and the rest would see transparent figures moving faster than usual. I could only see gray ghosts drifting around and through the colored figures of the living in the storage room. Two phantom men rolled a barrel out of the room.

"Hold." Luc's baritone rumbled through the air.

I paused the release of the time thread.

"Names," he demanded.

"That's William and me," squeaked the retainer standing with the steward.

"Name," Luc snapped.

"Bartholomew, m'lord," the retainer squeaked again.

"I told them to bring up a barrel of the local rose for dinner the night before the delivery," the steward offered.

"Luc," I said through gritted teeth.

"My apologies. Continue." At least he actually sounded sorry, but I don't think he truly understood the strain of what I was doing.

I let the string of time the onyx showed me slide forward. Several ghostly men rolled barrels down the ramp.

"Who are the three with Bartholomew?" Luc asked.

"The man on the barrel with him is Julian, one of the Duke's retainers," the steward answered. "The other two are the vineyard's transporters."

"Do you know them?"

The steward shook his head. "Rubio and his son normally bring the Orrin shipments. These two said Rubio had hurt his back, and they'd been hired to deliver the barrels."

"Names," Luc snapped again.

"Th-they didn't give their names." A green sheen of sweat appeared at the steward's hairline. "Their paperwork had the vineyard's seal."

Luc folded his arms. "Where did the shipment come from?"

"The Pana Valley," Lady Alessa and the steward answered at the same time.

"Lord Aleister DiGrove's estate," the duke's sister added.

Luc's concern matched my own. If this turned out to be a power play within the nobility, things could turn very ugly very fast.

I let the rest of the timeline slide through my grip. But once the barrel in question was stored, it remained in place until Bartholomew and the man he named as William tapped it this morning.

"Well, that wasn't a damn bit helpful," Luc murmured.

I thanked the onyx before I shook the feeling back into my fingers and rose to my feet. "Let's drain the barrel and get her out."

"Shame about the wine." Luc stepped out of the way.

I could hear DiCook's teeth grind, but he kept silent.

The steward and Bartholomew set buckets under the tap to drain the ruined red while the guardsman went off to fetch an old blanket. Once a sufficient amount had been removed that we wouldn't flood the cellar if we accidentally tipped it, Luc and I peered in the barrel once more.

I pulled my gloves back on. "Ready?"

"We can do it if her ladyship can't."

I didn't have to look at DiCook to hear the sneer in his voice. "My thanks, Magistrate, but I can't have you or your men vomit on the body and contaminate it." I hooked my arm under one of the corpse's shoulders. "Ready"

Luc grabbed the other shoulder. Together, Luc and I lifted the deceased out of the barrel. She was heavier than she should have been, her skin having absorbed a great deal of wine. On the shores of the Peaceful Sea, one couldn't help seeing their share of drowning victims. We carefully settled the nude body on the blanket.

I brushed the soaked locks away from the face. A sharp gasp came from Lady Katarina. I looked at noblewoman. "You recognize her?"

She stepped closer. "The face is distorted but—" She gave a sharp nod. "Sister Gretchen from the Temple of Love. She was my playmate when we were children."

I could feel Luc watching me, which was understandable. For the six months since my assignment to Orrin, I'd managed to avoid the chief priestess of the Temple of Love, but I couldn't any longer.

With one of her people dead, I was going to have to face my mother.

Acknowledgements

It's somehow fitting that I'm writing this the same day as Avengers: Endgame premieres in U.S. theaters. Just like the pinnacle of the Marvel Cinematic Universe, this book series is brought to you by an entire cast and crew of incredible people:

Jaye Manus of QA Productions, who has been much more of an emotional rock to me than she realizes.

Elaina Lee of For the Muse Design, who turns my poorly articulated ideas into real art.

Writers Angela Penrose, Joseph Bradshire, and Scott Dyson for their support when things went really wrong.

To all of my attorney friends, whose stories and experiences helped flesh out my cast of characters.

And most of all, to Darling Husband and Genius Kid. I love you.